Lupin Leaps In

GEORGIA DUNN

ELVIS
FIELD REPORTER

LUPIN
LEAD ANCHOR

PUCK
FIELD REPORTER

 A **BREAKING CAT NEWS** ADVENTURE

Andrews McMeel
PUBLISHING®

FOR THE REAL LIFE 'MAN,' MY HUSBAND RYAN.

THANK YOU FOR YOUR LOVE, SUPPORT, THE ADVENTURES

WE'VE HAD, AND THE ADVENTURES TO COME!

Andrews McMeel Publishing
a division of Andrews McMeel Universal
1130 Walnut Street, Kansas City, Missouri 64106

www.andrewsmcmeel.com
www.breakingcatnews.com

24 25 26 27 28 SDB 10 9 8 7 6 5 4 3

ISBN: 978-1-4494-9522-0

Library of Congress Control Number: 2018958236

Published under license from Universal Uclick
www.gocomics.com

Made by:
RR Donnelley (Guangdong) Printing Solutions Company Ltd
Address and location of manufacturer:
No. 2 Minzhu Road, Daning, Humen Town,
Dongguan City, Guangdong Province, China 523930
3rd Printing—11/25/24

ATTENTION: SCHOOLS AND BUSINESSES
Andrews McMeel books are available at quantity discounts with bulk purchase for educational, business, or sales promotional use. For information, please e-mail the Andrews McMeel Publishing Special Sales Department: sales@andrewsmcmeel.com.

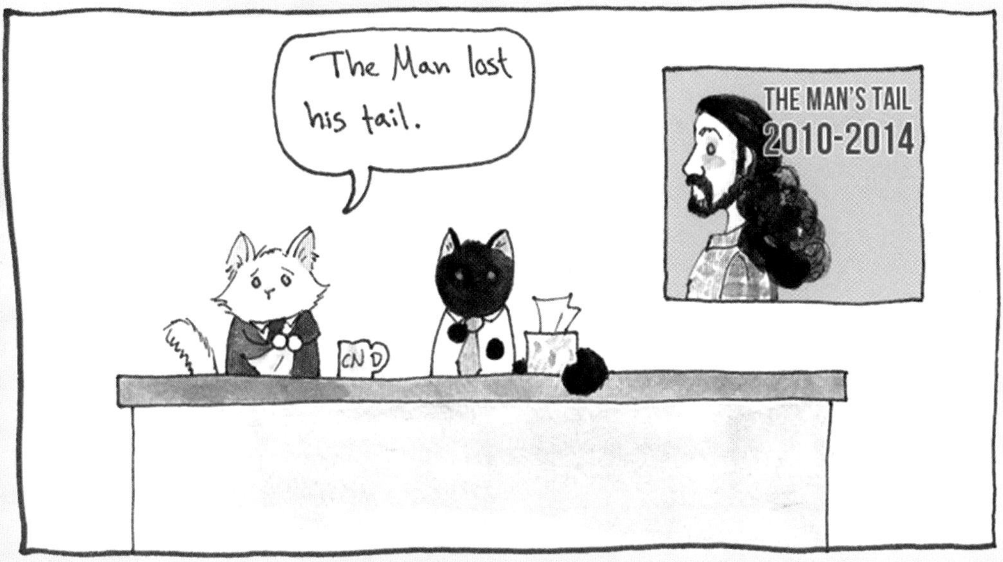
The Man lost his tail.
CND
THE MAN'S TAIL
2010-2014

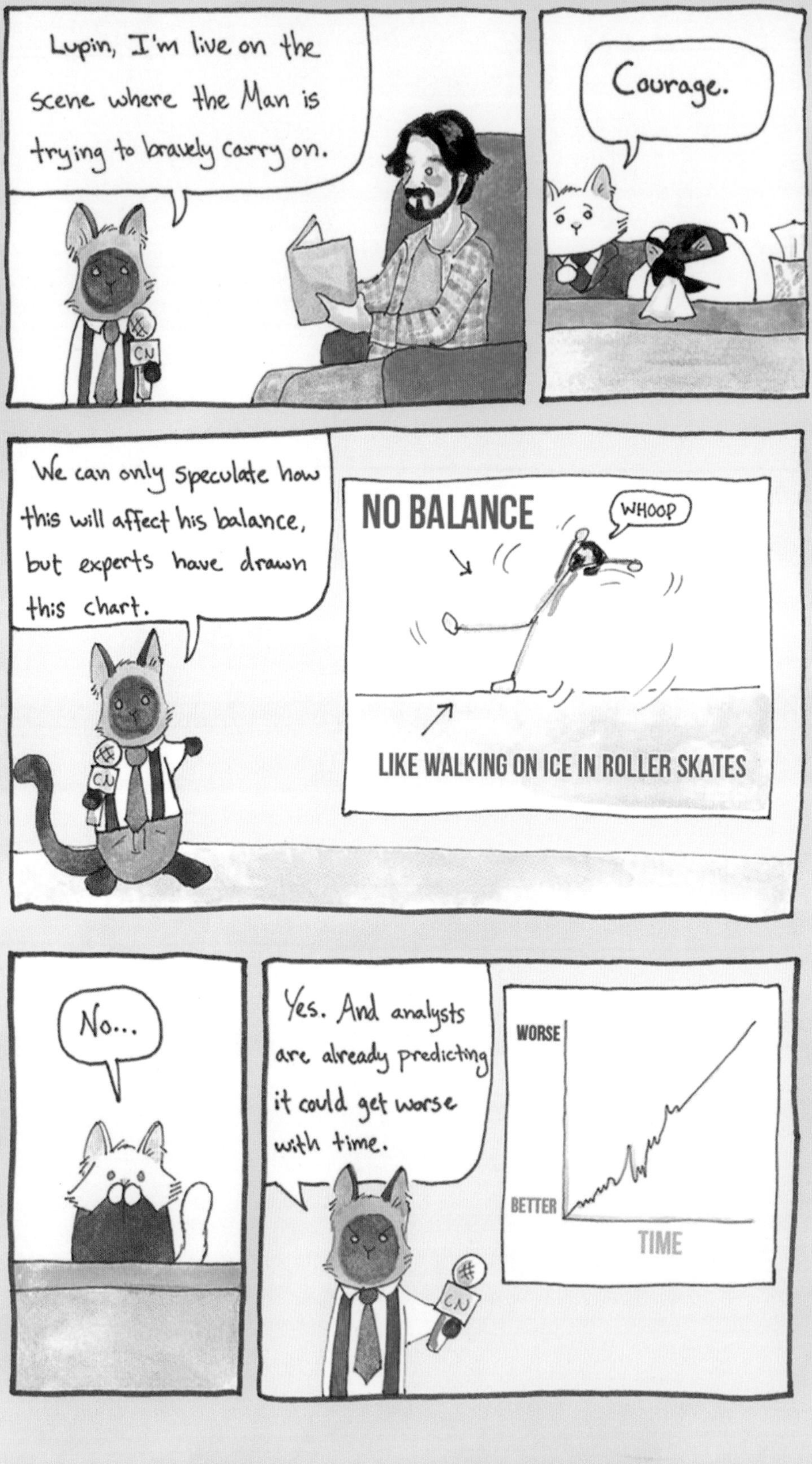
Lupin, I'm live on the scene where the Man is trying to bravely carry on.
Courage.
CN
We can only speculate how this will affect his balance, but experts have drawn this chart.
NO BALANCE
WHOOP
LIKE WALKING ON ICE IN ROLLER SKATES
CN
No...
Yes. And analysts are already predicting it could get worse with time.
WORSE
BETTER
TIME
CN

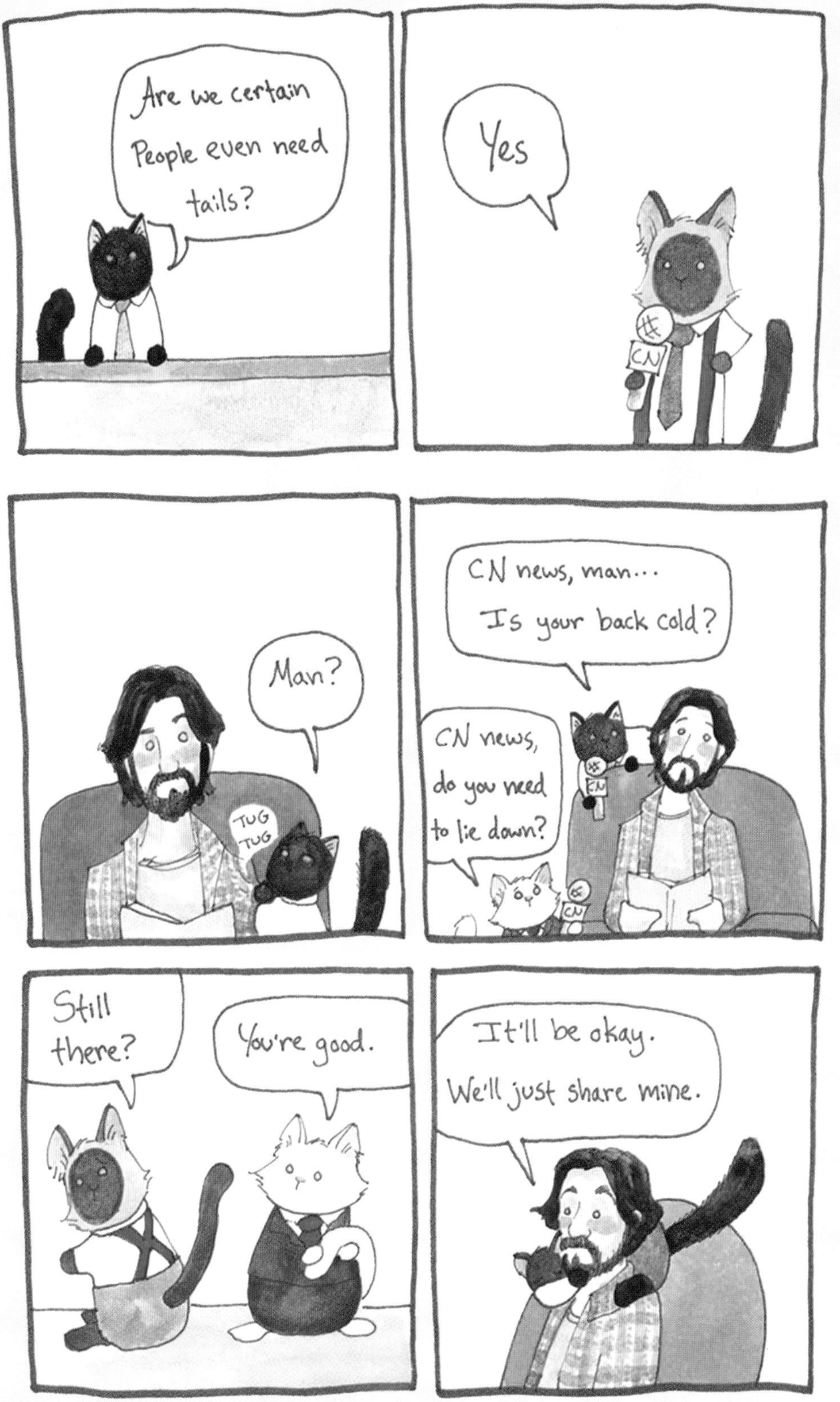
Are we certain People even need tails?
Yes
CN
Man?
TUG TUG
CN news, man... Is your back cold?
CN news, do you need to lie down?
CN
CN
Still there?
You're good.
It'll be okay. We'll just share mine.

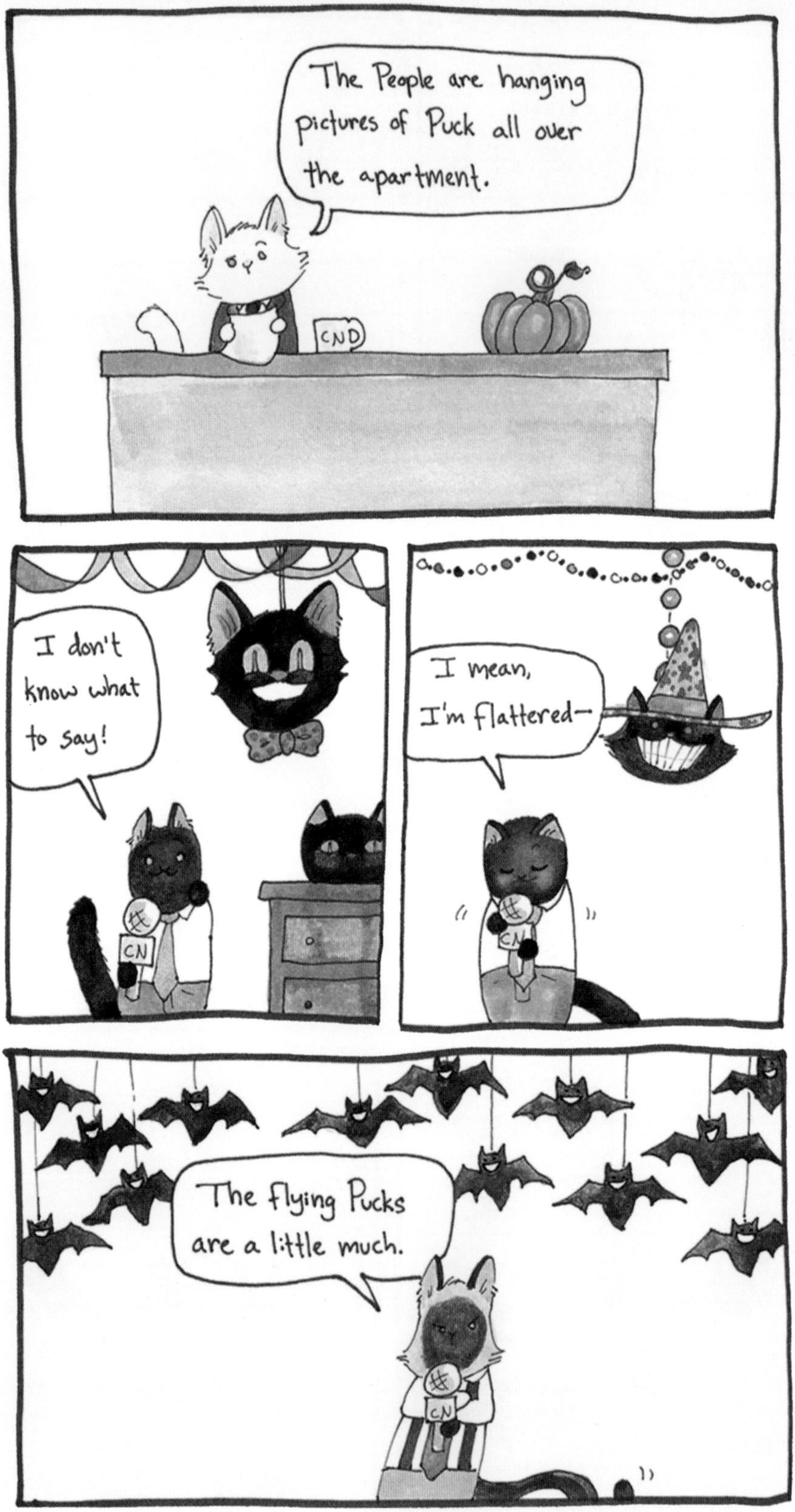
The People are hanging pictures of Puck all over the apartment.
CND
I don't know what to say!
CN
I mean, I'm flattered—
CN
The flying Pucks are a little much.
CN

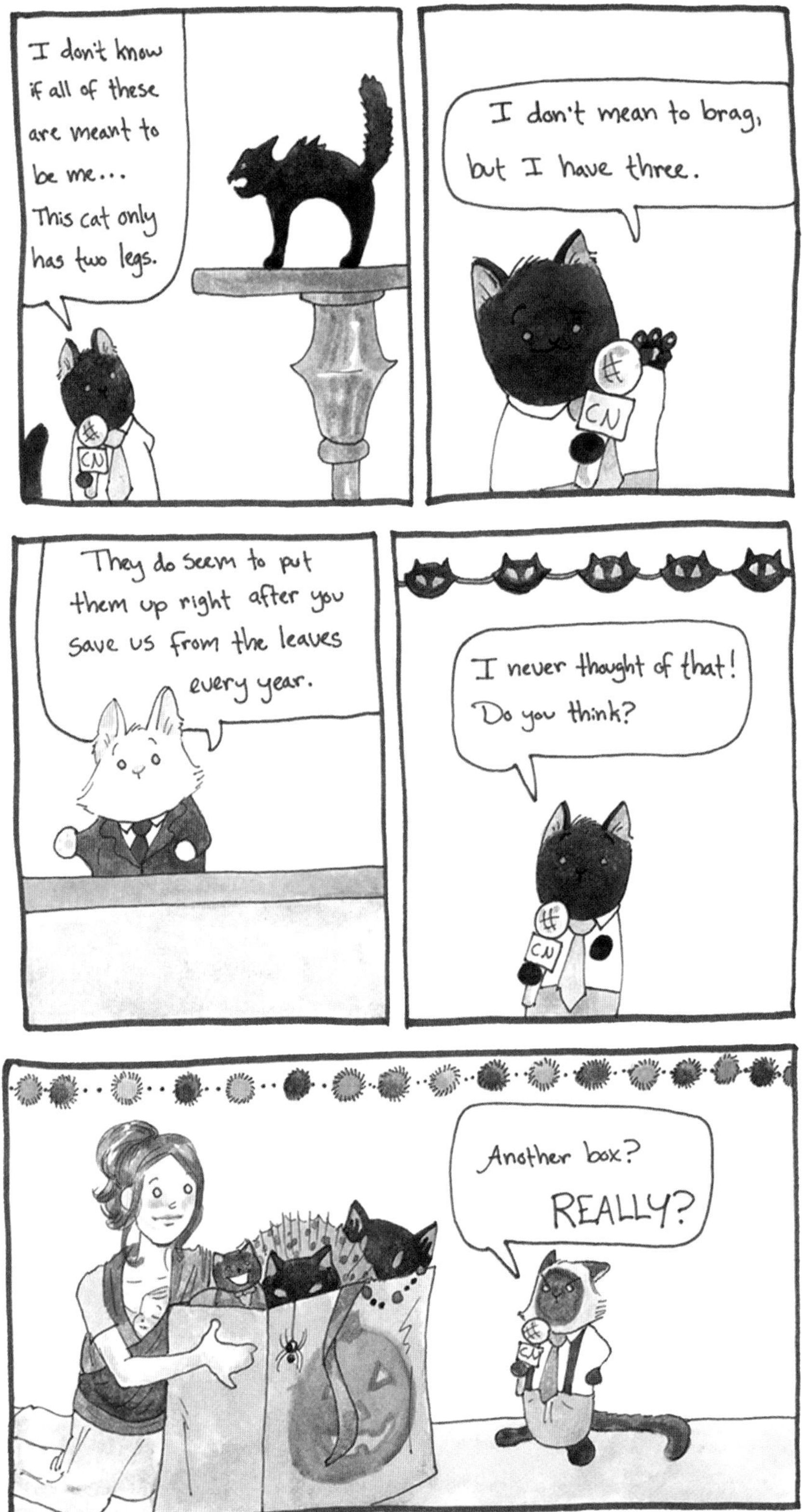
I don't know if all of these are meant to be me... This cat only has two legs.
I don't mean to brag, but I have three.
CN
They do seem to put them up right after you save us from the leaves every year.
I never thought of that! Do you think?
CN
Another box? REALLY?
CN

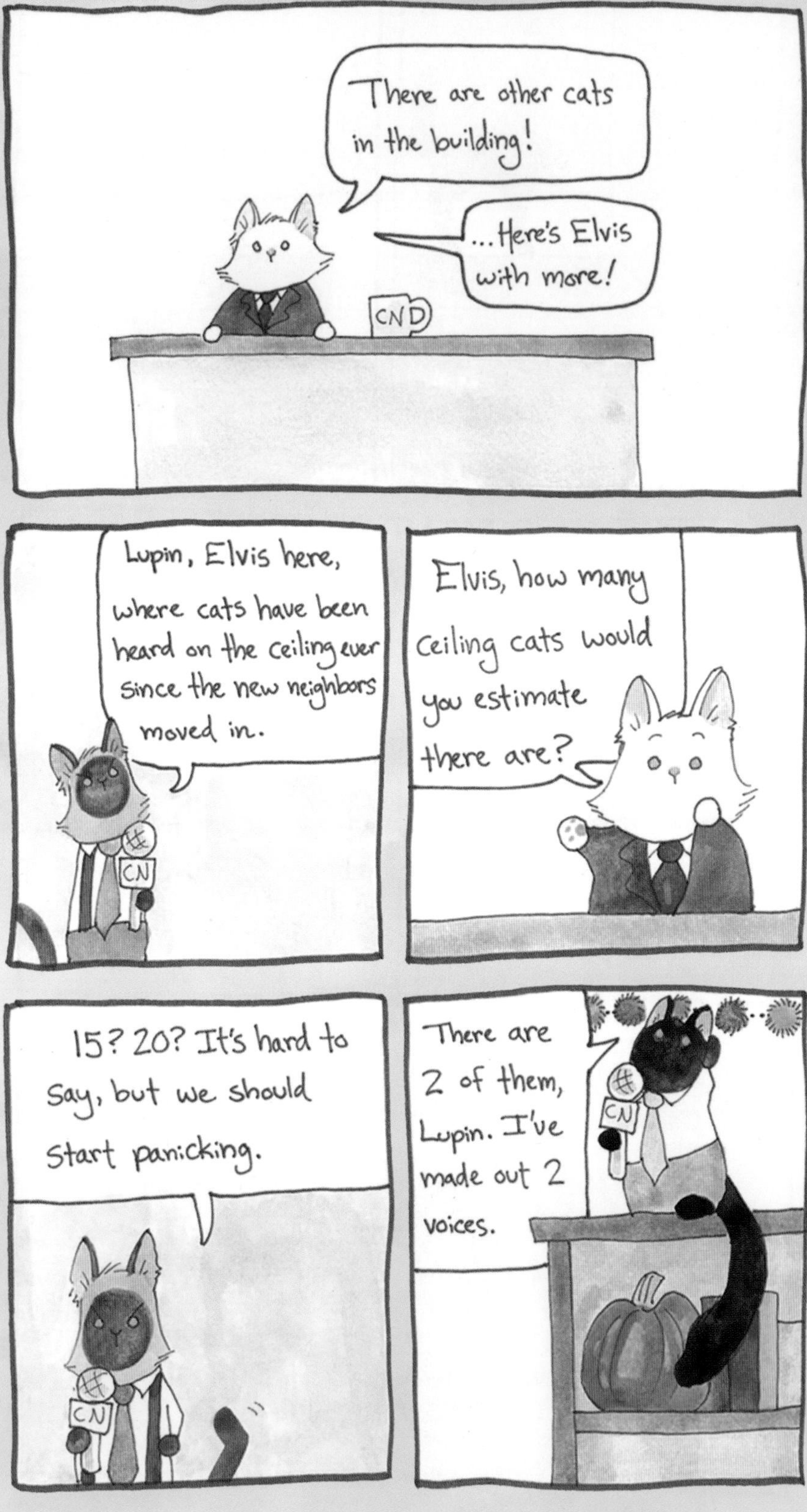
There are other cats in the building!
...Here's Elvis with more!
CND
Lupin, Elvis here, where cats have been heard on the ceiling ever since the new neighbors moved in.
CN
Elvis, how many ceiling cats would you estimate there are?
15? 20? It's hard to say, but we should start panicking.
CN
There are 2 of them, Lupin. I've made out 2 voices.
CN

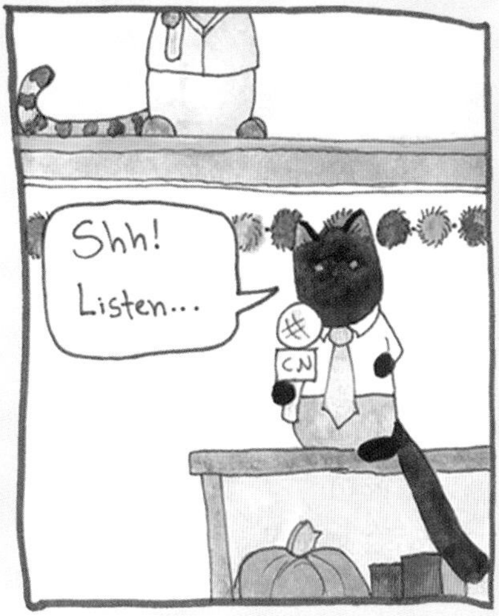
Shh! Listen...
CN

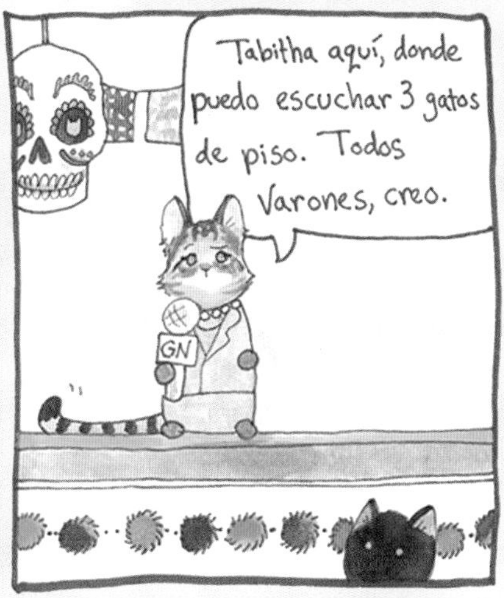
Tabitha aquí, donde puedo escuchar 3 gatos de piso. Todos Varones, creo.
GN

Tabitha here, where we can hear 3 cats in the floor. All males, I believe.

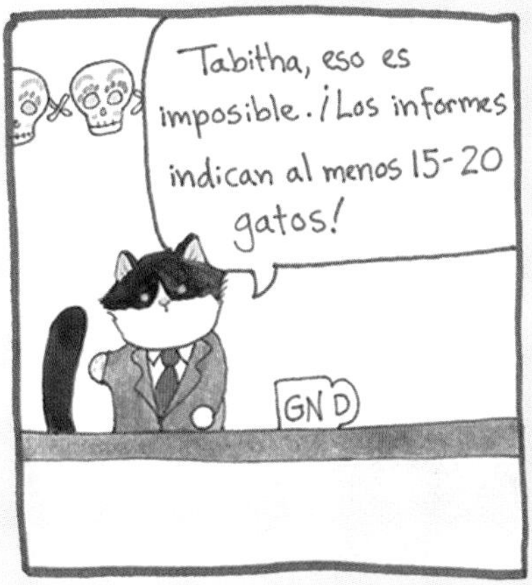
Tabitha, eso es imposible. ¡Los informes indican al menos 15-20 gatos!
GN D

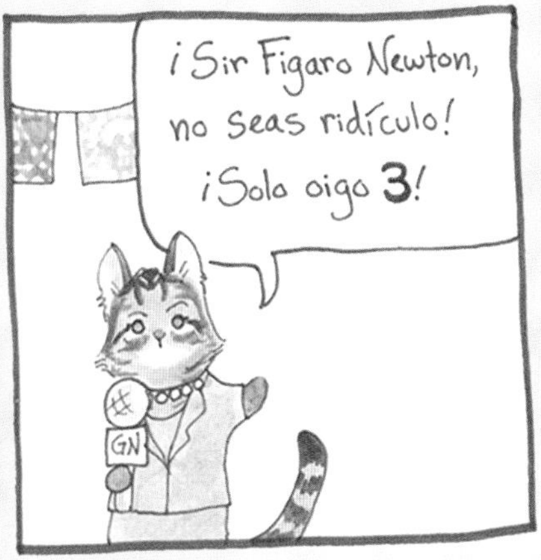
¡Sir Figaro Newton, no seas ridículo! ¡Solo oigo 3!
GN

Tabitha, it's impossible. Reports indicate at least 15-20 cats!

Sir Figaro Newton, don't be ridiculous! I only hear 3!

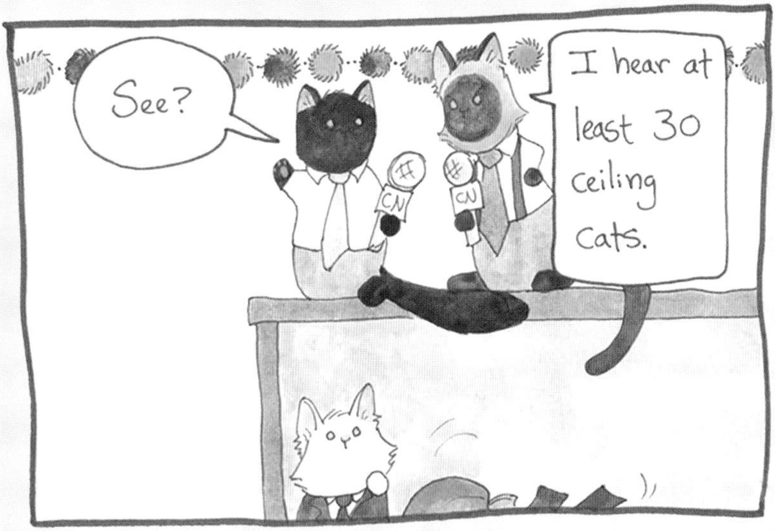
See?
I hear at least 30 ceiling cats.
CN
CN

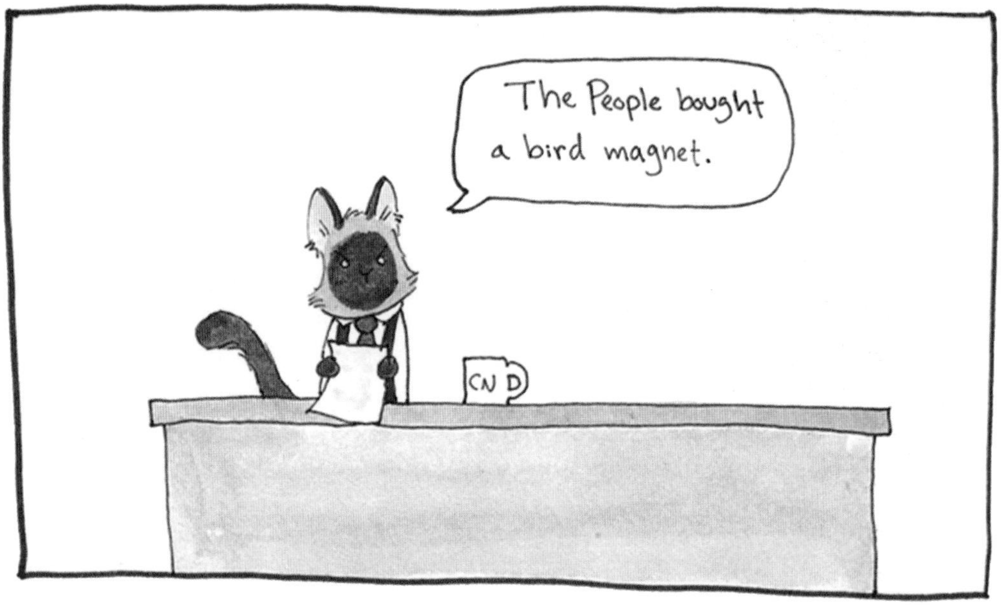
The People bought a bird magnet.
CN D

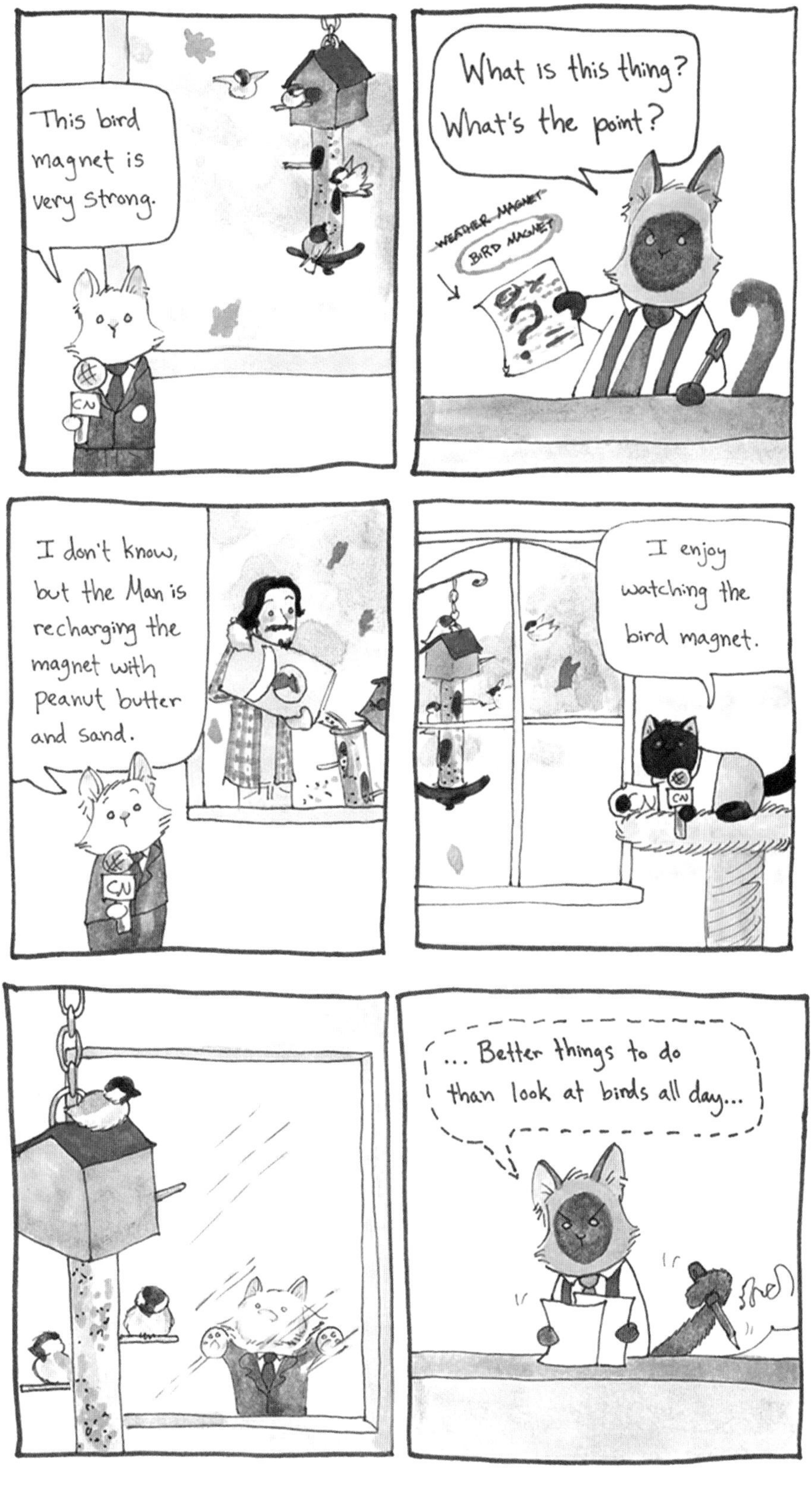
This bird magnet is very strong.
What is this thing? What's the point?
WEATHER MAGNET
BIRD MAGNET
I don't know, but the Man is recharging the magnet with peanut butter and sand.
I enjoy watching the bird magnet.
... Better things to do than look at birds all day...

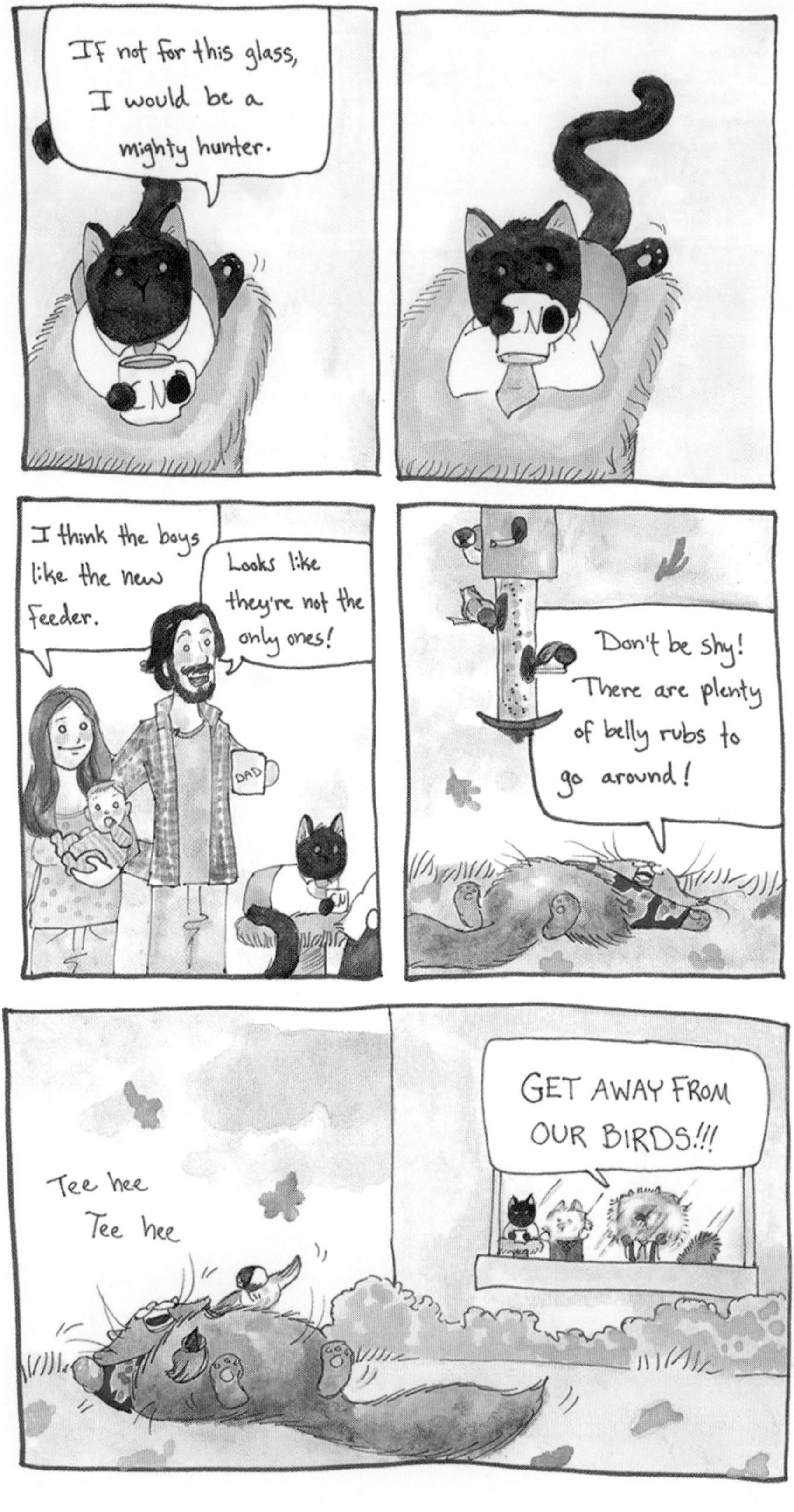
If not for this glass,
I would be a
mighty hunter.
I think the boys
like the new
feeder.
Looks like
they're not the
only ones!
DAD
Don't be shy!
There are plenty
of belly rubs to
go around!
Tee hee
Tee hee
GET AWAY FROM
OUR BIRDS!!!

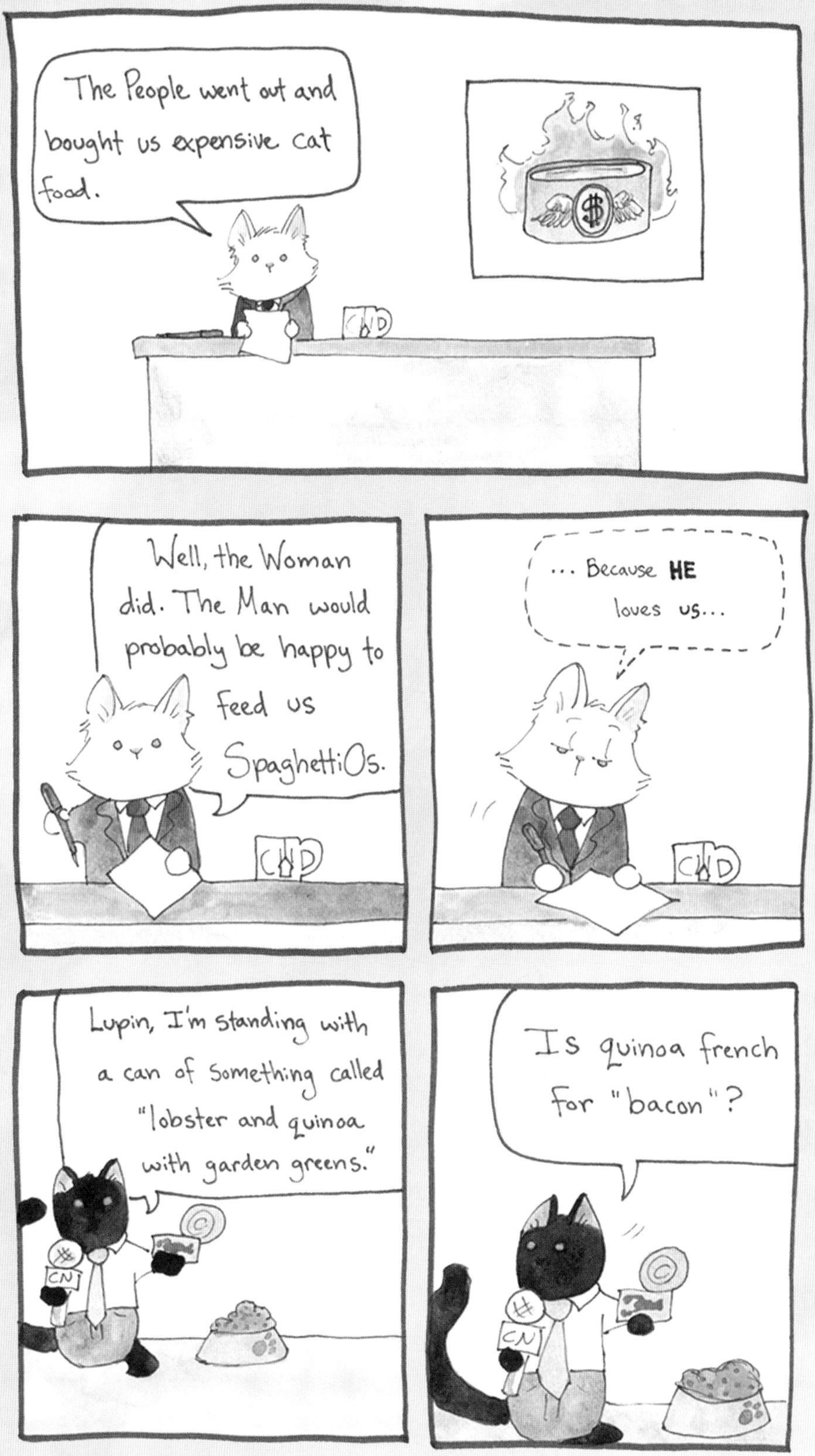
The People went out and bought us expensive cat food.
Well, the Woman did. The Man would probably be happy to feed us SpaghettiOs.
... Because HE loves us...
Lupin, I'm standing with a can of something called "lobster and quinoa with garden greens."
Is quinoa french for "bacon"?

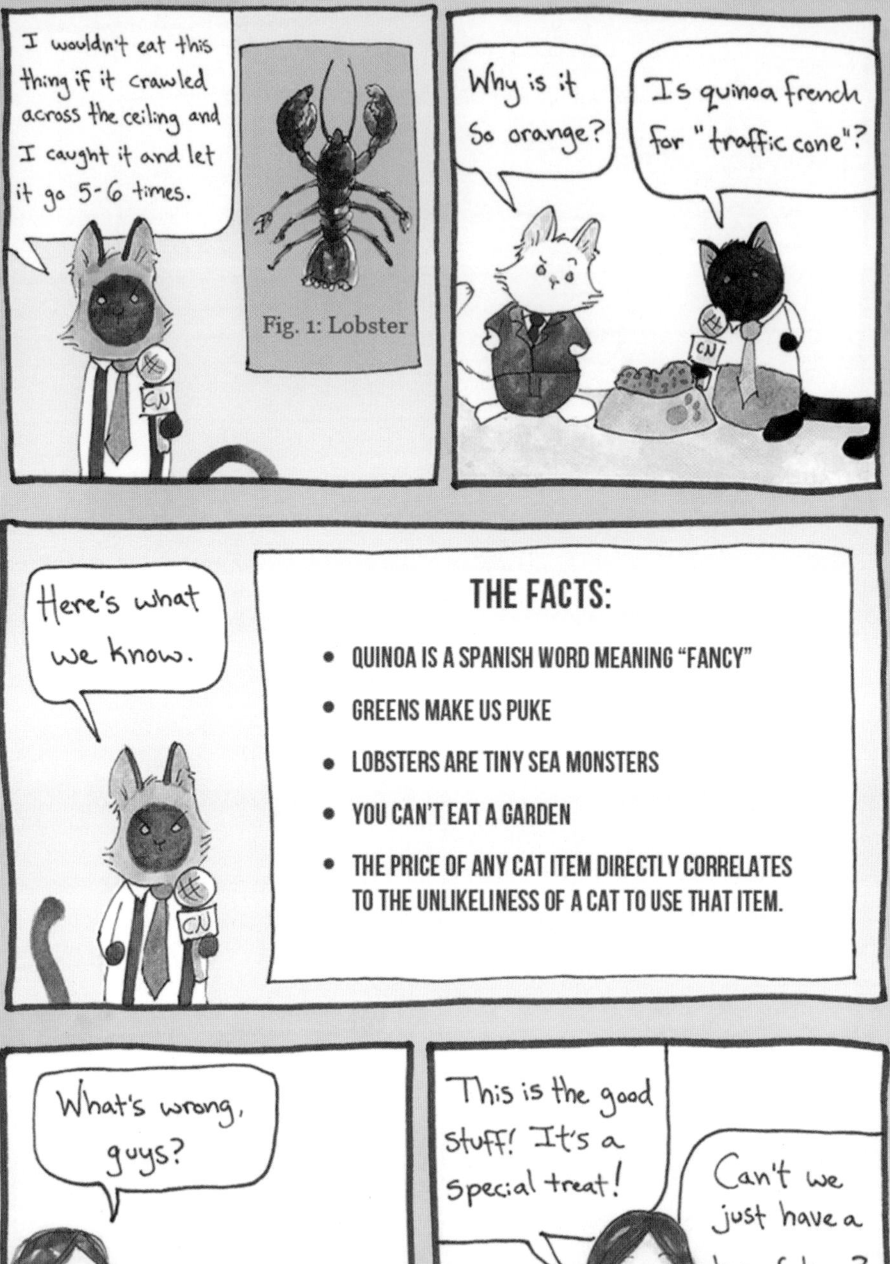
I wouldn't eat this thing if it crawled across the ceiling and I caught it and let it go 5-6 times.
Fig. 1: Lobster
CN
Why is it So orange?
Is quinoa french for "traffic cone"?
CN
Here's what we know.
CN
THE FACTS:
QUINOA IS A SPANISH WORD MEANING "FANCY"
GREENS MAKE US PUKE
LOBSTERS ARE TINY SEA MONSTERS
YOU CAN'T EAT A GARDEN
THE PRICE OF ANY CAT ITEM DIRECTLY CORRELATES TO THE UNLIKELINESS OF A CAT TO USE THAT ITEM.
What's wrong, guys?
SHRUG
Sigh.
This is the good stuff! It's a Special treat!
Can't we just have a box of ham?
CN

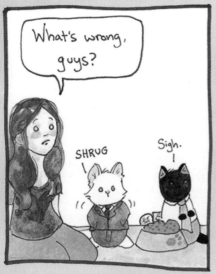

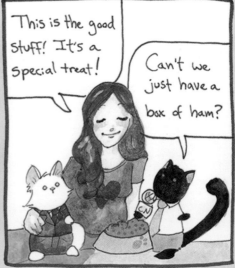

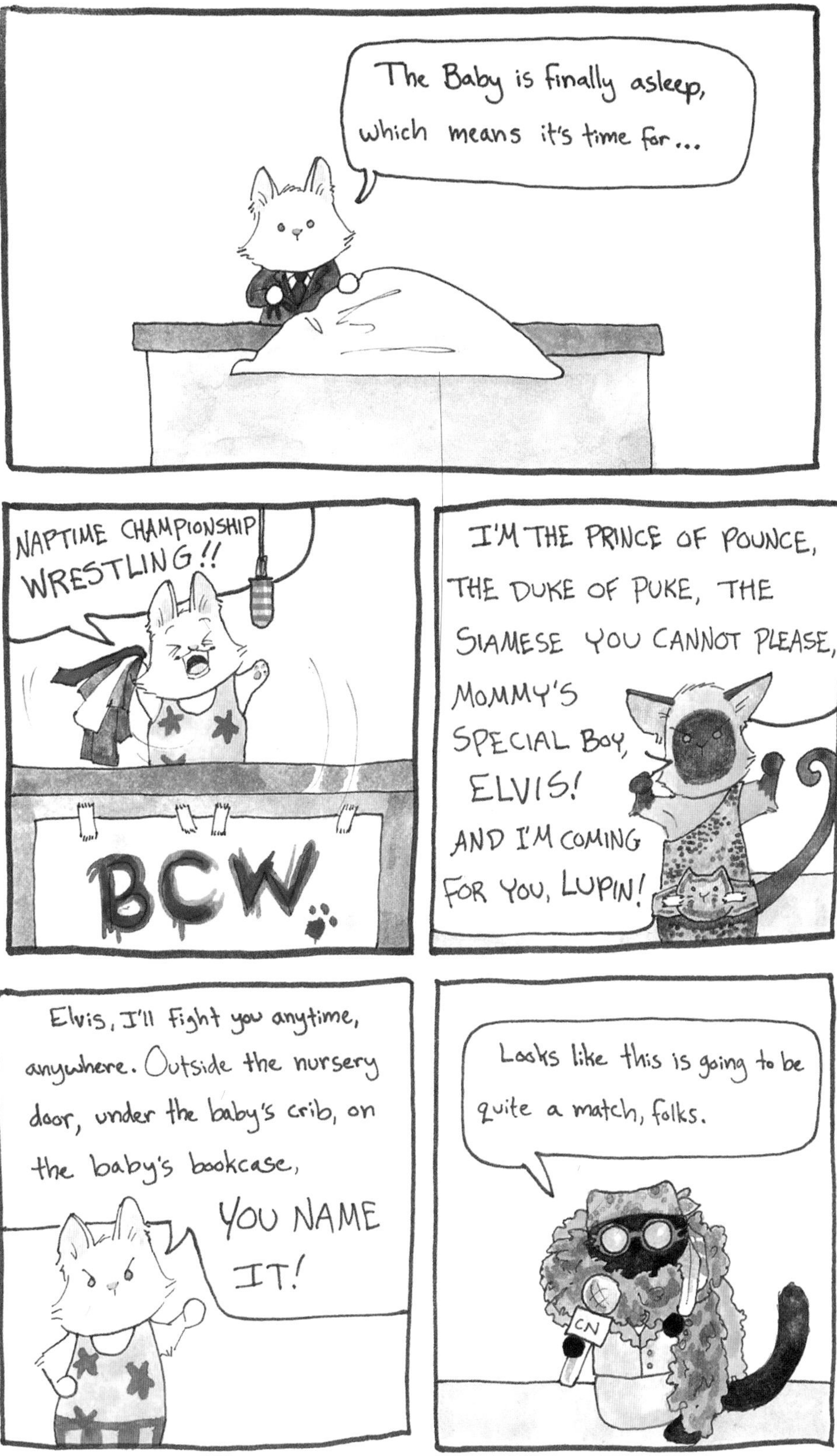

The Baby is finally asleep, which means it's time for...
NAPTIME CHAMPIONSHIP WRESTLING!!
BCW
I'M THE PRINCE OF POUNCE, THE DUKE OF PUKE, THE SIAMESE YOU CANNOT PLEASE, MOMMY'S SPECIAL BOY, ELVIS! AND I'M COMING FOR YOU, LUPIN!
Elvis, I'll fight you anytime, anywhere. Outside the nursery door, under the baby's crib, on the baby's bookcase, YOU NAME IT!
Looks like this is going to be quite a match, folks.
CN

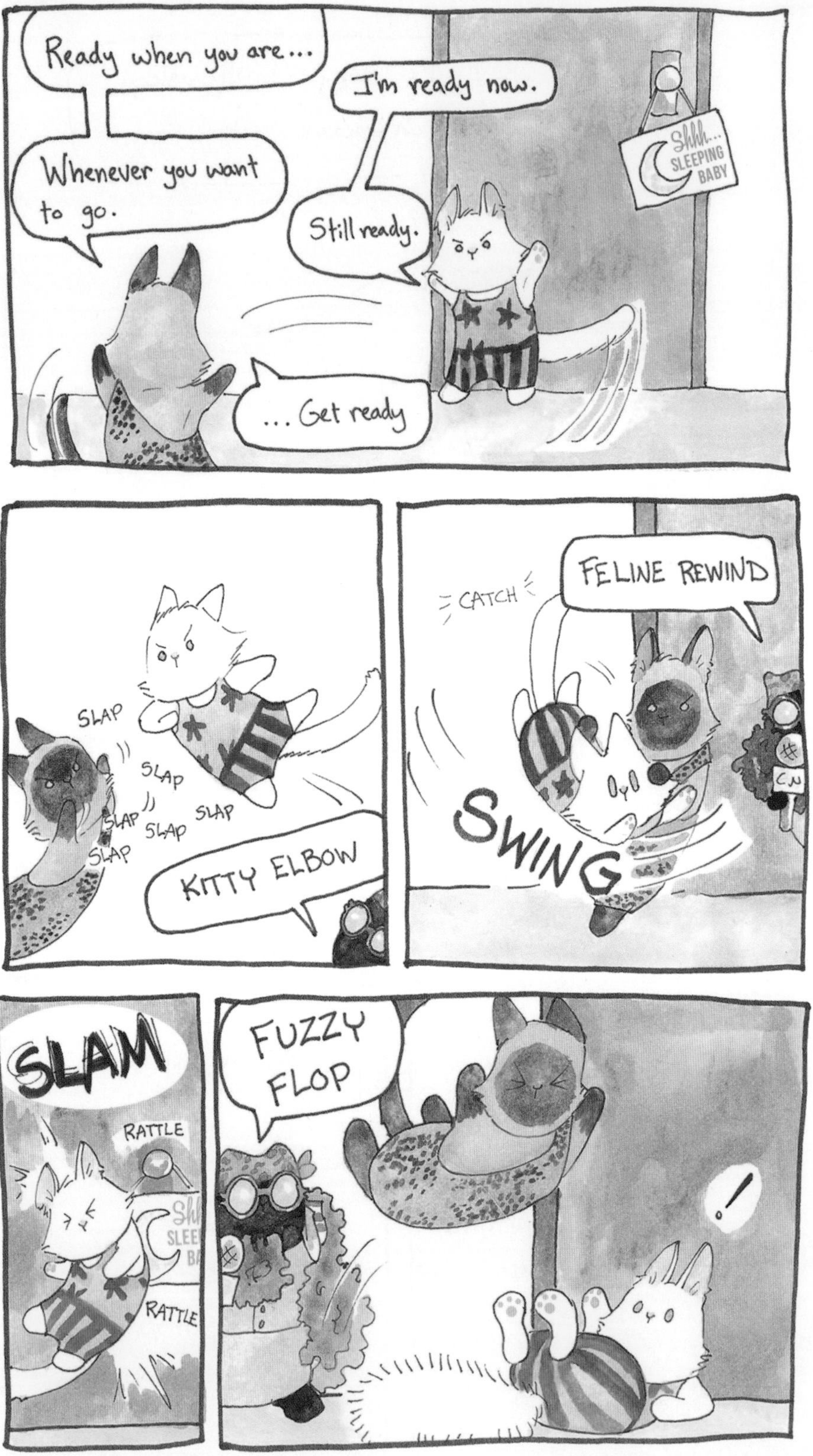
Ready when you are...
Whenever you want to go.
I'm ready now.
Still ready.
Shhh... SLEEPING BABY
... Get ready
SLAP
SLAP
SLAP SLAP SLAP
SLAP
KITTY ELBOW
CATCH
FELINE REWIND
SWING
SLAM
RATTLE
RATTLE
FUZZY FLOP
!

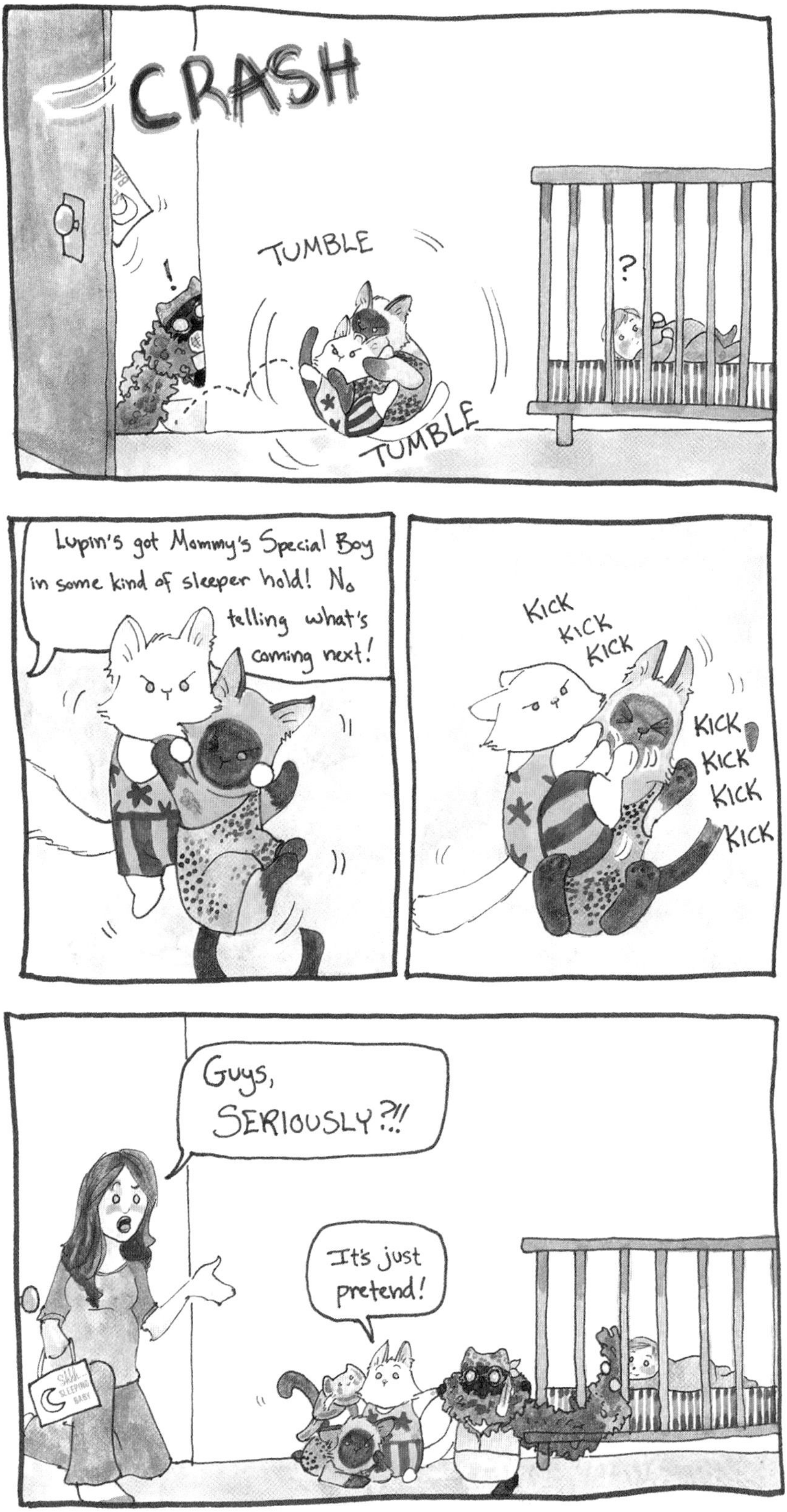
CRASH
TUMBLE
TUMBLE
!
?
Lupin's got Mommy's Special Boy in some kind of sleeper hold! No telling what's coming next!
KICK KICK KICK
KICK KICK KICK KICK
Guys, SERIOUSLY?!!
It's just pretend!

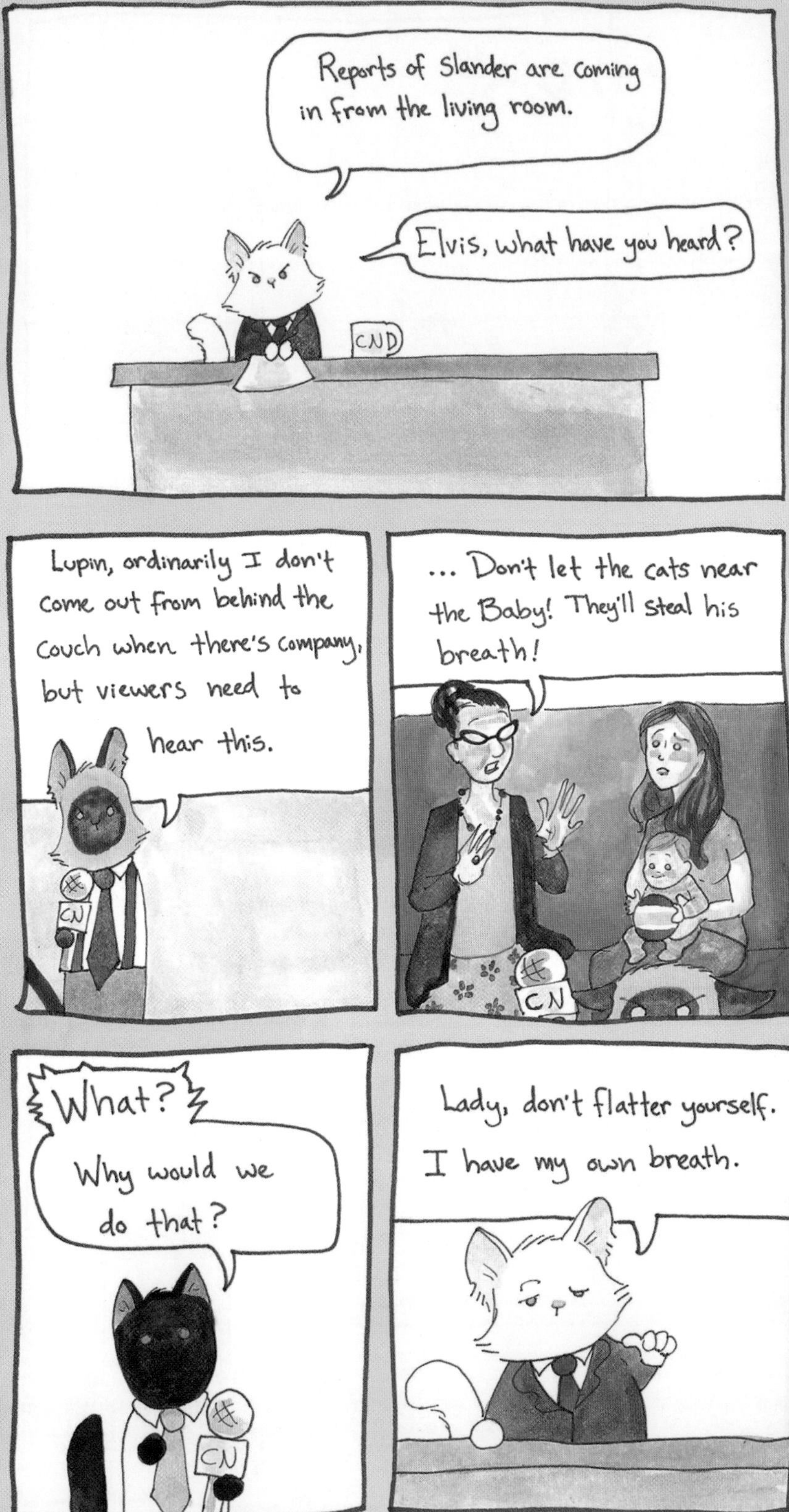
Reports of Slander are coming in from the living room.
Elvis, what have you heard?
CND
Lupin, ordinarily I don't come out from behind the couch when there's company, but viewers need to hear this.
CN
... Don't let the cats near the Baby! They'll steal his breath!
CN
What?
Why would we do that?
CN
Lady, don't flatter yourself. I have my own breath.

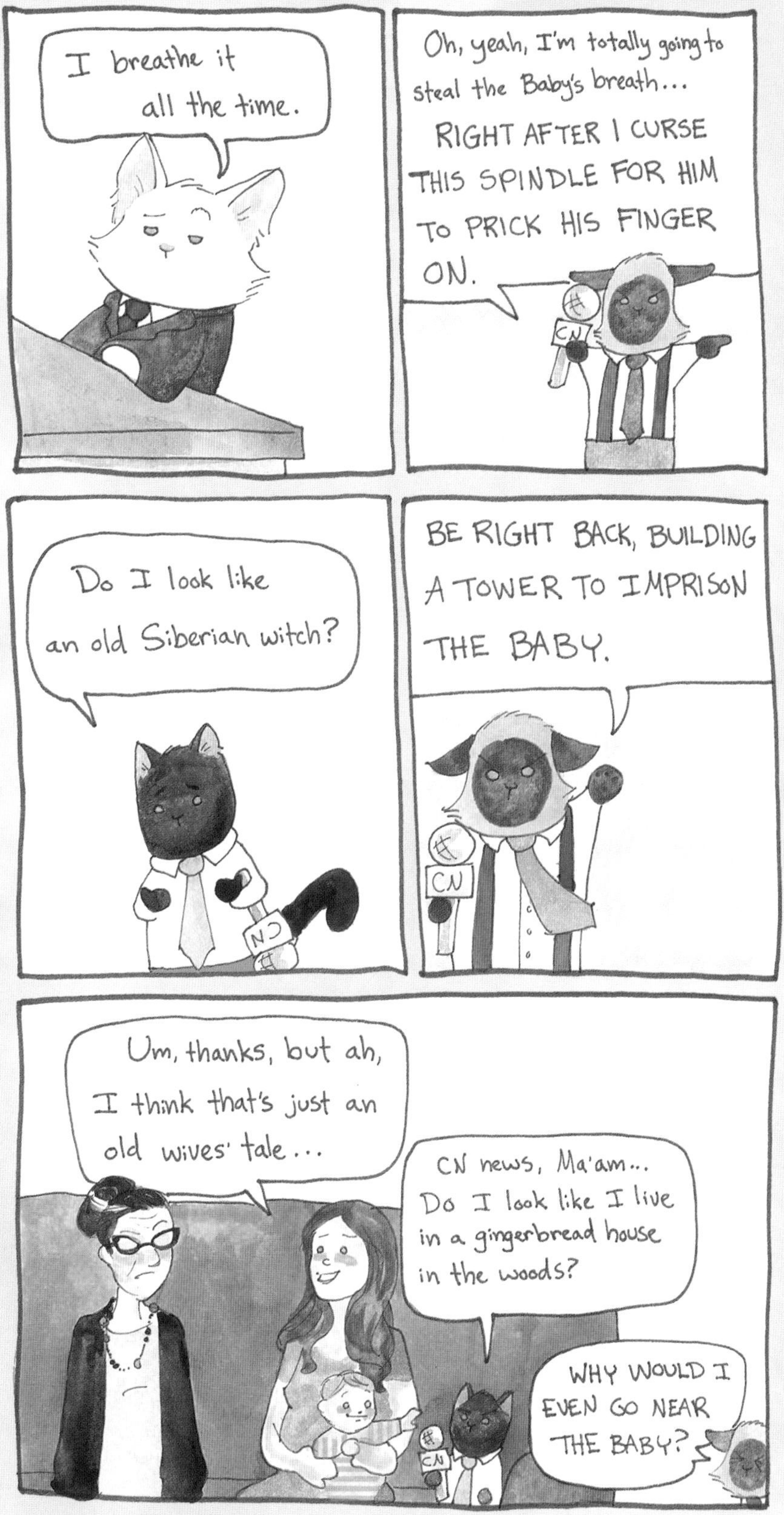
I breathe it all the time.
Oh, yeah, I'm totally going to steal the Baby's breath... RIGHT AFTER I CURSE THIS SPINDLE FOR HIM TO PRICK HIS FINGER ON.
CN
Do I look like an old Siberian witch?
CN
BE RIGHT BACK, BUILDING A TOWER TO IMPRISON THE BABY.
CN
Um, thanks, but ah, I think that's just an old wives' tale...
CN news, Ma'am... Do I look like I live in a gingerbread house in the woods?
WHY WOULD I EVEN GO NEAR THE BABY?
CN

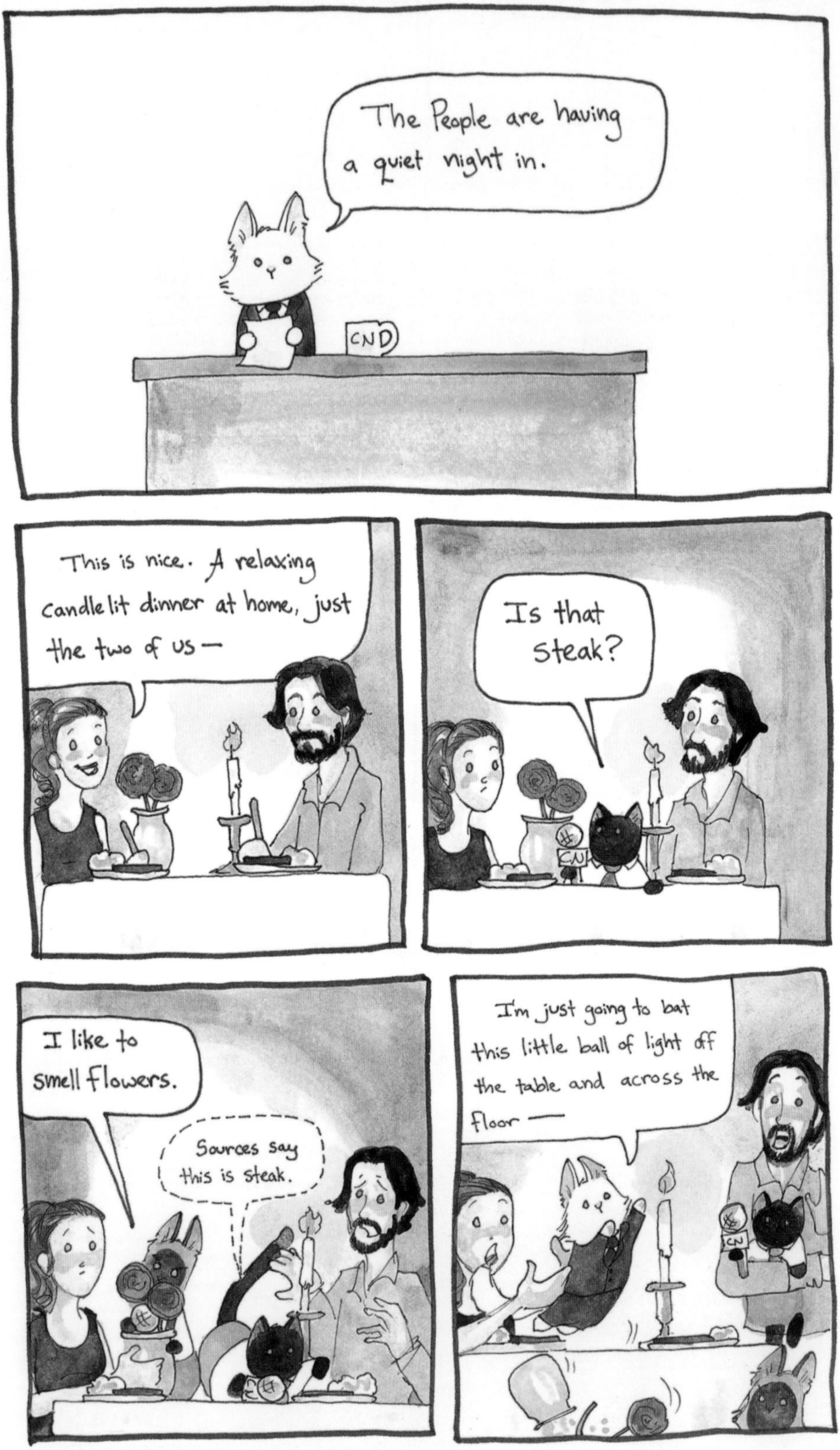
The People are having a quiet night in.
CND
This is nice. A relaxing candlelit dinner at home, just the two of us —
Is that steak?
I like to smell flowers.
Sources say this is steak.
I'm just going to bat this little ball of light off the table and across the floor —

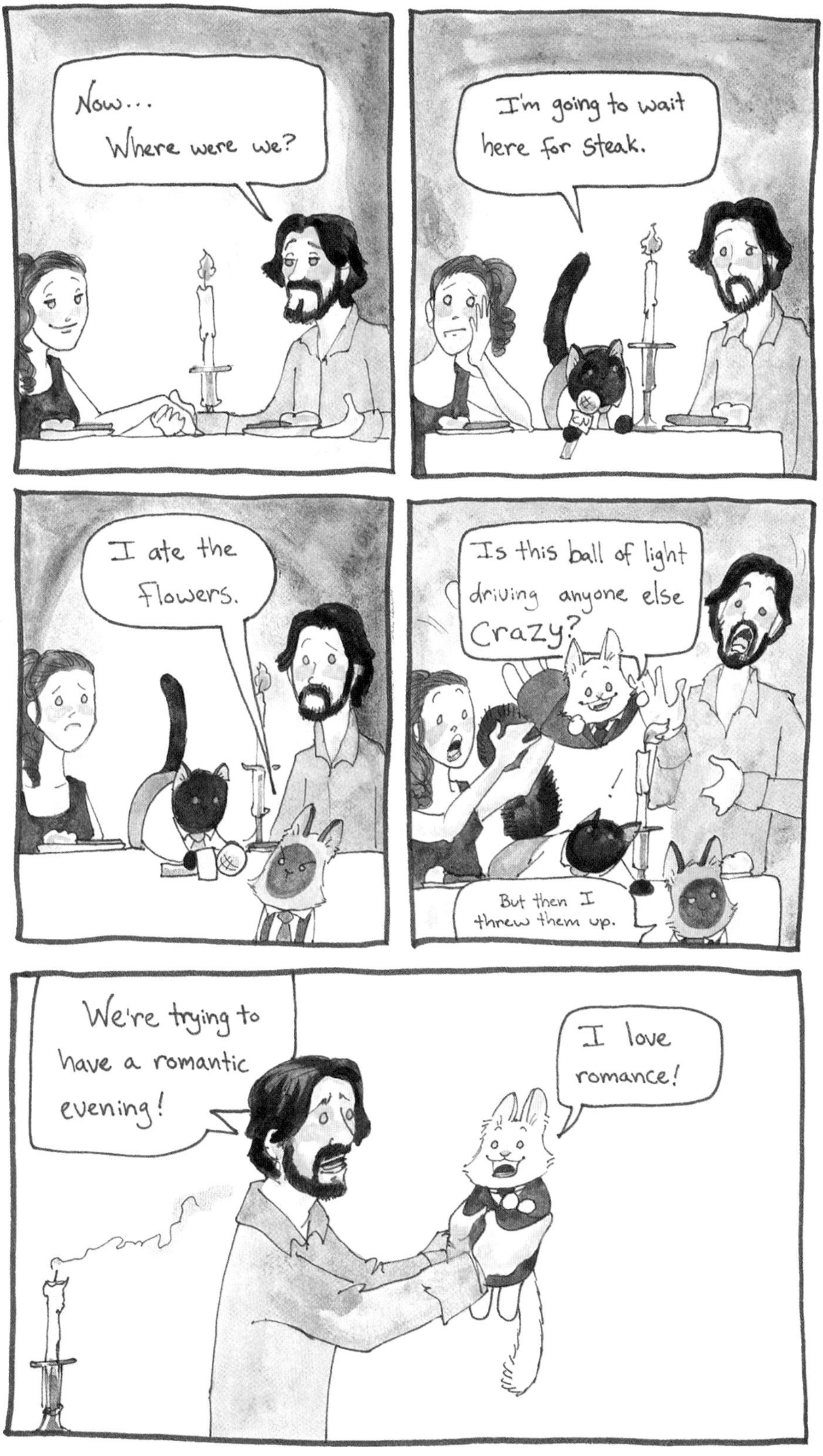
Now...
Where were we?
I'm going to wait here for steak.
CN
I ate the flowers.
Is this ball of light driving anyone else crazy?
But then I threw them up.
We're trying to have a romantic evening!
I love romance!

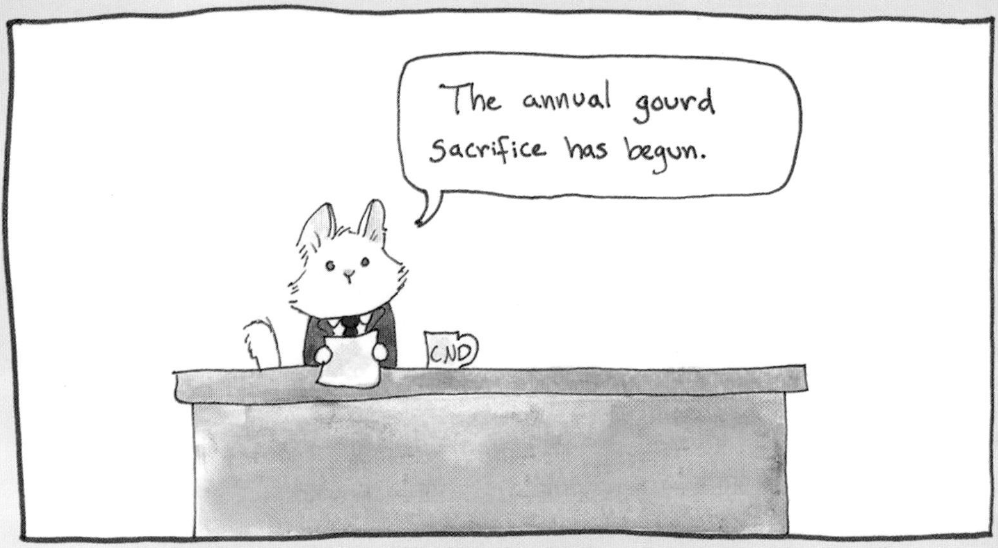
The annual gourd sacrifice has begun.
CND

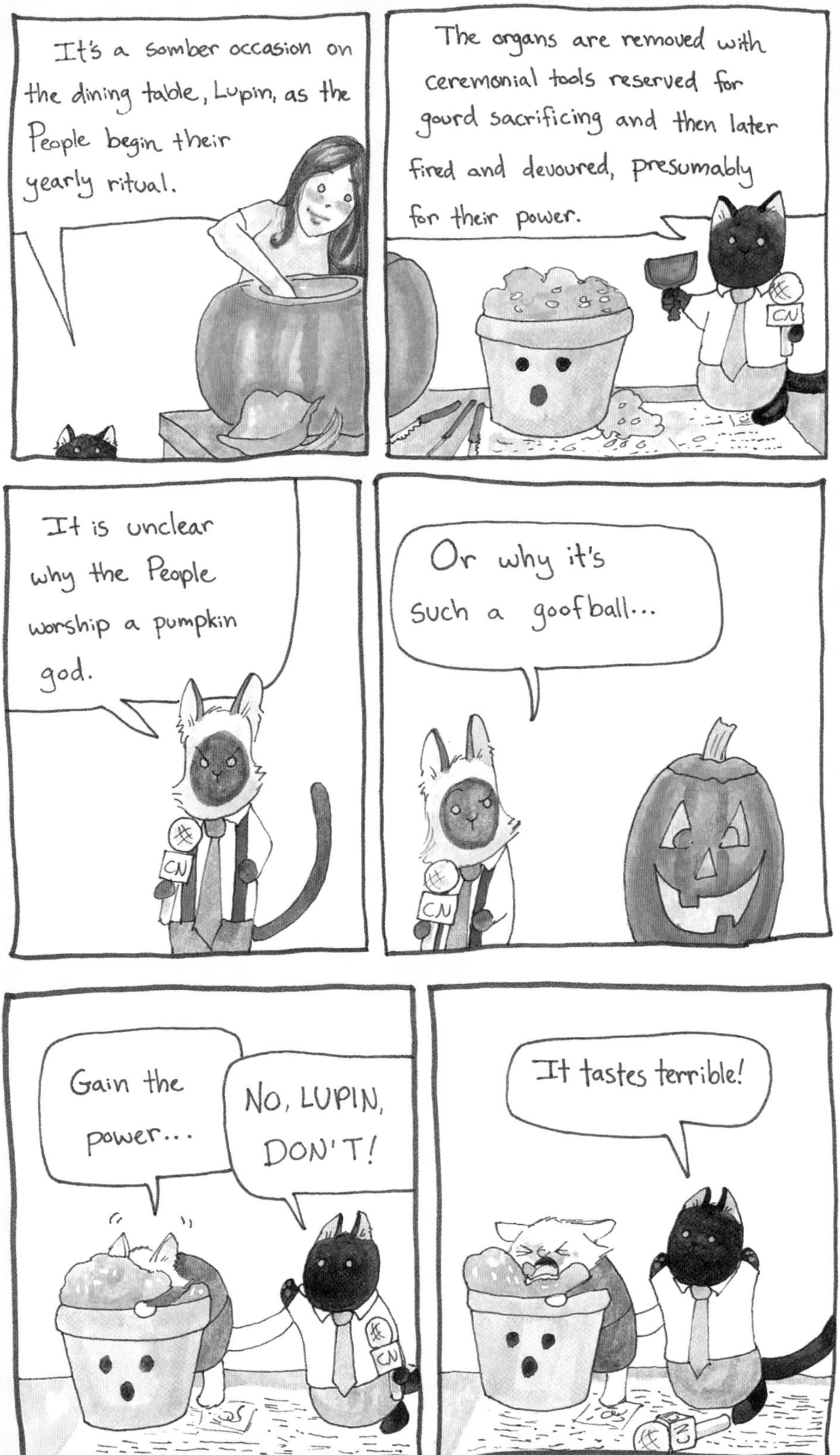

It's a somber occasion on the dining table, Lupin, as the People begin their yearly ritual.
The organs are removed with ceremonial tools reserved for gourd sacrificing and then later fired and devoured, presumably for their power.
CN
It is unclear why the People worship a pumpkin god.
CN
Or why it's such a goofball...
CN
Gain the power...
NO, LUPIN, DON'T!
CN
It tastes terrible!
CN

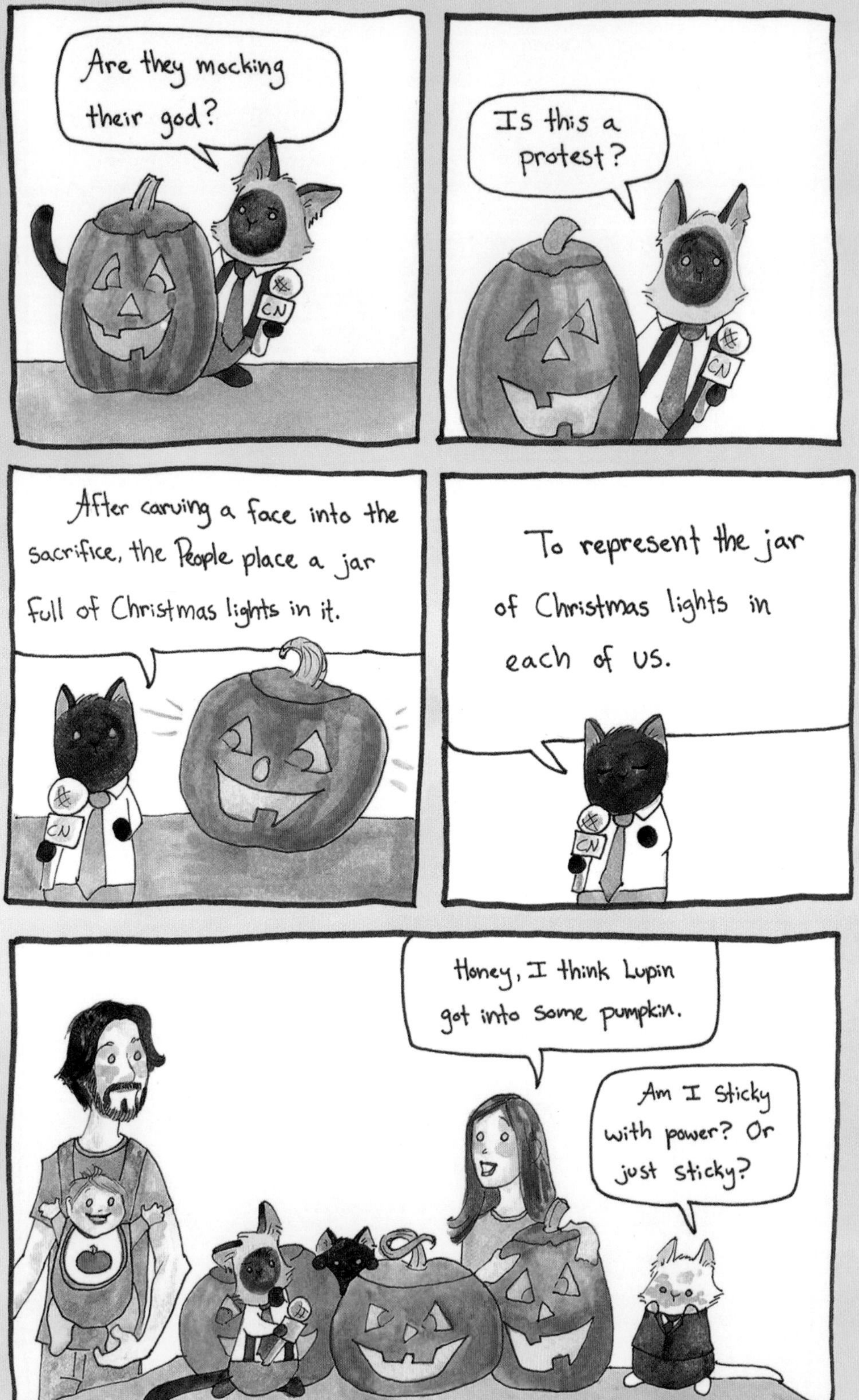

Are they mocking their god?
Is this a protest?
CN
After carving a face into the sacrifice, the People place a jar full of Christmas lights in it.
To represent the jar of Christmas lights in each of us.
Honey, I think Lupin got into some pumpkin.
Am I sticky with power? Or just sticky?

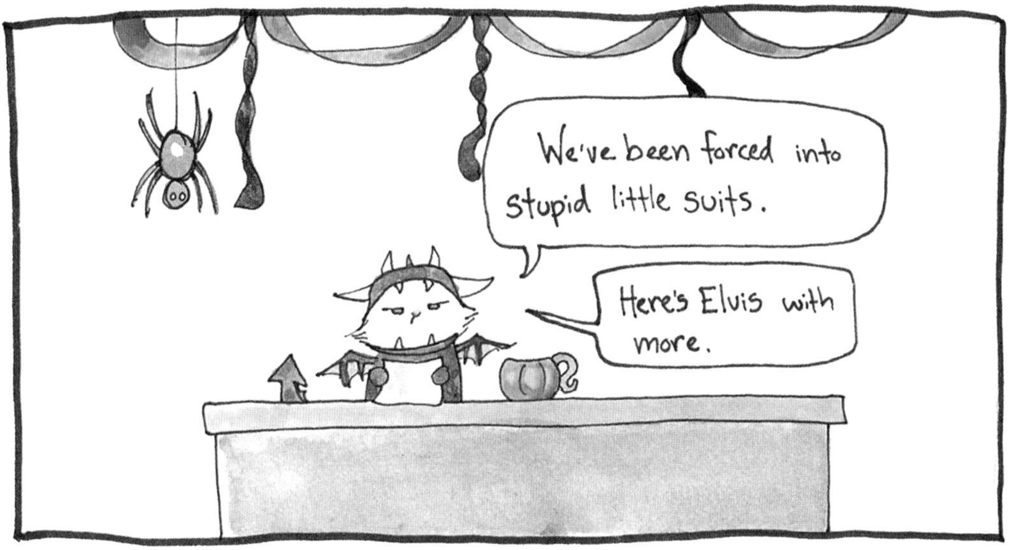
We've been forced into stupid little suits.
Here's Elvis with more.

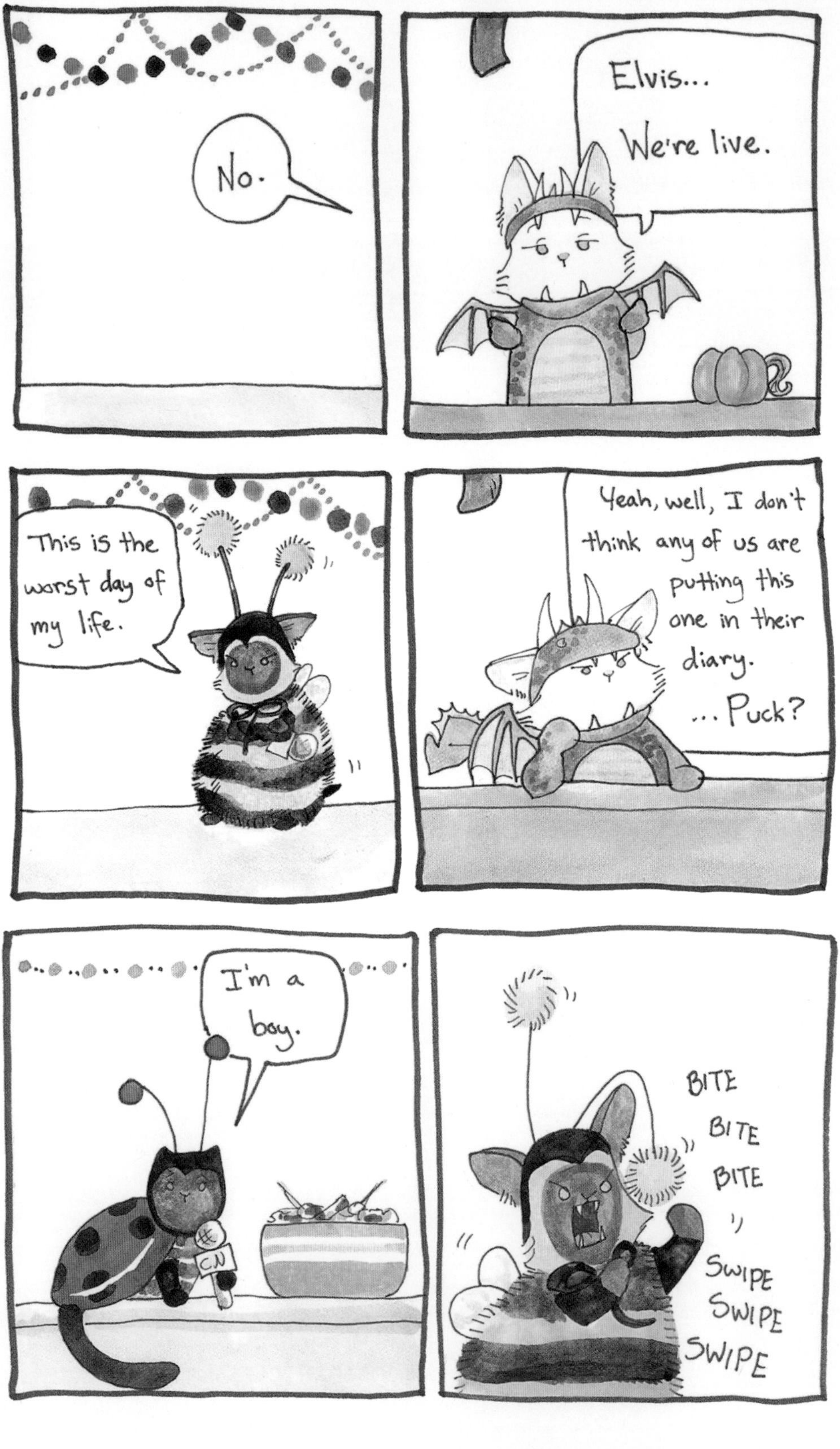
No.
Elvis... We're live.
This is the worst day of my life.
Yeah, well, I don't think any of us are putting this one in their diary.
... Puck?
I'm a boy.
CN
BITE
BITE
BITE
SWIPE
SWIPE
SWIPE

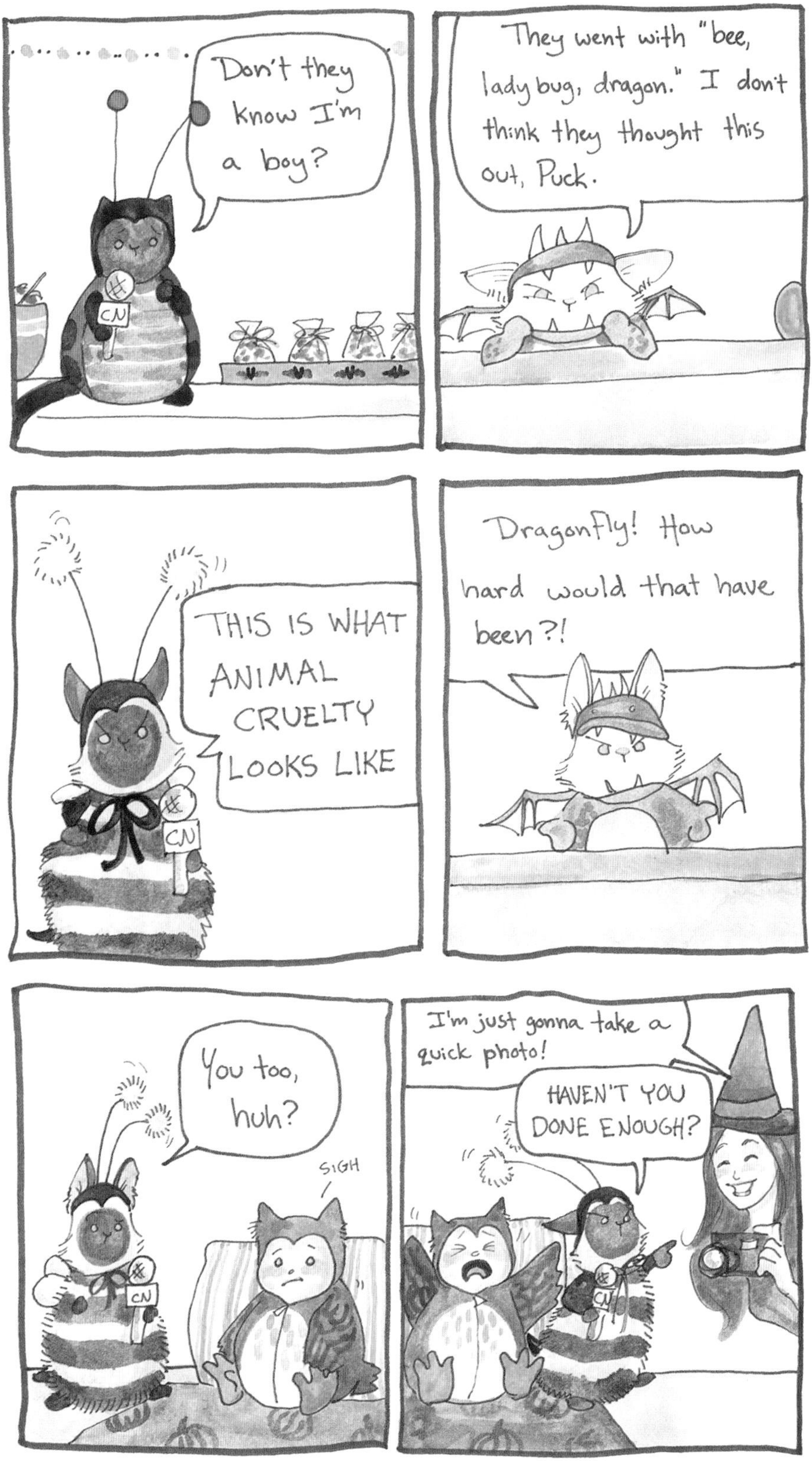
Don't they know I'm a boy?
They went with "bee, lady bug, dragon." I don't think they thought this out, Puck.
THIS IS WHAT ANIMAL CRUELTY LOOKS LIKE
Dragonfly! How hard would that have been?!
You too, huh?
SIGH
I'm just gonna take a quick photo!
HAVEN'T YOU DONE ENOUGH?

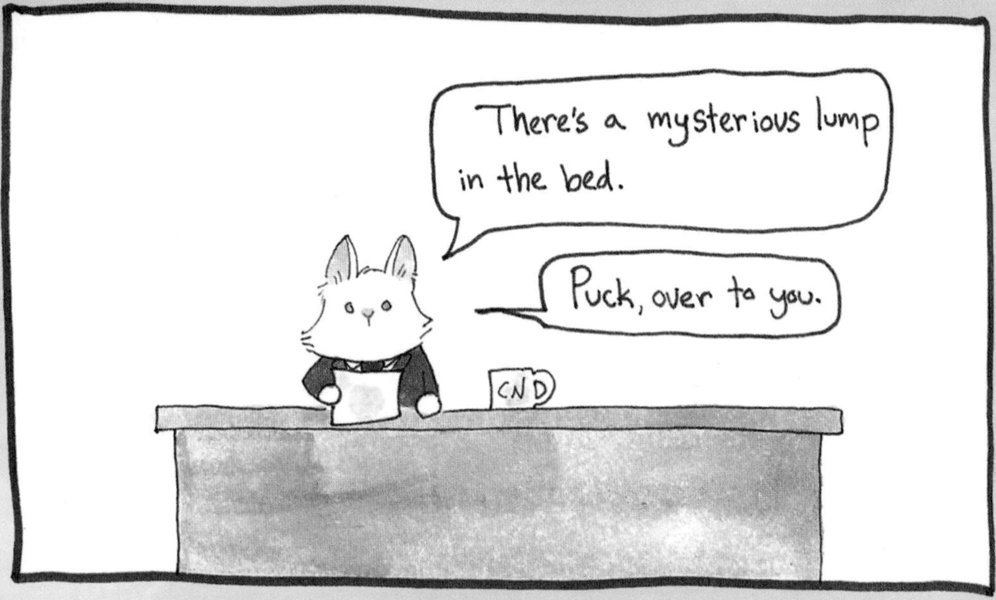
There's a mysterious lump in the bed.
Puck, over to you.
CND

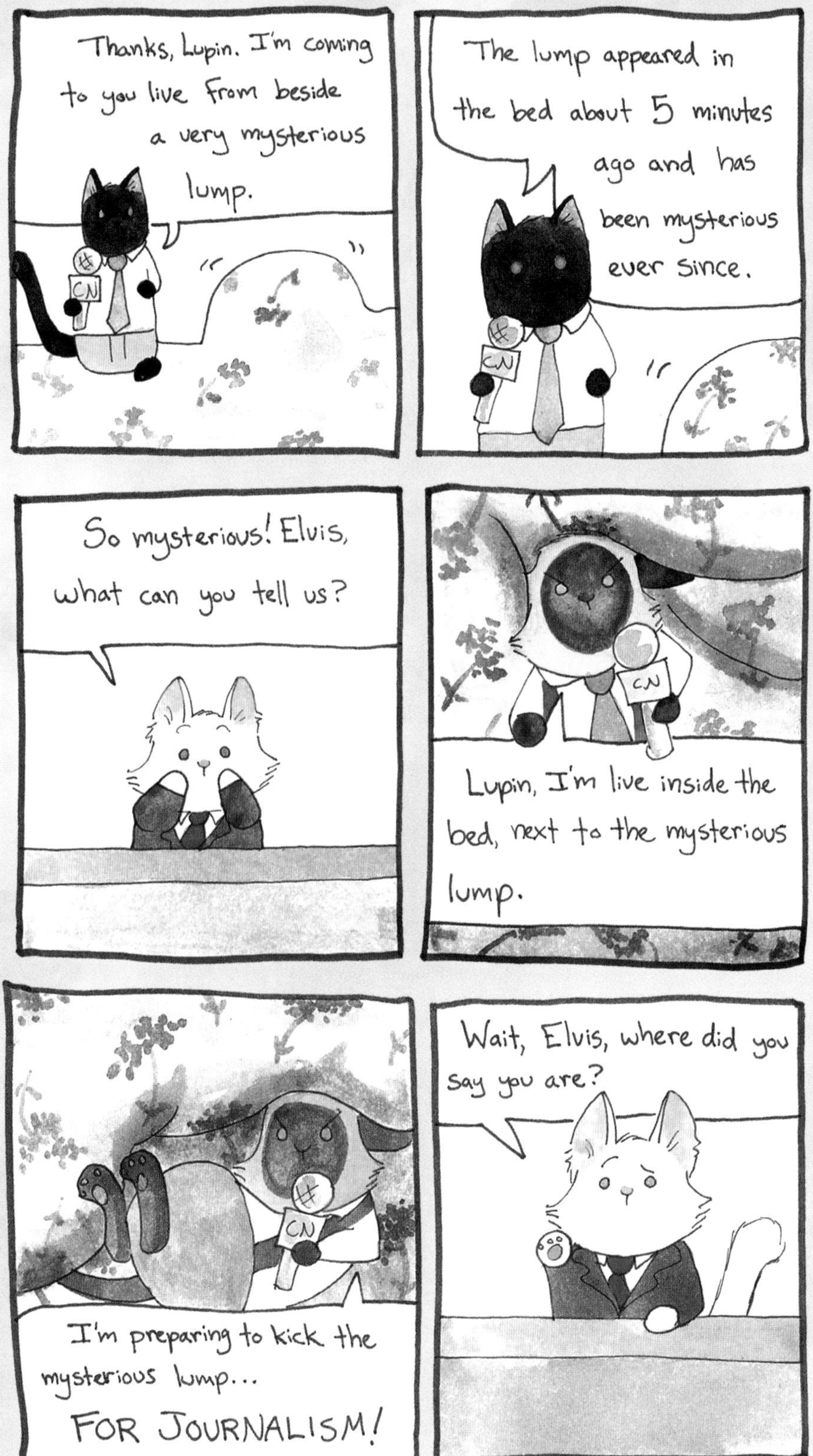
Thanks, Lupin. I'm coming to you live from beside a very mysterious lump.
CN
The lump appeared in the bed about 5 minutes ago and has been mysterious ever since.
CN
So mysterious! Elvis, what can you tell us?
CN
Lupin, I'm live inside the bed, next to the mysterious lump.
CN
I'm preparing to kick the mysterious lump... FOR JOURNALISM!
Wait, Elvis, where did you say you are?

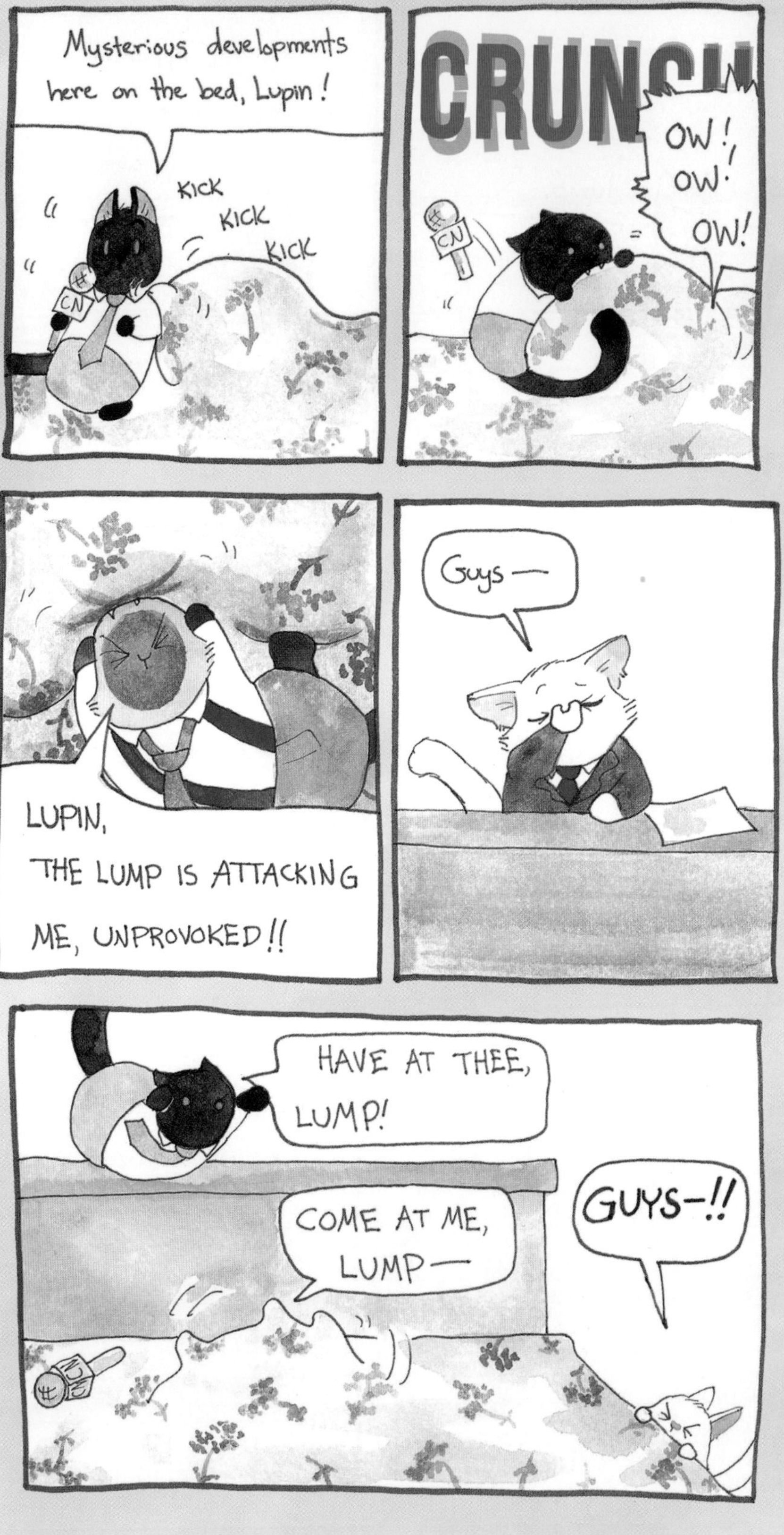
Mysterious developments here on the bed, Lupin!
KICK
KICK
KICK
CN
CRUNCH
OW!
OW!
OW!
CN
LUPIN,
THE LUMP IS ATTACKING ME, UNPROVOKED!!
Guys—
HAVE AT THEE, LUMP!
COME AT ME, LUMP—
GUYS—!!
CN
CN

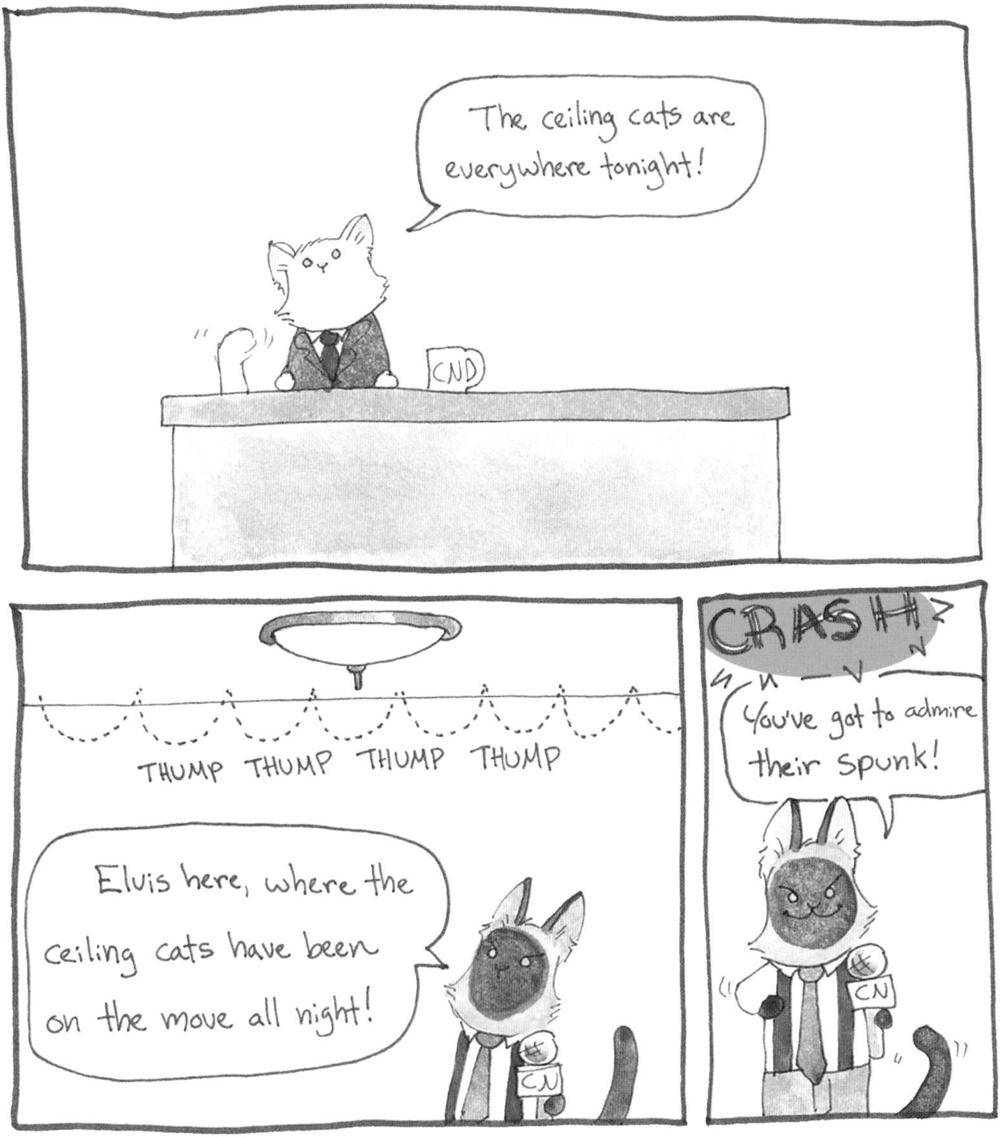
The ceiling cats are everywhere tonight!
CND
THUMP THUMP THUMP THUMP
Elvis here, where the ceiling cats have been on the move all night!
CN
CRASH
You've got to admire their spunk!
CN

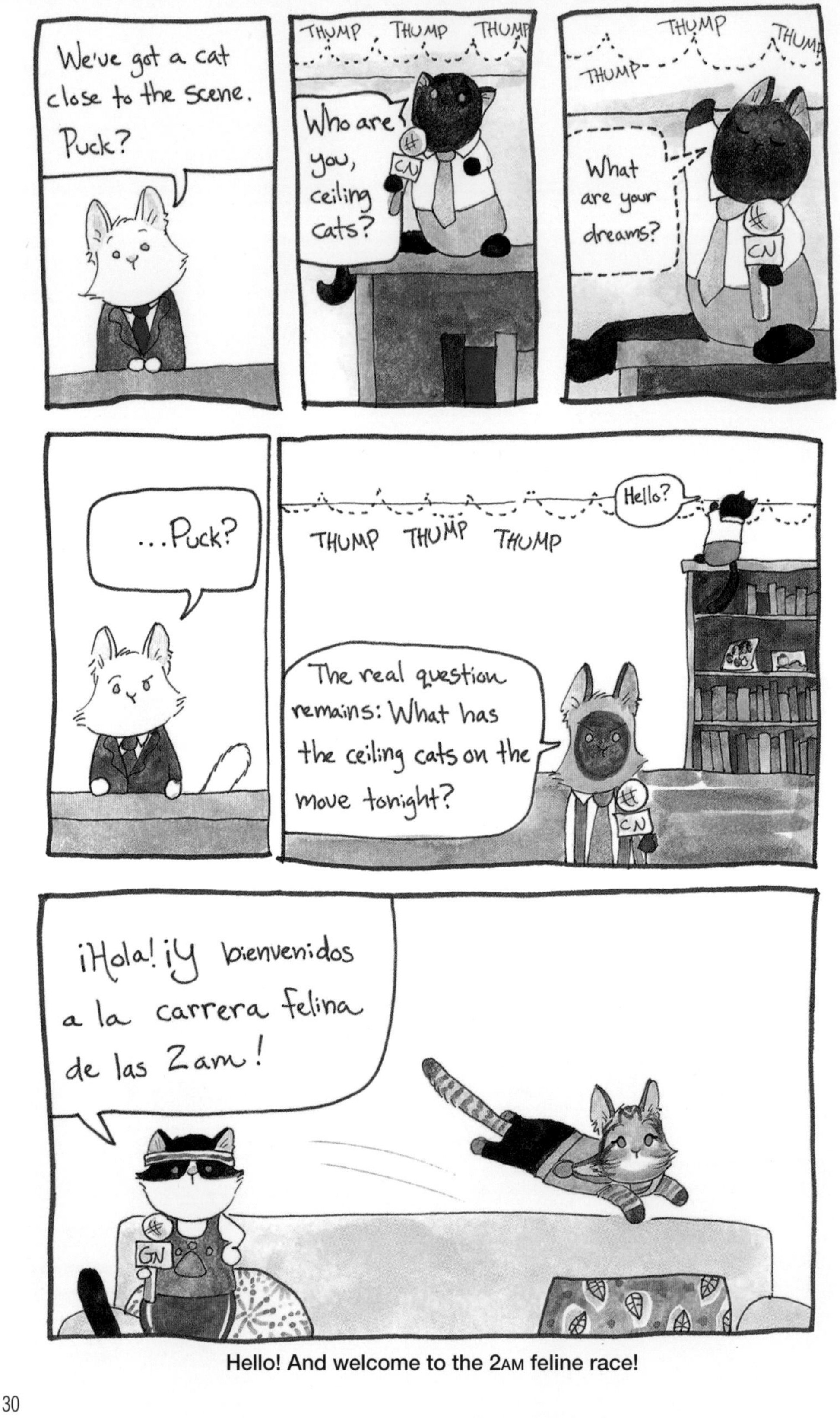

We've got a cat close to the scene. Puck?
THUMP THUMP THUMP
Who are you, ceiling cats?
CN
THUMP THUMP THUMP THUMP
What are your dreams?
CN
...Puck?
Hello?
THUMP THUMP THUMP
The real question remains: What has the ceiling cats on the move tonight?
CN
¡Hola! ¡Y bienvenidos a la carrera felina de las 2am!
GN

Hello! And welcome to the 2AM feline race!

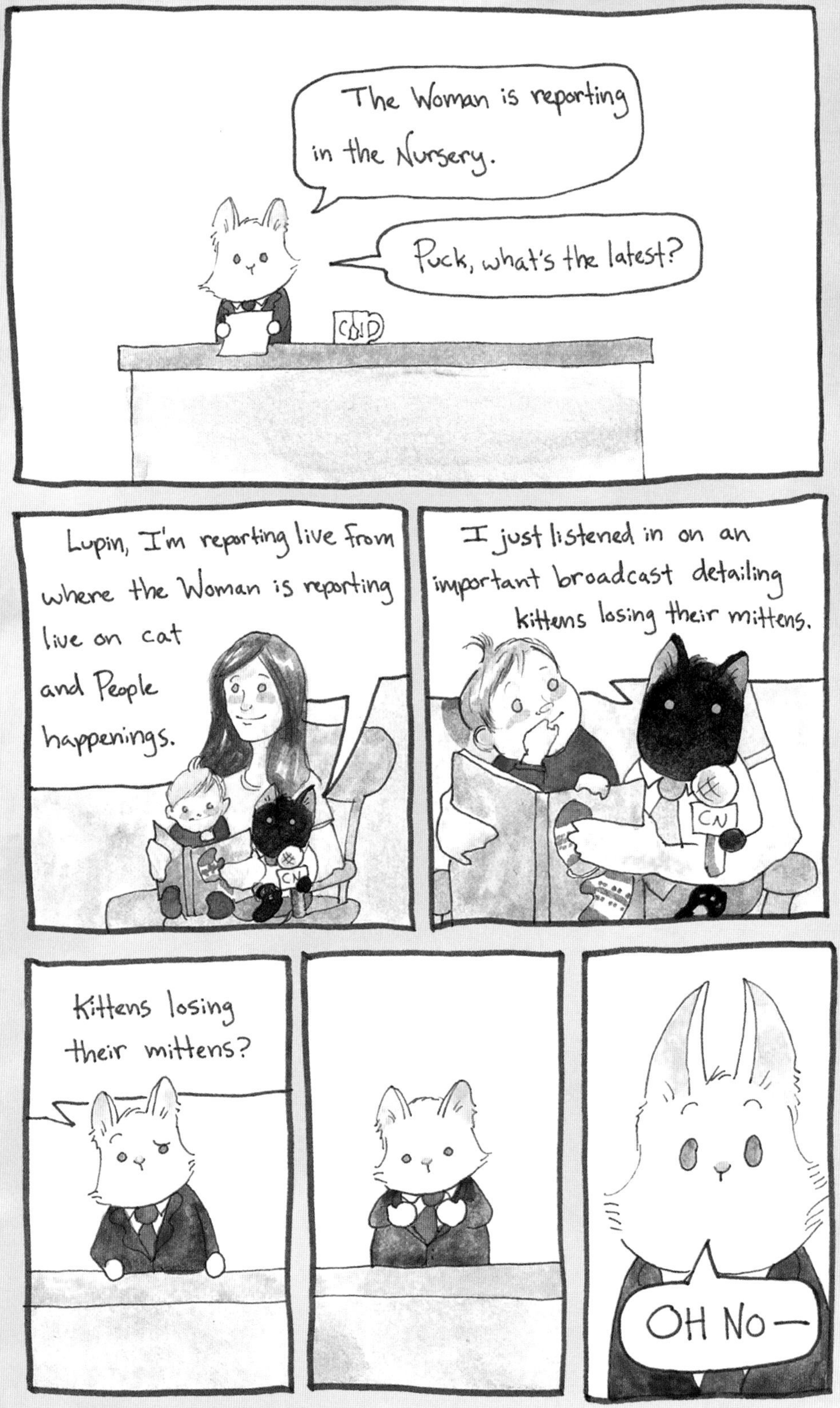
The Woman is reporting in the Nursery.
Puck, what's the latest?
CNID
Lupin, I'm reporting live from where the Woman is reporting live on cat and People happenings.
CN
I just listened in on an important broadcast detailing kittens losing their mittens.
CN
Kittens losing their mittens?
OH No—

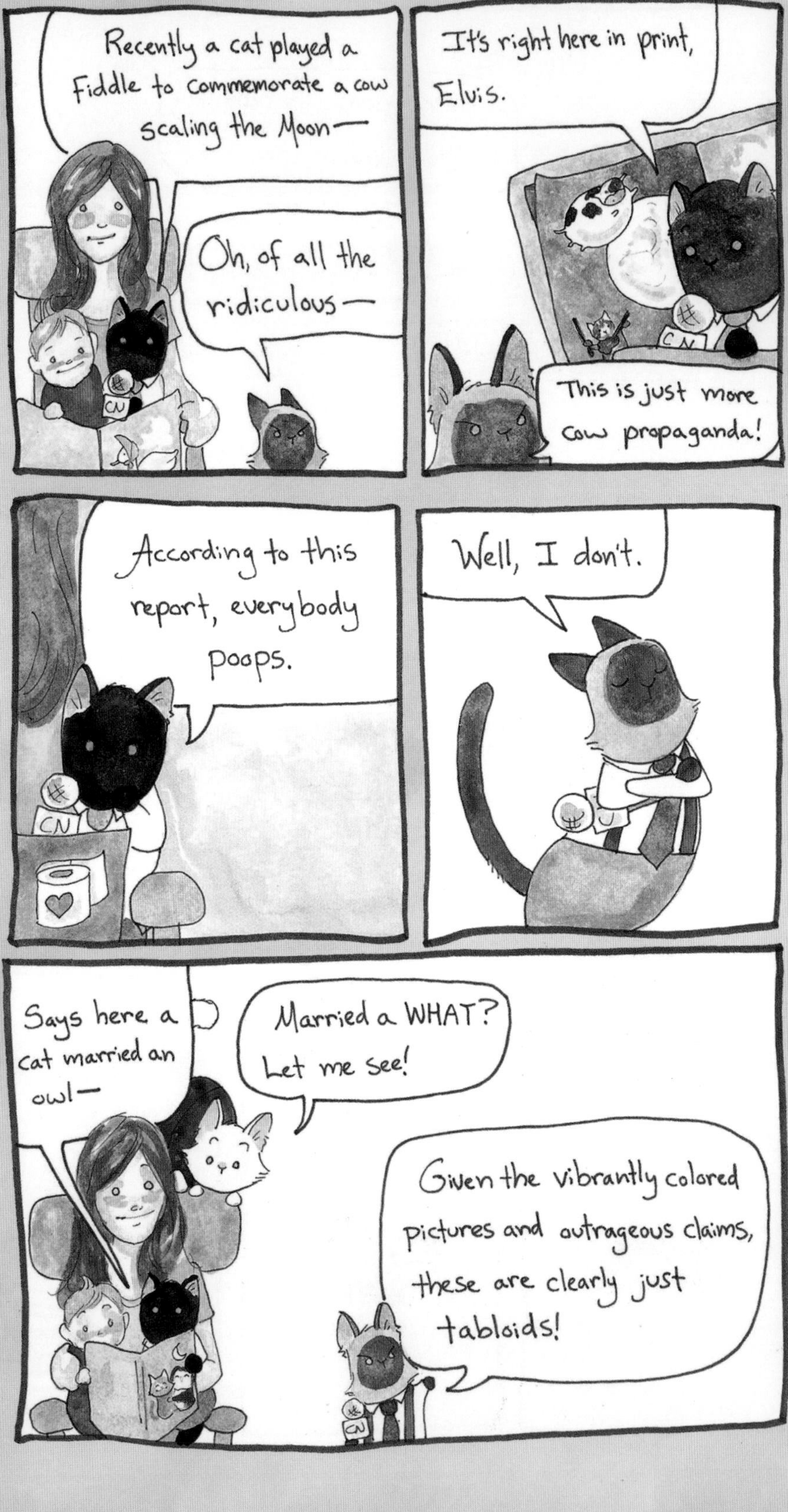
Recently a cat played a Fiddle to commemorate a cow scaling the Moon—
Oh, of all the ridiculous—
It's right here in print, Elvis.
This is just more cow propaganda!
According to this report, everybody poops.
Well, I don't.
Says here a cat married an owl—
Married a WHAT? Let me see!
Given the vibrantly colored pictures and outrageous claims, these are clearly just tabloids!

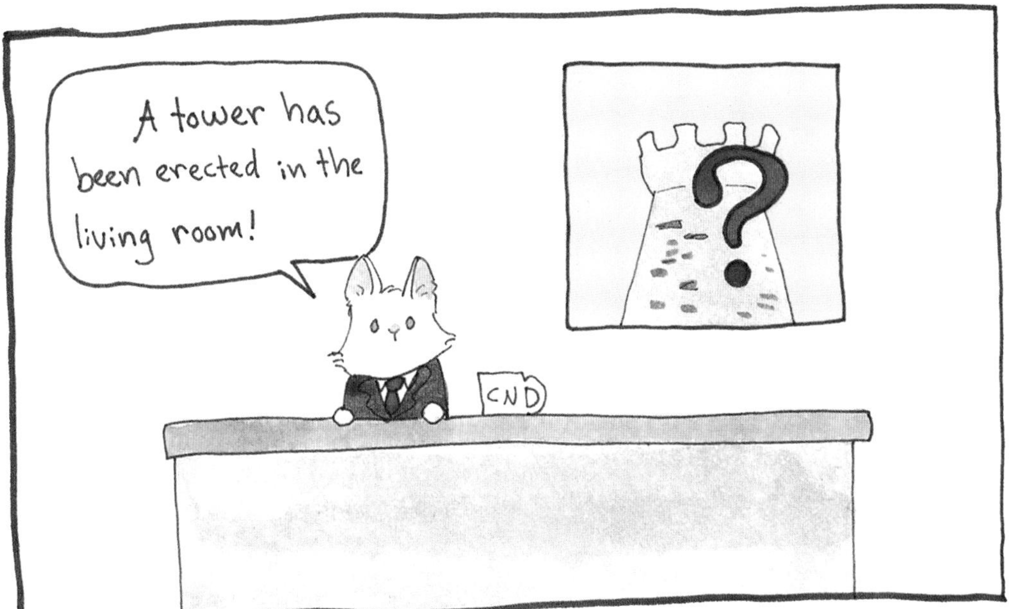
A tower has been erected in the living room!
CND

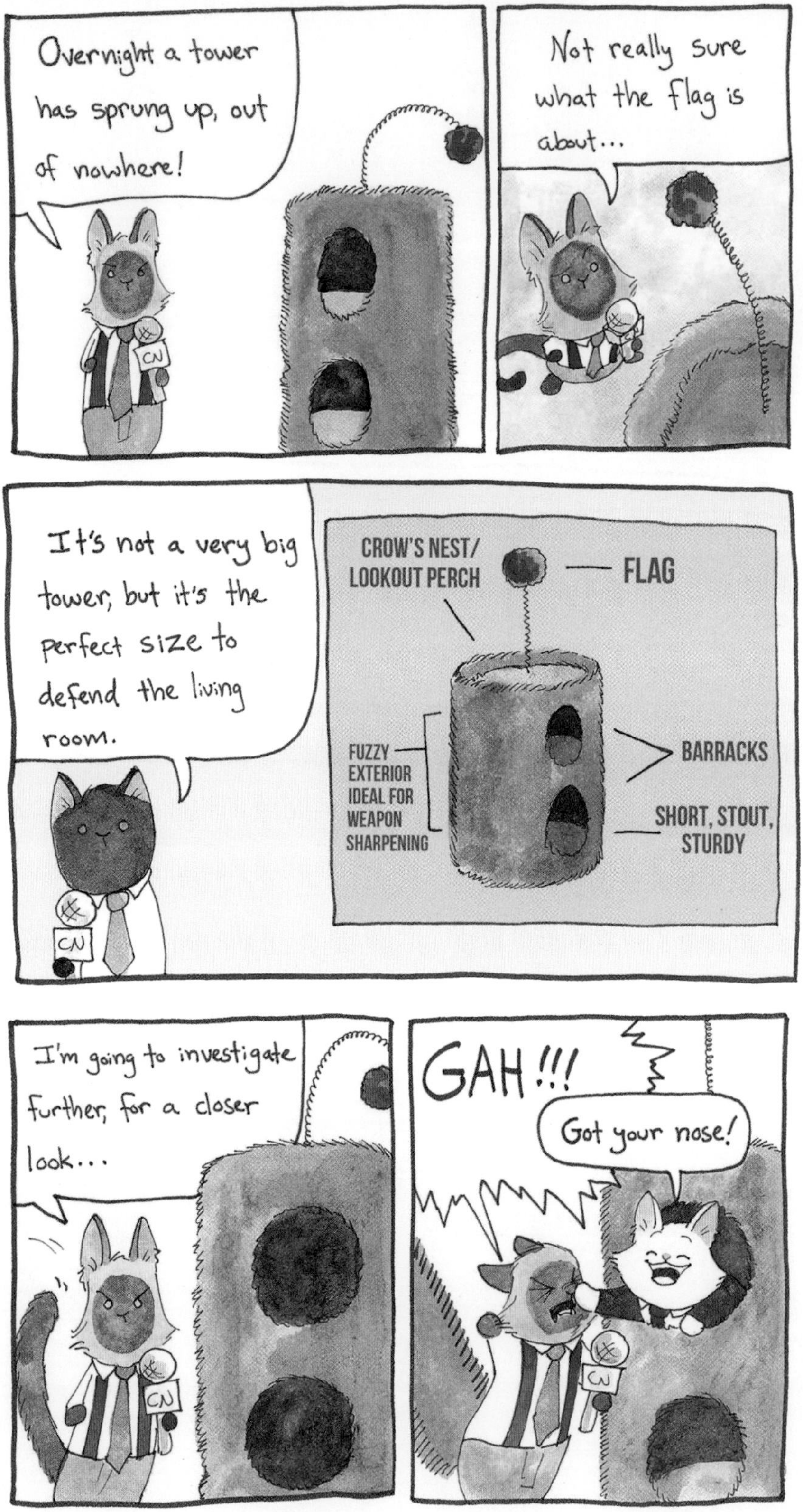
Overnight a tower has sprung up, out of nowhere!
Not really sure what the flag is about...
It's not a very big tower, but it's the perfect size to defend the living room.
CROW'S NEST/ LOOKOUT PERCH
FLAG
FUZZY EXTERIOR IDEAL FOR WEAPON SHARPENING
BARRACKS
SHORT, STOUT, STURDY
I'm going to investigate further, for a closer look...
GAH!!!
Got your nose!

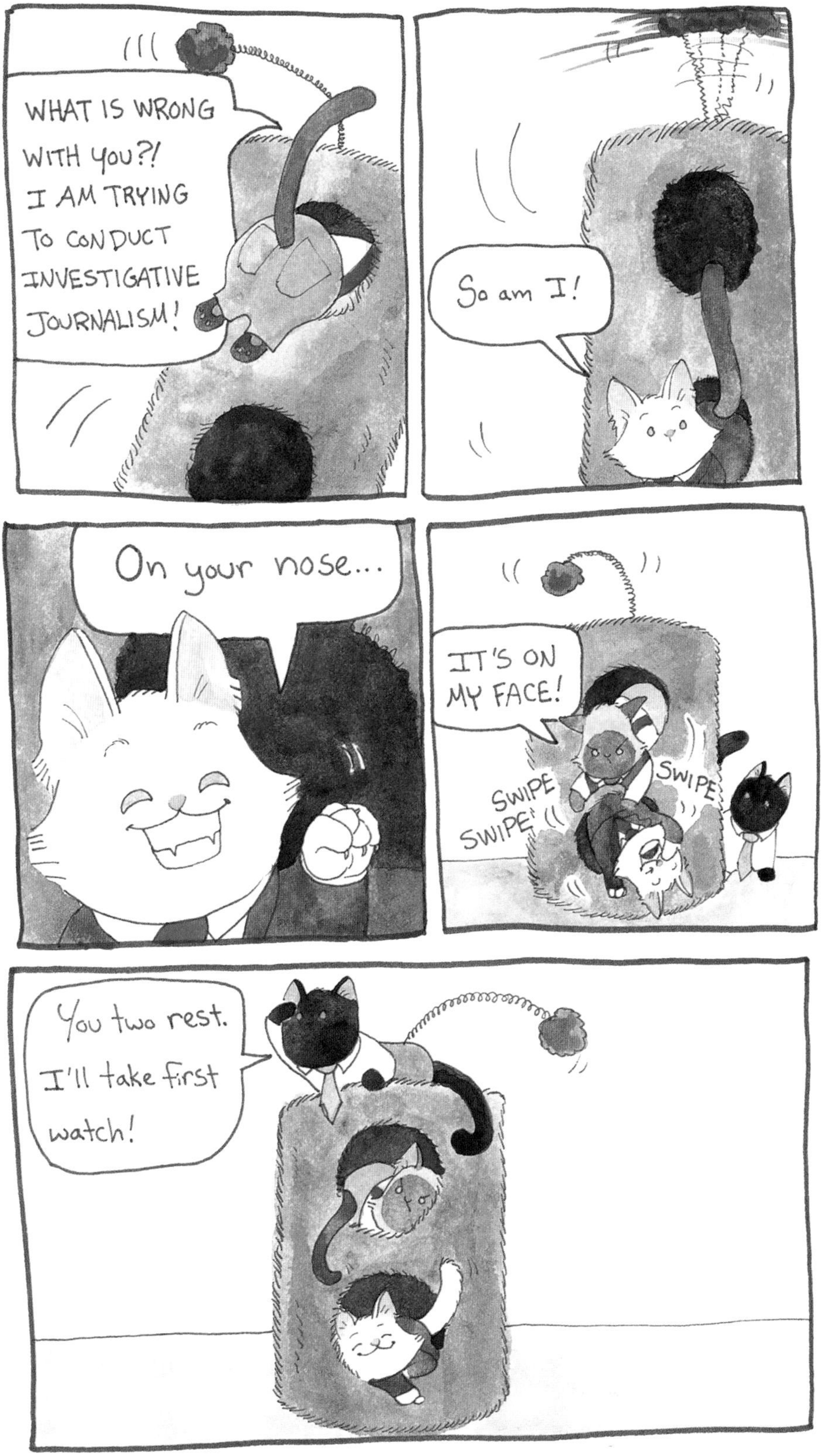
WHAT IS WRONG WITH YOU?! I AM TRYING TO CONDUCT INVESTIGATIVE JOURNALISM!
So am I!
On your nose...
IT'S ON MY FACE!
SWIPE
SWIPE
SWIPE
You two rest. I'll take first watch!

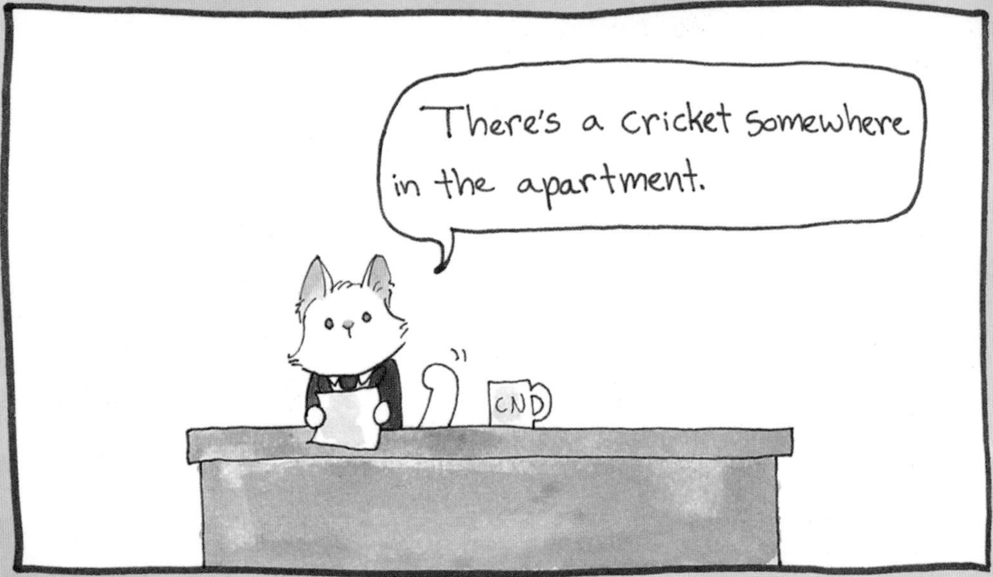
There's a cricket somewhere in the apartment.
CND

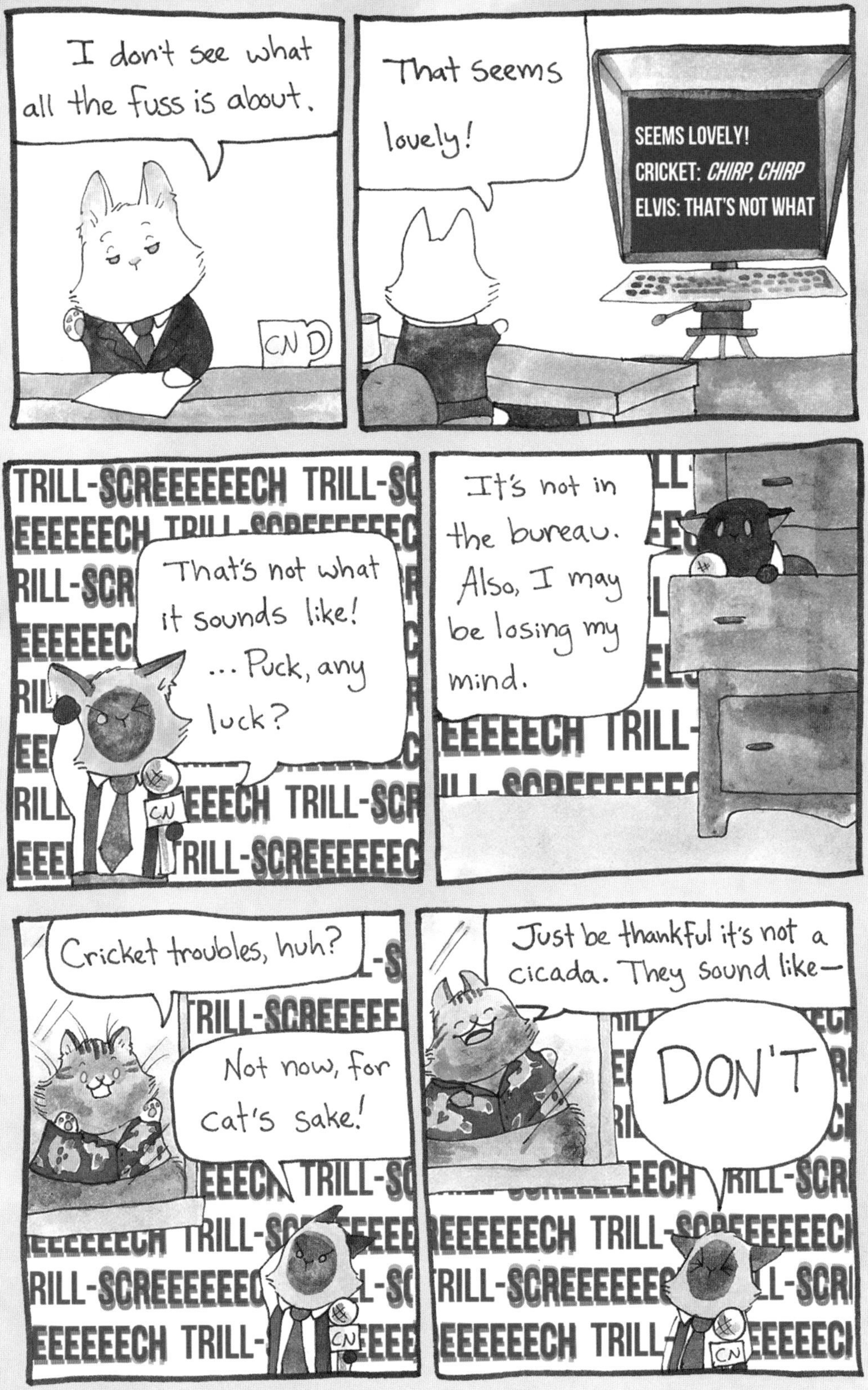
I don't see what all the fuss is about.
That seems lovely!
SEEMS LOVELY!
CRICKET: CHIRP, CHIRP
ELVIS: THAT'S NOT WHAT
CN
TRILL-SCREEEEEEECH
That's not what it sounds like! ... Puck, any luck?
CN
It's not in the bureau. Also, I may be losing my mind.
Cricket troubles, huh?
Not now, for cat's sake!
CN
Just be thankful it's not a cicada. They sound like—
DON'T
CN

TOMMY: *CHITTER, CHITTER*

REENEGH
REENEGH
RENEGHH
HHHHHHH
HHHHHHH
HHHHHH

LUPIN, THE TELEPROMPTER IS LYING TO YOU!

Lupin, the teleprompter is...

GASP

TREACHERY!

TRILL-SCREEEEEECH
EEEEEECH TRILL
RILL-SCREEEEEE
EEEEECH TRILL

It's not under the bed.

TRILL-SCREEEEE
REEEEEECH TR
RILL-SCREEEE

Elvis, do you remember how great it was in the before-cricket times?

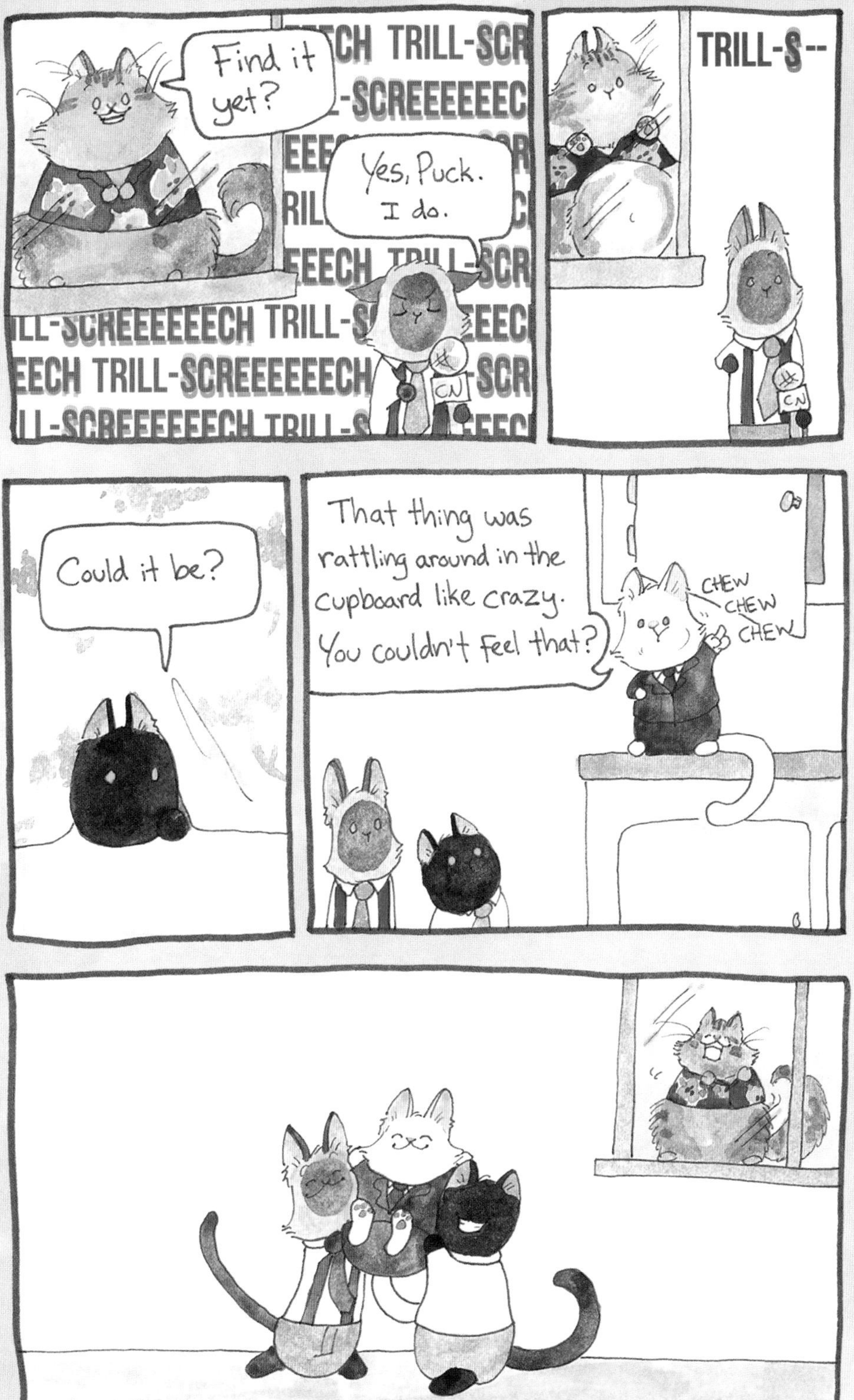
TRILL-SCREEEEEEECH
Find it yet?
Yes, Puck. I do.
TRILL-S--
Could it be?
That thing was rattling around in the cupboard like crazy. You couldn't feel that?
CHEW CHEW CHEW

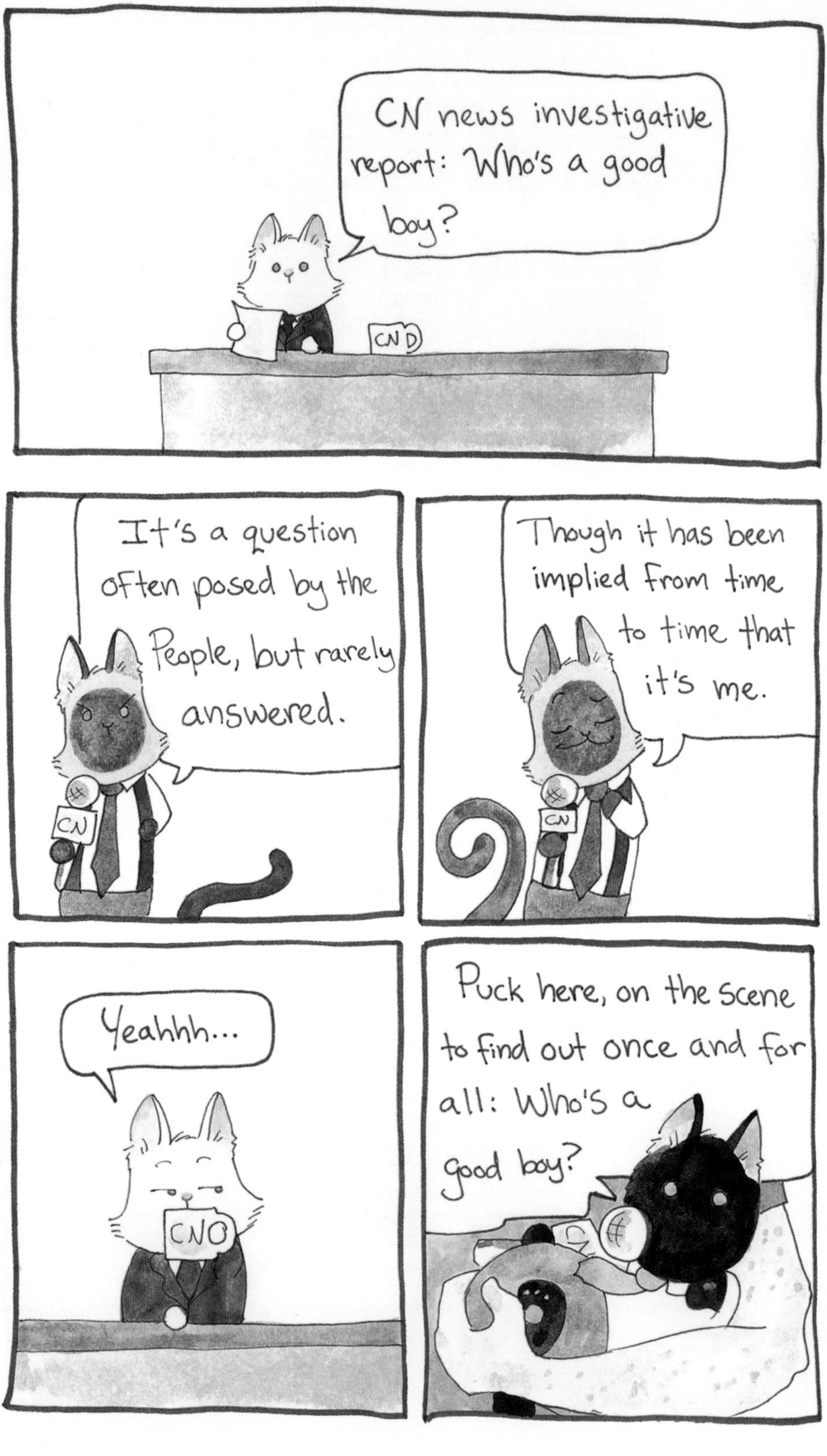
CN news investigative report: Who's a good boy?
CND
It's a question often posed by the People, but rarely answered.
CN
Though it has been implied from time to time that it's me.
CN
Yeahhh...
CNO
Puck here, on the scene to find out once and for all: Who's a good boy?

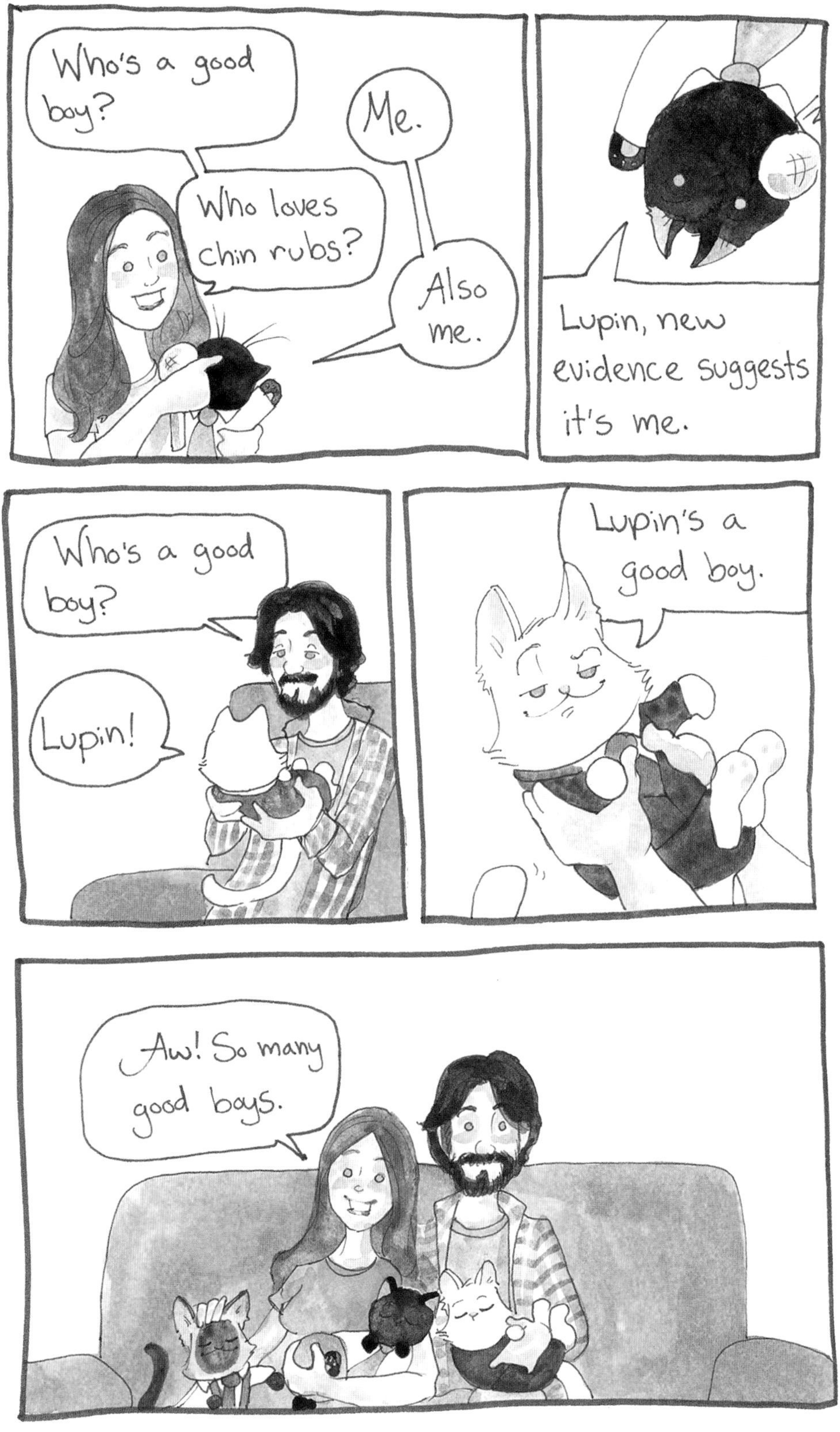
Who's a good boy?
Me.
Who loves chin rubs?
Also me.
Lupin, new evidence suggests it's me.
Who's a good boy?
Lupin!
Lupin's a good boy.
Aw! So many good boys.

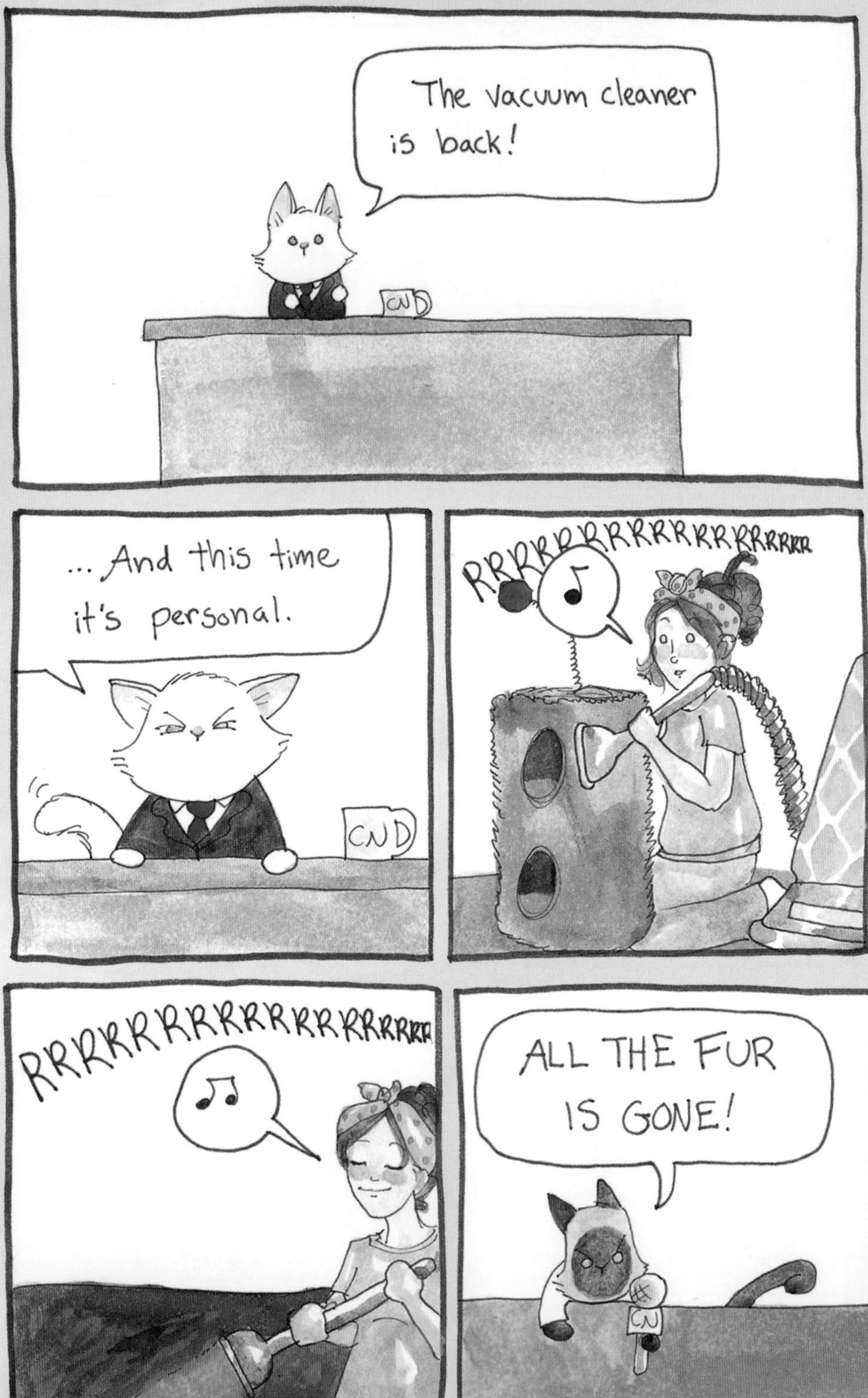
The vacuum cleaner is back!
CND
...And this time it's personal.
CND
RRRRRRRRRRRRRRRRRR
RRRRRRRRRRRRRRRRRR
ALL THE FUR IS GONE!
CN

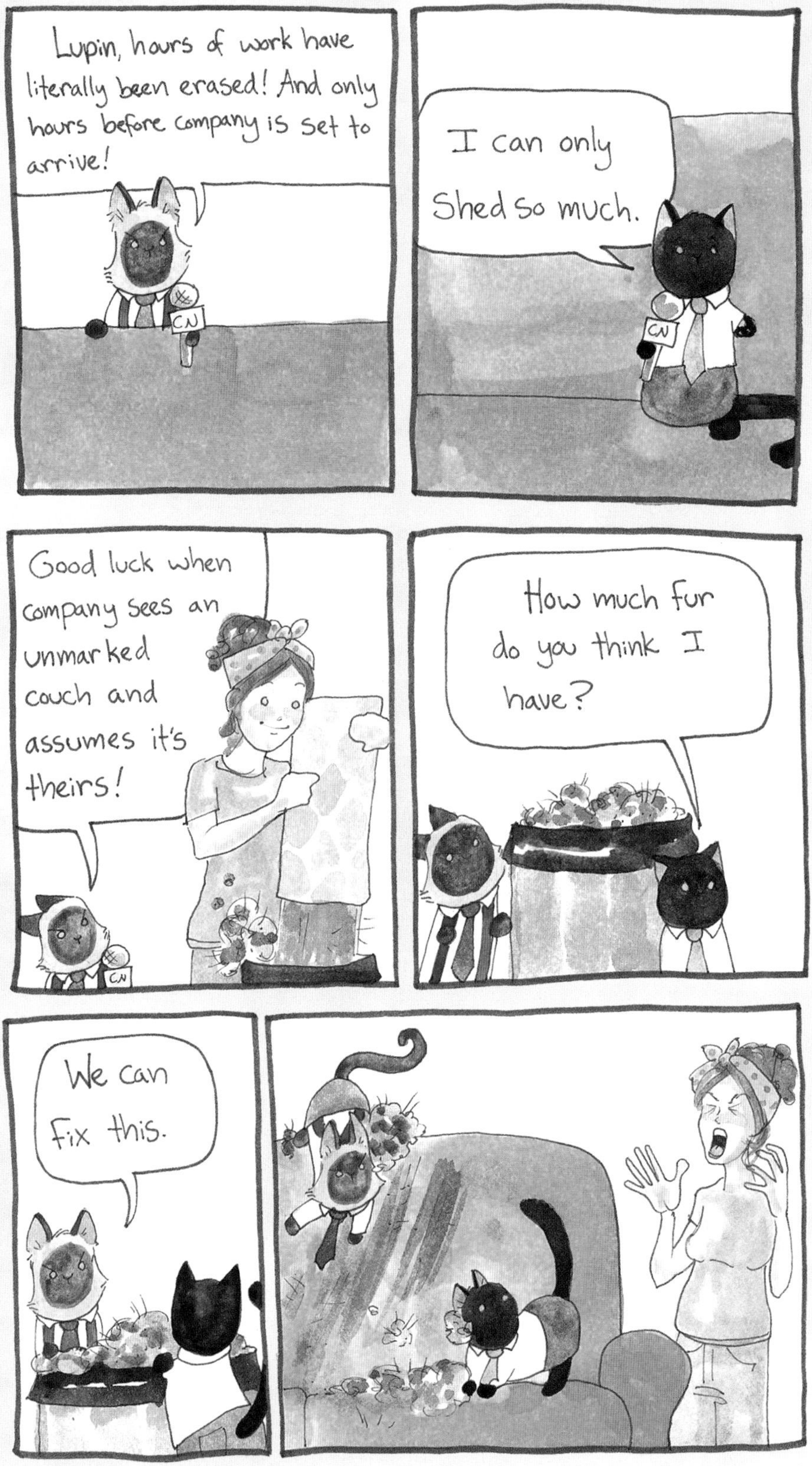
Lupin, hours of work have literally been erased! And only hours before company is set to arrive!
CN
I can only Shed so much.
CN
Good luck when company sees an unmarked couch and assumes it's theirs!
CN
How much fur do you think I have?
We can Fix this.

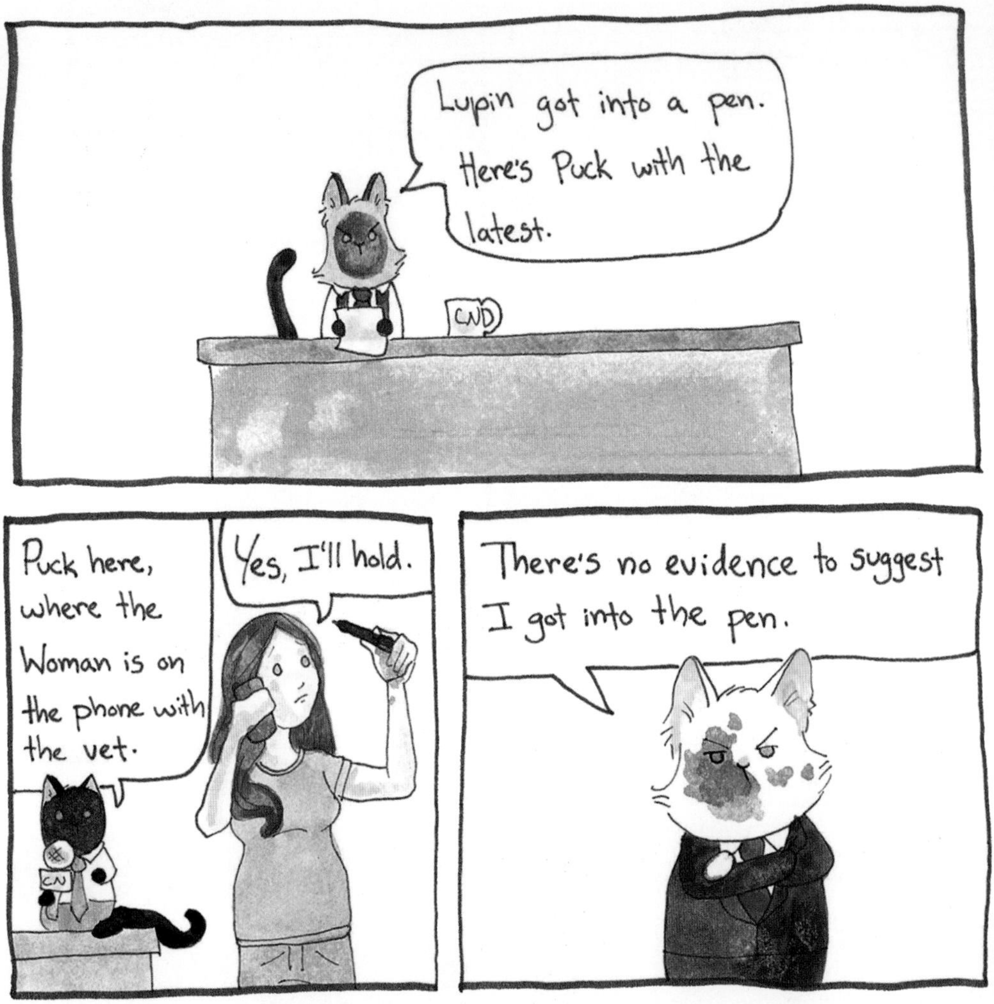
Lupin got into a pen. Here's Puck with the latest.
CND
Puck here, where the Woman is on the phone with the vet.
CN
Yes, I'll hold.
There's no evidence to suggest I got into the pen.

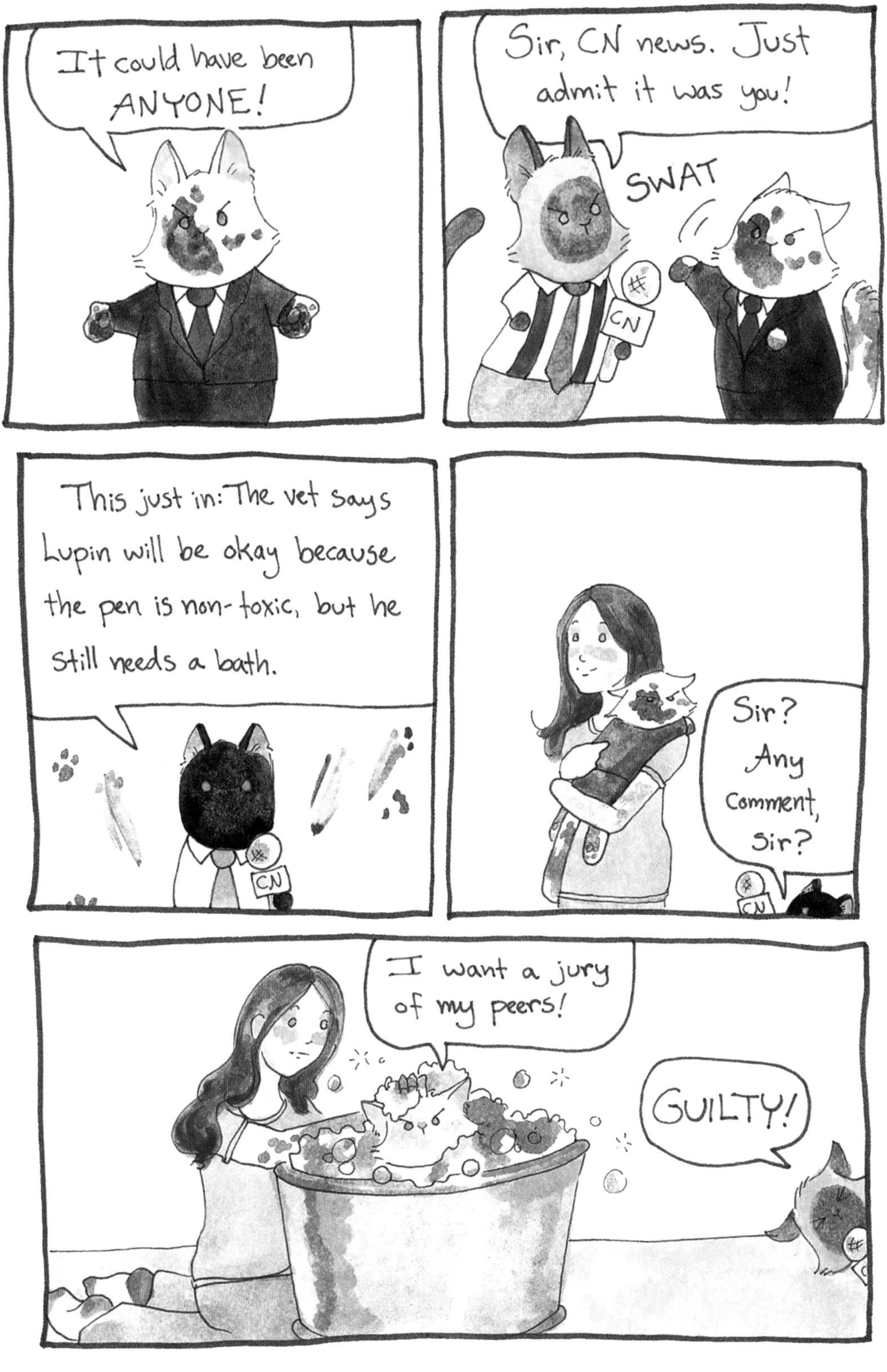
It could have been ANYONE!
Sir, CN news. Just admit it was you!
SWAT
CN
This just in: The vet says Lupin will be okay because the pen is non-toxic, but he still needs a bath.
CN
Sir? Any Comment, Sir?
CN
I want a jury of my peers!
GUILTY!

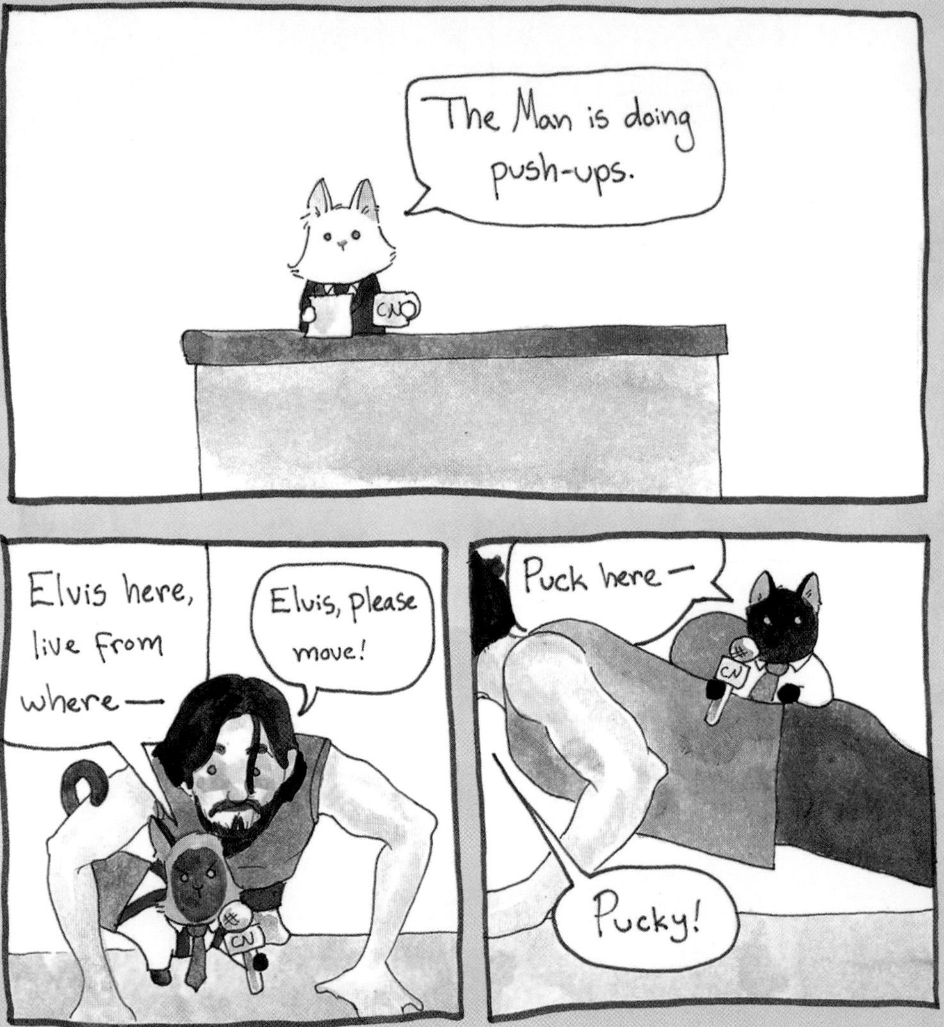
The Man is doing push-ups.
CN
Elvis here, live from where—
Elvis, please move!
CN
Puck here—
CN
Pucky!

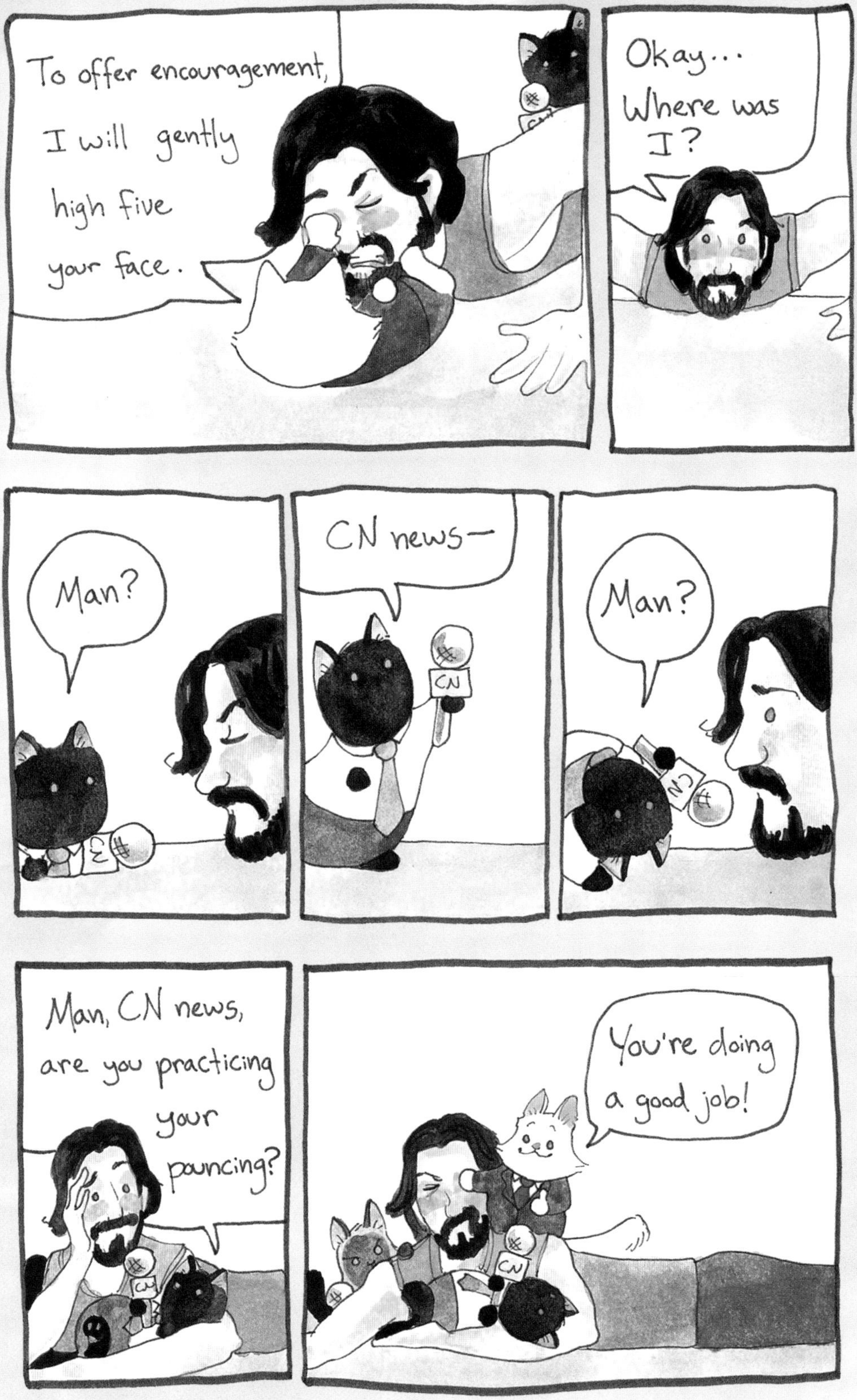
To offer encouragement, I will gently high five your face.
Okay... Where was I?
Man?
CN news—
Man?
Man, CN news, are you practicing your pouncing?
You're doing a good job!

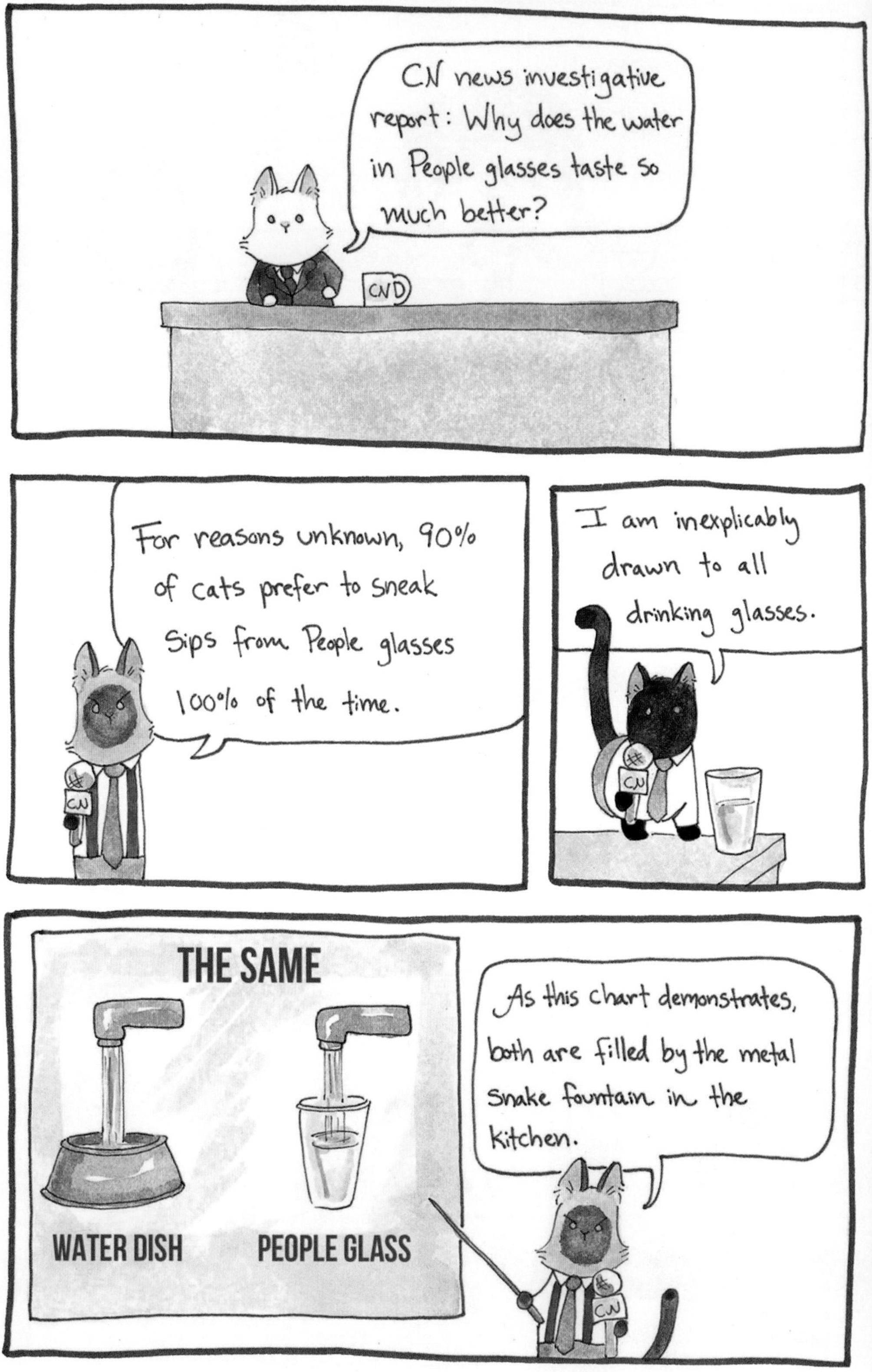
CN news investigative report: Why does the water in People glasses taste so much better?
CND
For reasons unknown, 90% of cats prefer to sneak Sips from People glasses 100% of the time.
CN
I am inexplicably drawn to all drinking glasses.
CN
THE SAME
WATER DISH
PEOPLE GLASS
As this chart demonstrates, both are filled by the metal Snake fountain in the kitchen.
CN

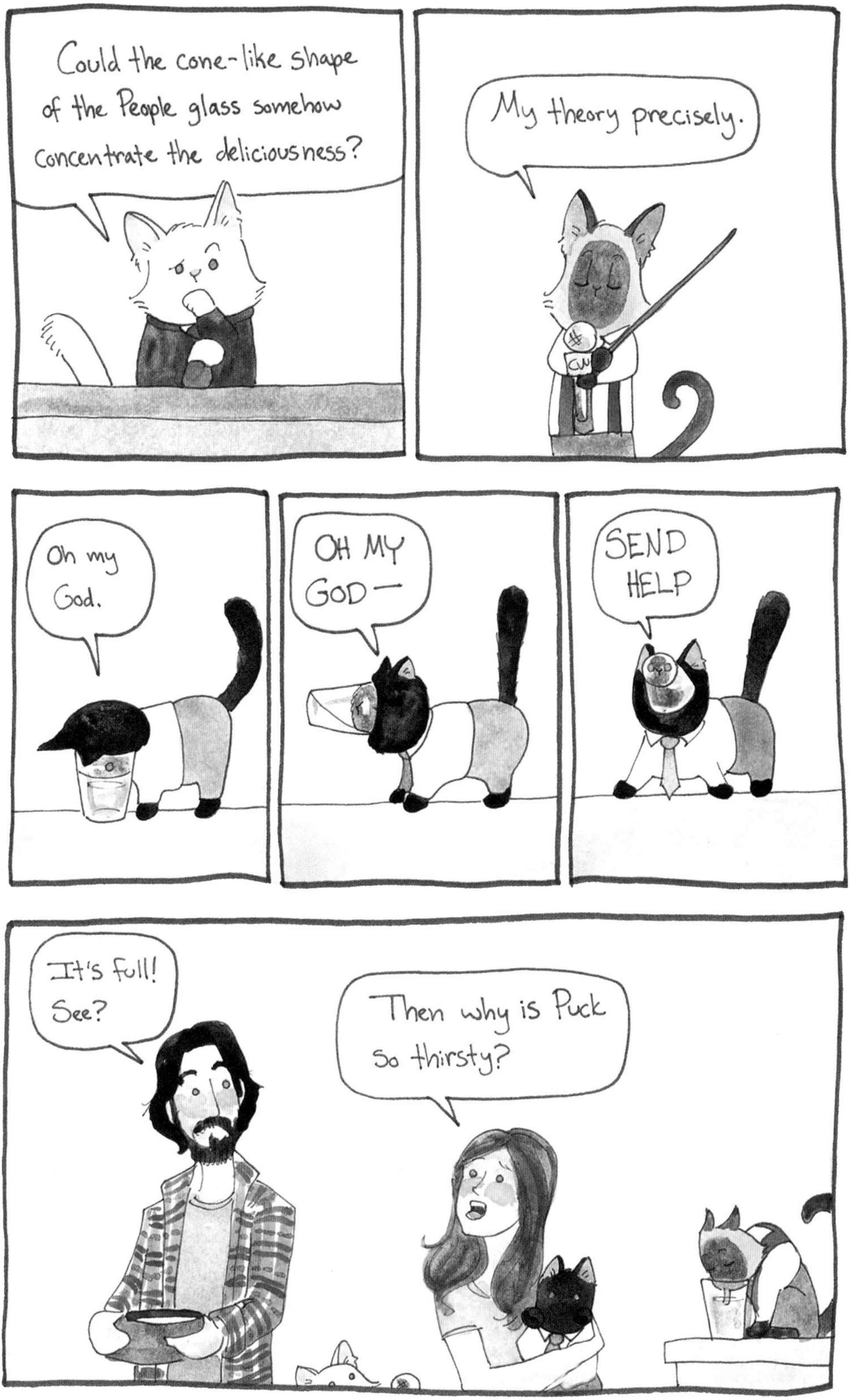
Could the cone-like shape of the People glass somehow concentrate the deliciousness?
My theory precisely.
Oh my God.
OH MY GOD—
SEND HELP
It's full! See?
Then why is Puck so thirsty?

Delicious smells are coming in from the kitchen.
CND
Elvis?
Thanks, Lupin. Elvis here, overseeing all of the feast preparations in the kitchen.
CN
I am vital to this process.
CN
Elvis, get down.

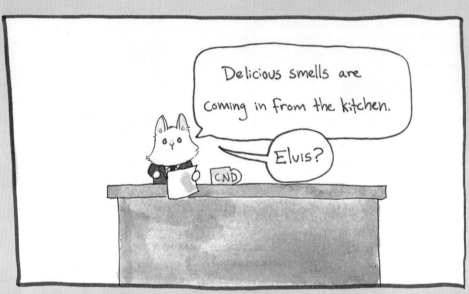

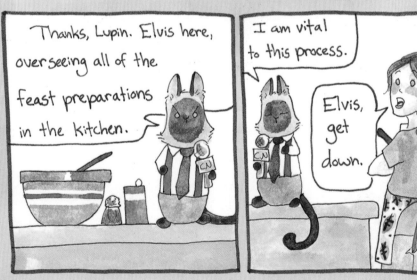

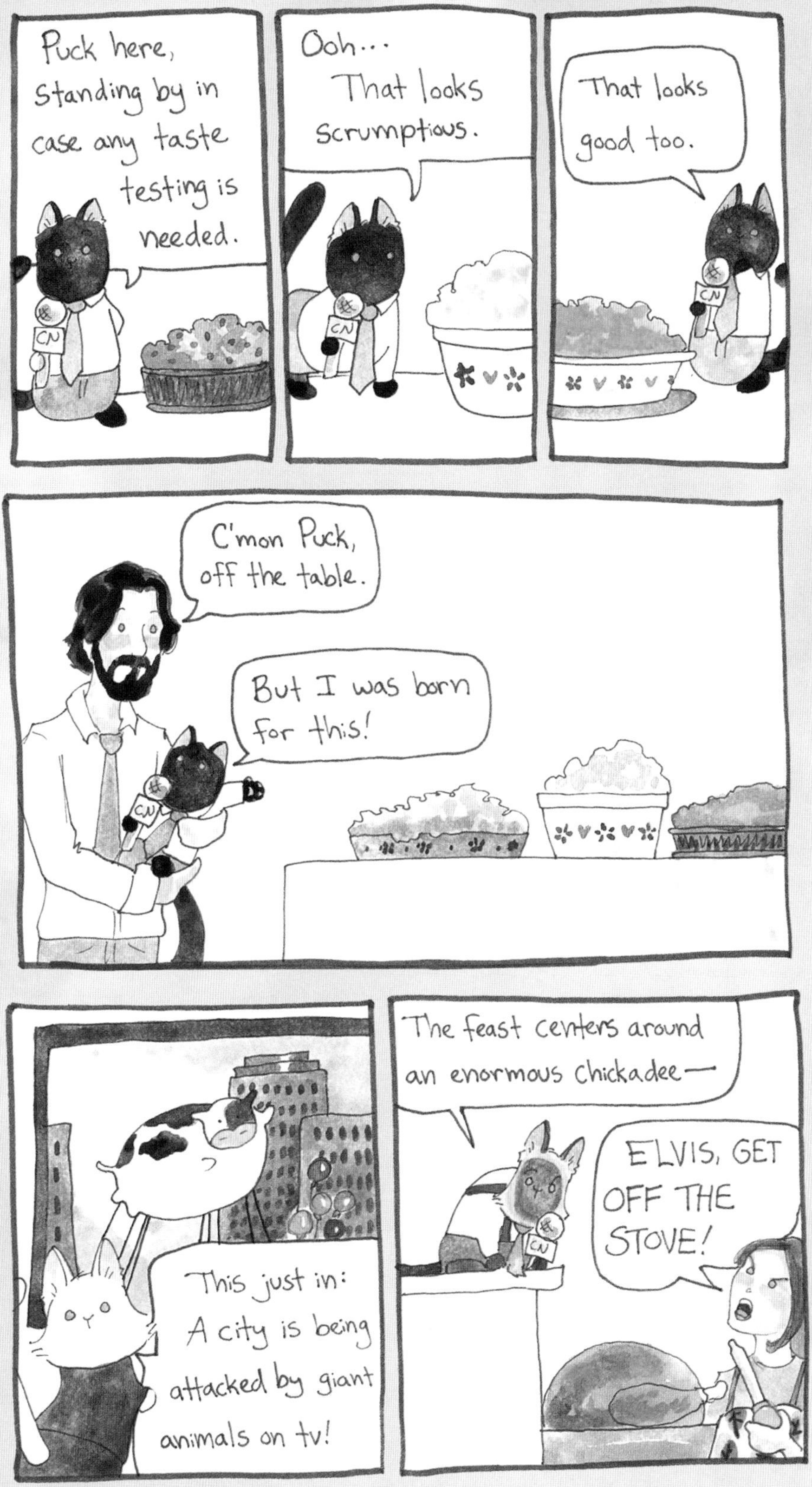
Puck here, Standing by in case any taste testing is needed.
Ooh... That looks Scrumptious.
That looks good too.
C'mon Puck, off the table.
But I was born for this!
This just in: A city is being attacked by giant animals on tv!
The feast centers around an enormous Chickadee—
ELVIS, GET OFF THE STOVE!

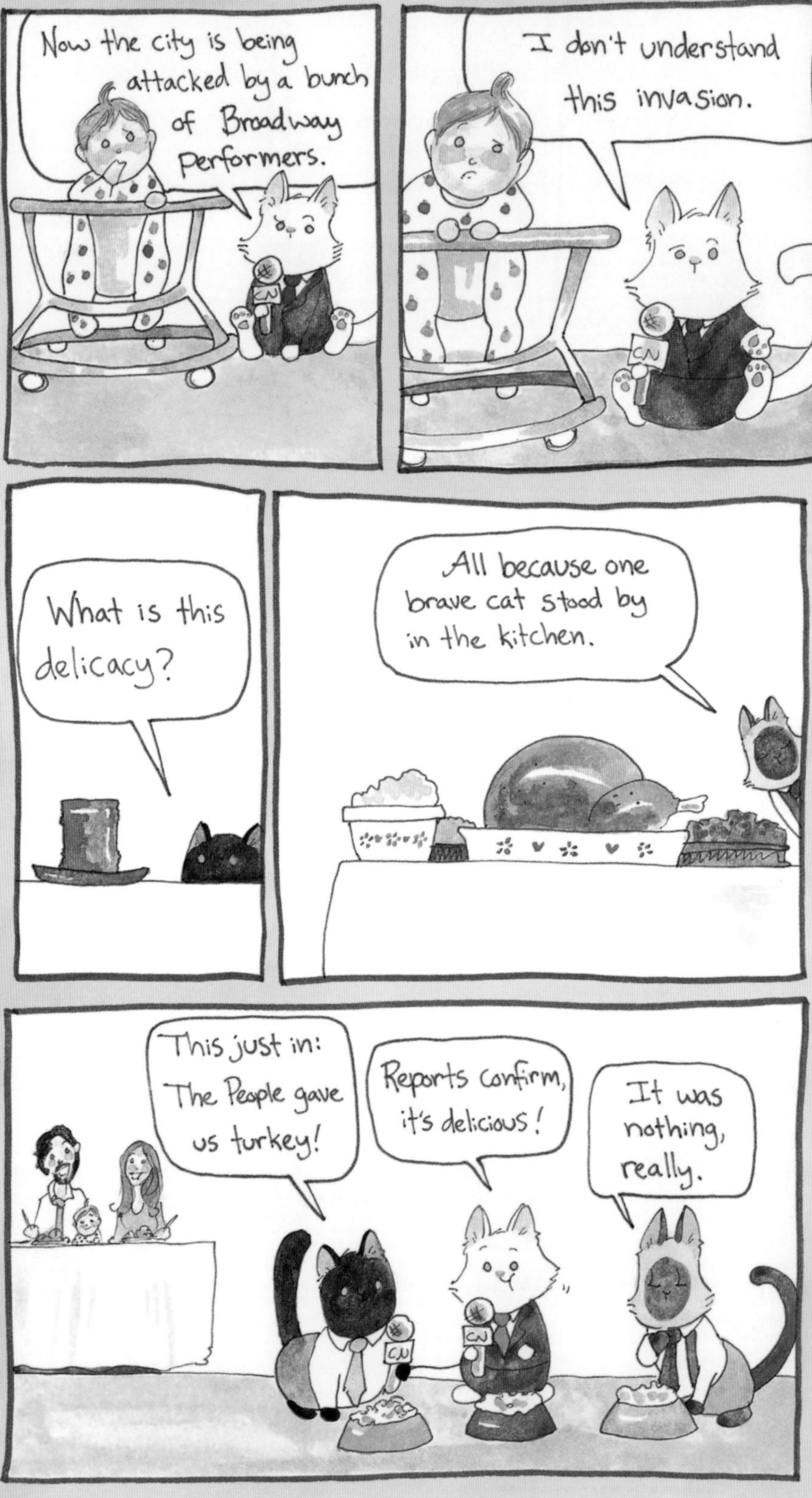
Now the city is being attacked by a bunch of Broadway Performers.
I don't understand this invasion.
What is this delicacy?
All because one brave cat stood by in the kitchen.
This just in: The People gave us turkey!
Reports confirm, it's delicious!
It was nothing, really.
CN

A tree grew in the living room! Here's Puck with more!

Lupin, as you can see behind me, an entire tree grew overnight!

Judging by the glass bulbs and bright lights, I'd guess this fir is native to Las Vegas.

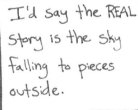

I'd say the REAL story is the sky falling to pieces outside.

Elvis, that happens in these little winter traps all the time!

SHAKE SHAKE SHAKE

It'll stop in a few minutes.

53

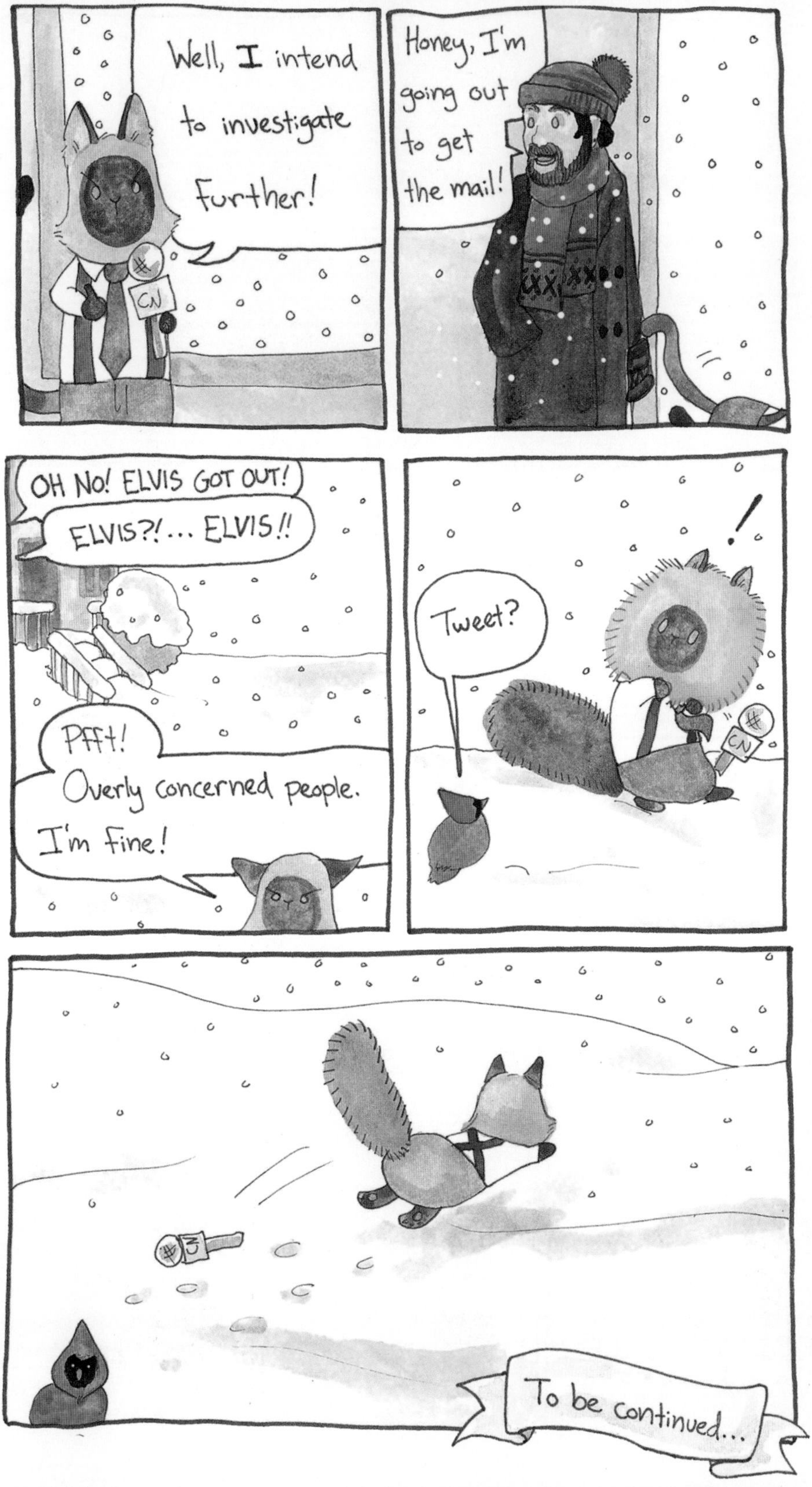
Well, I intend to investigate further!
Honey, I'm going out to get the mail!
OH NO! ELVIS GOT OUT!
ELVIS?!... ELVIS!!
Pfft! Overly concerned people. I'm fine!
Tweet?
!
To be continued...

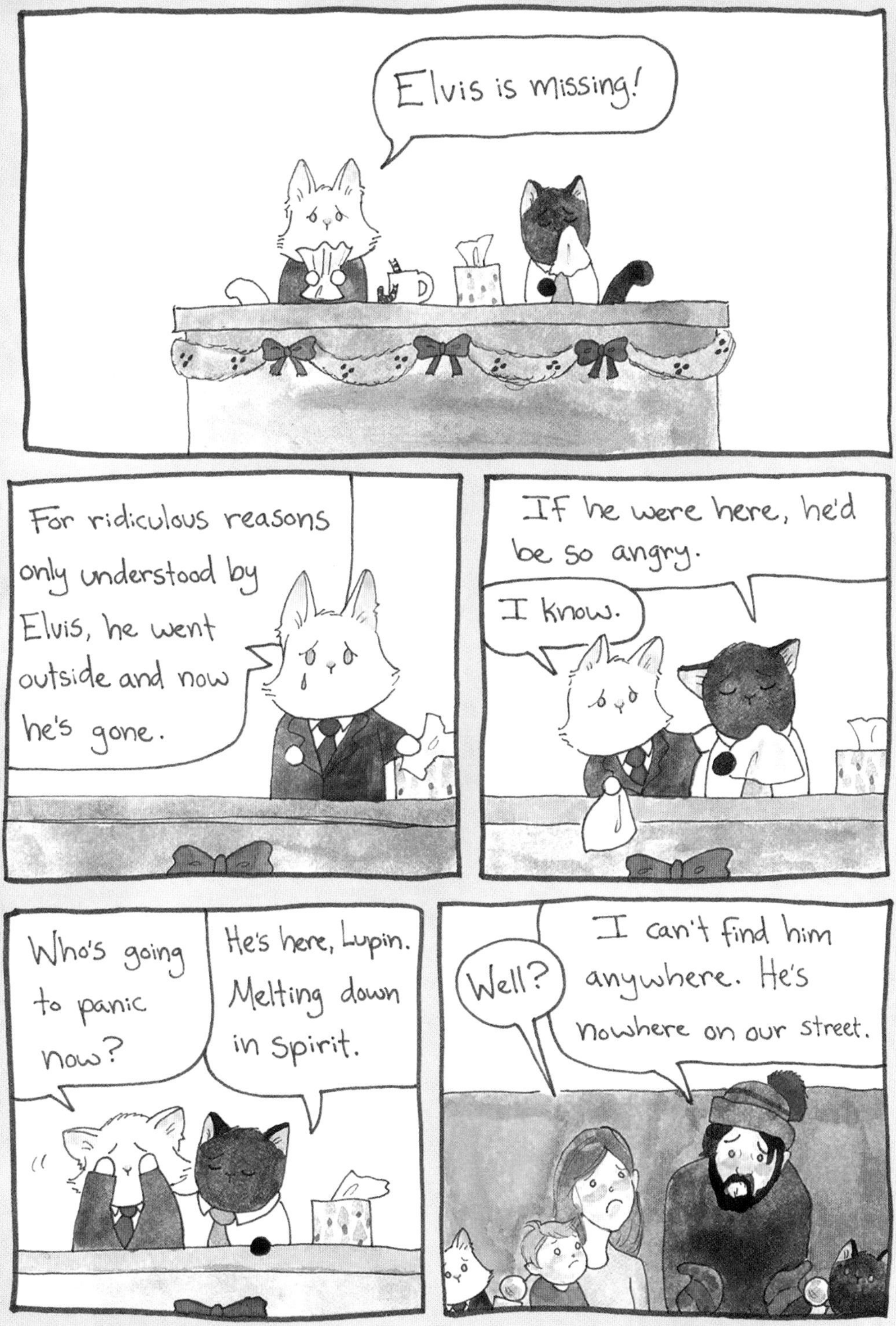
Elvis is missing!
For ridiculous reasons only understood by Elvis, he went outside and now he's gone.
If he were here, he'd be so angry.
I know.
Who's going to panic now?
He's here, Lupin. Melting down in spirit.
Well?
I can't find him anywhere. He's nowhere on our street.

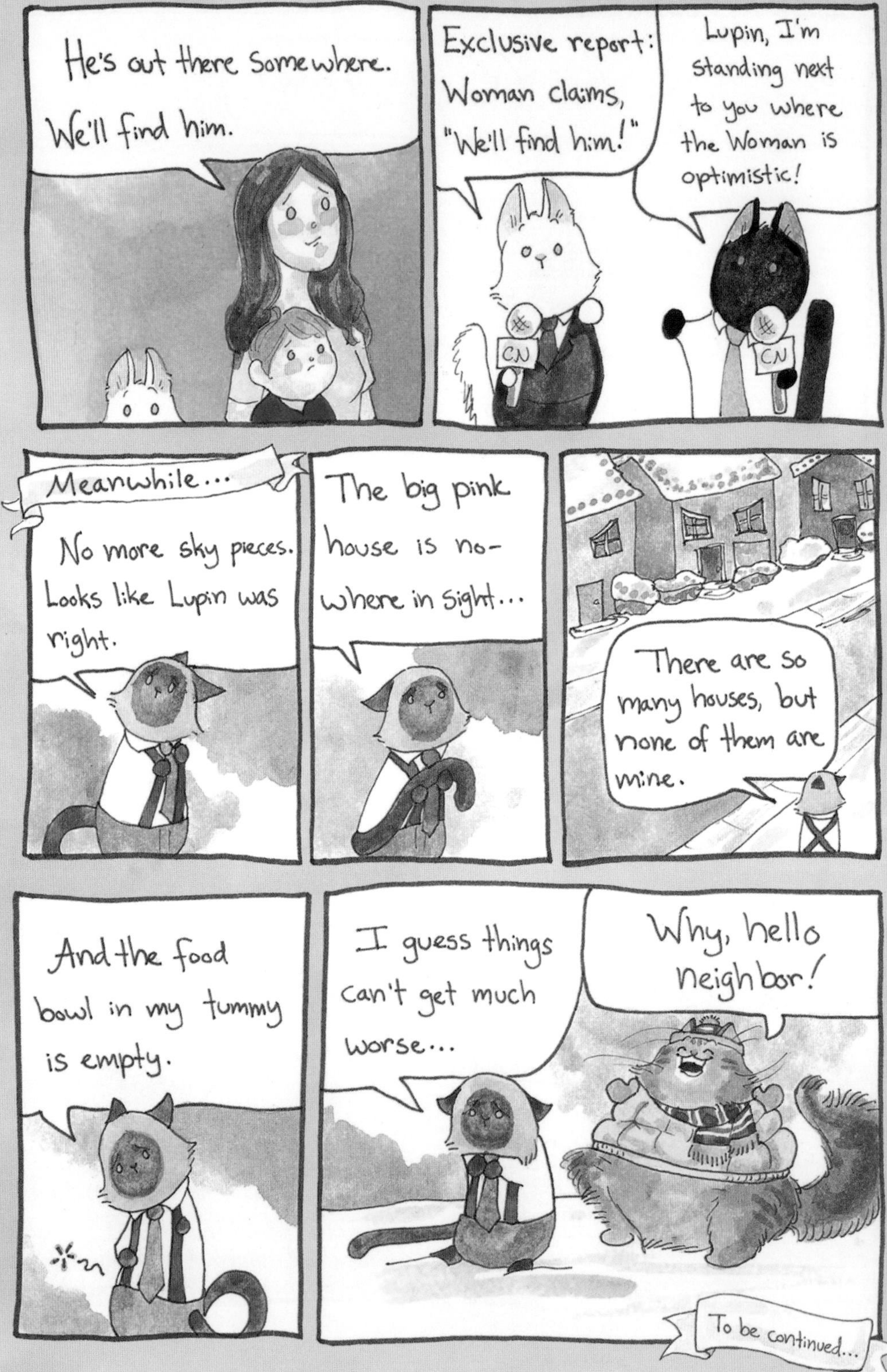
He's out there Somewhere. We'll find him.
Exclusive report: Woman claims, "We'll find him!"
Lupin, I'm standing next to you where the Woman is optimistic!
CN
CN
Meanwhile...
No more sky pieces. Looks like Lupin was right.
The big pink house is no-where in sight...
There are so many houses, but none of them are mine.
And the food bowl in my tummy is empty.
I guess things can't get much worse...
Why, hello neighbor!
To be continued...

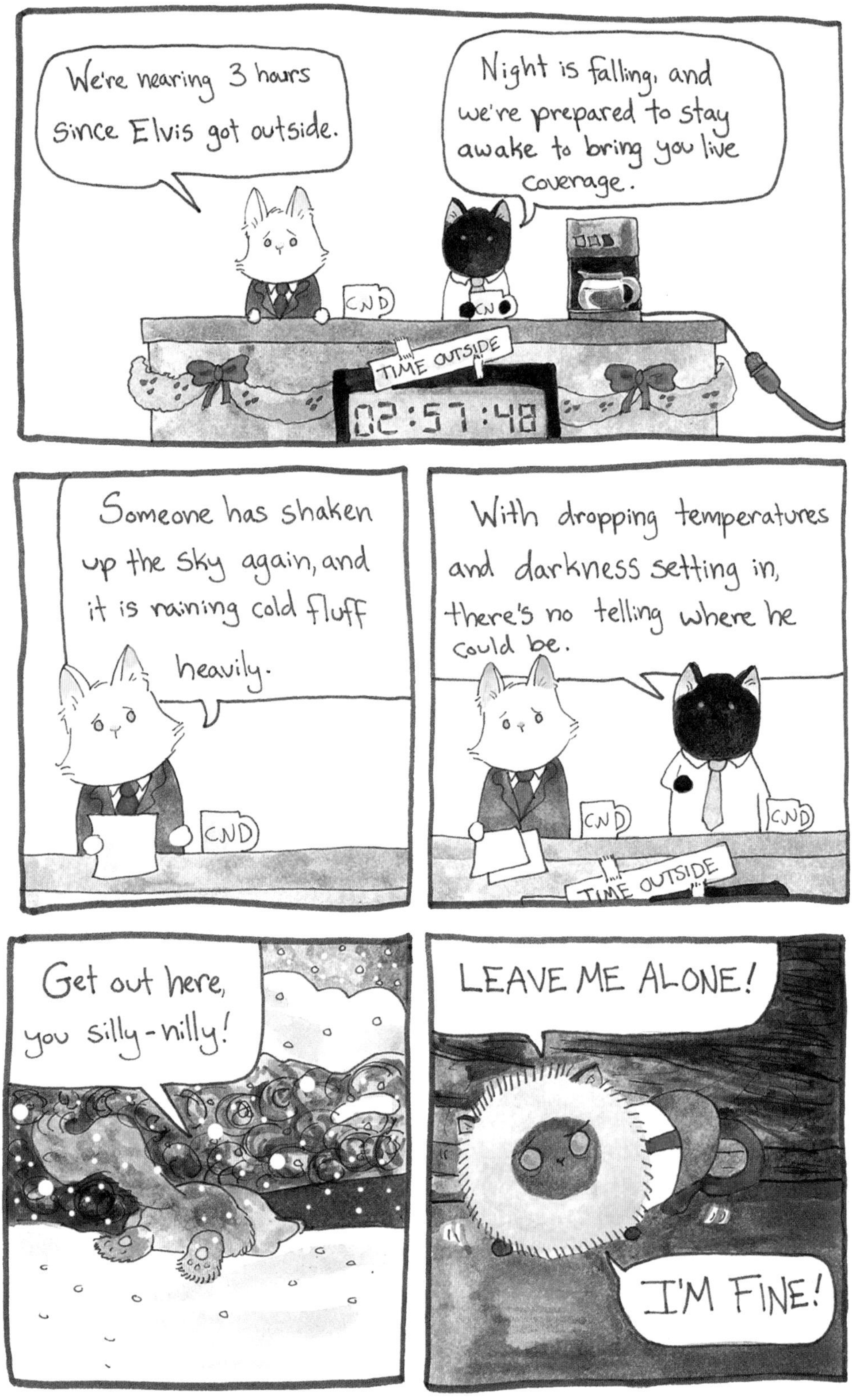
We're nearing 3 hours since Elvis got outside.
Night is falling, and we're prepared to stay awake to bring you live coverage.
CND
TIME OUTSIDE
02:57:48
Someone has shaken up the sky again, and it is raining cold fluff heavily.
CND
With dropping temperatures and darkness setting in, there's no telling where he could be.
CND
CND
TIME OUTSIDE
Get out here, you silly-nilly!
LEAVE ME ALONE!
I'M FINE!

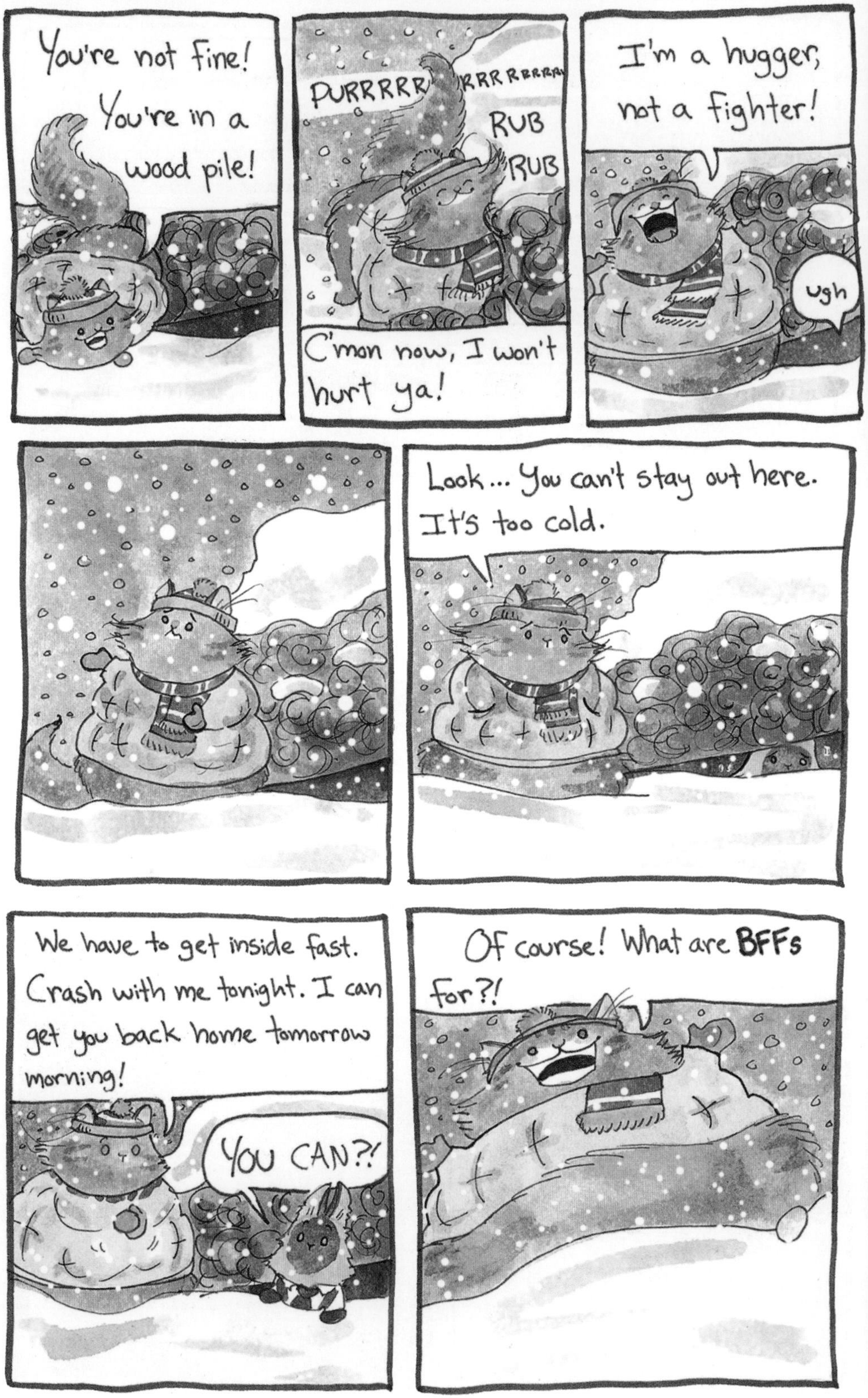
You're not fine! You're in a wood pile!
PURRRRRRRRRRRRRR
RUB RUB
C'mon now, I won't hurt ya!
I'm a hugger, not a fighter!
ugh
Look... You can't stay out here. It's too cold.
We have to get inside fast. Crash with me tonight. I can get you back home tomorrow morning!
YOU CAN?!
Of course! What are **BFFs** for?!

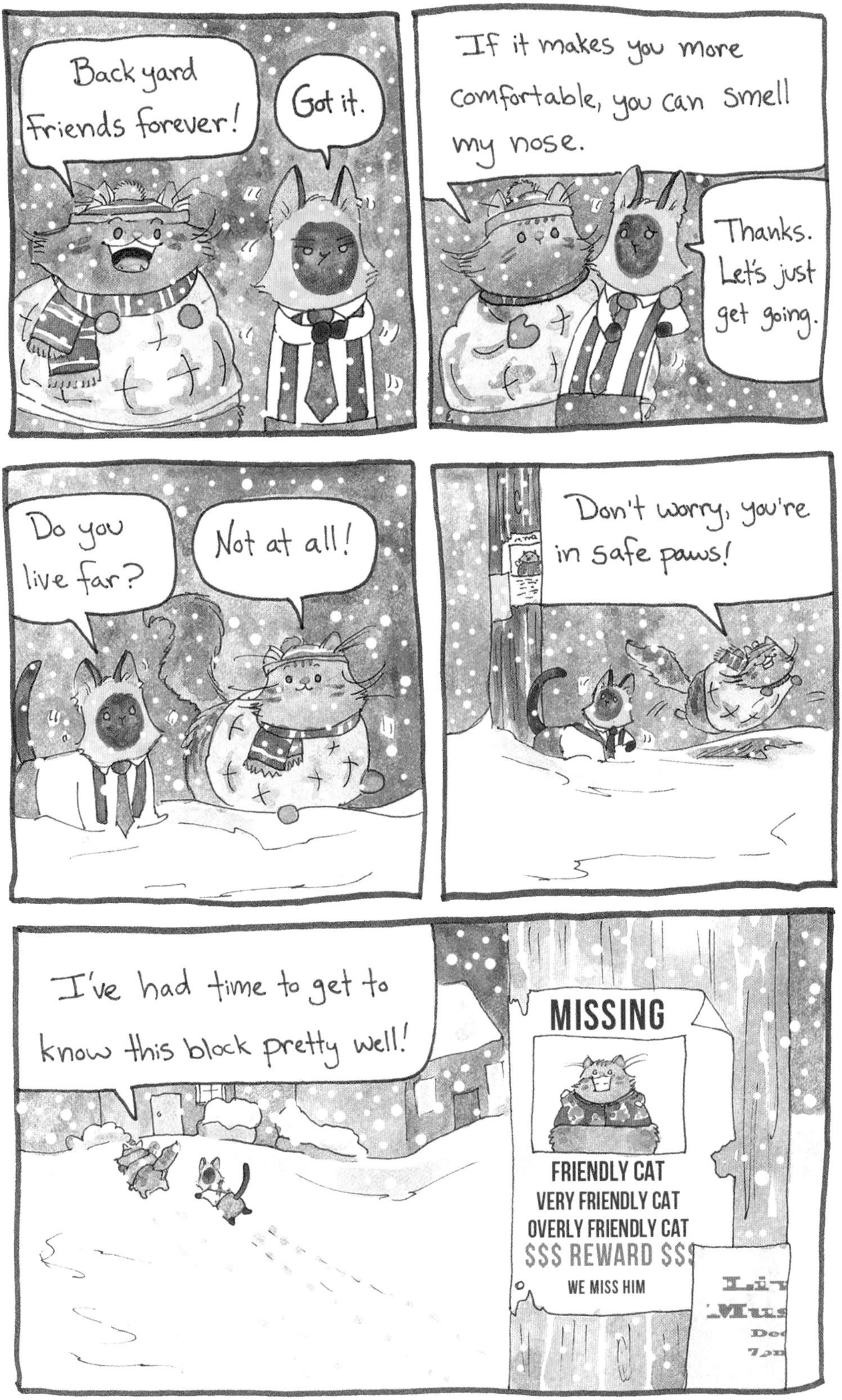
Back yard Friends forever!
Got it.
If it makes you more comfortable, you can smell my nose.
Thanks. Let's just get going.
Do you live far?
Not at all!
Don't worry, you're in safe paws!
I've had time to get to know this block pretty well!
MISSING
FRIENDLY CAT
VERY FRIENDLY CAT
OVERLY FRIENDLY CAT
$$$ REWARD $$$
WE MISS HIM

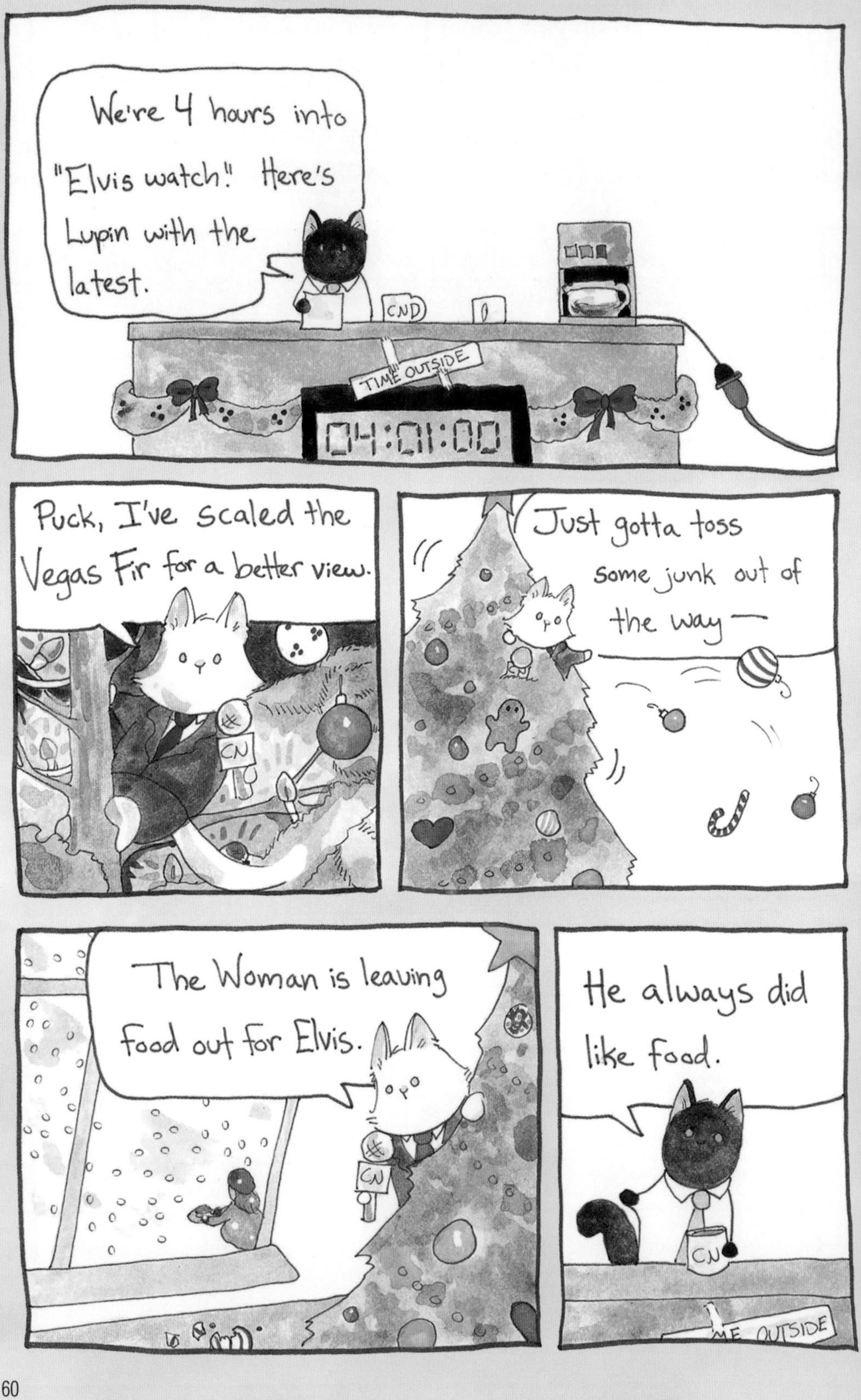
We're 4 hours into "Elvis watch!" Here's Lupin with the latest.
CND
TIME OUTSIDE
04:01:00
Puck, I've scaled the Vegas Fir for a better view.
CN
Just gotta toss some junk out of the way—
The Woman is leaving food out for Elvis.
CN
He always did like food.
CN
ME OUTSIDE

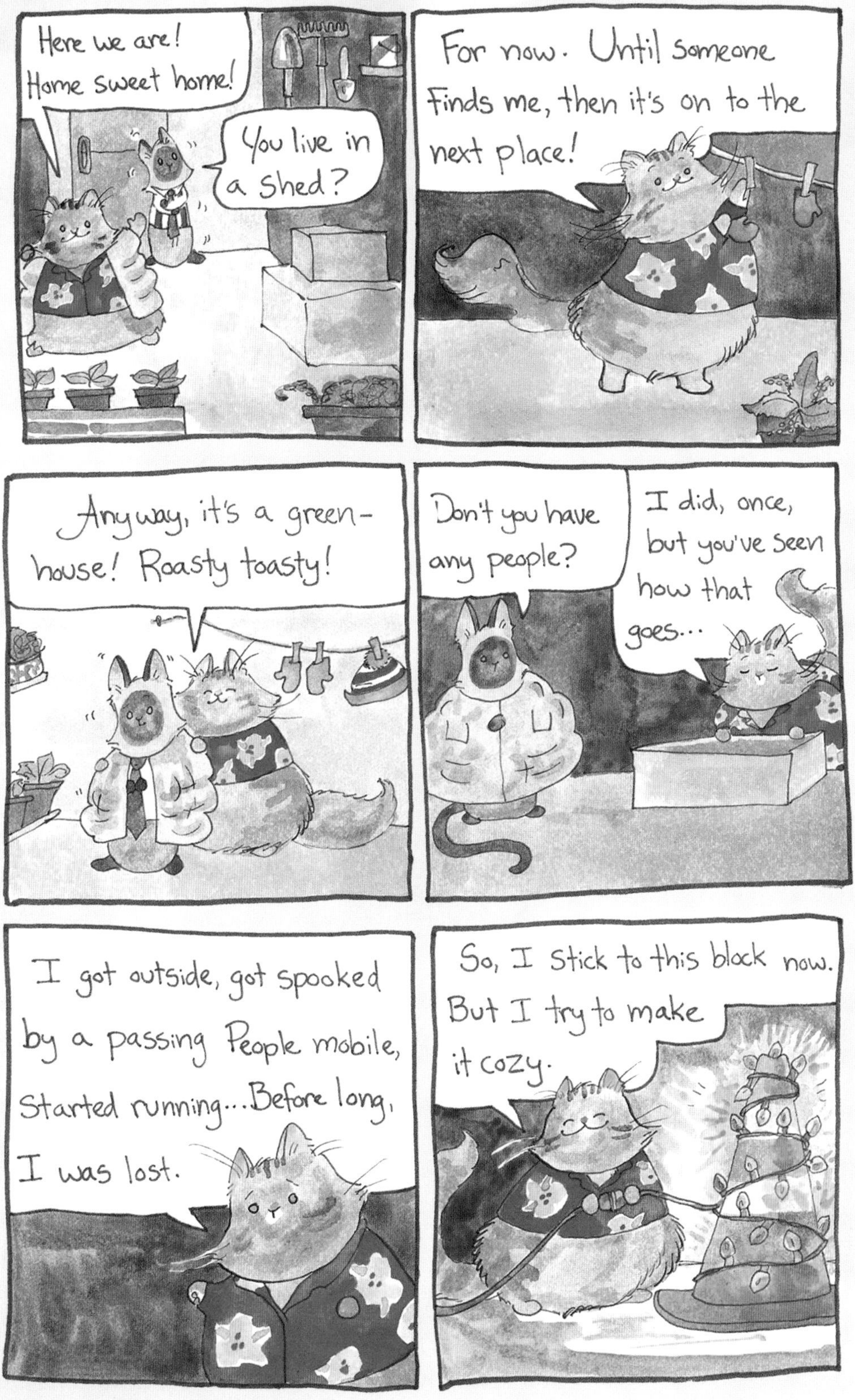
Here we are! Home sweet home!
You live in a shed?
For now. Until someone finds me, then it's on to the next place!
Anyway, it's a green-house! Roasty toasty!
Don't you have any people?
I did, once, but you've seen how that goes...
I got outside, got spooked by a passing People mobile, Started running... Before long, I was lost.
So, I stick to this block now. But I try to make it cozy.

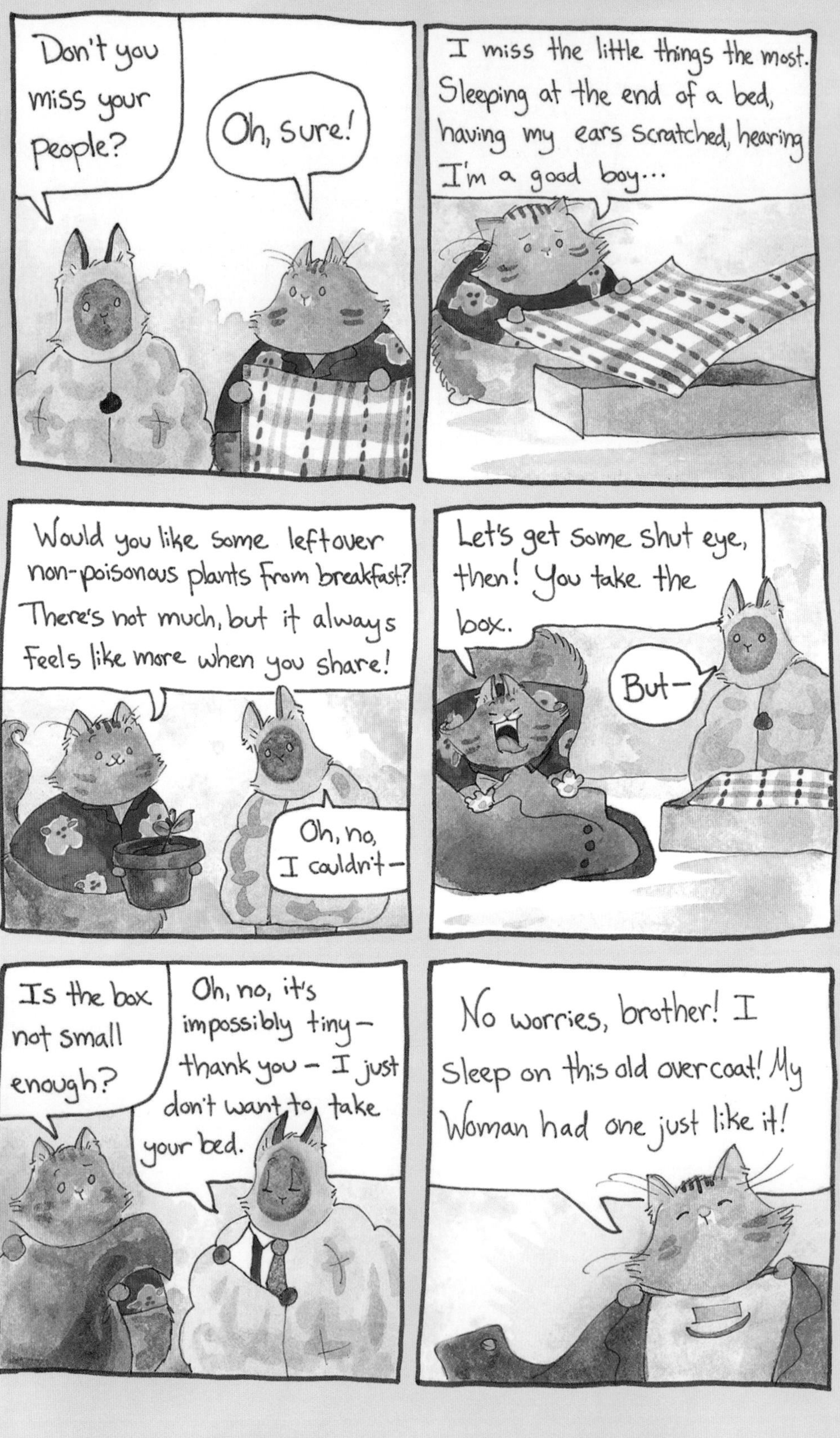
Don't you miss your people?
Oh, sure!
I miss the little things the most. Sleeping at the end of a bed, having my ears scratched, hearing I'm a good boy...
Would you like some leftover non-poisonous plants from breakfast? There's not much, but it always feels like more when you share!
Oh, no, I couldn't—
Let's get some shut eye, then! You take the box.
But—
Is the box not small enough?
Oh, no, it's impossibly tiny—thank you—I just don't want to take your bed.
No worries, brother! I sleep on this old overcoat! My Woman had one just like it!

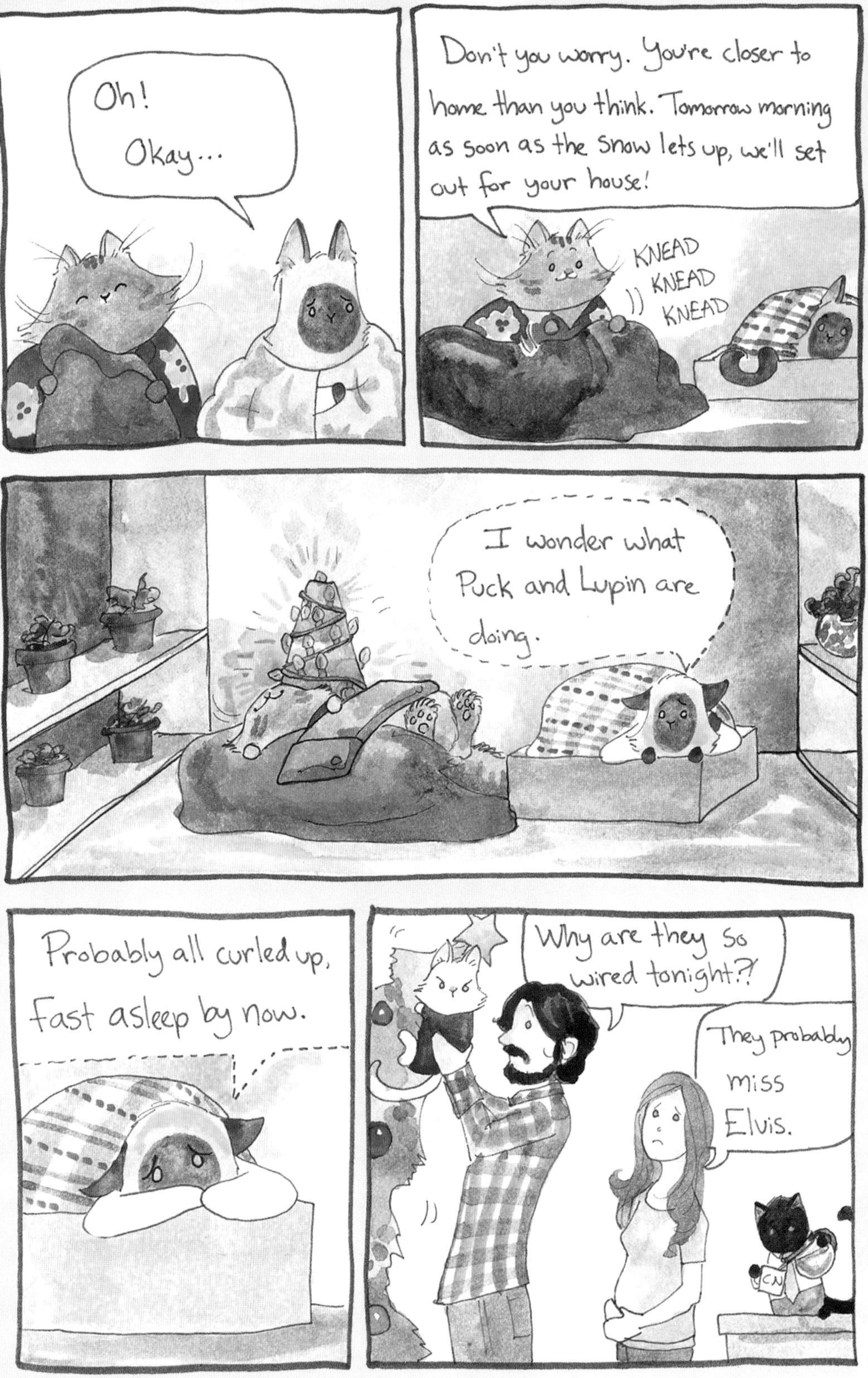
Oh!
Okay...
Don't you worry. You're closer to home than you think. Tomorrow morning as soon as the snow lets up, we'll set out for your house!
KNEAD
KNEAD
KNEAD
I wonder what Puck and Lupin are doing.
Probably all curled up, fast asleep by now.
Why are they so wired tonight?!
They probably miss Elvis.
CN

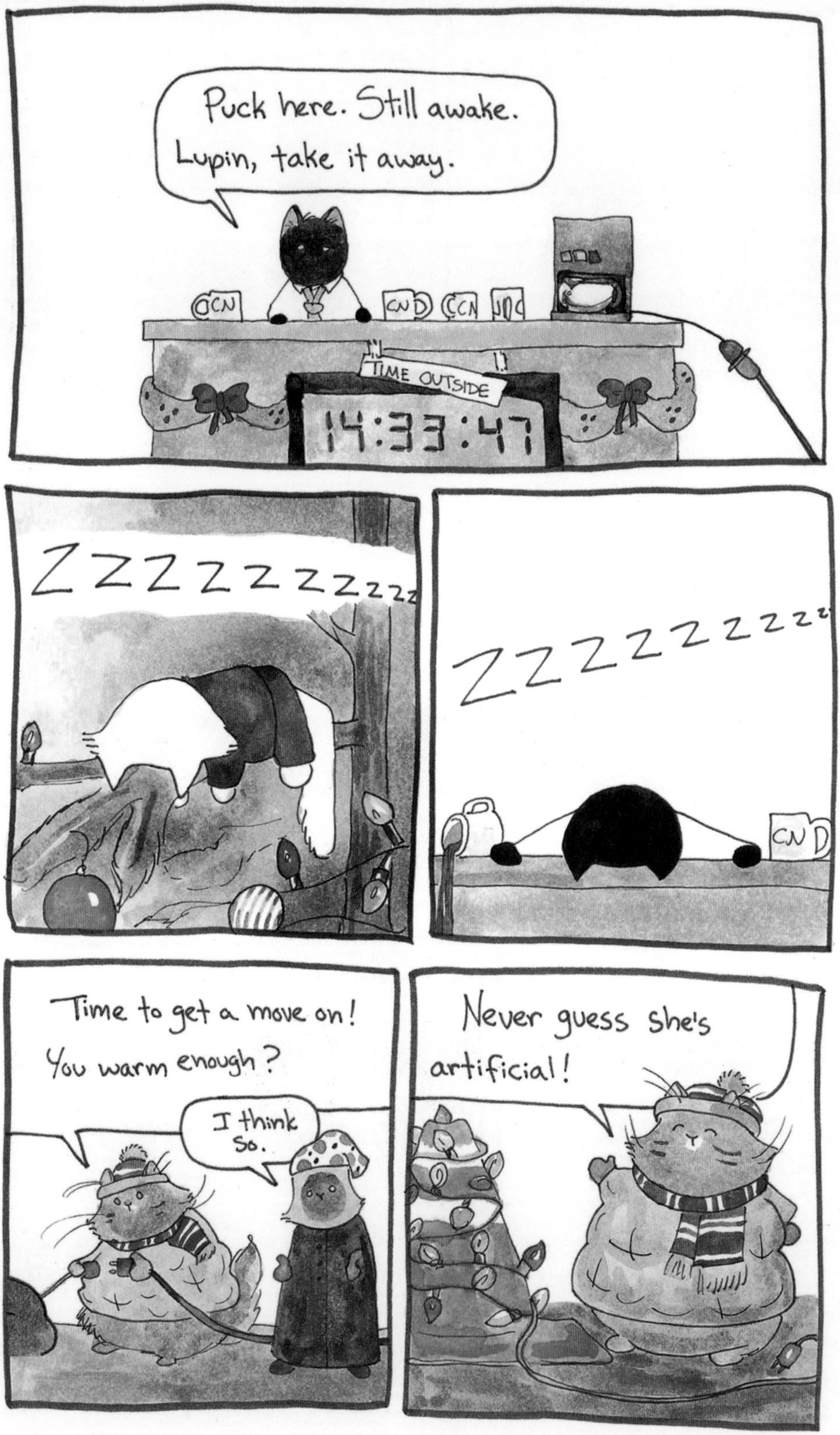
Puck here. Still awake.
Lupin, take it away.
OCN
CND
CCN
TIME OUTSIDE
14:33:47
ZZZZZZZzzz
ZZZZZZZZZz
CND
Time to get a move on!
You warm enough?
I think so.
Never guess she's artificial!

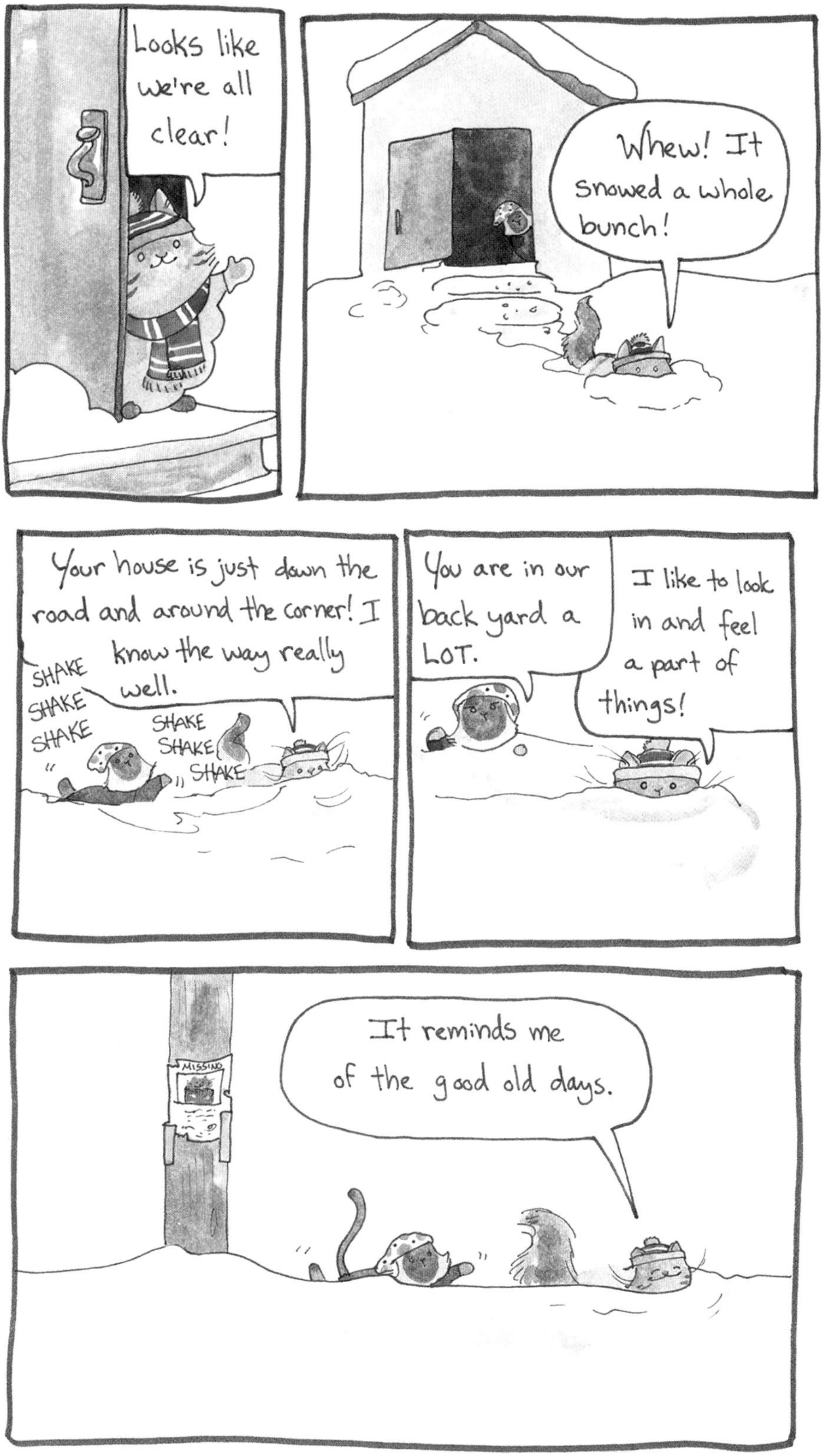
Looks like we're all clear!
Whew! It snowed a whole bunch!
Your house is just down the road and around the corner! I know the way really well.
SHAKE SHAKE SHAKE
SHAKE SHAKE SHAKE
You are in our back yard a LOT.
I like to look in and feel a part of things!
MISSING
It reminds me of the good old days.

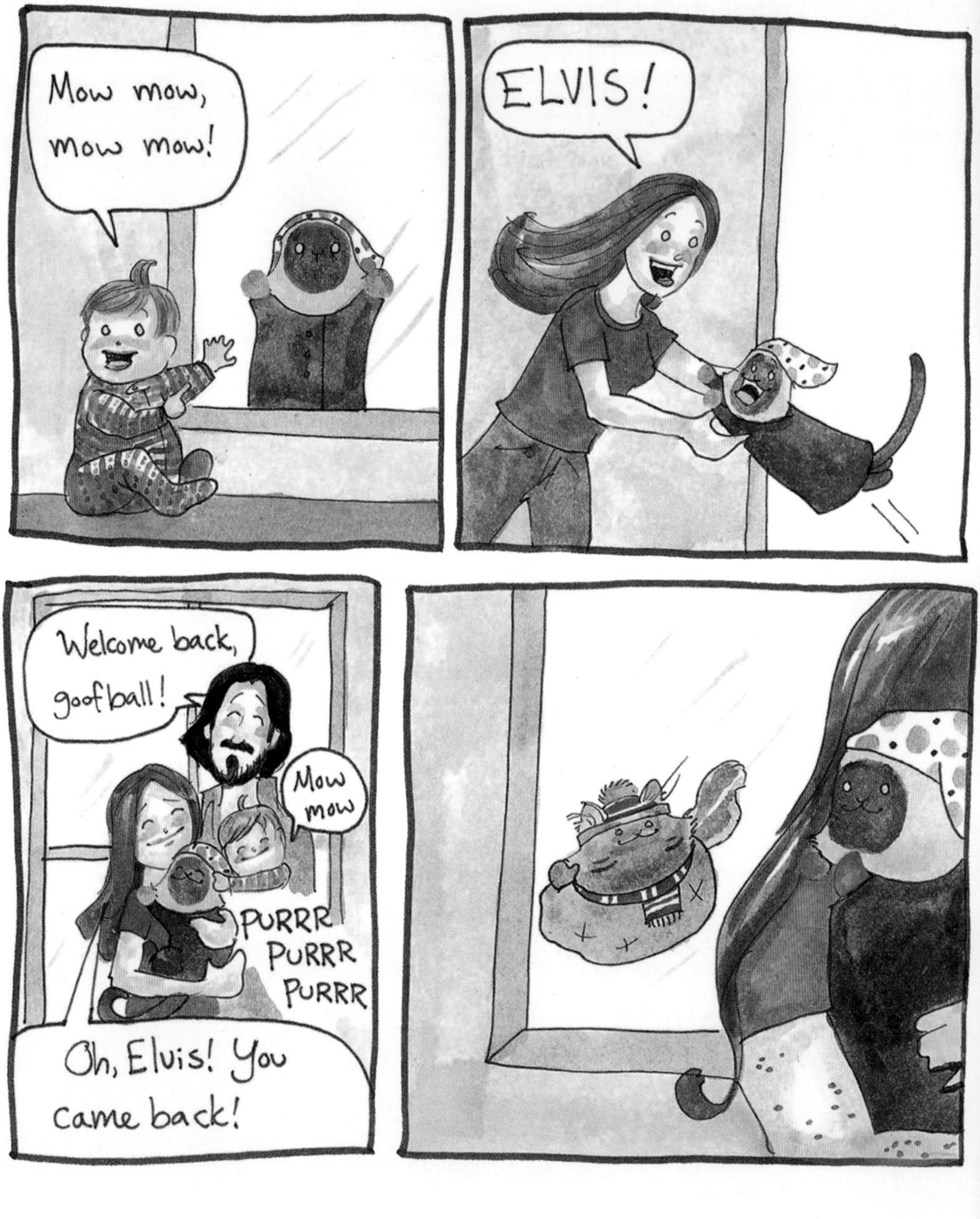
Mow mow,
mow mow!
ELVIS!
Welcome back,
goofball!
Mow
mow
PURRR
PURRR
PURRR
Oh, Elvis! You
came back!

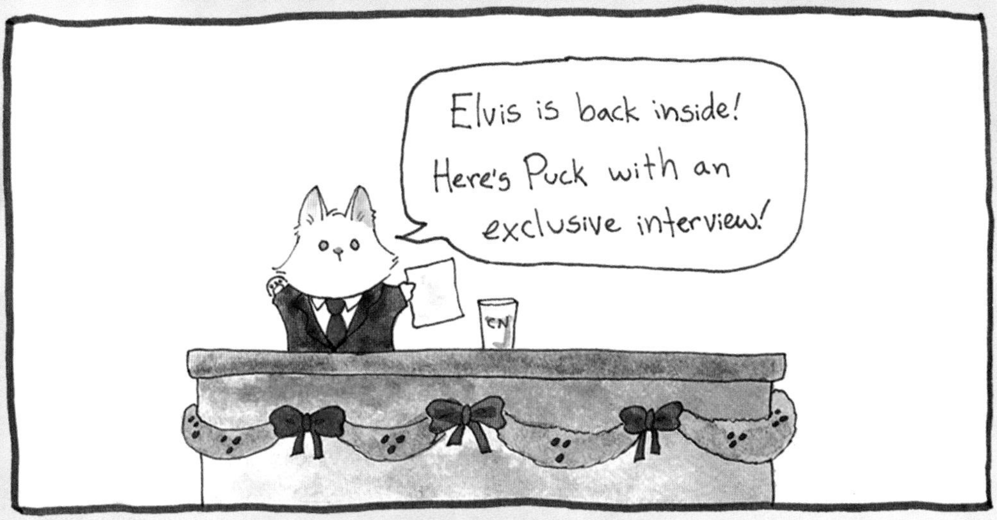
Elvis is back inside! Here's Puck with an exclusive interview!
CN

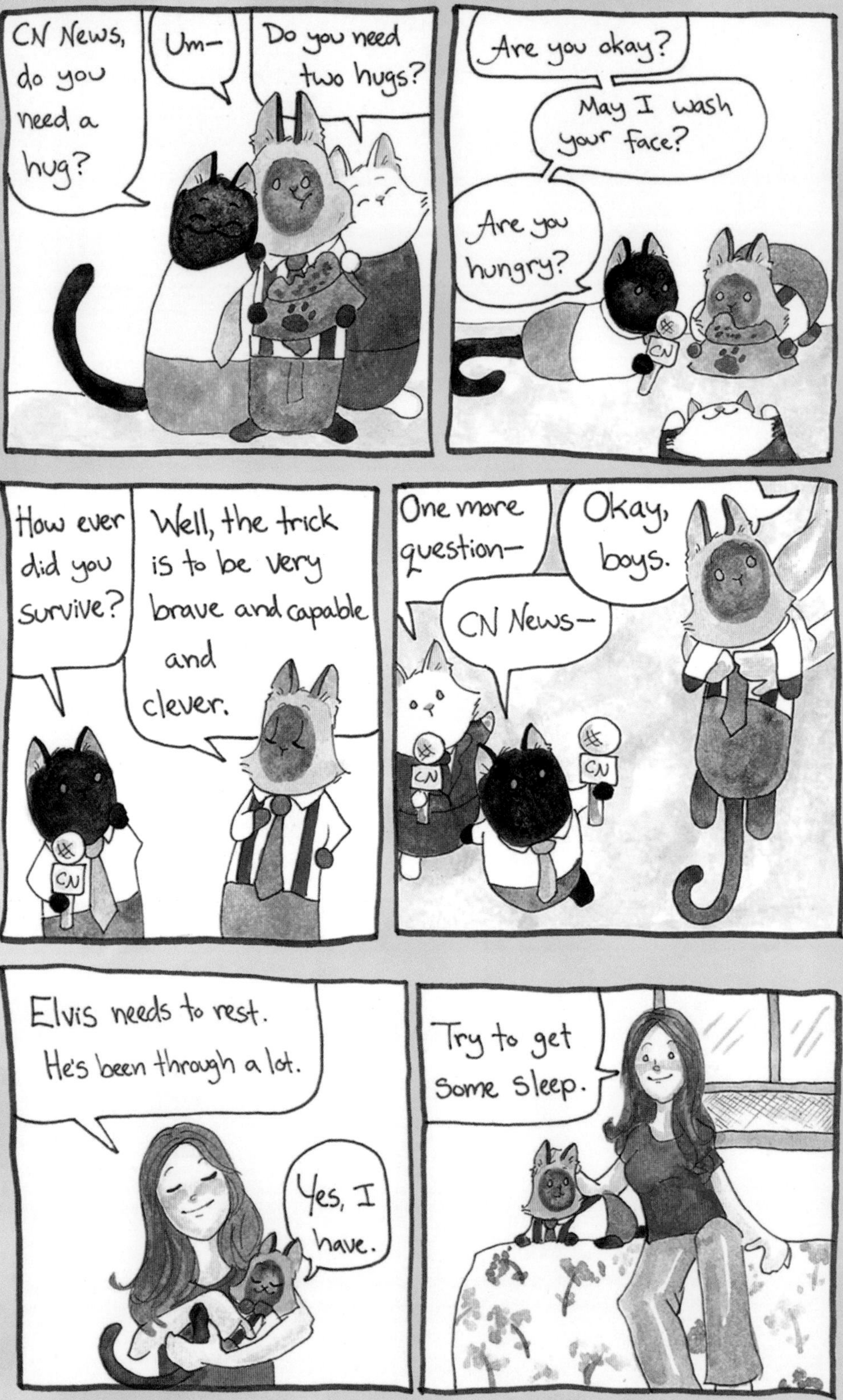
CN News, do you need a hug?
Um—
Do you need two hugs?
Are you okay?
May I wash your face?
Are you hungry?
CN
How ever did you survive?
Well, the trick is to be very brave and capable and clever.
CN
One more question—
CN News—
Okay, boys.
CN
CN
Elvis needs to rest. He's been through a lot.
Yes, I have.
Try to get some sleep.

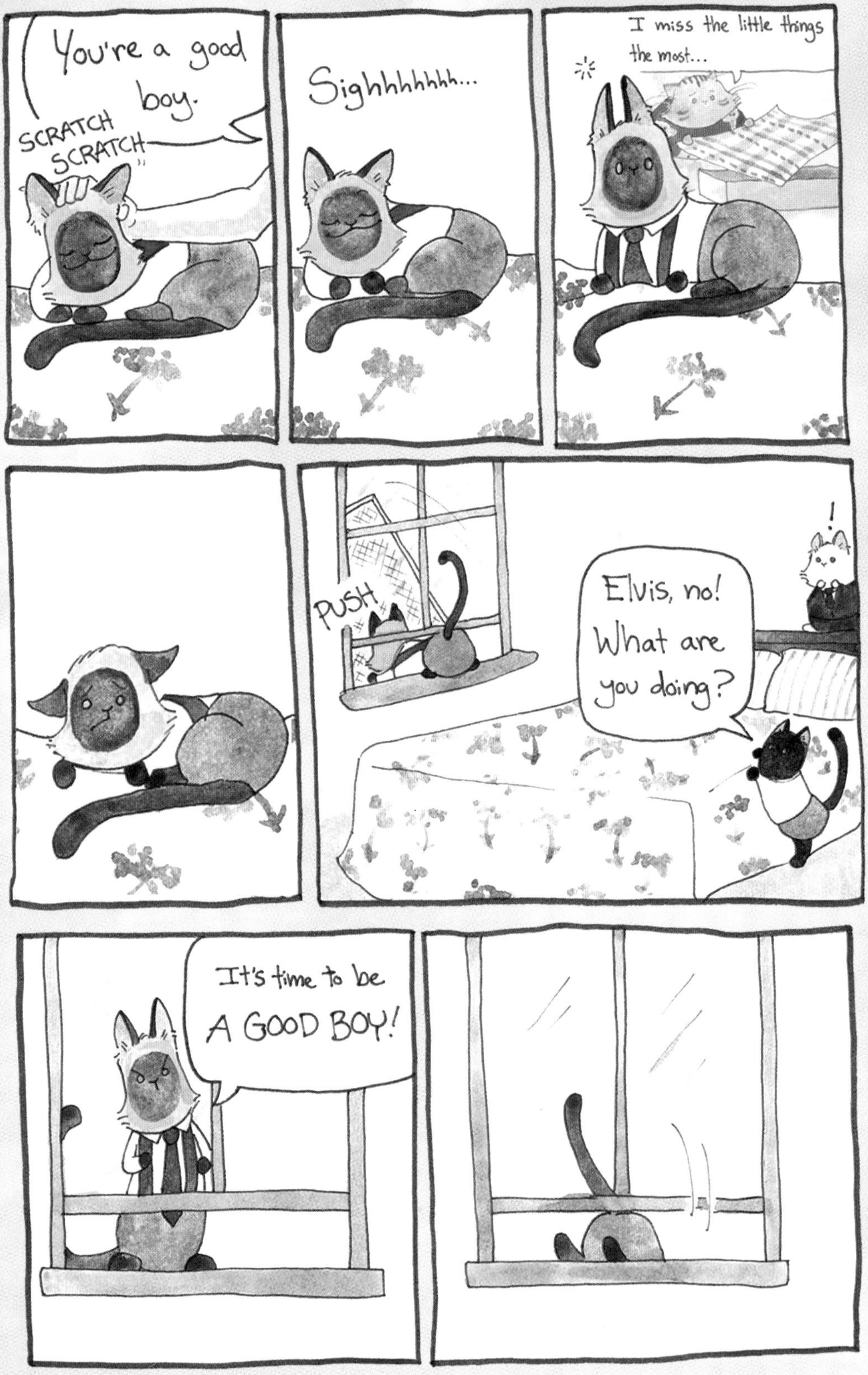
You're a good boy.
SCRATCH SCRATCH
Sighhhhhhh...
I miss the little things the most...
PUSH
Elvis, no! What are you doing?
!
It's time to be A GOOD BOY!

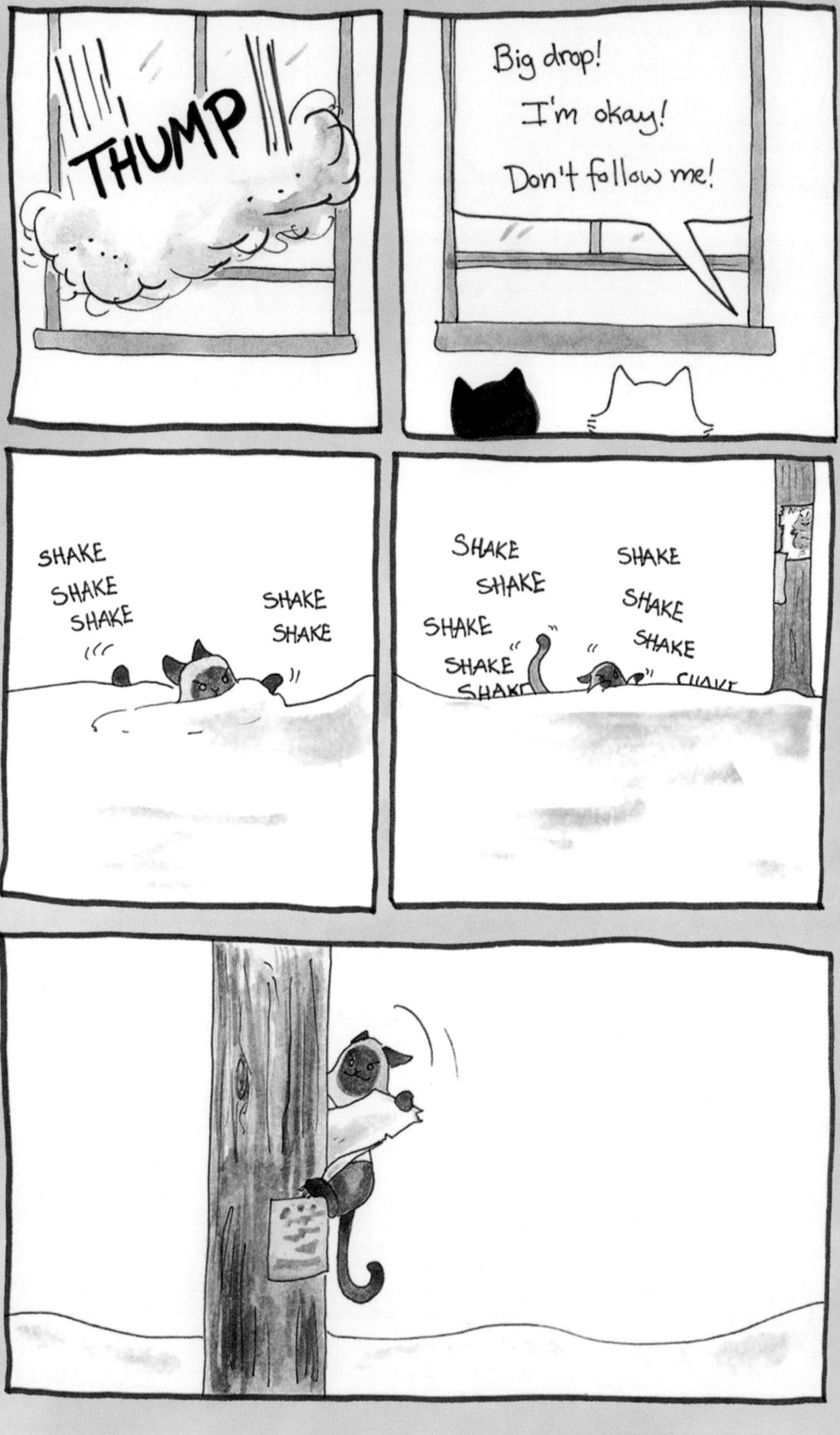
THUMP
Big drop!
I'm okay!
Don't follow me!
SHAKE
SHAKE
SHAKE
SHAKE
SHAKE
SHAKE
SHAKE
SHAKE
SHAKE
SHAKE
SHAKE
SHAKE

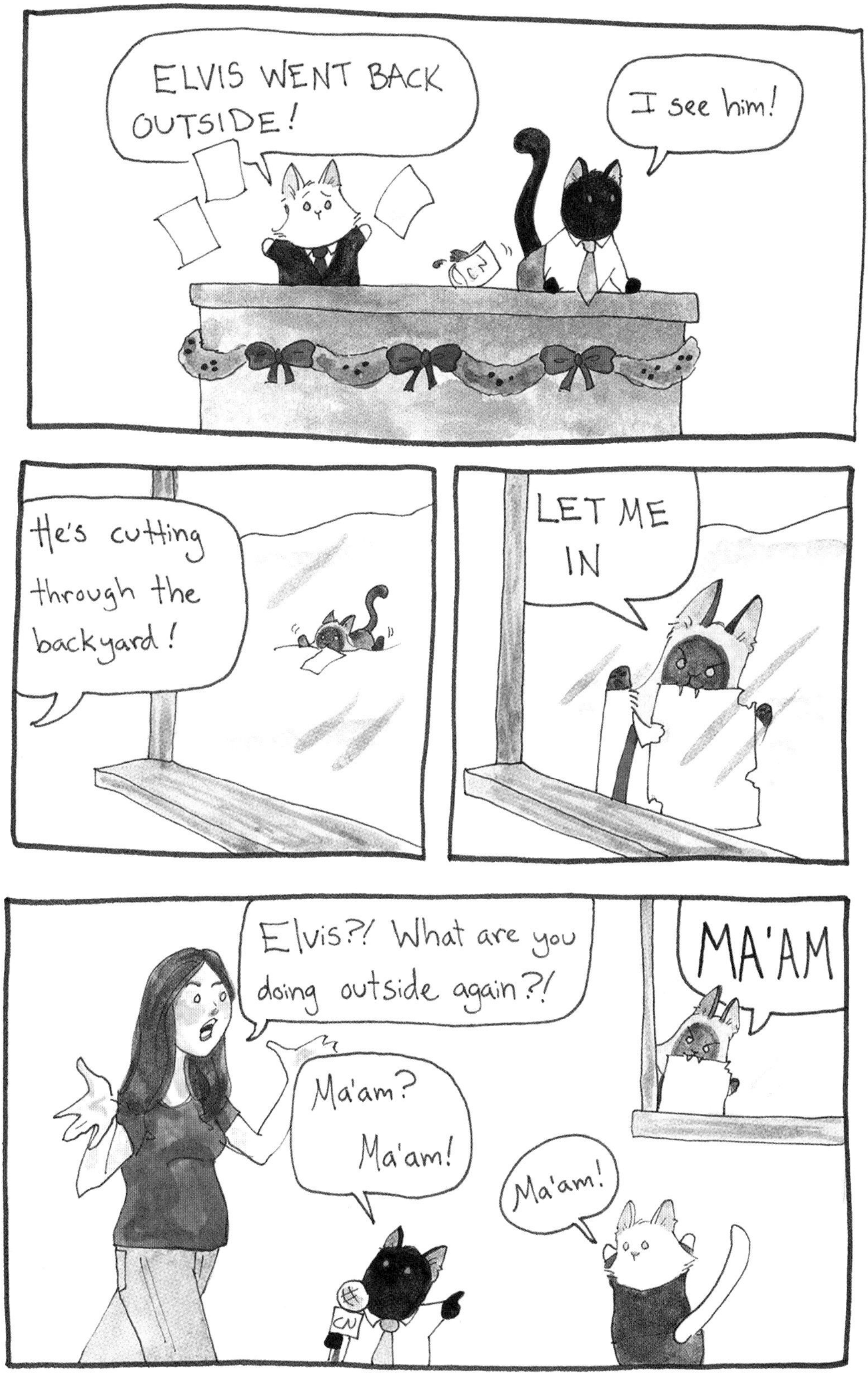
ELVIS WENT BACK OUTSIDE!
I see him!
He's cutting through the backyard!
LET ME IN
Elvis?! What are you doing outside again?!
MA'AM
Ma'am? Ma'am!
Ma'am!

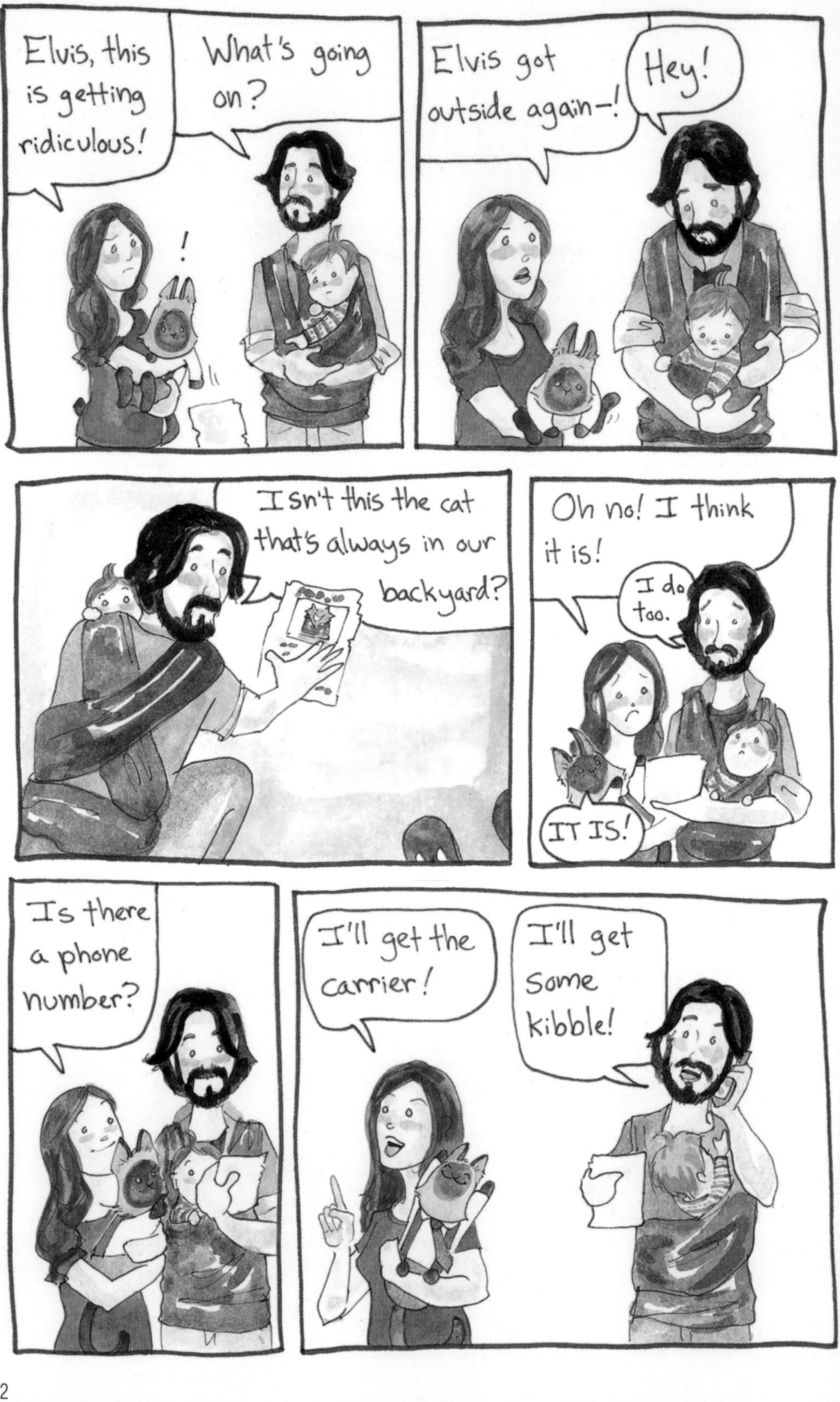
Elvis, this is getting ridiculous!
What's going on?
Elvis got outside again—!
Hey!
Isn't this the cat that's always in our backyard?
Oh no! I think it is!
I do too.
IT IS!
Is there a phone number?
I'll get the carrier!
I'll get some kibble!

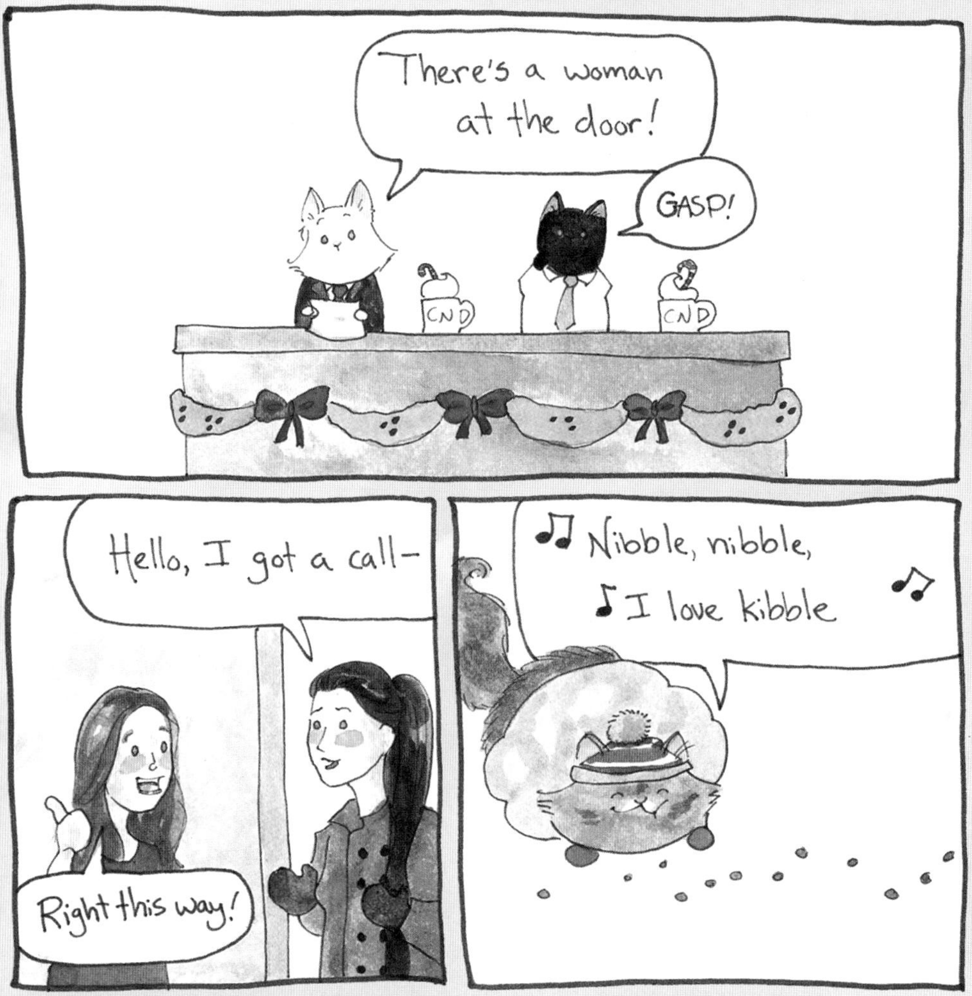
There's a woman at the door!
GASP!
CND
CND
Hello, I got a call-
Right this way!
Nibble, nibble, I love kibble

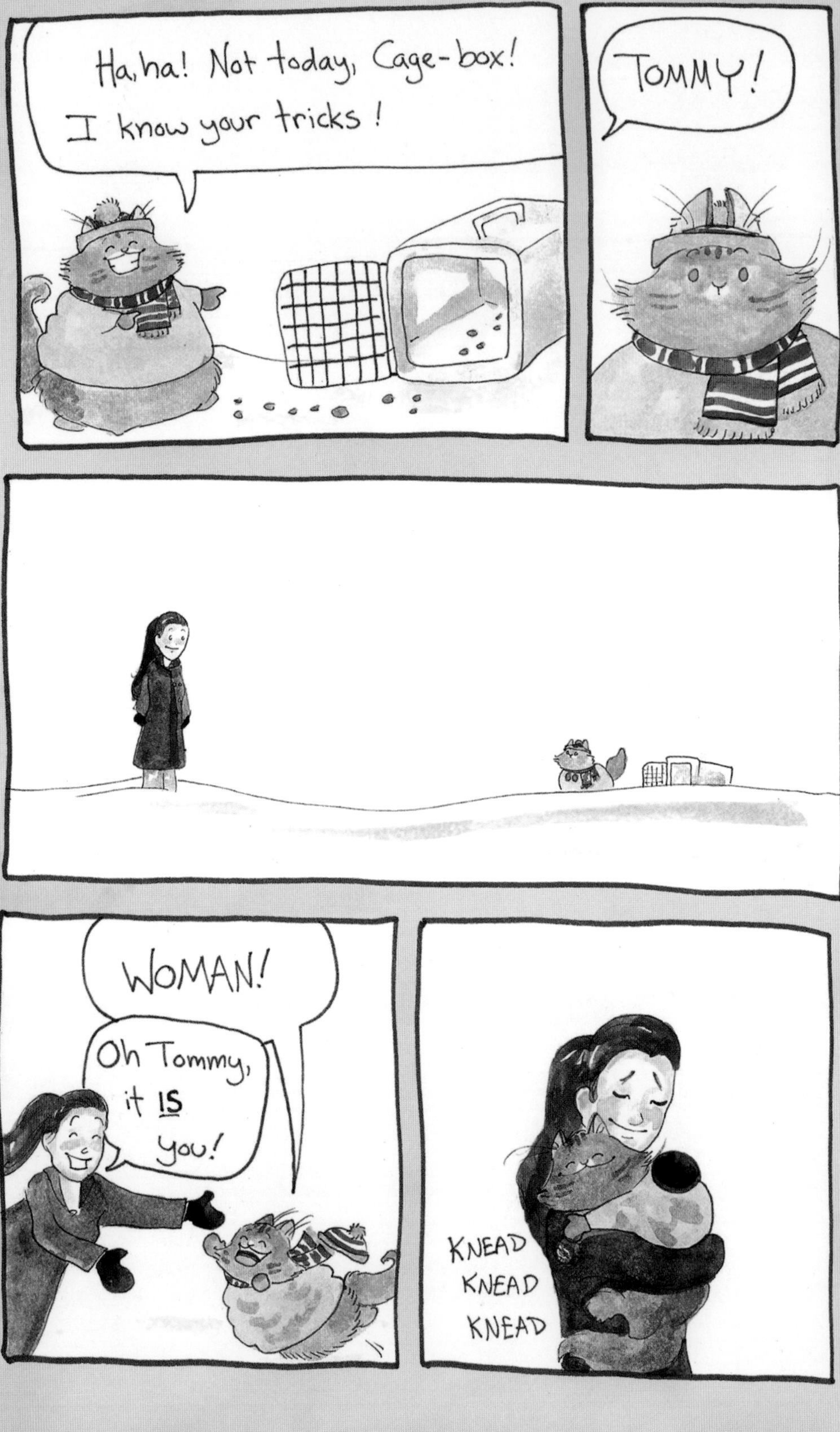
Ha, ha! Not today, Cage-box! I know your tricks!
TOMMY!
WOMAN!
Oh Tommy, it IS you!
KNEAD KNEAD KNEAD

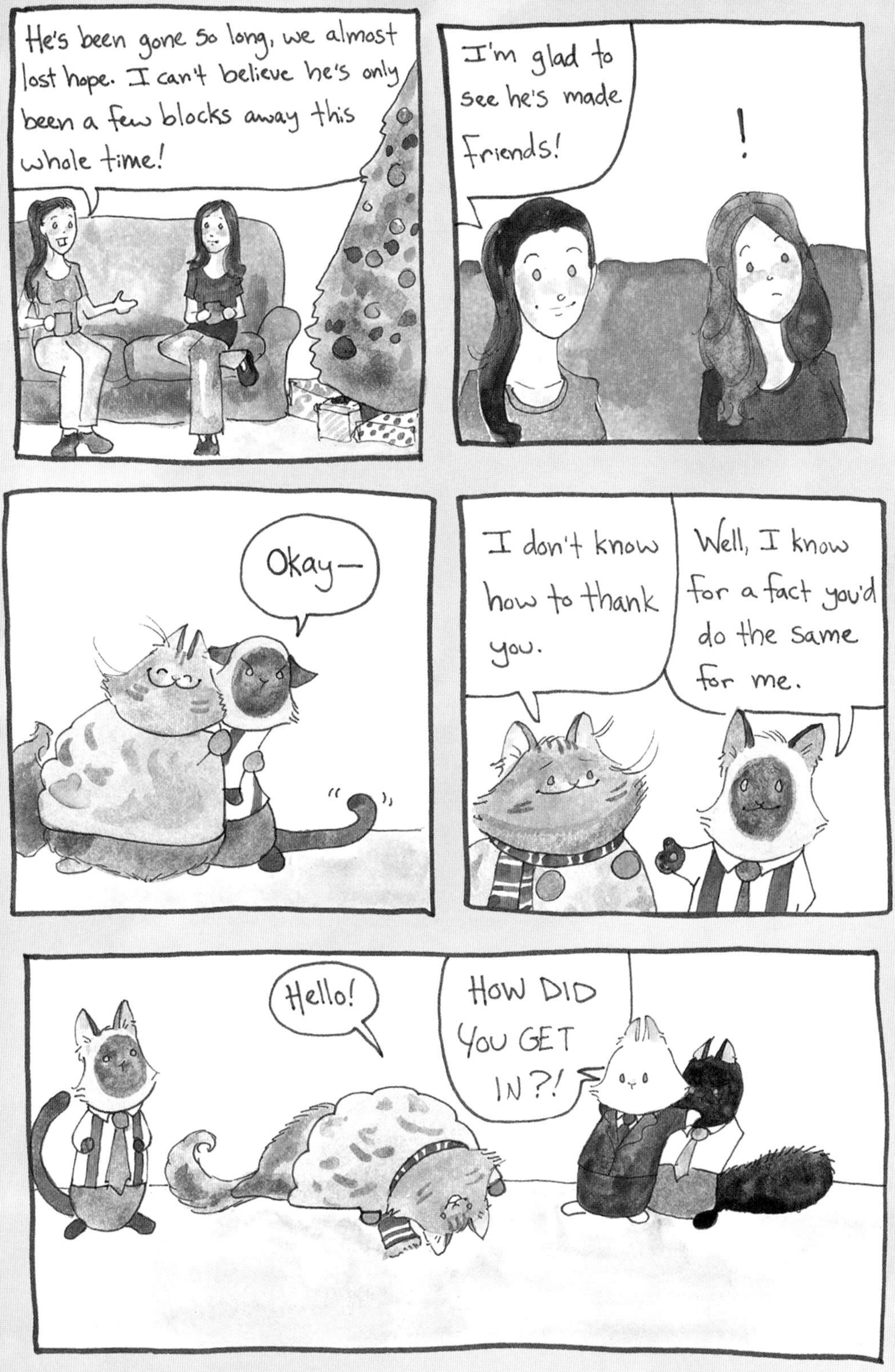
He's been gone so long, we almost lost hope. I can't believe he's only been a few blocks away this whole time!
I'm glad to see he's made friends!
!
Okay—
I don't know how to thank you.
Well, I know for a fact you'd do the same for me.
Hello!
HOW DID YOU GET IN?!

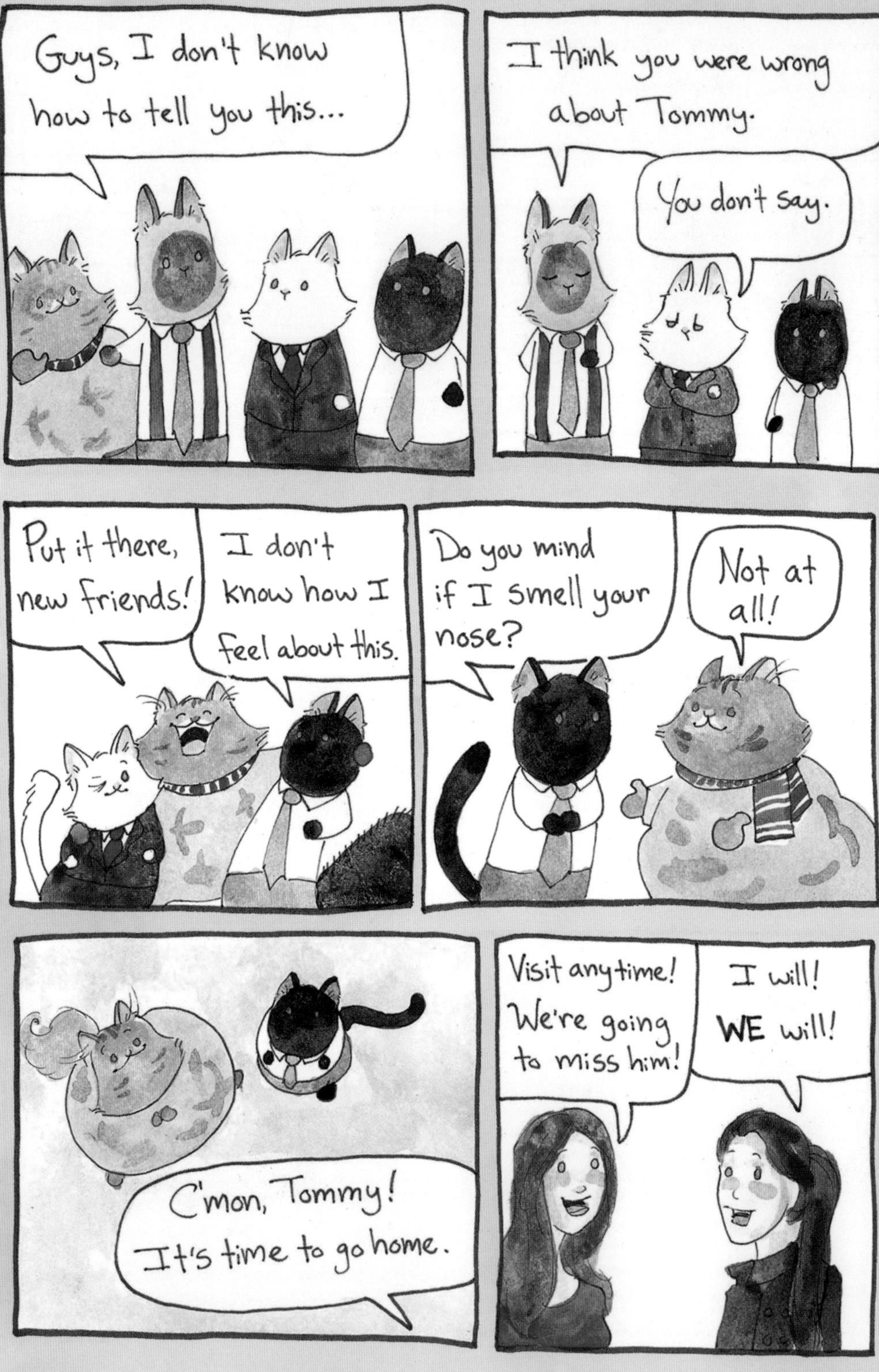
Guys, I don't know how to tell you this...
I think you were wrong about Tommy.
You don't say.
Put it there, new friends!
I don't know how I feel about this.
Do you mind if I smell your nose?
Not at all!
C'mon, Tommy! It's time to go home.
Visit anytime! We're going to miss him!
I will! WE will!

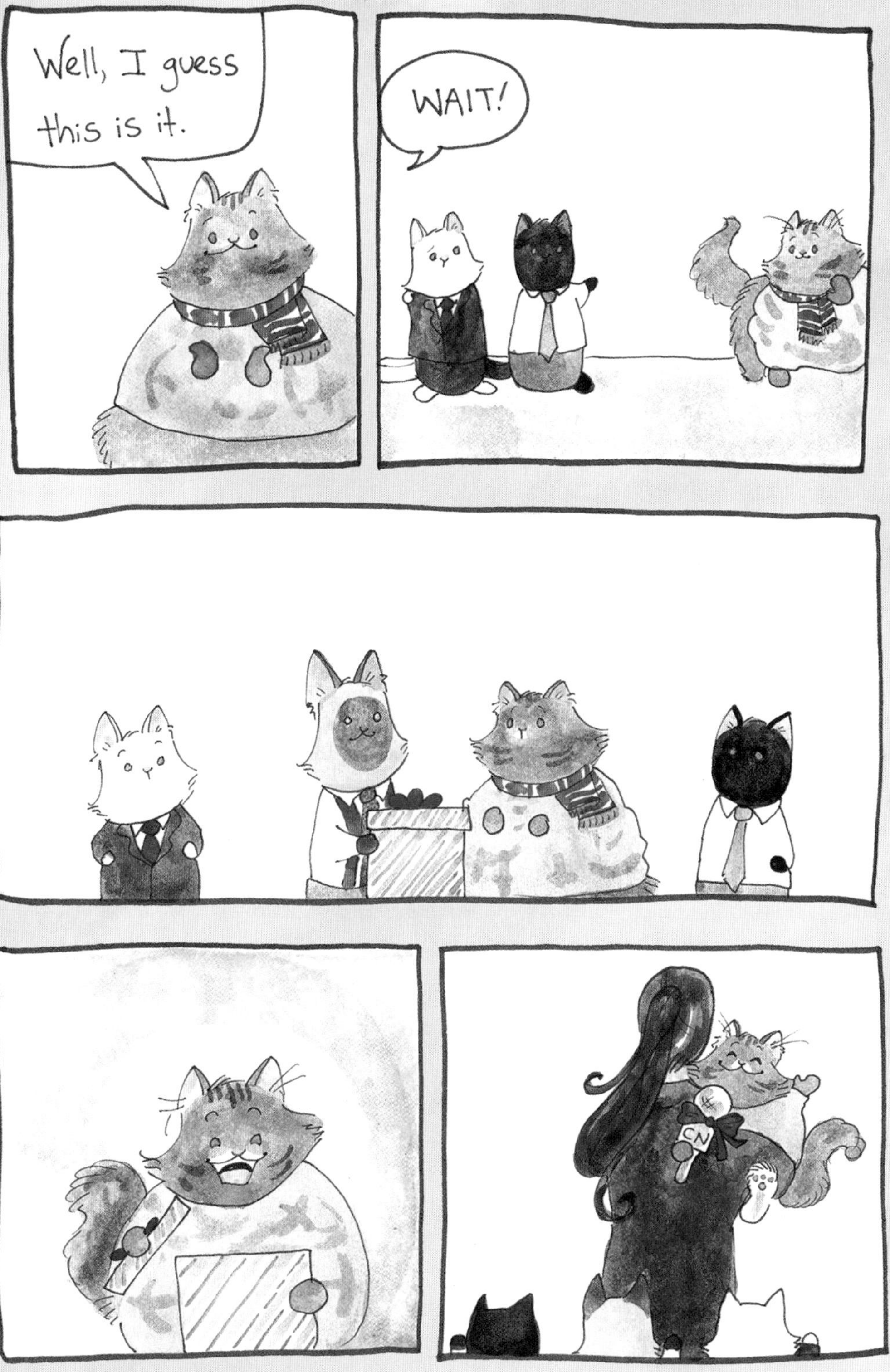
Well, I guess this is it.
WAIT!
CN

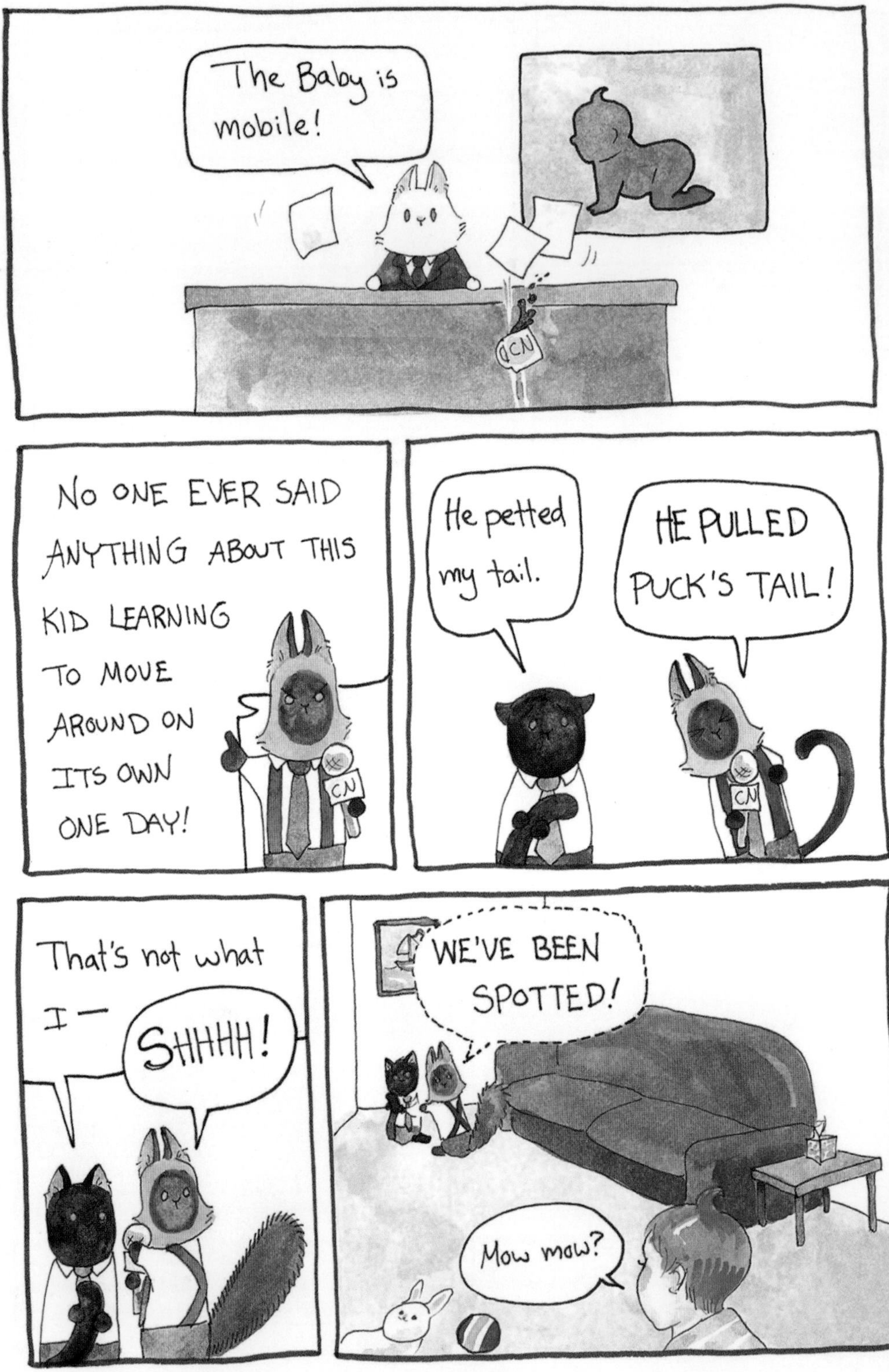
The Baby is mobile!
CN
NO ONE EVER SAID ANYTHING ABOUT THIS KID LEARNING TO MOVE AROUND ON ITS OWN ONE DAY!
CN
He petted my tail.
HE PULLED PUCK'S TAIL!
CN
That's not what I—
SHHHH!
WE'VE BEEN SPOTTED!
Mow mow?

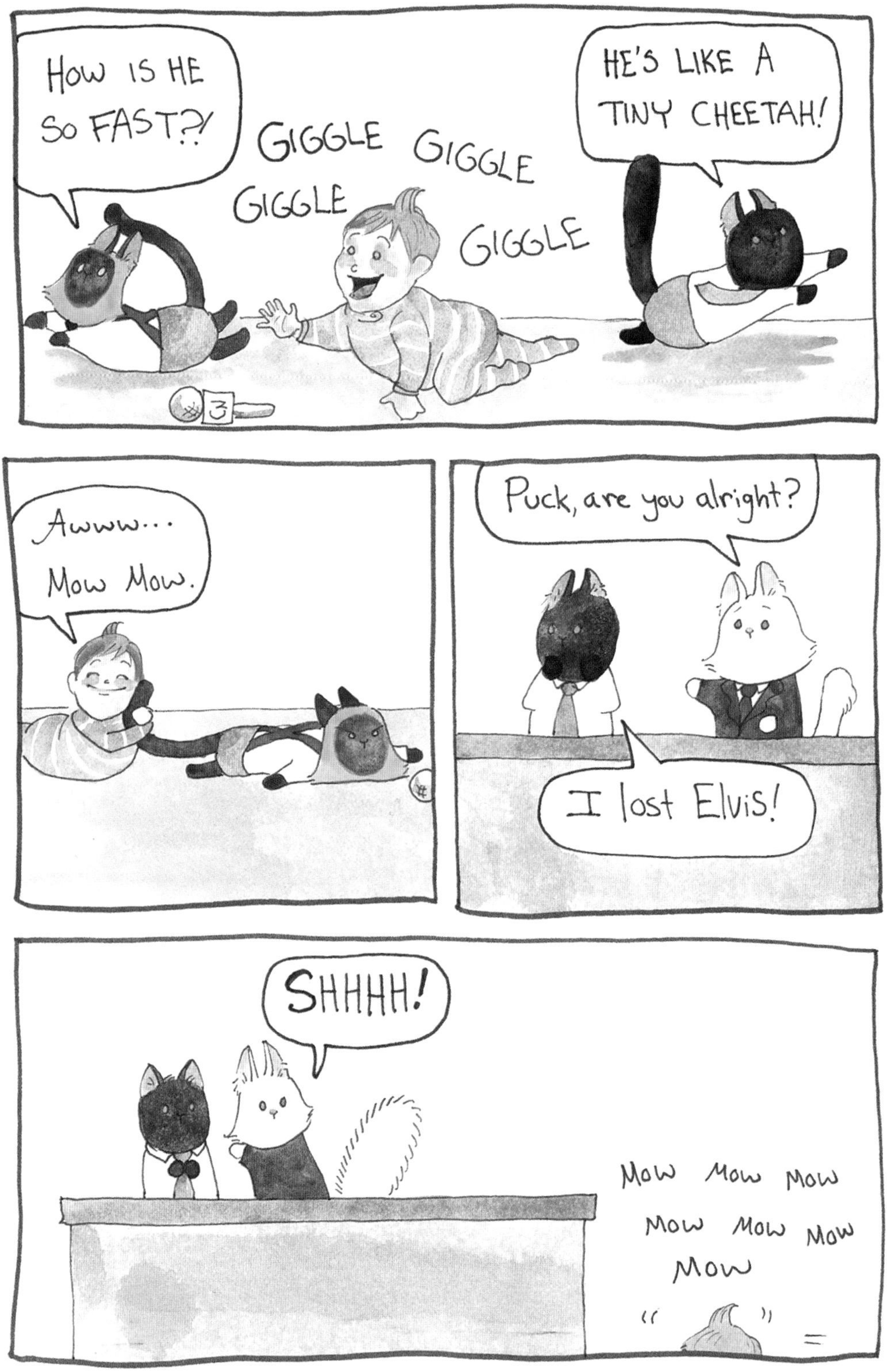
HOW IS HE SO FAST?!
GIGGLE GIGGLE
GIGGLE GIGGLE
HE'S LIKE A TINY CHEETAH!
Awww... Mow Mow.
Puck, are you alright?
I lost Elvis!
SHHHH!
Mow Mow Mow
Mow Mow Mow
Mow

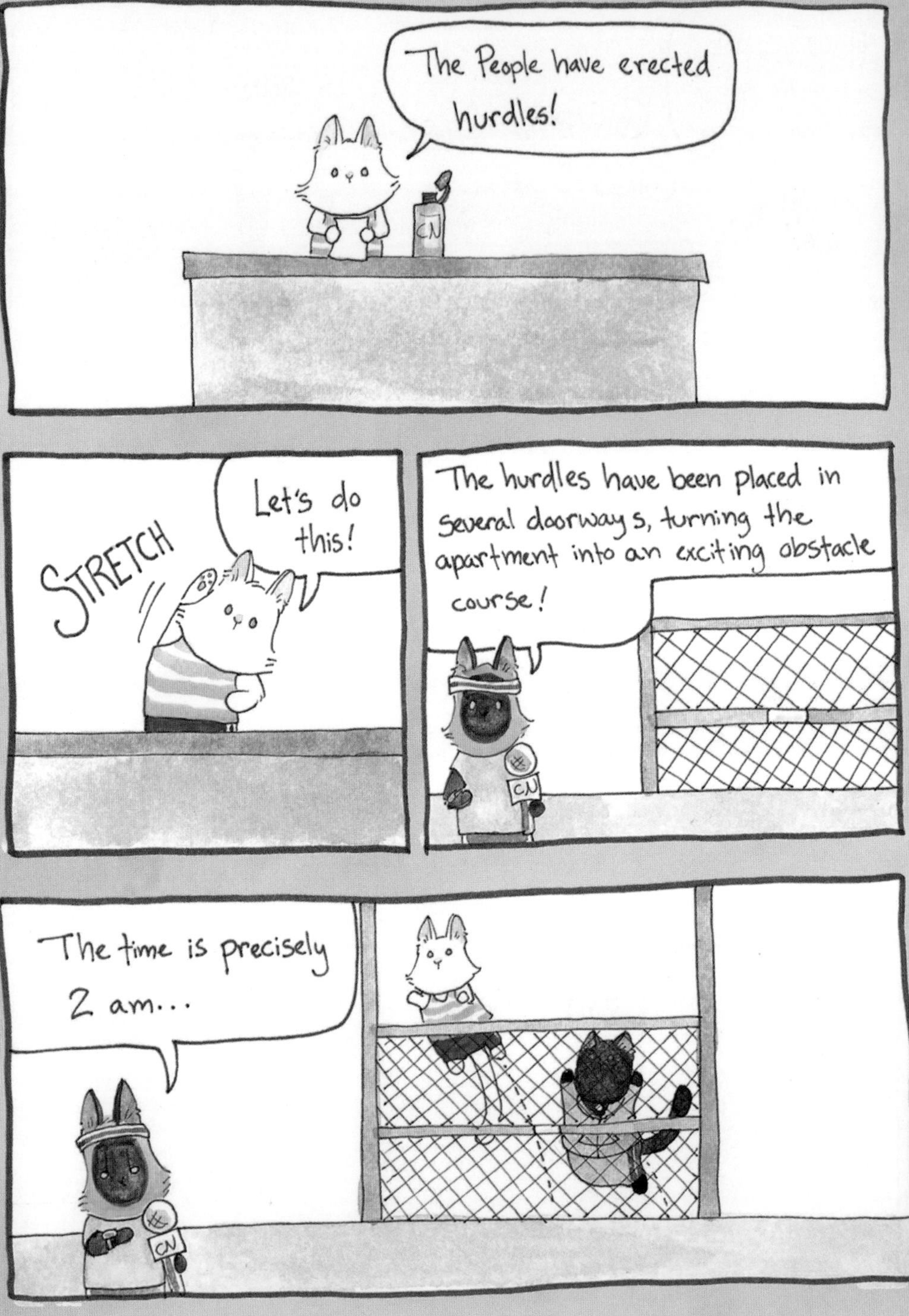
The People have erected hurdles!
STRETCH
Let's do this!
The hurdles have been placed in several doorways, turning the apartment into an exciting obstacle course!
The time is precisely 2 am...

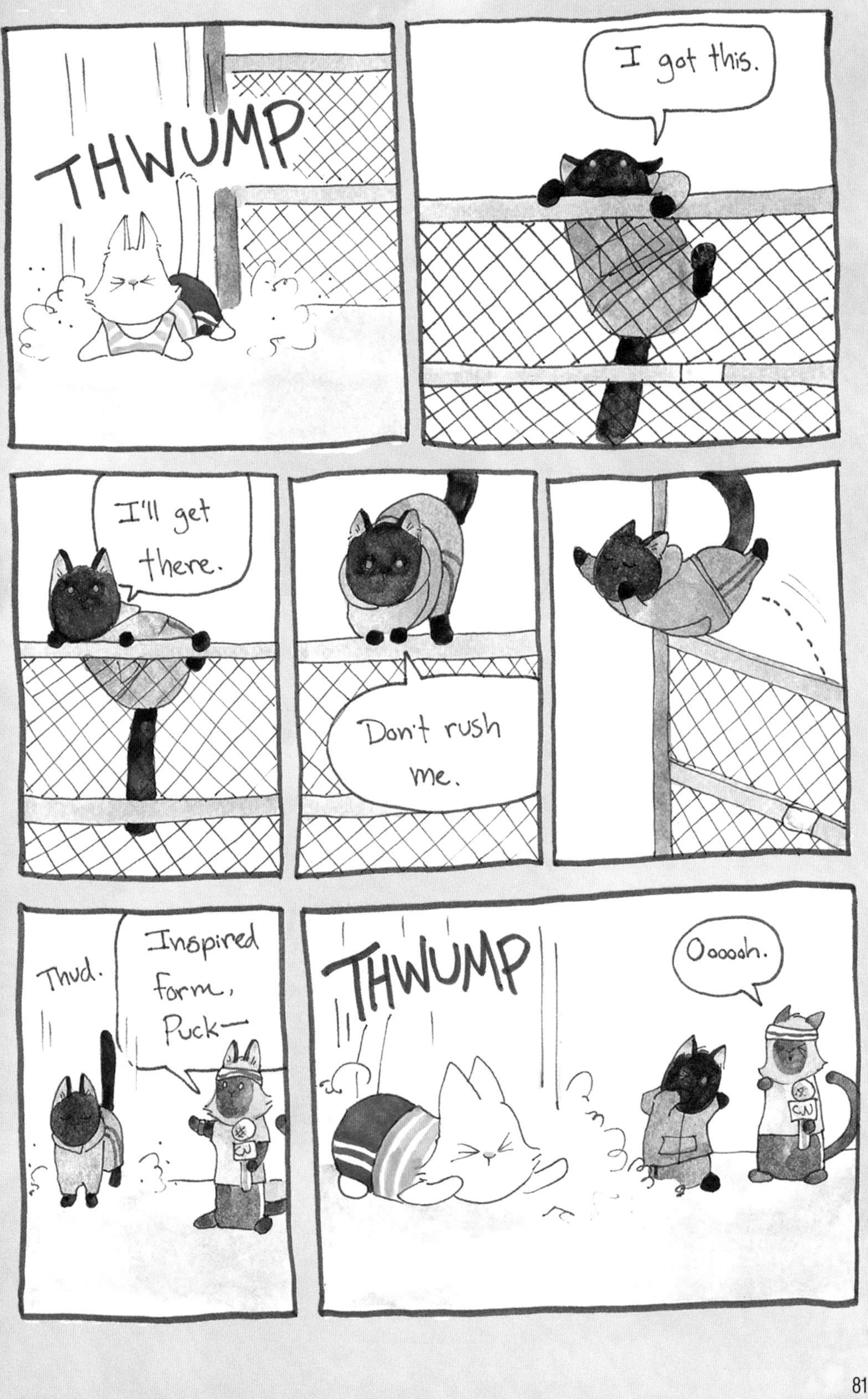
THWUMP
I got this.
I'll get there.
Don't rush me.
Thud.
Inspired form, Puck—
THWUMP
Oooooh.

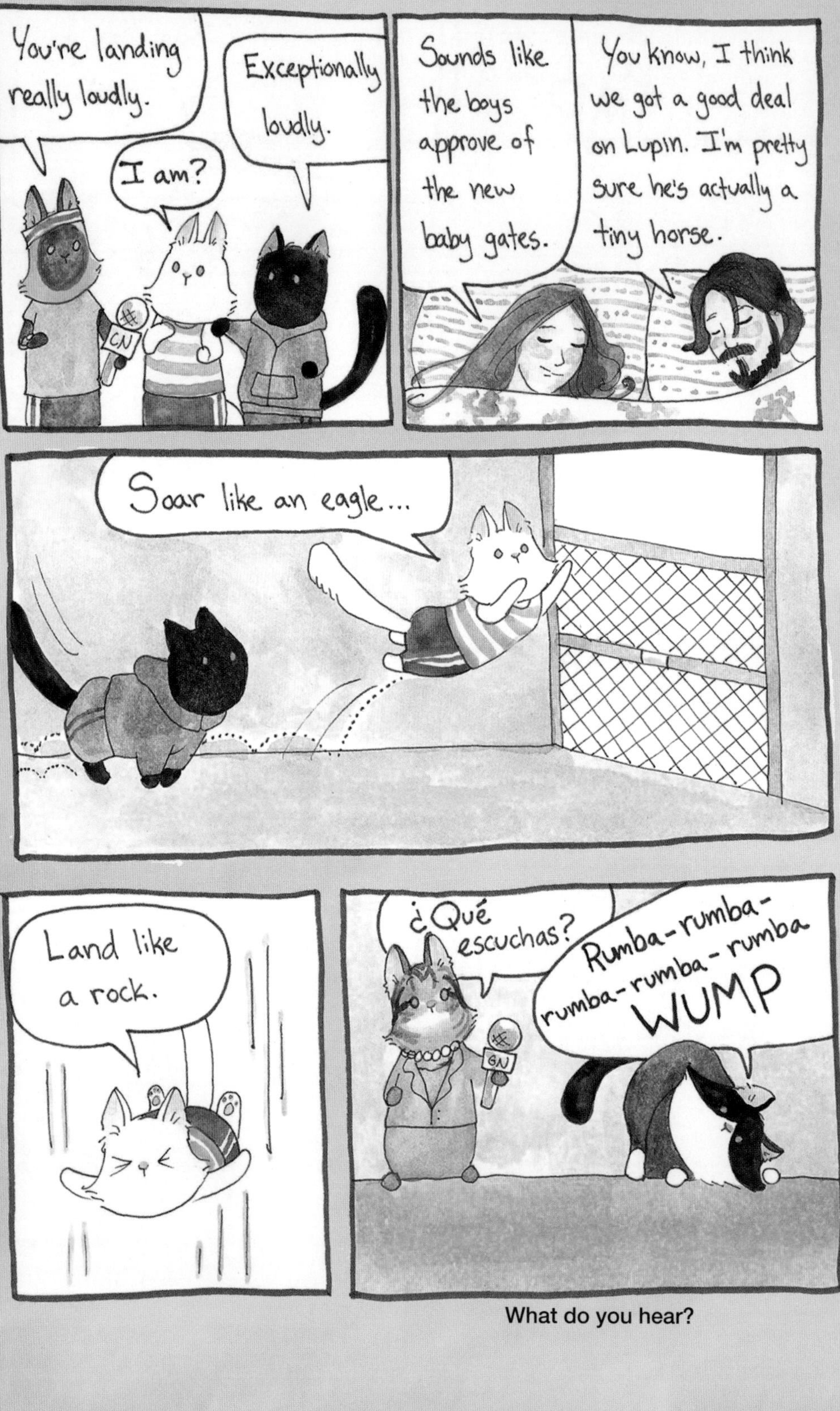
You're landing really loudly.
I am?
Exceptionally loudly.
Sounds like the boys approve of the new baby gates.
You know, I think we got a good deal on Lupin. I'm pretty sure he's actually a tiny horse.
Soar like an eagle...
Land like a rock.
¿Qué escuchas?
Rumba-rumba-rumba-rumba-rumba-rumba WUMP

What do you hear?

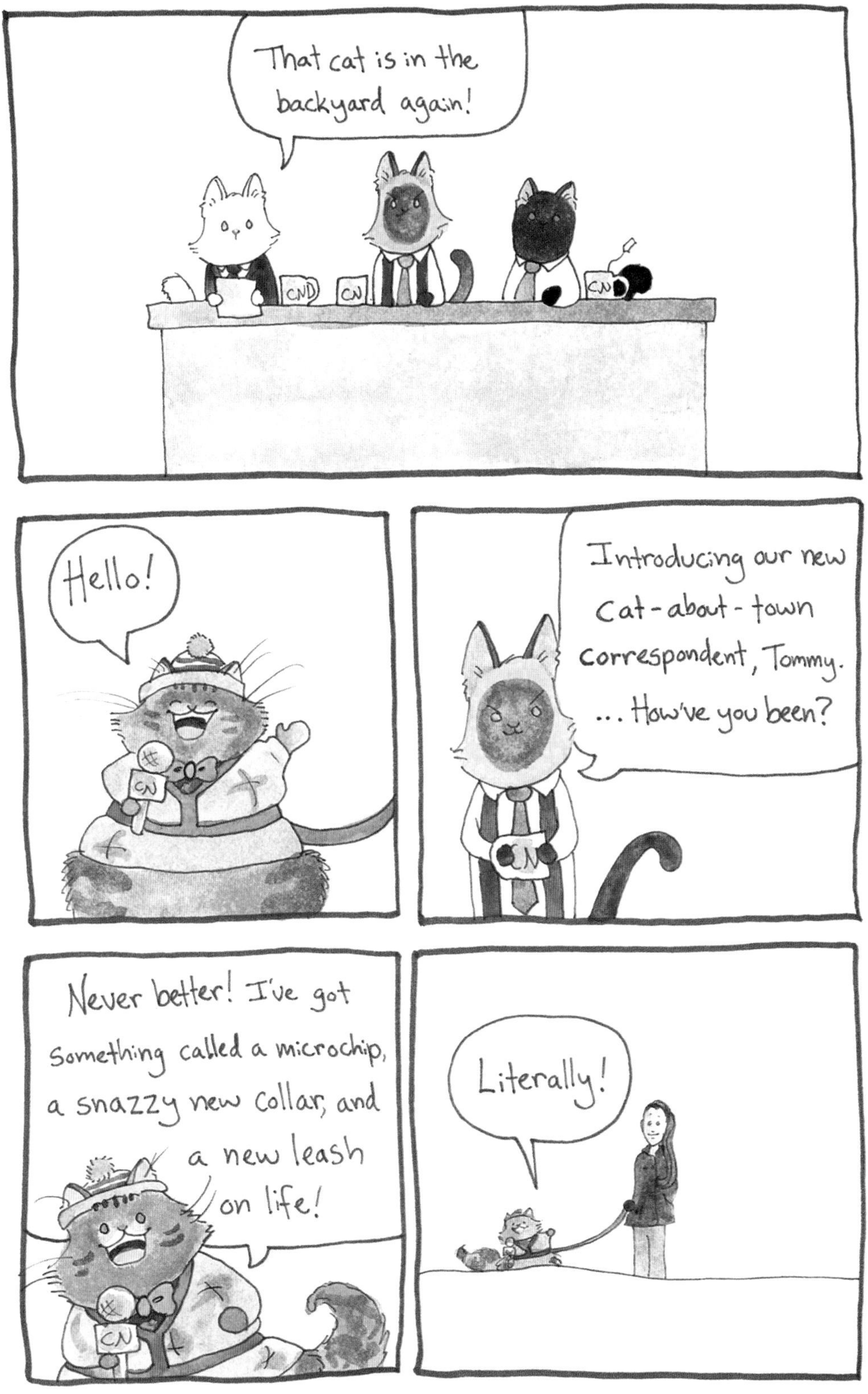
That cat is in the backyard again!
CND
CN
CN
Hello!
CN
Introducing our new cat-about-town correspondent, Tommy. ...How've you been?
CN
Never better! I've got something called a microchip, a snazzy new collar, and a new leash on life!
CN
Literally!

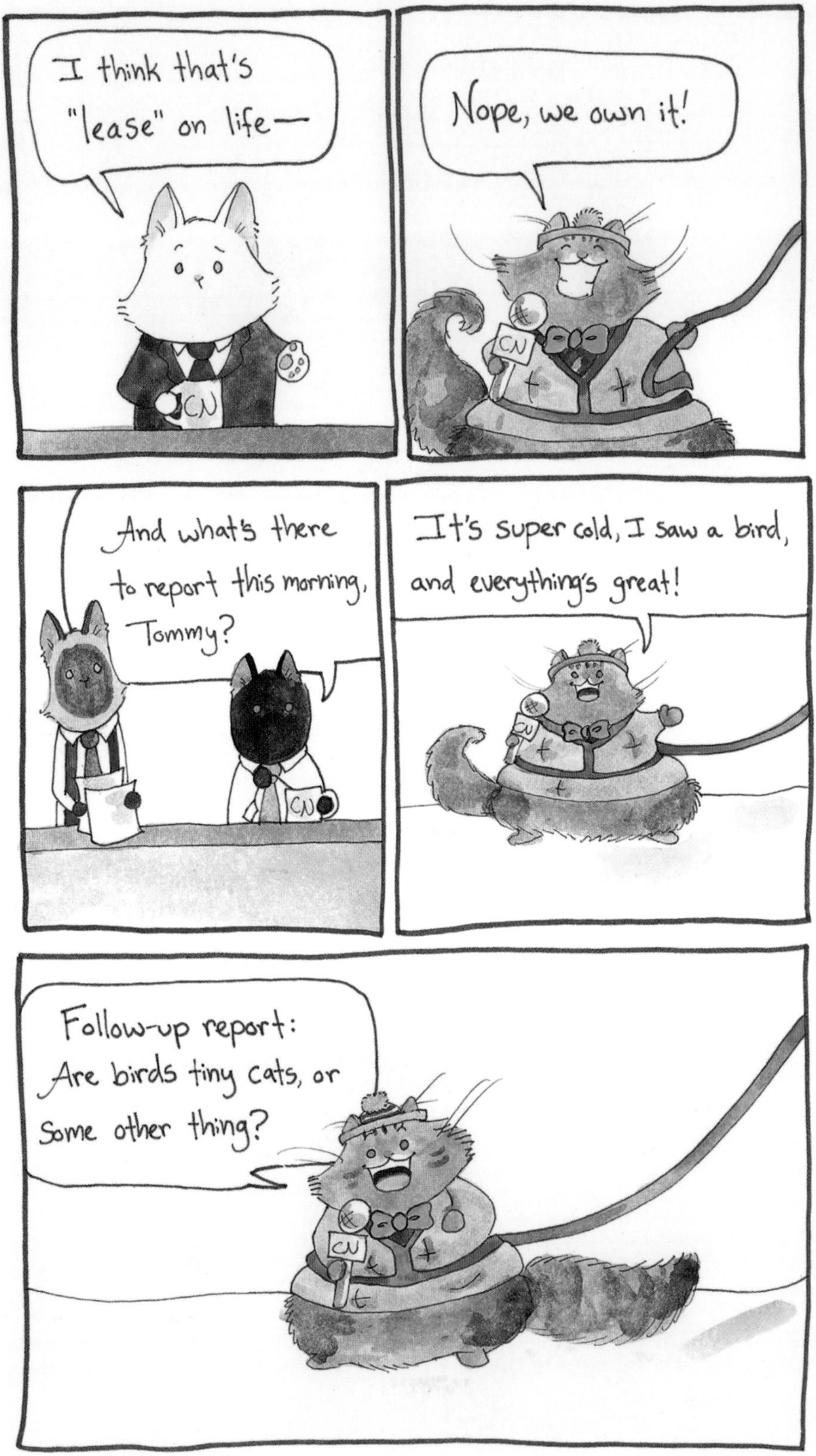
I think that's "lease" on life—
Nope, we own it!
CN
And what's there to report this morning, Tommy?
CN
It's super cold, I saw a bird, and everything's great!
CN
Follow-up report: Are birds tiny cats, or Some other thing?
CN

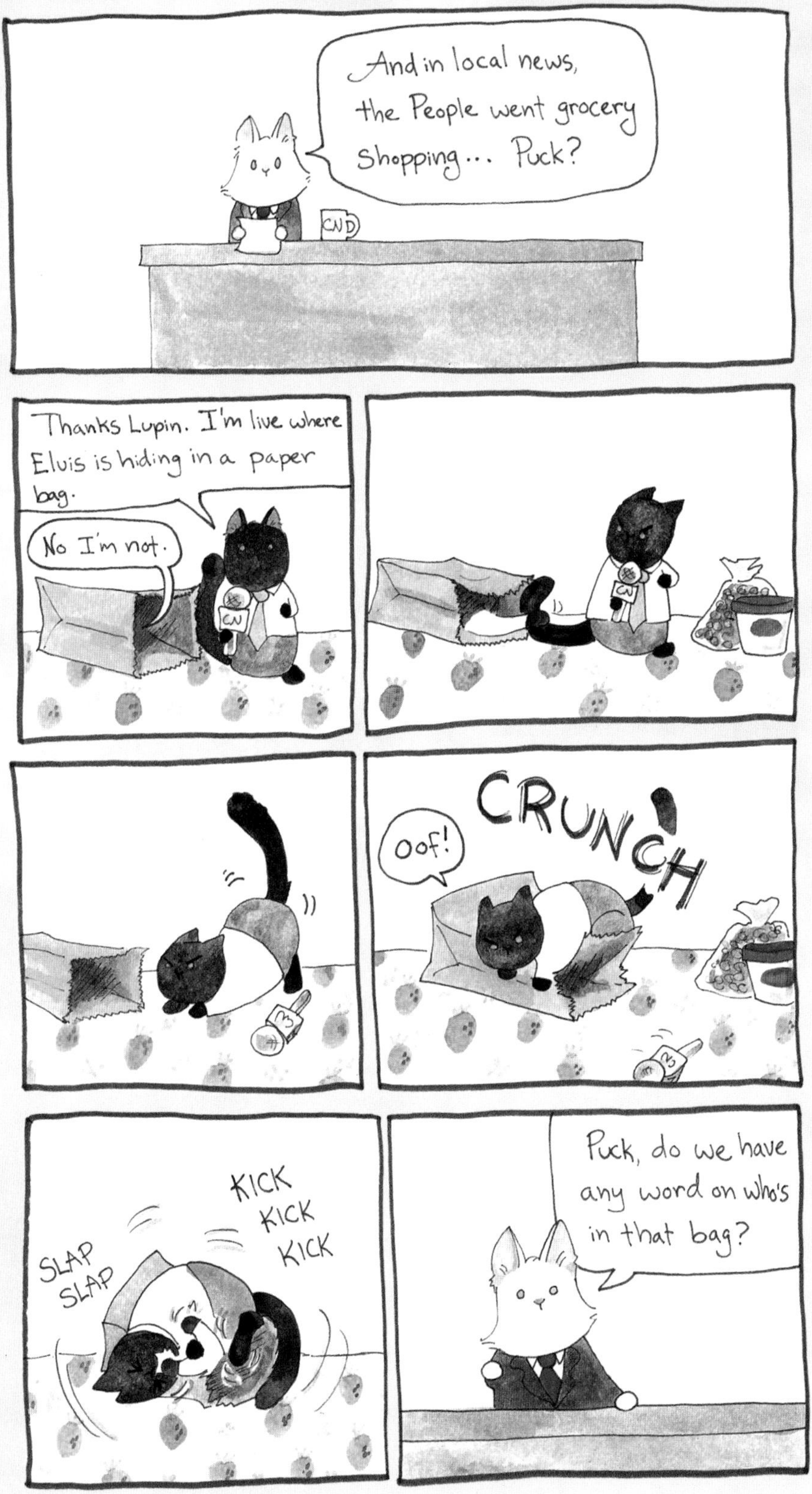
And in local news, the People went grocery shopping... Puck?
Thanks Lupin. I'm live where Elvis is hiding in a paper bag.
No I'm not.
CN
Oof!
CRUNCH
SLAP SLAP
KICK KICK KICK
Puck, do we have any word on who's in that bag?

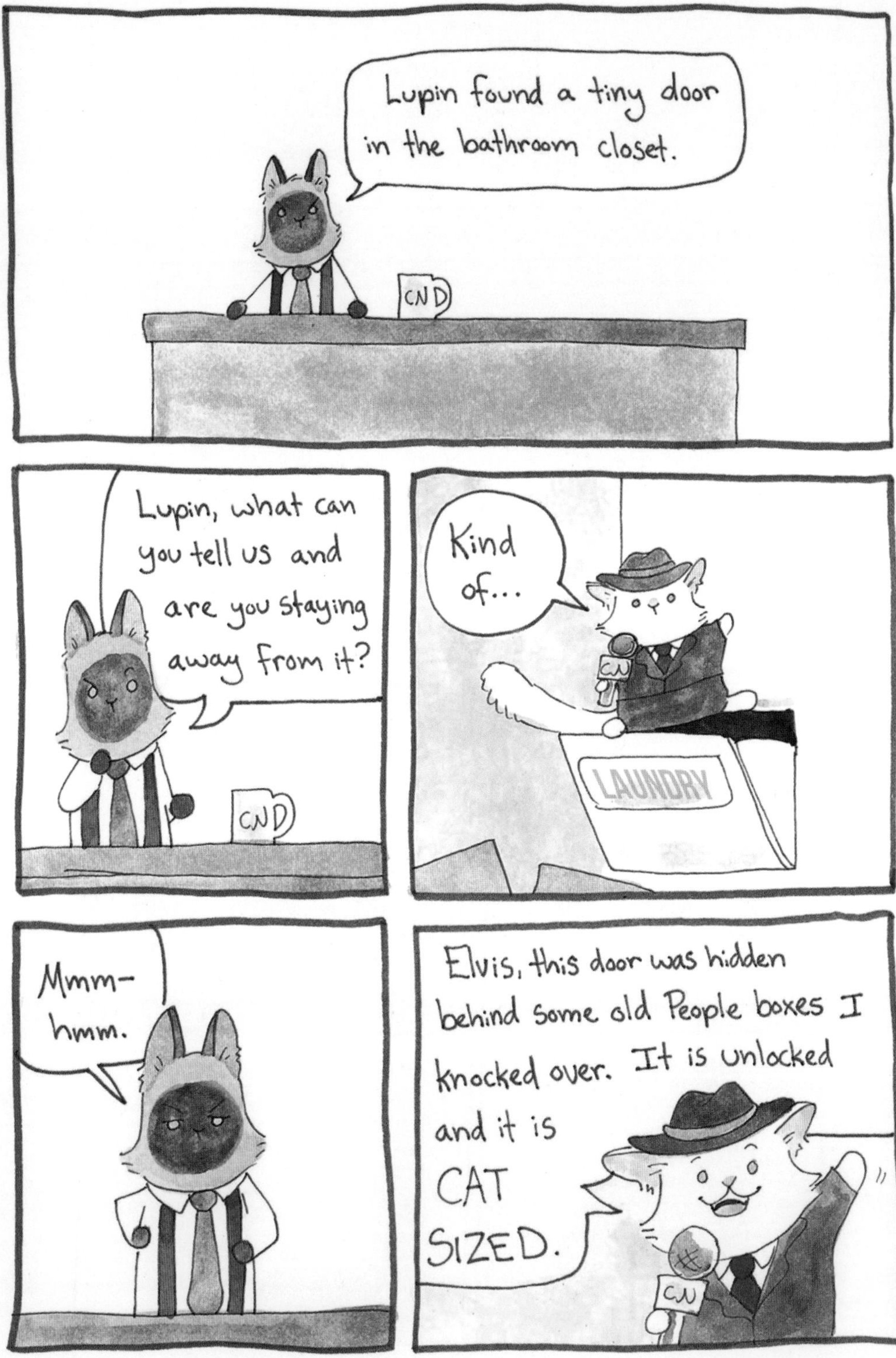
Lupin found a tiny door in the bathroom closet.
CND
Lupin, what can you tell us and are you staying away from it?
CND
Kind of...
CN
LAUNDRY
Mmm-hmm.
Elvis, this door was hidden behind some old People boxes I knocked over. It is unlocked and it is CAT SIZED.
CN

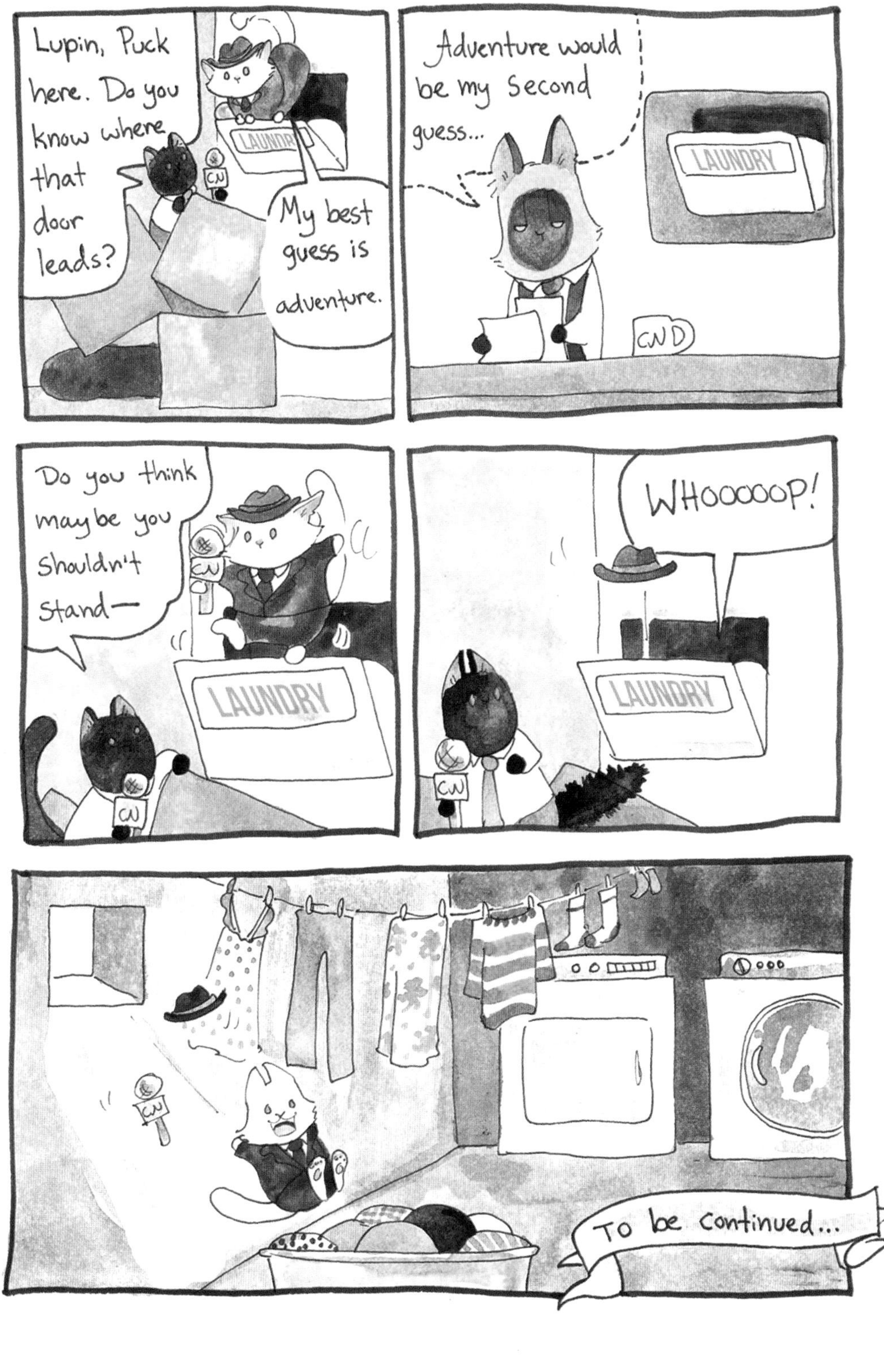
Lupin, Puck here. Do you know where that door leads?
LAUNDRY
CW
My best guess is adventure.
Adventure would be my second guess...
LAUNDRY
CWD
Do you think maybe you shouldn't stand—
LAUNDRY
CW
WHOOOOOP!
LAUNDRY
CW
CW
To be continued...

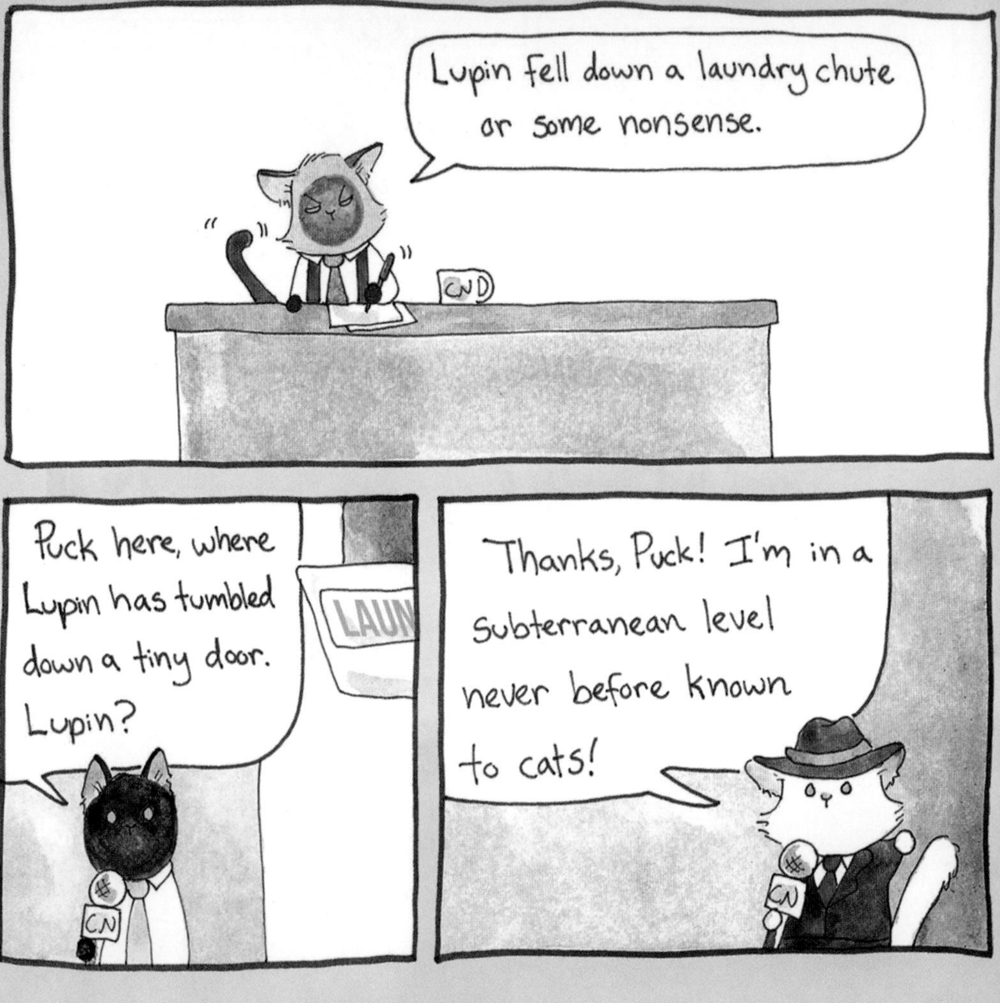
Lupin fell down a laundry chute or some nonsense.
Puck here, where Lupin has tumbled down a tiny door. Lupin?
LAUN
Thanks, Puck! I'm in a subterranean level never before known to cats!

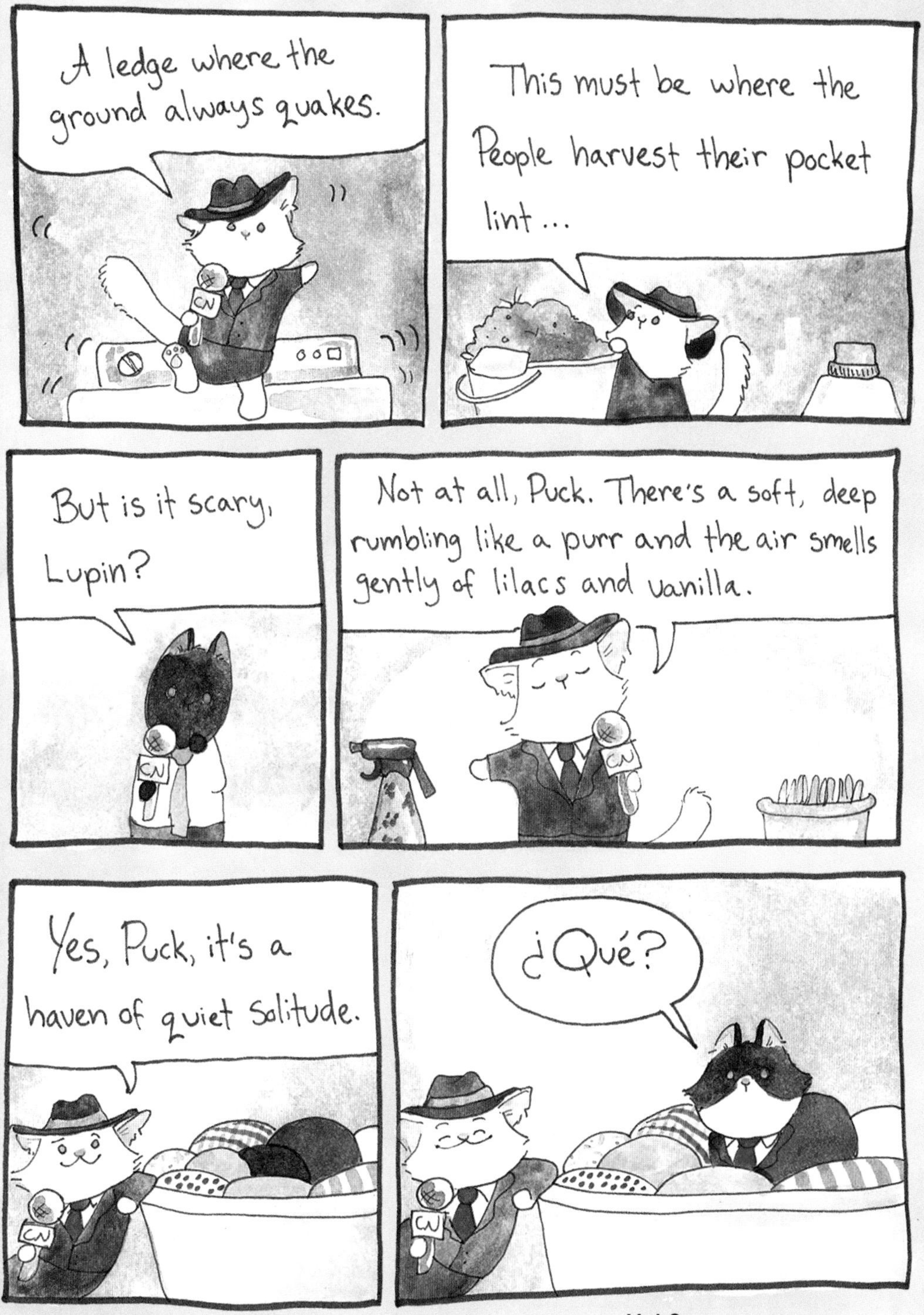
A ledge where the ground always quakes.
This must be where the People harvest their pocket lint...
CN
But is it scary, Lupin?
Not at all, Puck. There's a soft, deep rumbling like a purr and the air smells gently of lilacs and vanilla.
Yes, Puck, it's a haven of quiet solitude.
¿Qué?

Huh?

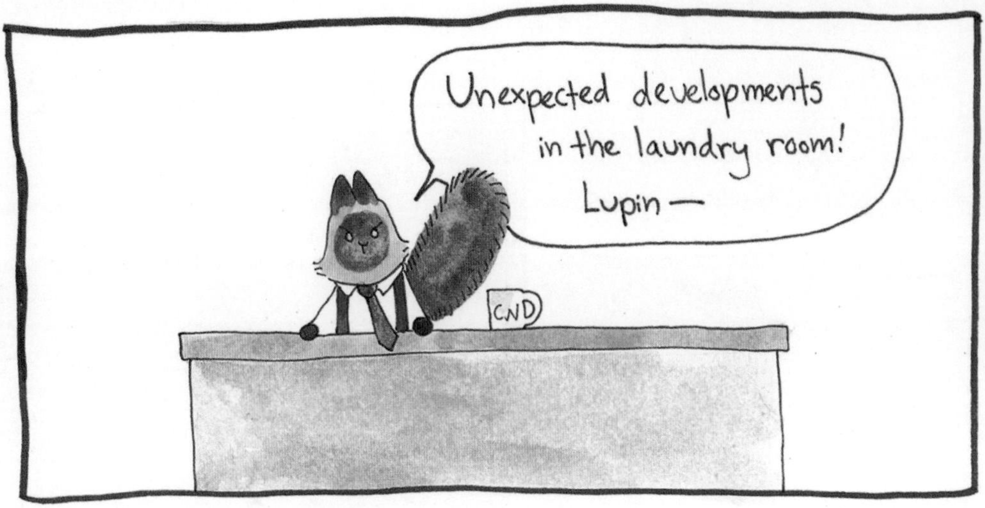
Unexpected developments in the laundry room! Lupin—
CND

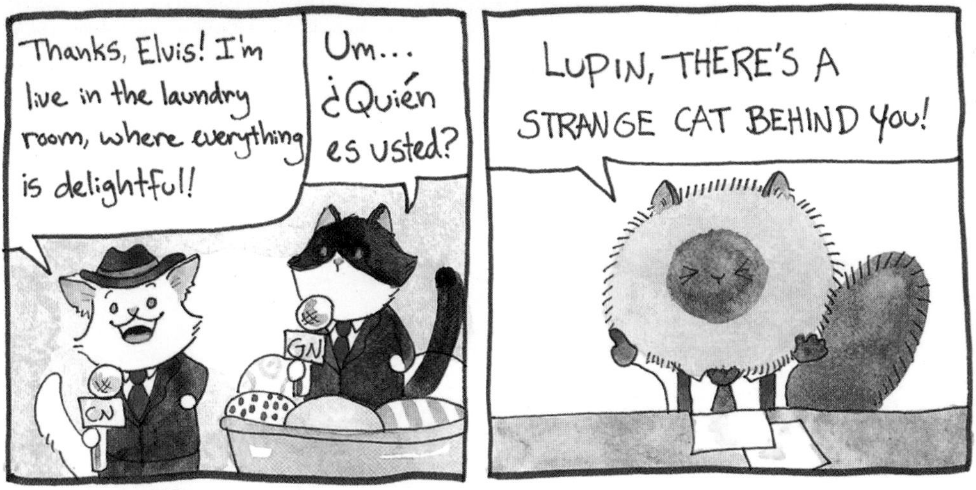
Thanks, Elvis! I'm live in the laundry room, where everything is delightful!
Um... ¿Quién es usted?
LUPIN, THERE'S A STRANGE CAT BEHIND YOU!
CN
GN

Who are you?

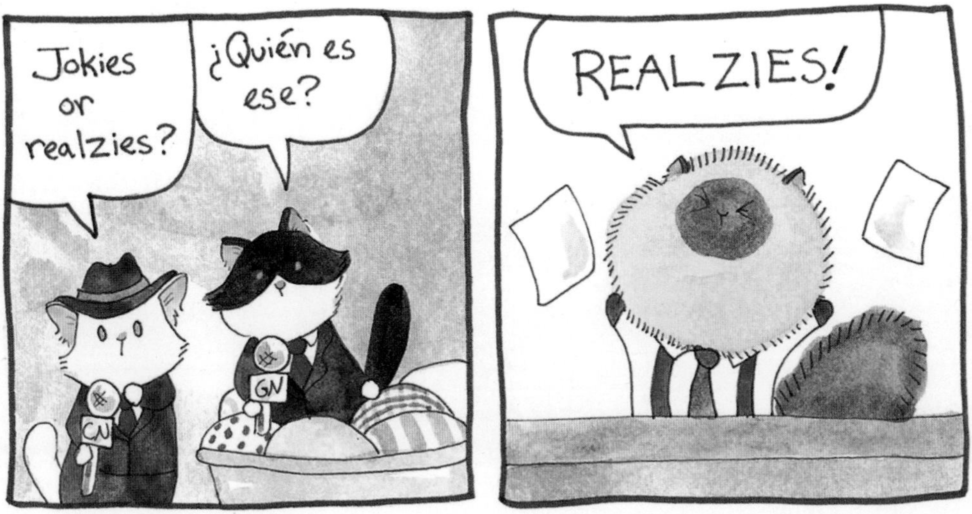
Jokies or realzies?
¿Quién es ese?
REALZIES!
CN
GN

Who is that?

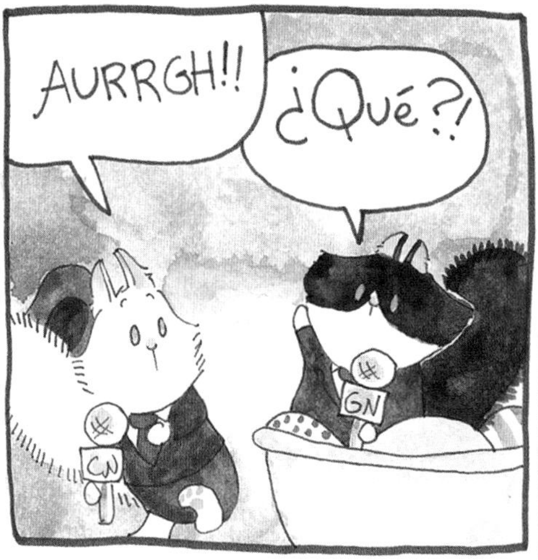
AURRGH!!
¿Qué?!

What?!

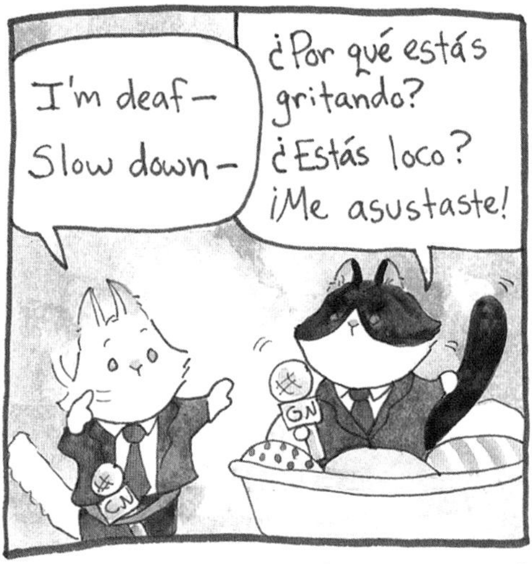
I'm deaf—
Slow down—
¿Por qué estás gritando? ¿Estás loco? ¡Me asustaste!

Why are you shouting? Are you crazy?
You scared me!

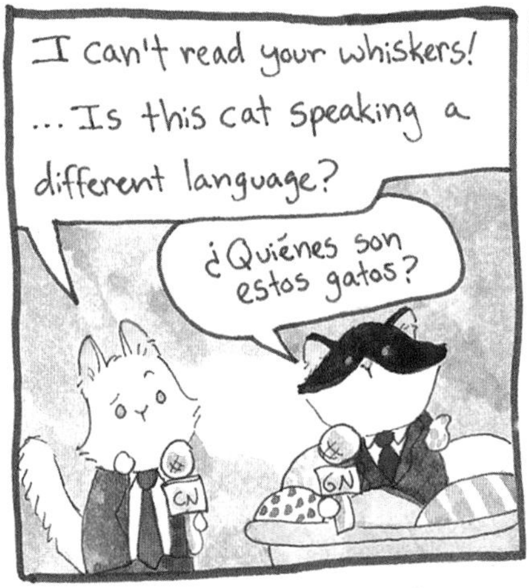
I can't read your whiskers! ...Is this cat speaking a different language?
¿Quiénes son estos gatos?

Who are these cats?

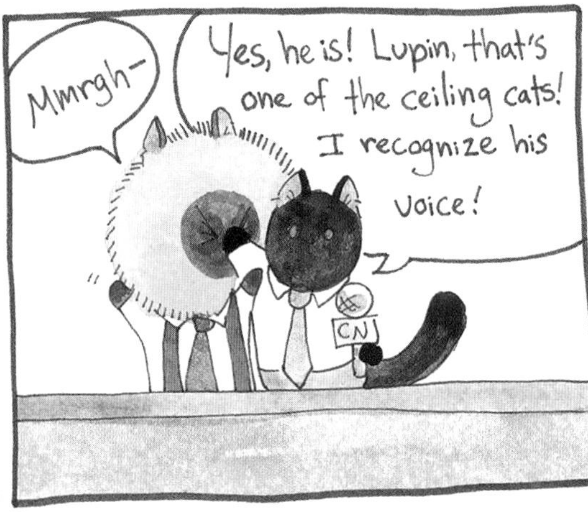
Mmrgh—
Yes, he is! Lupin, that's one of the ceiling cats! I recognize his voice!

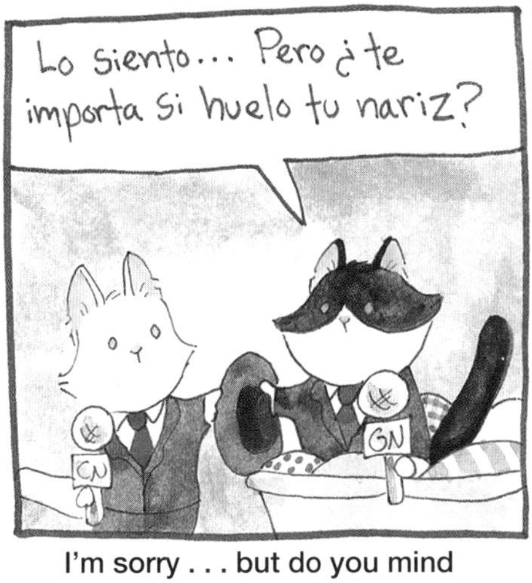
Lo siento... Pero ¿te importa si huelo tu nariz?

I'm sorry . . . but do you mind
if I smell your nose?

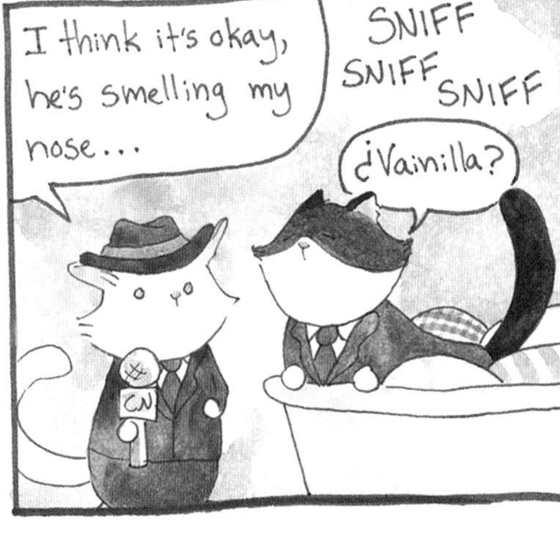
I think it's okay, he's smelling my nose...
SNIFF
SNIFF
SNIFF
¿Vainilla?

Vanilla?

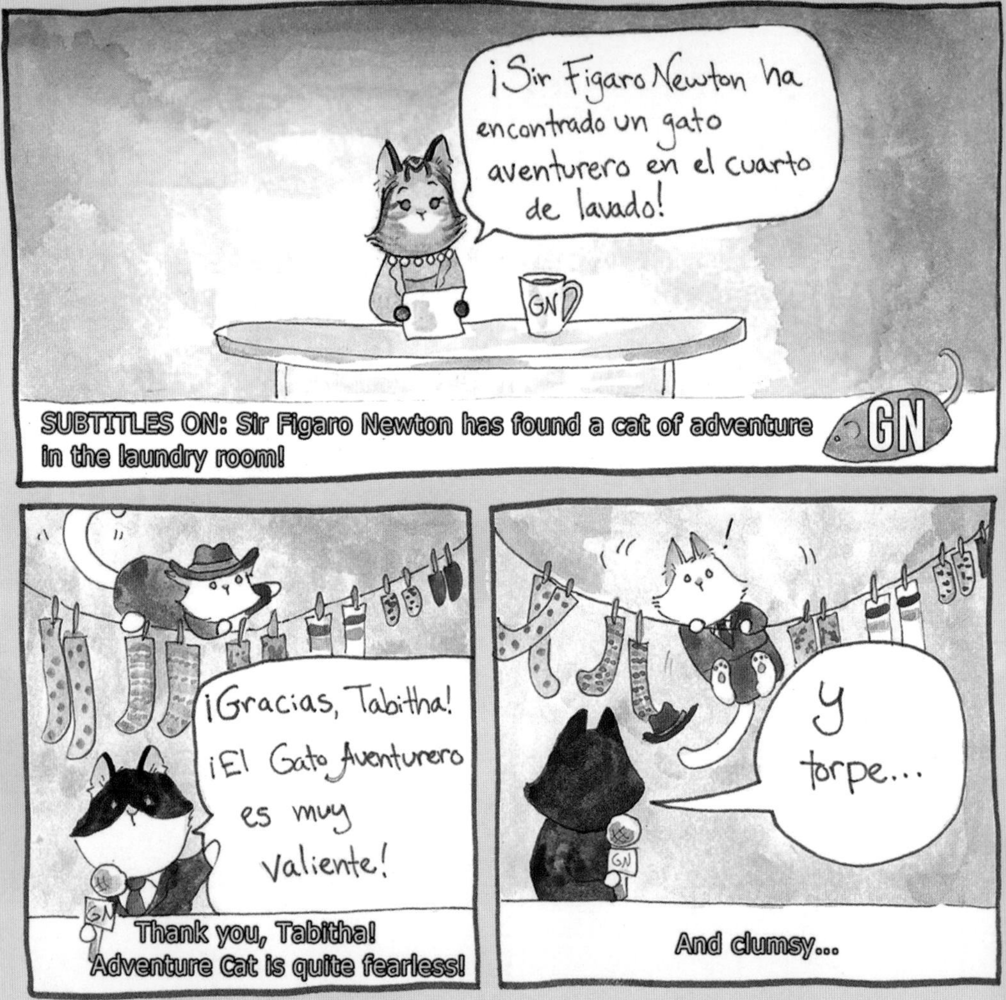
¡Sir Figaro Newton ha encontrado un gato aventurero en el cuarto de lavado!
GN
SUBTITLES ON: Sir Figaro Newton has found a cat of adventure in the laundry room!
GN
¡Gracias, Tabitha! ¡El Gato Aventurero es muy valiente!
GN
Thank you, Tabitha! Adventure Cat is quite fearless!
Y torpe...
GN
And clumsy...

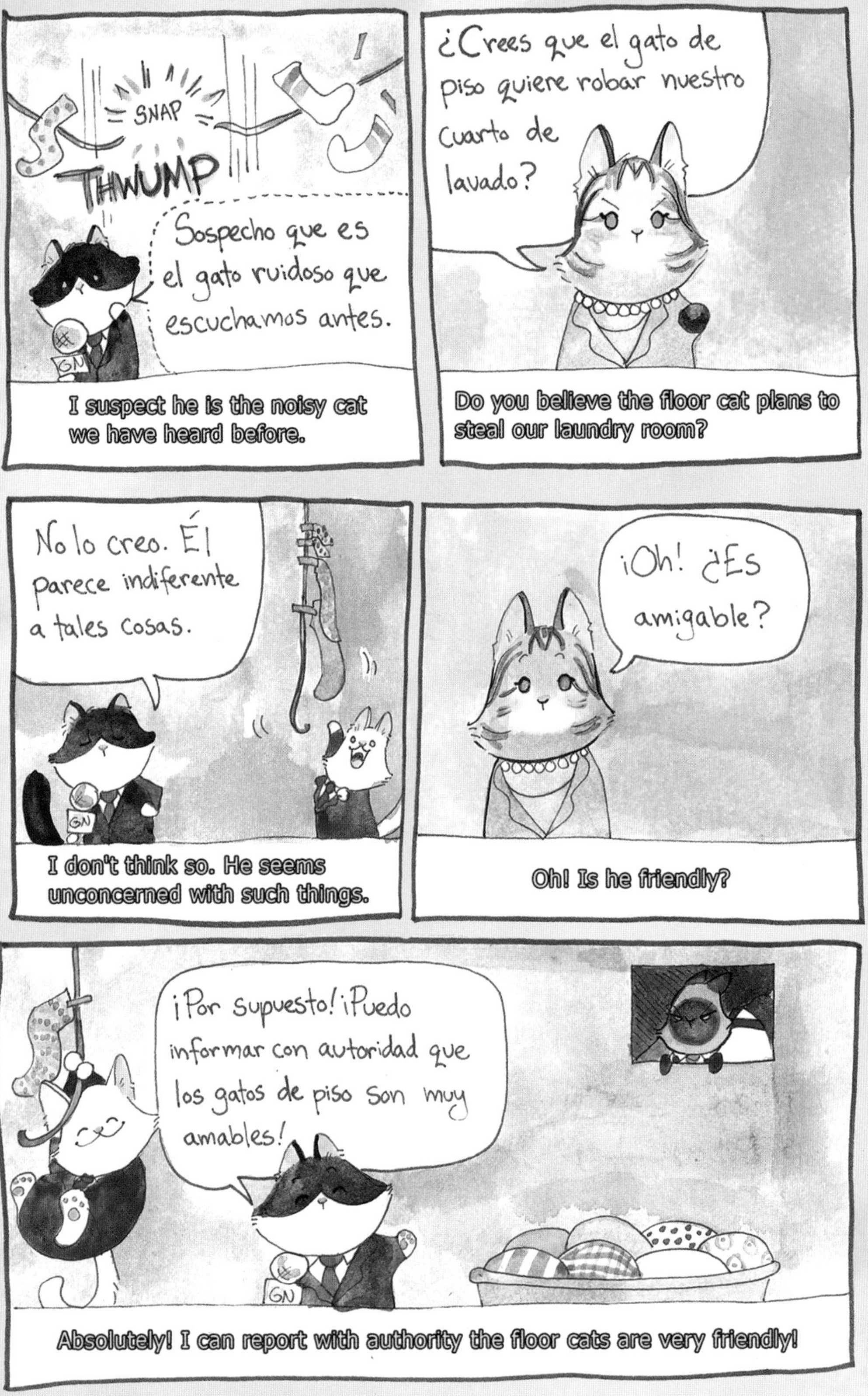
SNAP
THWUMP
Sospecho que es el gato ruidoso que escuchamos antes.
I suspect he is the noisy cat we have heard before.
¿Crees que el gato de piso quiere robar nuestro cuarto de lavado?
Do you believe the floor cat plans to steal our laundry room?
No lo creo. Él parece indiferente a tales cosas.
I don't think so. He seems unconcerned with such things.
¡Oh! ¿Es amigable?
Oh! Is he friendly?
¡Por supuesto! ¡Puedo informar con autoridad que los gatos de piso son muy amables!
Absolutely! I can report with authority the floor cats are very friendly!

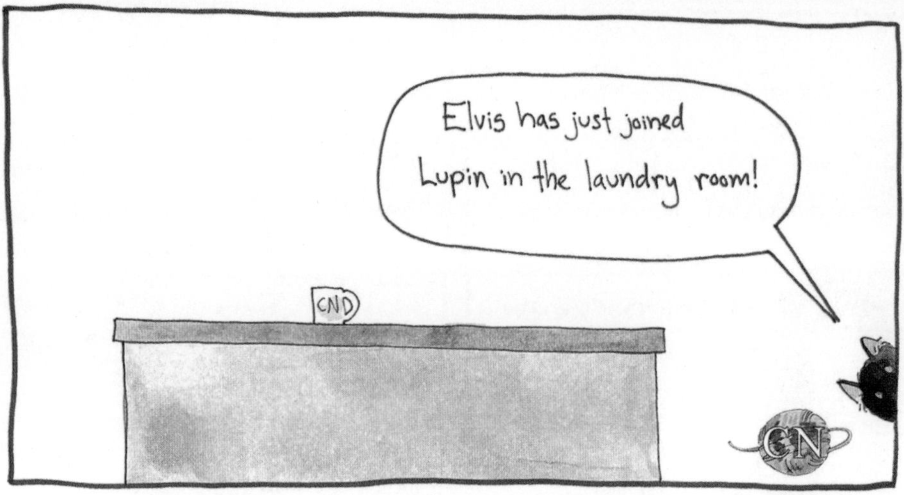
Elvis has just joined Lupin in the laundry room!

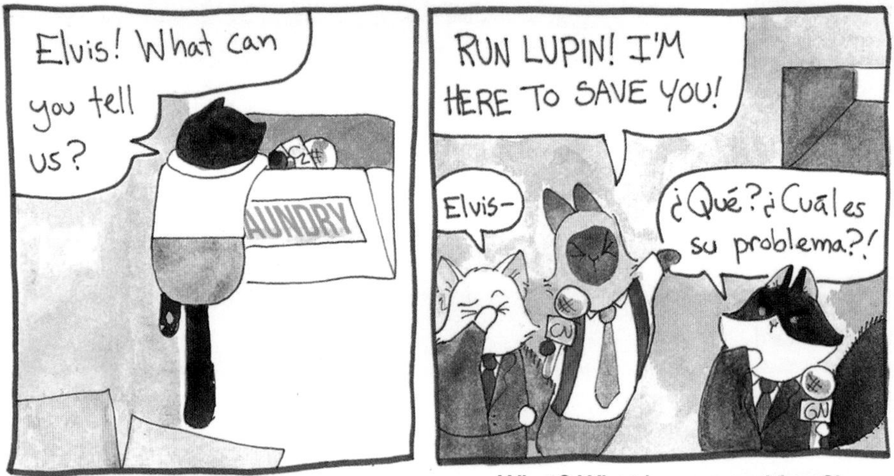
Elvis! What can you tell us?
RUN LUPIN! I'M HERE TO SAVE YOU!
Elvis-
¿Qué? ¿Cuál es su problema?!

What? What is your problem?!

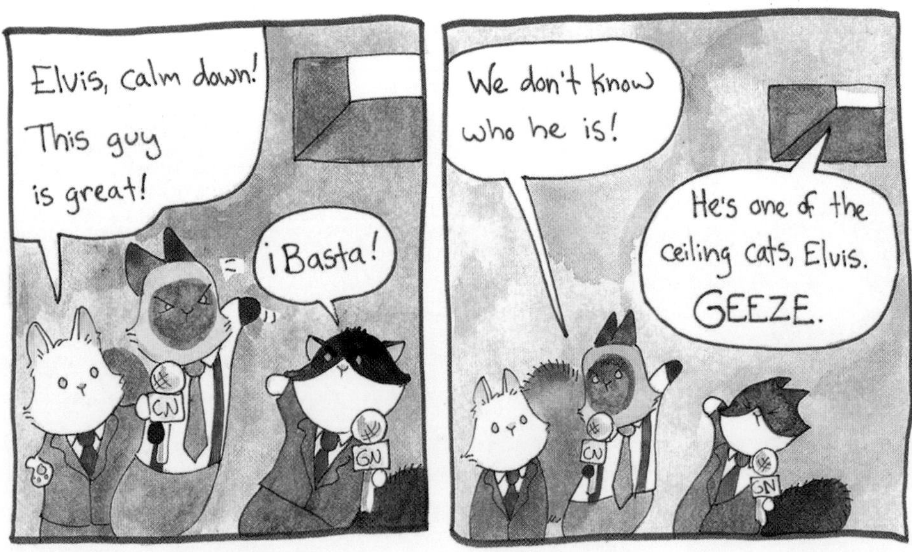
Elvis, calm down! This guy is great!
¡Basta!
We don't know who he is!
He's one of the ceiling cats, Elvis. GEEZE.

Enough!

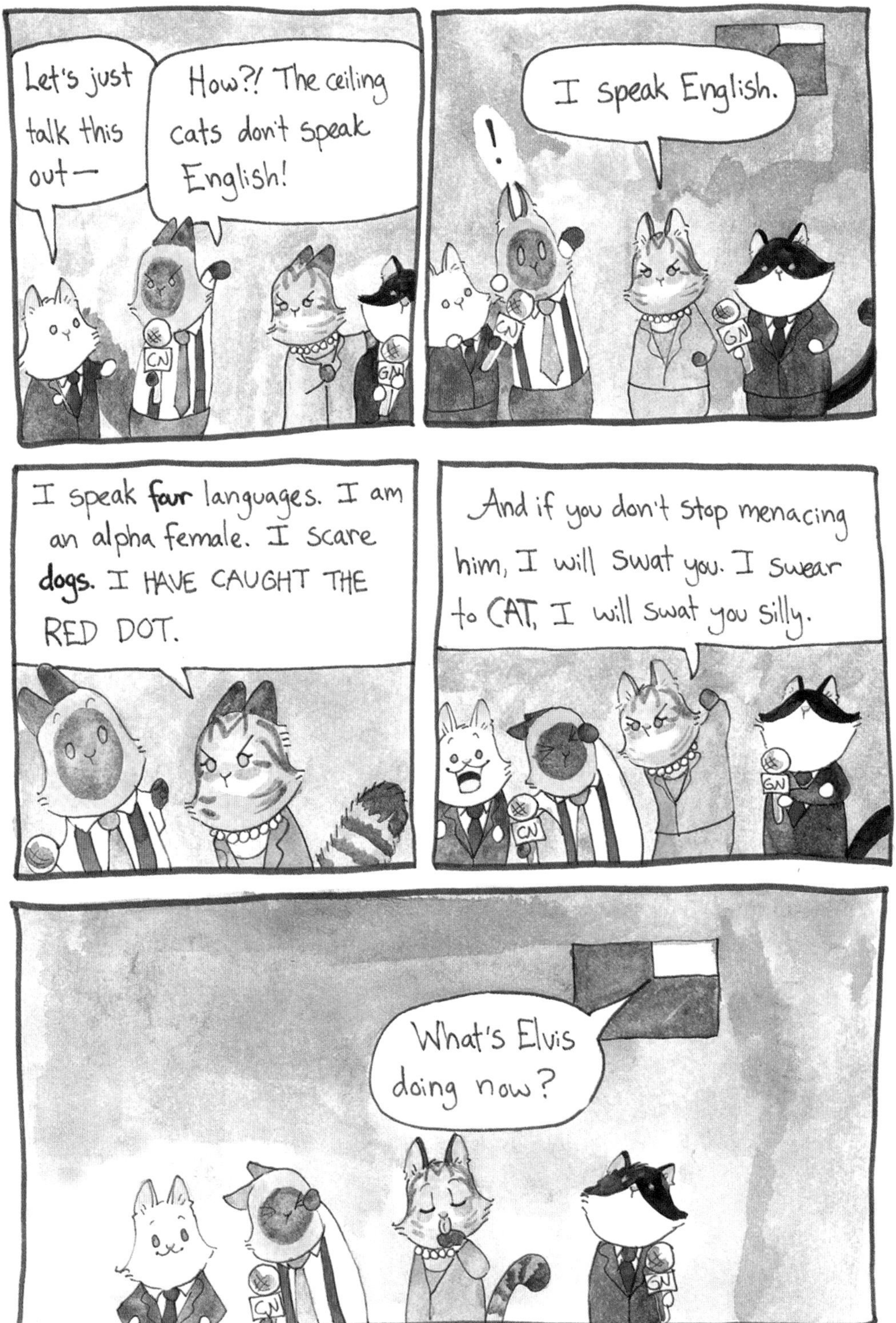
Let's just talk this out—
How?! The ceiling cats don't speak English!
!
I speak English.
I speak **four** languages. I am an alpha female. I scare **dogs**. I HAVE CAUGHT THE RED DOT.
And if you don't stop menacing him, I will swat you. I swear to CAT, I will swat you silly.
CN
GN
What's Elvis doing now?

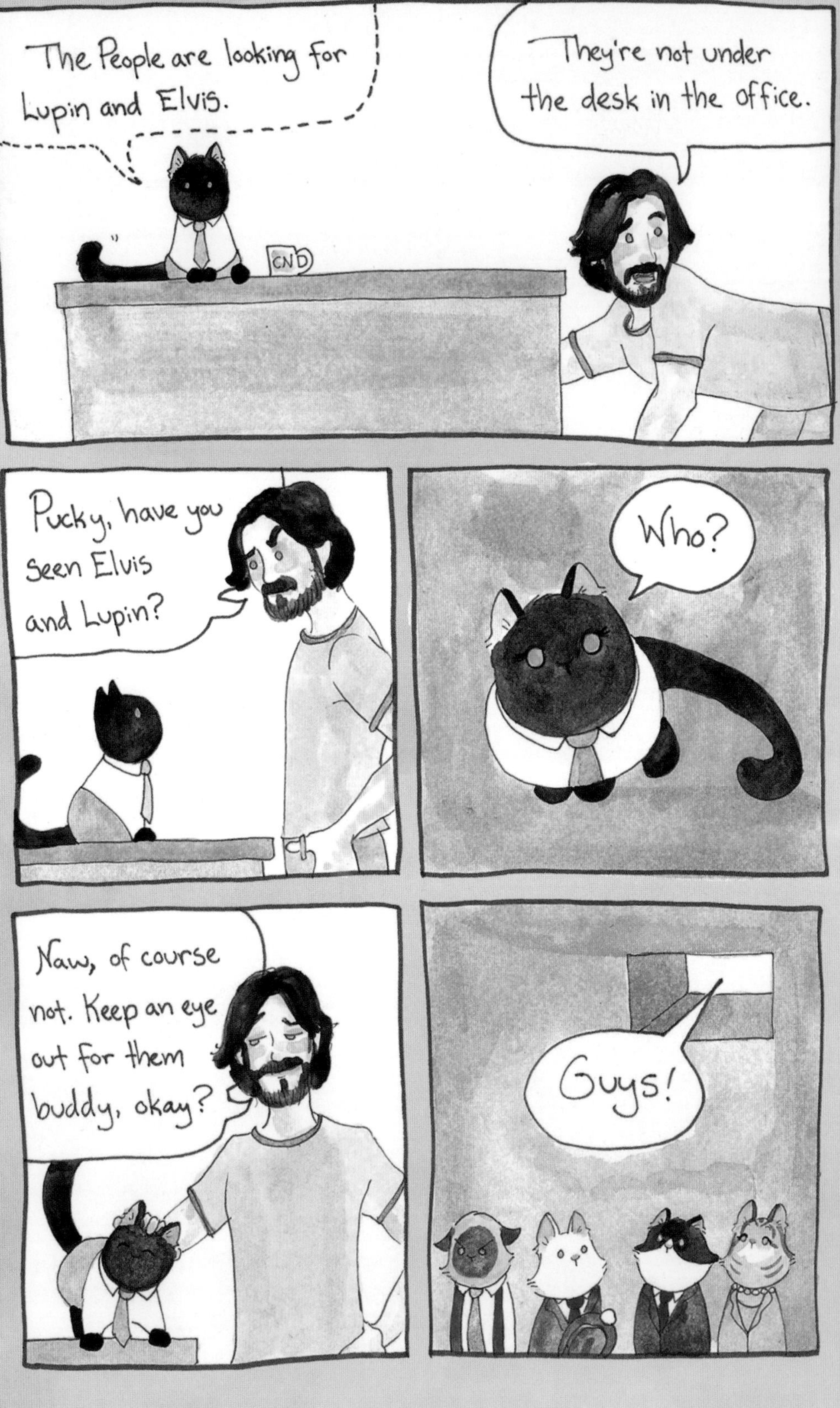
The People are looking for Lupin and Elvis.
They're not under the desk in the office.
CND
Pucky, have you seen Elvis and Lupin?
Who?
Naw, of course not. Keep an eye out for them buddy, okay?
Guys!

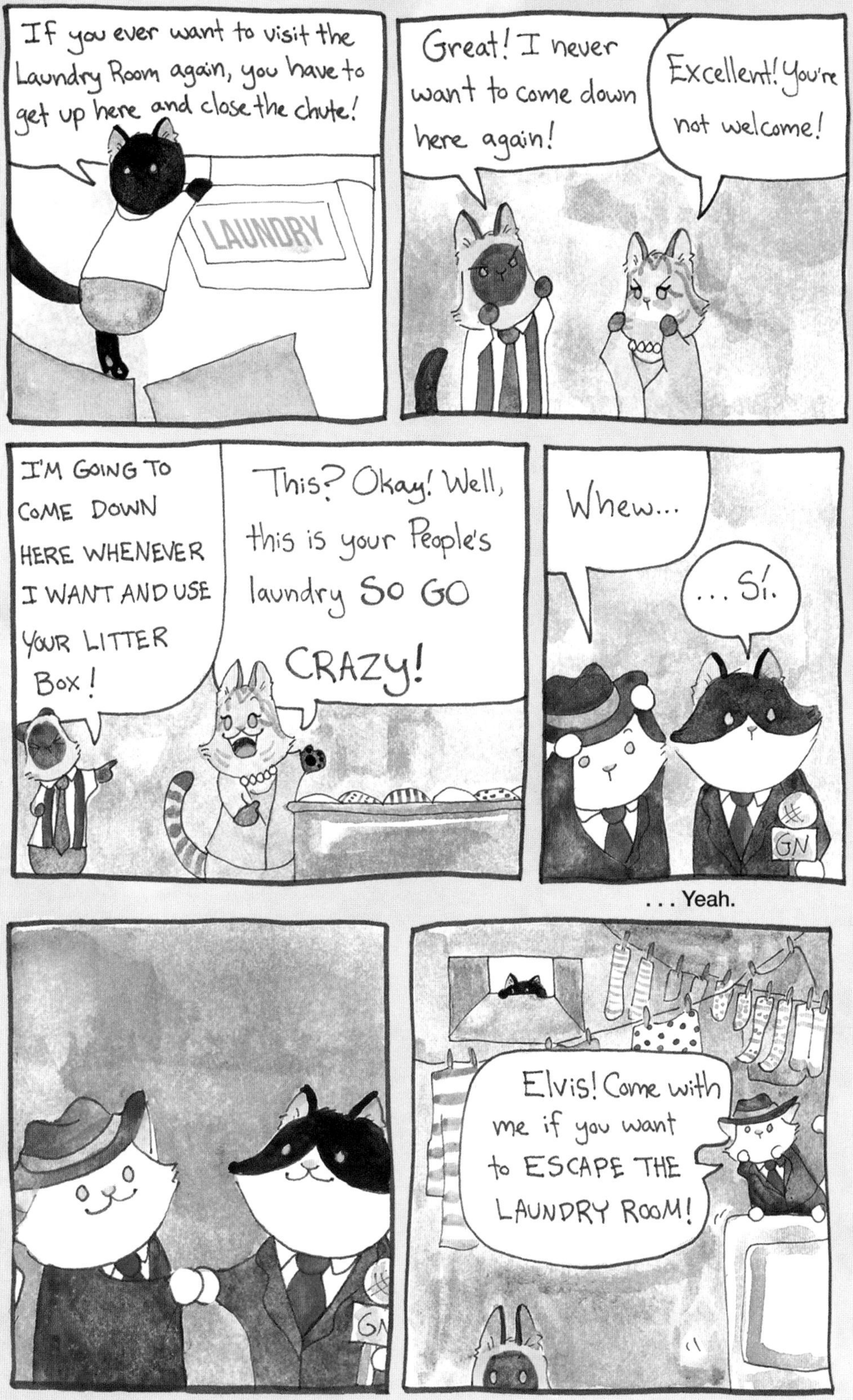
If you ever want to visit the Laundry Room again, you have to get up here and close the chute!
LAUNDRY
Great! I never want to come down here again!
Excellent! You're not welcome!
I'M GOING TO COME DOWN HERE WHENEVER I WANT AND USE YOUR LITTER BOX!
This? Okay! Well, this is your People's laundry SO GO CRAZY!
Whew...
... Sí.
GN
. . . Yeah.
Elvis! Come with me if you want to ESCAPE THE LAUNDRY ROOM!

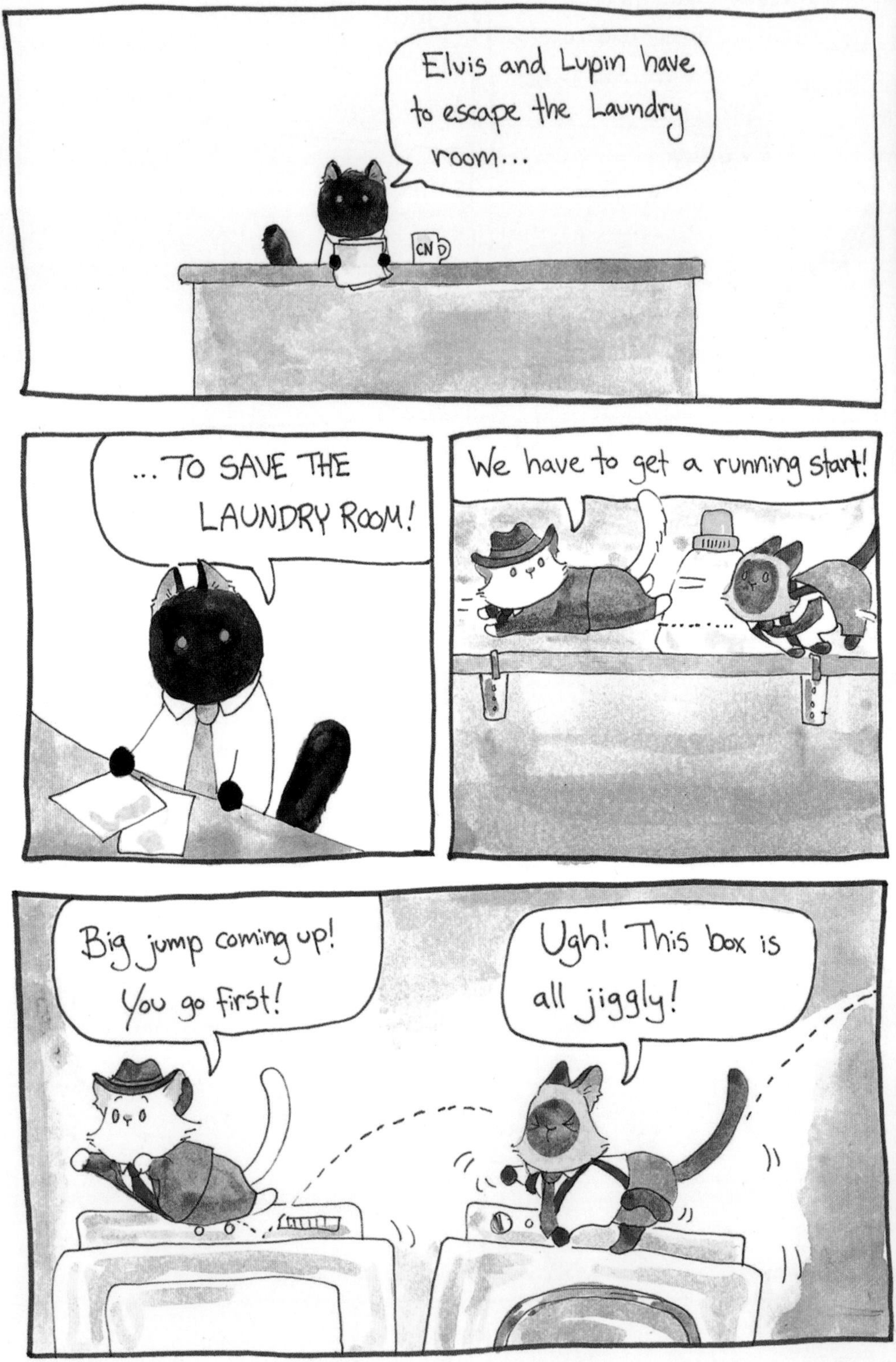
Elvis and Lupin have to escape the Laundry room...
CN
...TO SAVE THE LAUNDRY ROOM!
We have to get a running start!
Big jump coming up! You go first!
Ugh! This box is all jiggly!

FLOP

SCRAMBLE
SCRAMBLE

SHOVE

TWIST

LAUNDRY

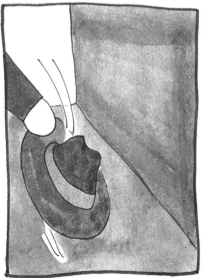

SNAP

LAUNDRY

CLICK

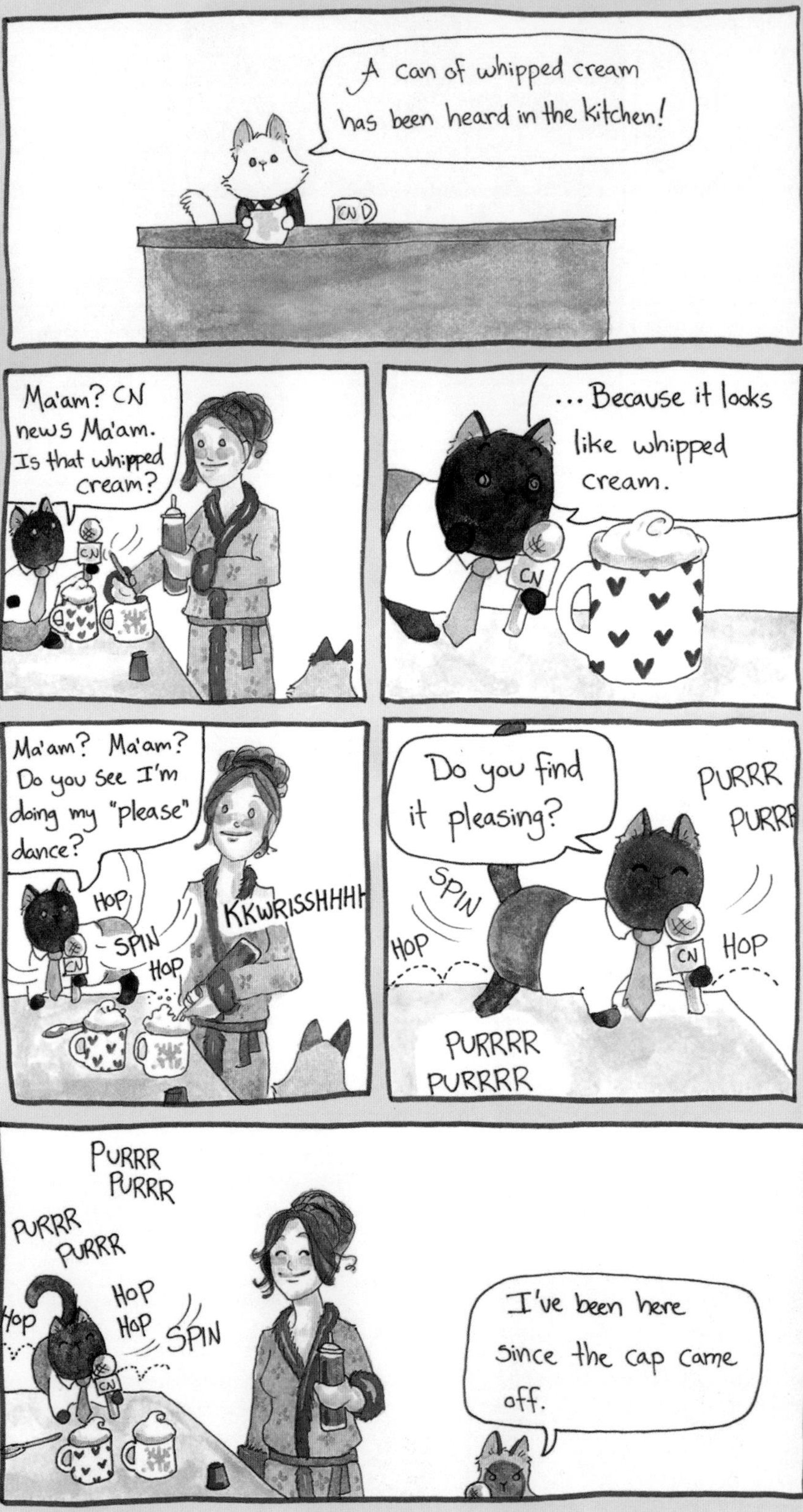
A can of whipped cream has been heard in the kitchen!
Ma'am? CN news Ma'am. Is that whipped cream?
CN
...Because it looks like whipped cream.
CN
Ma'am? Ma'am? Do you see I'm doing my "please" dance?
HOP
SPIN
HOP
KKWRISSHHHH
CN
Do you find it pleasing?
PURRR PURRR
SPIN
HOP
HOP
CN
PURRRR PURRRR
PURRR PURRR
PURRR PURRR
Hop
Hop Hop
SPIN
CN
I've been here since the cap came off.

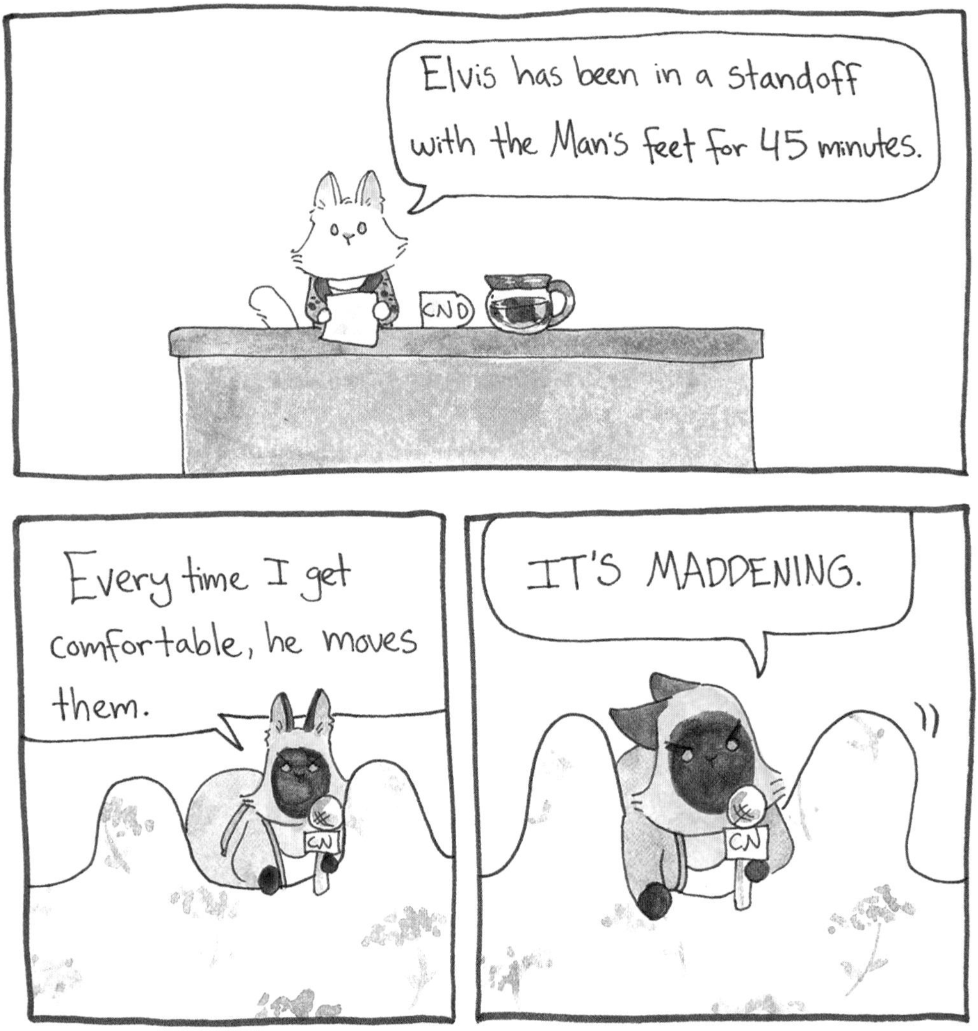
Elvis has been in a standoff with the Man's feet for 45 minutes.
CND
Every time I get comfortable, he moves them.
CN
IT'S MADDENING.
CN

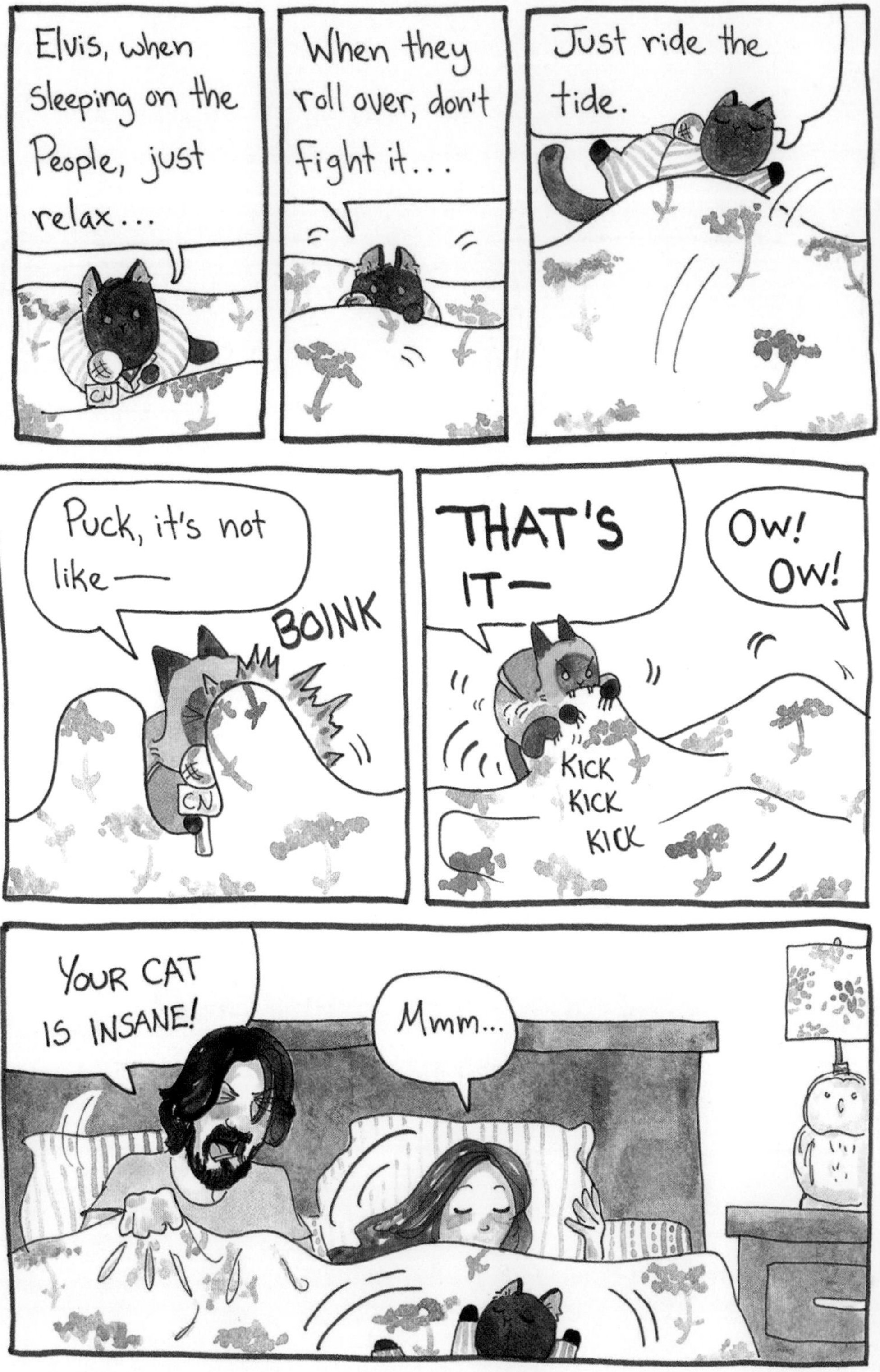
Elvis, when Sleeping on the People, just relax...
When they roll over, don't fight it...
Just ride the tide.
Puck, it's not like—
BOINK
THAT'S IT—
Ow! Ow!
KICK KICK KICK
YOUR CAT IS INSANE!
Mmm...

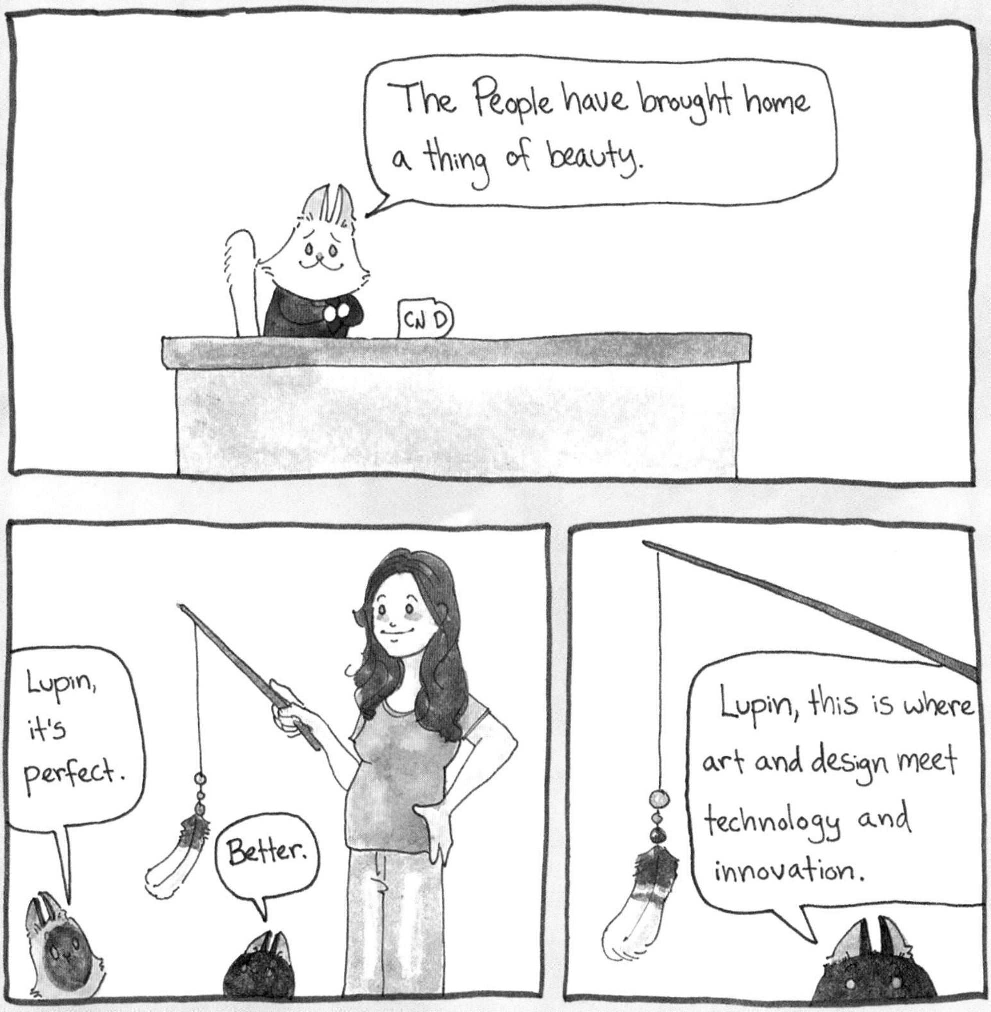
The People have brought home a thing of beauty.
CND
Lupin, it's perfect.
Better.
Lupin, this is where art and design meet technology and innovation.

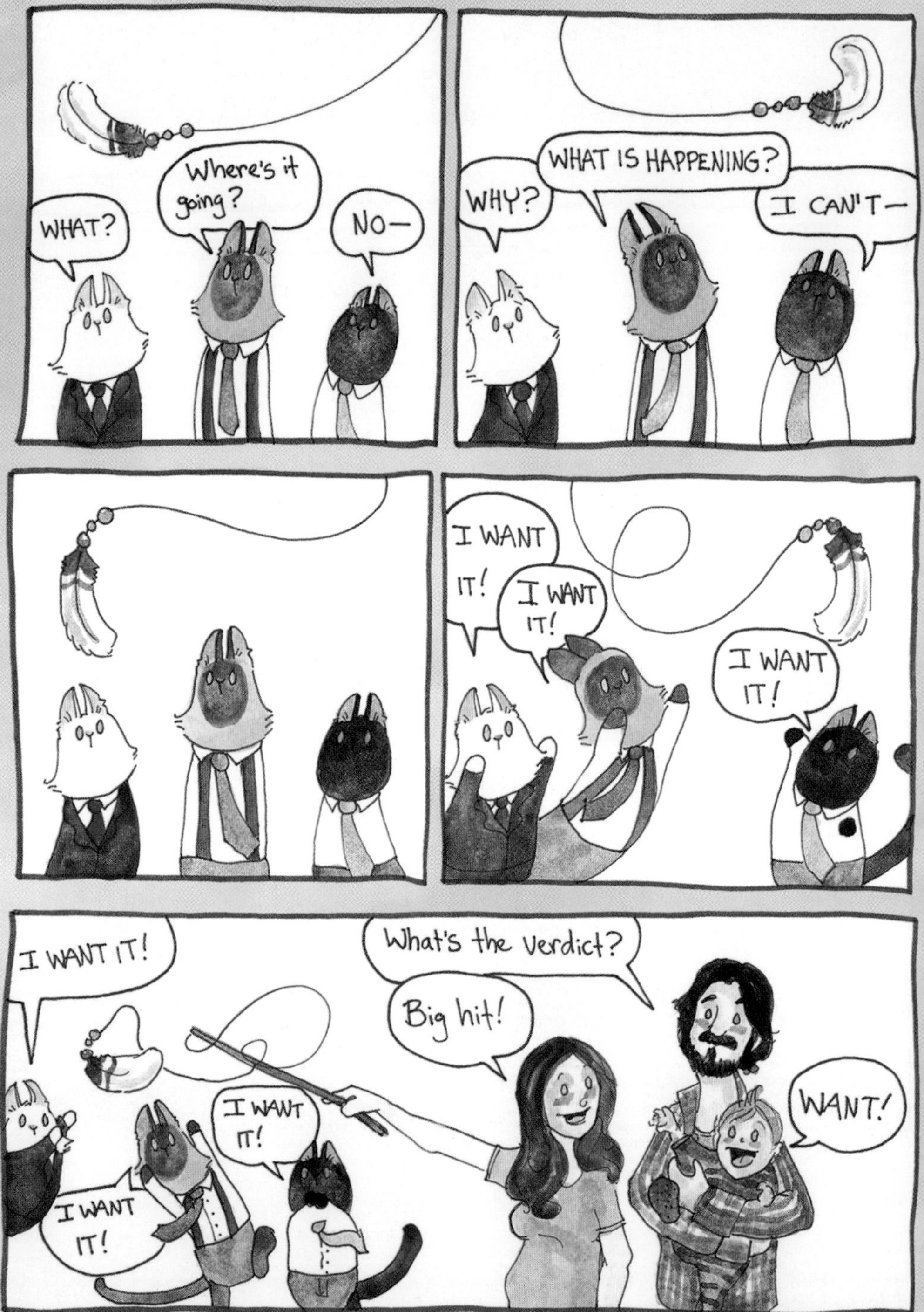
WHAT?
Where's it going?
No—
WHY?
WHAT IS HAPPENING?
I CAN'T—
I WANT IT!
I WANT IT!
I WANT IT!
I WANT IT!
What's the verdict?
Big hit!
I WANT IT!
I WANT IT!
WANT!

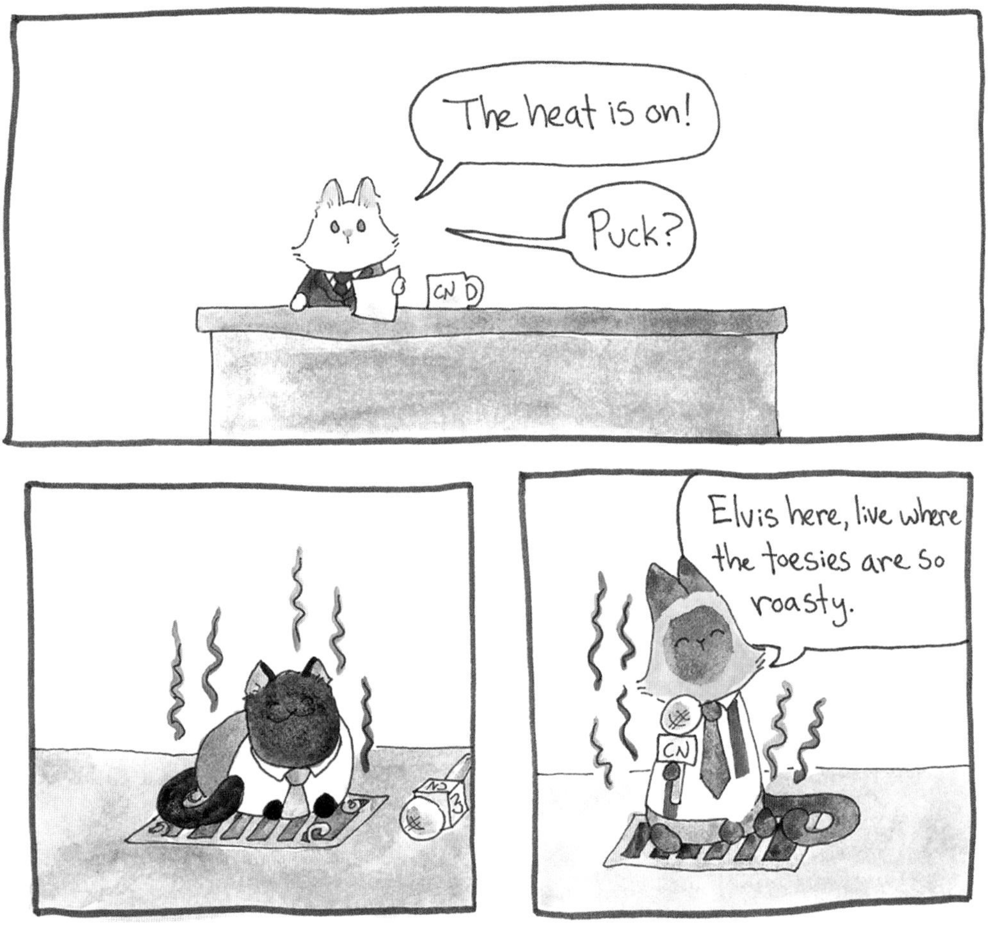
The heat is on!
Puck?
CN D
CN 3
CN
Elvis here, live where the toesies are so roasty.

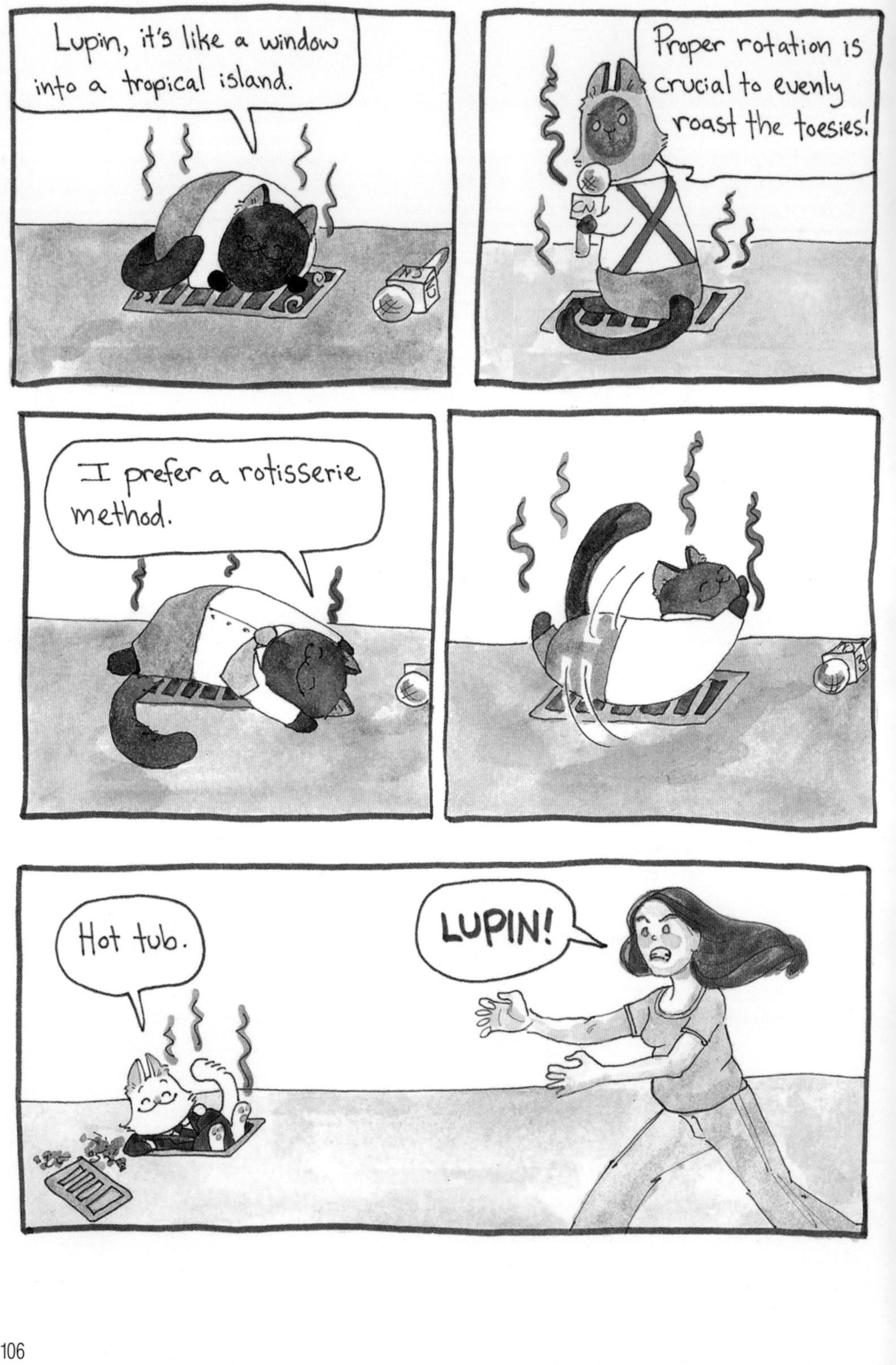
Lupin, it's like a window into a tropical island.
Proper rotation is crucial to evenly roast the toesies!
I prefer a rotisserie method.
Hot tub.
LUPIN!

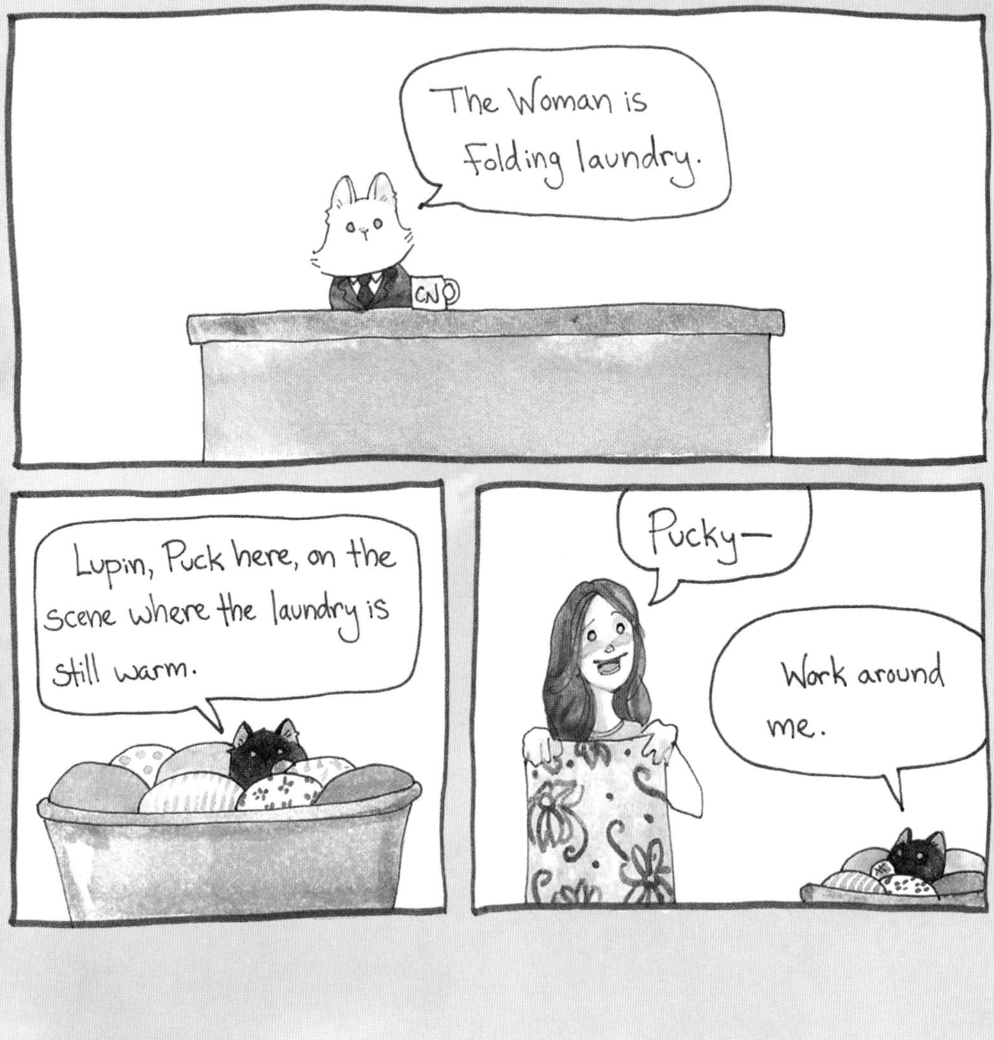
The Woman is folding laundry.
CN
Lupin, Puck here, on the scene where the laundry is still warm.
Pucky—
Work around me.

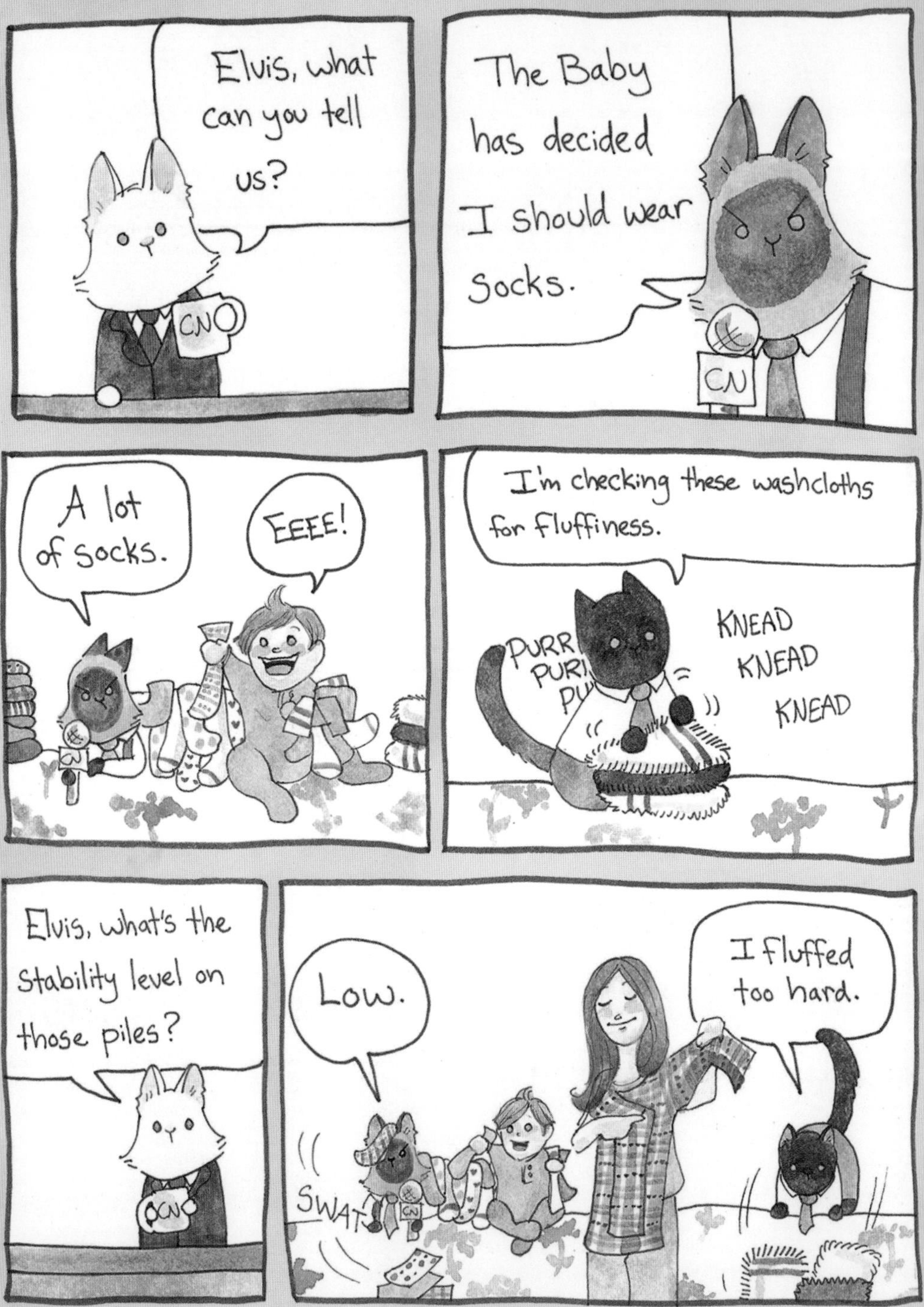
Elvis, what can you tell us?
CN
The Baby has decided I should wear socks.
CN
A lot of socks.
EEEE!
I'm checking these washcloths for fluffiness.
PURR PURR PU
KNEAD KNEAD KNEAD
Elvis, what's the stability level on those piles?
CN
Low.
SWAT
CN
I fluffed too hard.

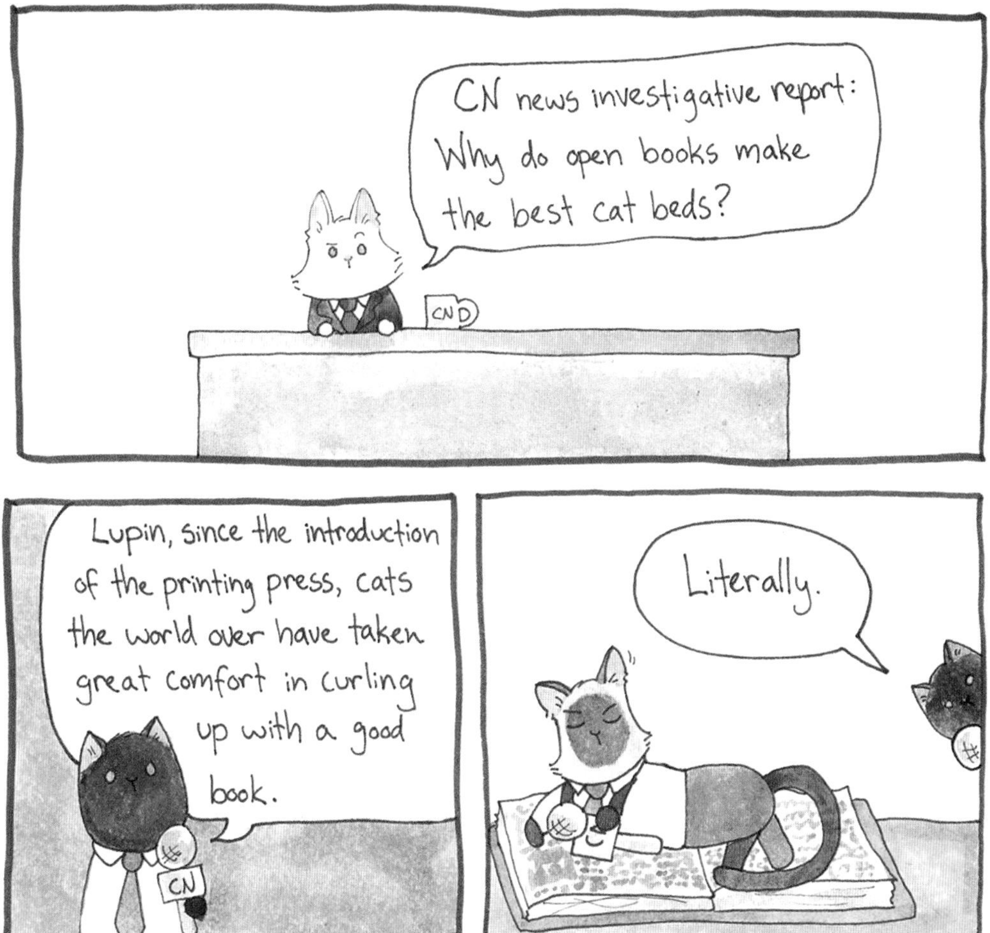
CN news investigative report: Why do open books make the best cat beds?
Lupin, since the introduction of the printing press, cats the world over have taken great comfort in curling up with a good book.
Literally.
CN
CN

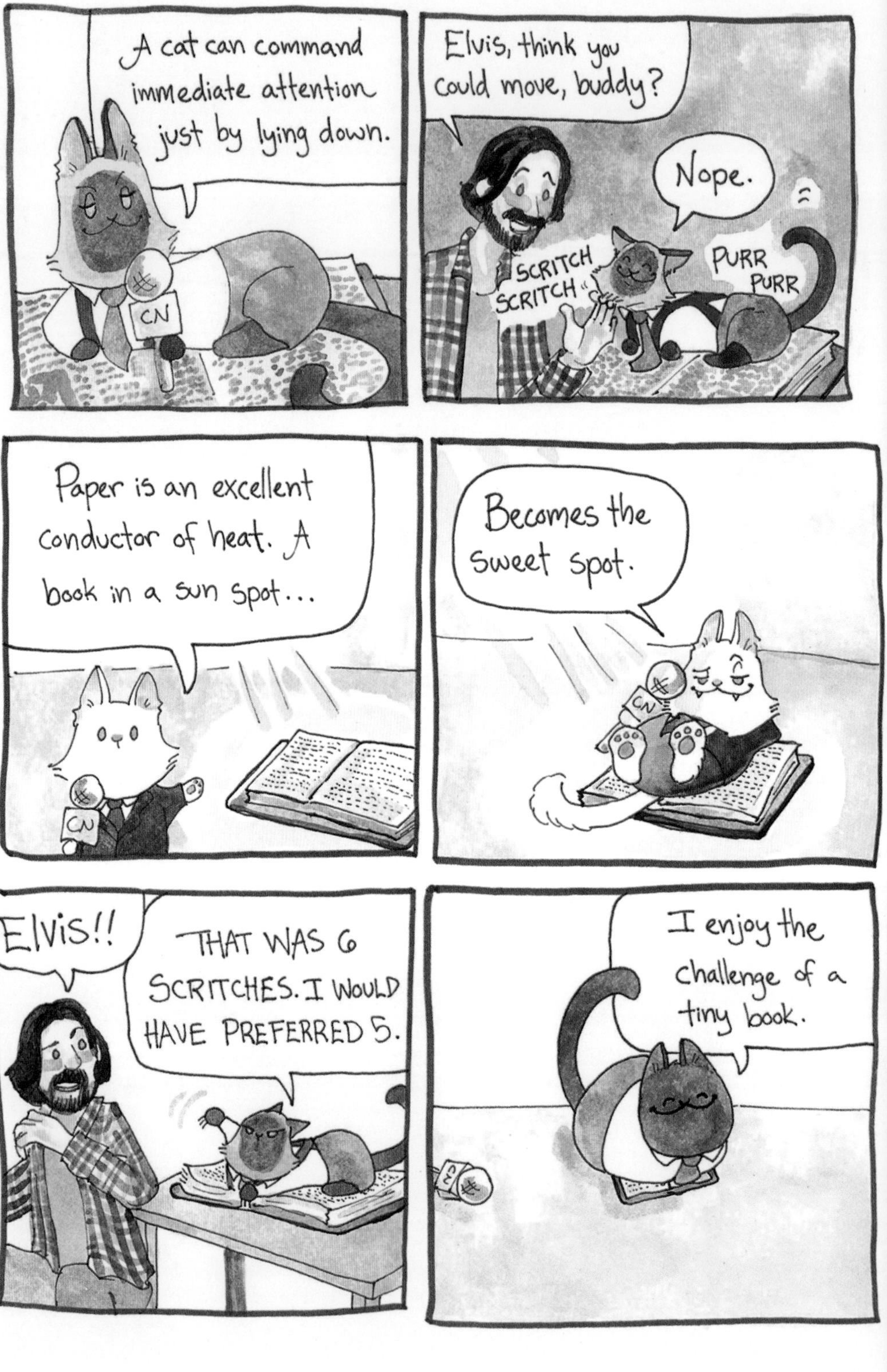
A cat can command immediate attention just by lying down.
CN
Elvis, think you could move, buddy?
Nope.
SCRITCH SCRITCH
PURR PURR
Paper is an excellent conductor of heat. A book in a sun spot...
CN
Becomes the sweet spot.
CN
Elvis!!
THAT WAS 6 SCRITCHES. I WOULD HAVE PREFERRED 5.
I enjoy the challenge of a tiny book.
CN

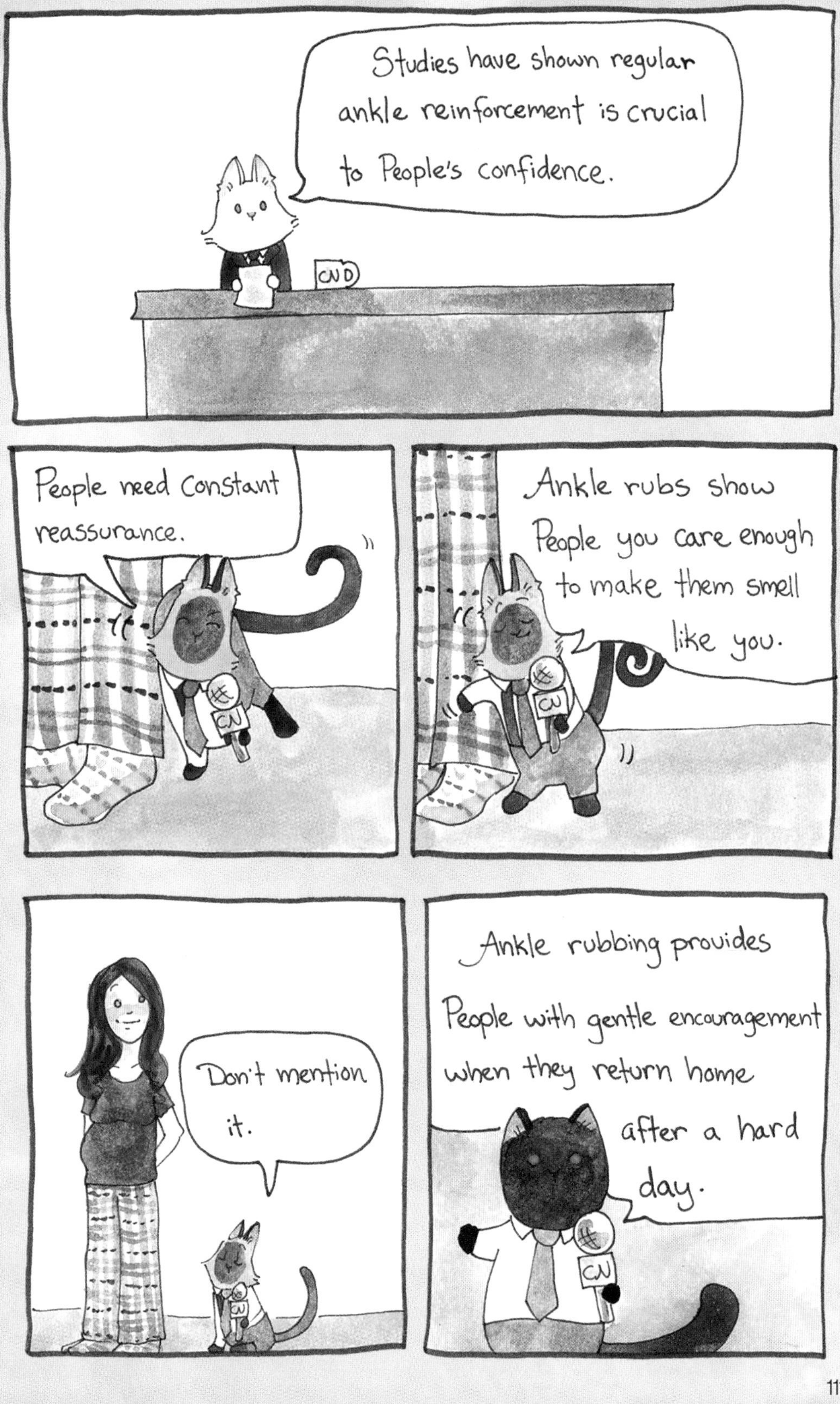
Studies have shown regular ankle reinforcement is crucial to People's confidence.
CND
People need constant reassurance.
CN
Ankle rubs show People you care enough to make them smell like you.
CN
Don't mention it.
CN
Ankle rubbing provides People with gentle encouragement when they return home after a hard day.
CN

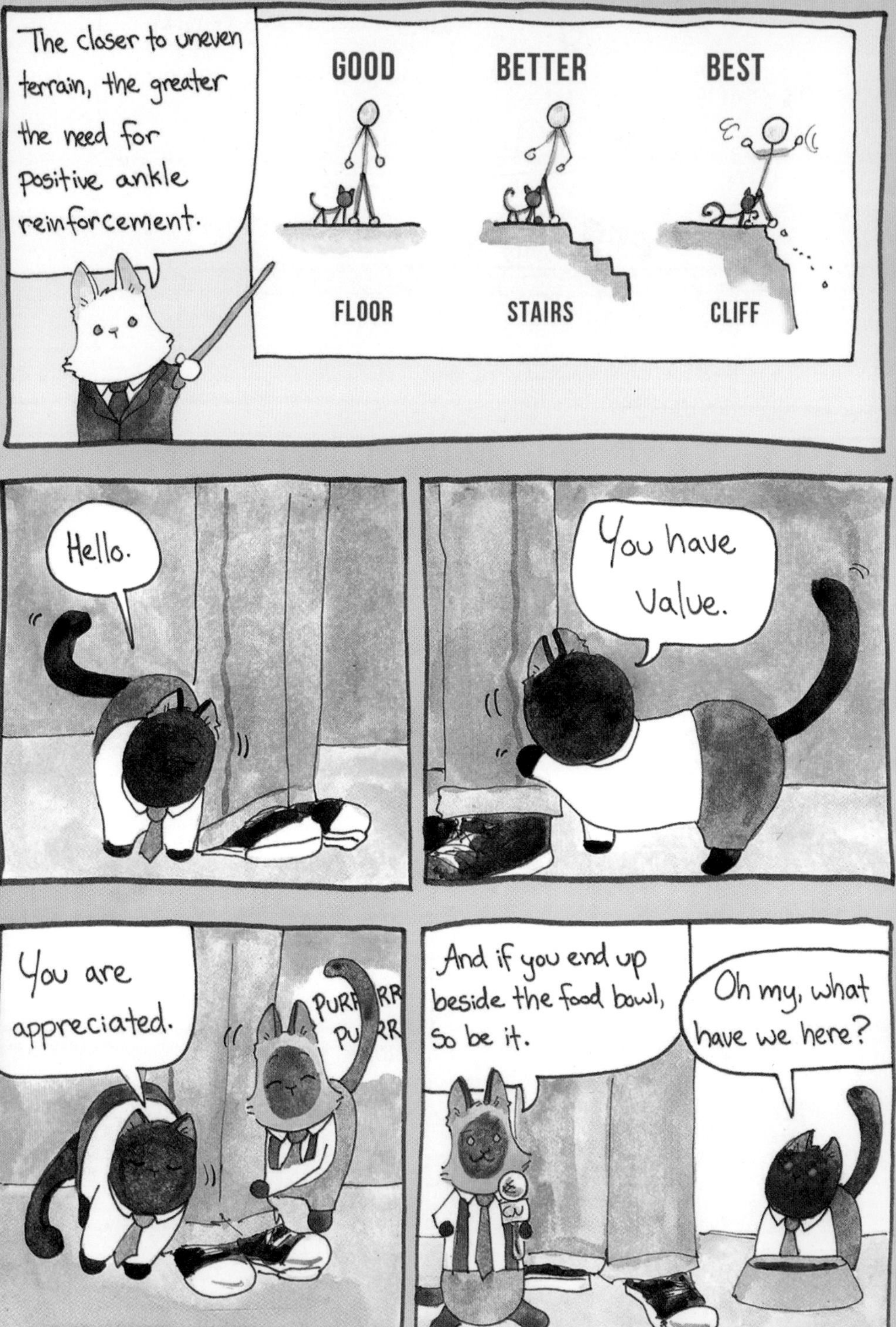
The closer to uneven terrain, the greater the need for positive ankle reinforcement.
GOOD
BETTER
BEST
FLOOR
STAIRS
CLIFF
Hello.
You have value.
You are appreciated.
PURRRR PURRRR
And if you end up beside the food bowl, so be it.
Oh my, what have we here?

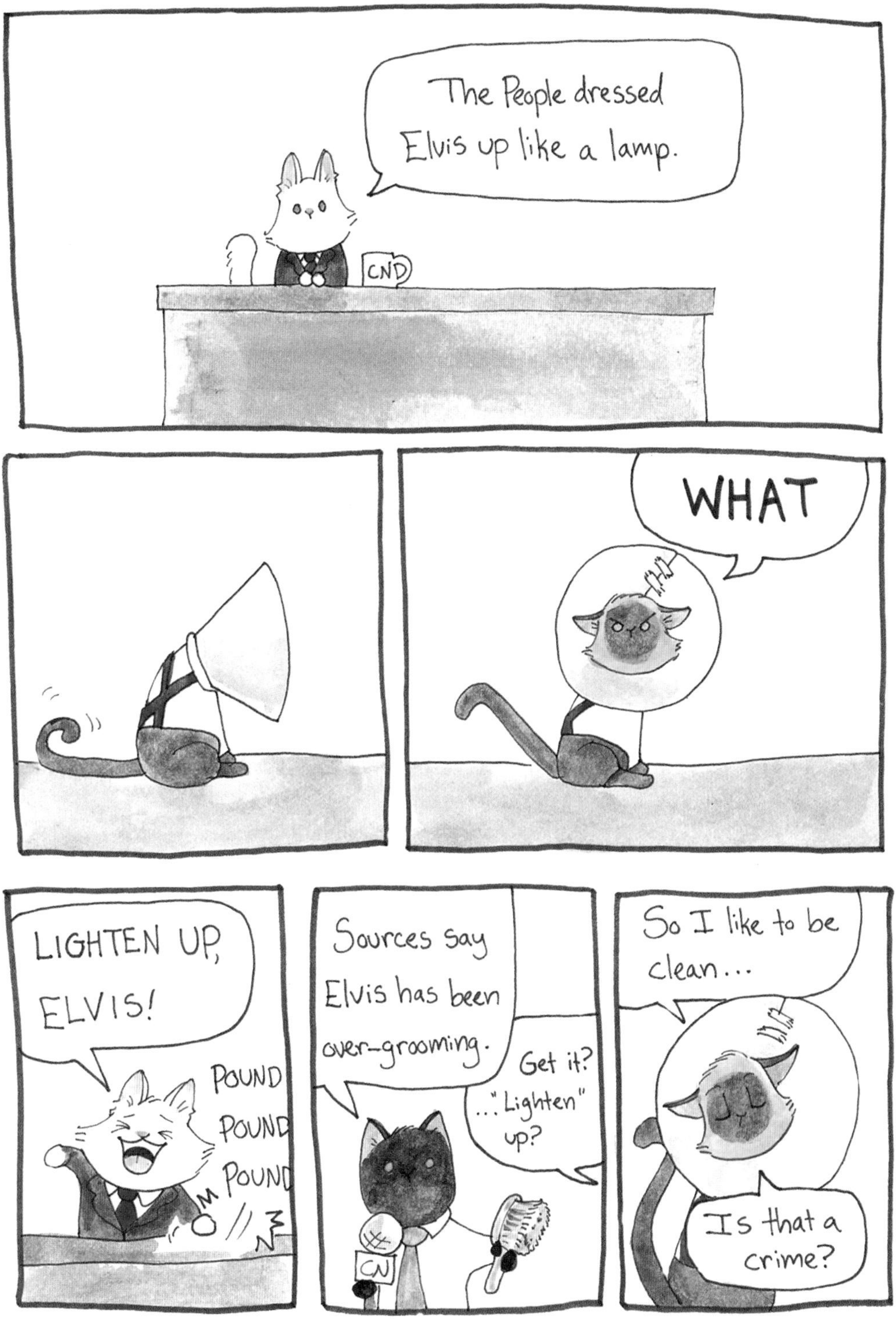
The People dressed Elvis up like a lamp.
CND
WHAT
LIGHTEN UP, ELVIS!
POUND
POUND
POUND
Sources say Elvis has been over-grooming.
Get it? ..."Lighten" up?
CN
So I like to be clean...
Is that a crime?

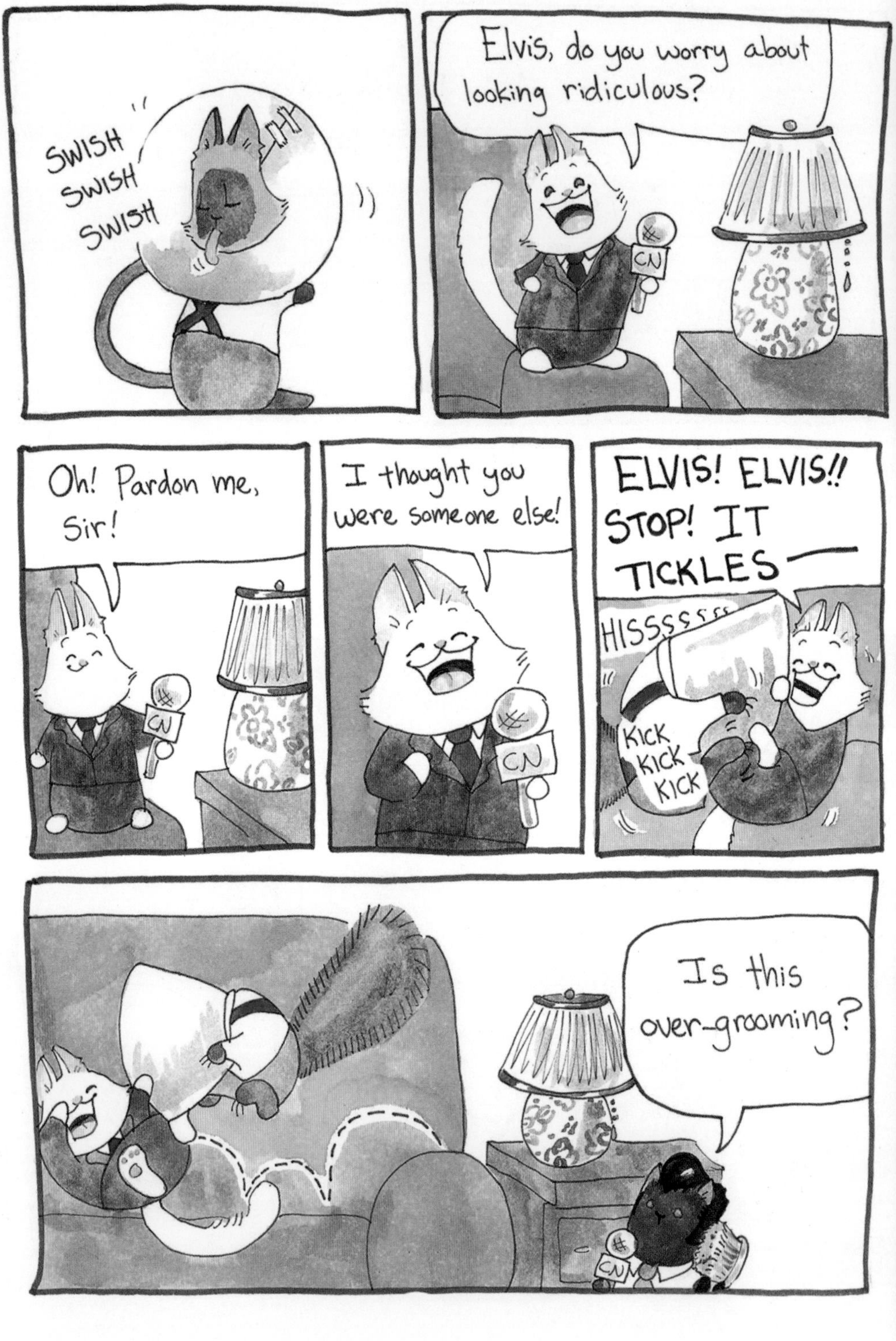
SWISH
SWISH
SWISH
Elvis, do you worry about looking ridiculous?
CN
Oh! Pardon me, Sir!
CN
I thought you were someone else!
CN
ELVIS! ELVIS!! STOP! IT TICKLES—
HISSSSSSS
KICK
KICK
KICK
Is this over-grooming?
CN

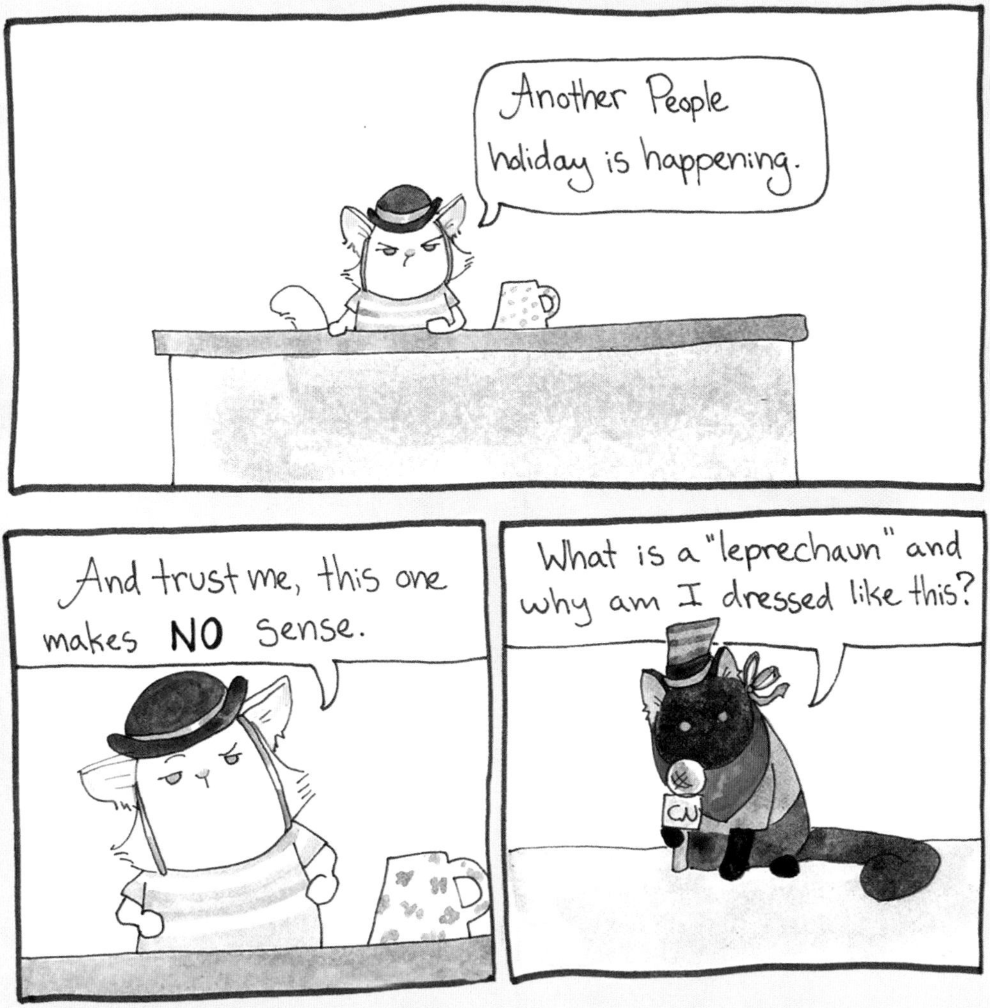
Another People holiday is happening.
And trust me, this one makes NO sense.
What is a "leprechaun" and why am I dressed like this?
CN

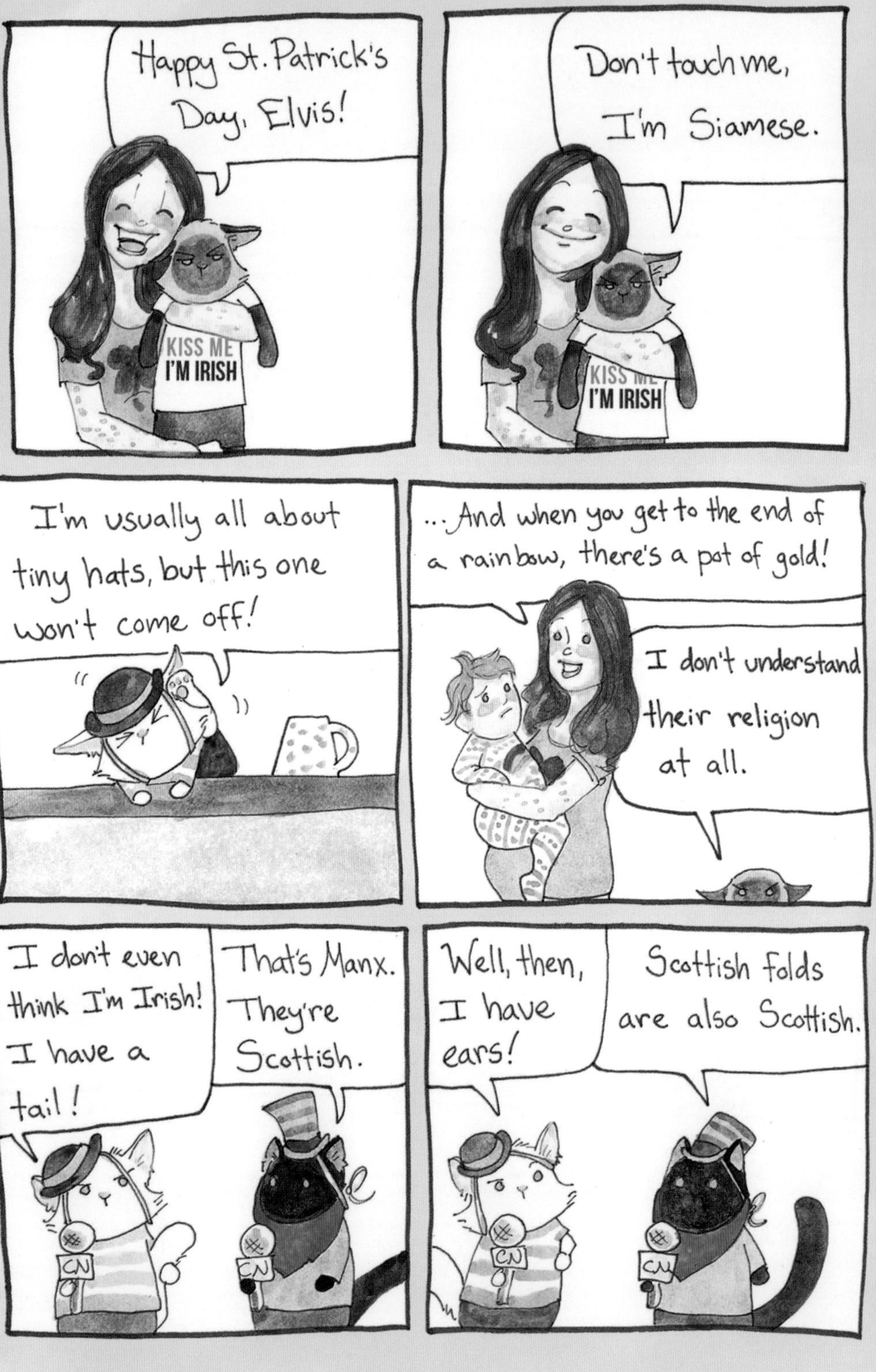
Happy St. Patrick's Day, Elvis!
KISS ME I'M IRISH
Don't touch me, I'm Siamese.
KISS ME I'M IRISH
I'm usually all about tiny hats, but this one won't come off!
...And when you get to the end of a rainbow, there's a pot of gold!
I don't understand their religion at all.
I don't even think I'm Irish! I have a tail!
That's Manx. They're Scottish.
CN
CN
Well, then, I have ears!
Scottish folds are also Scottish.
CN
CN

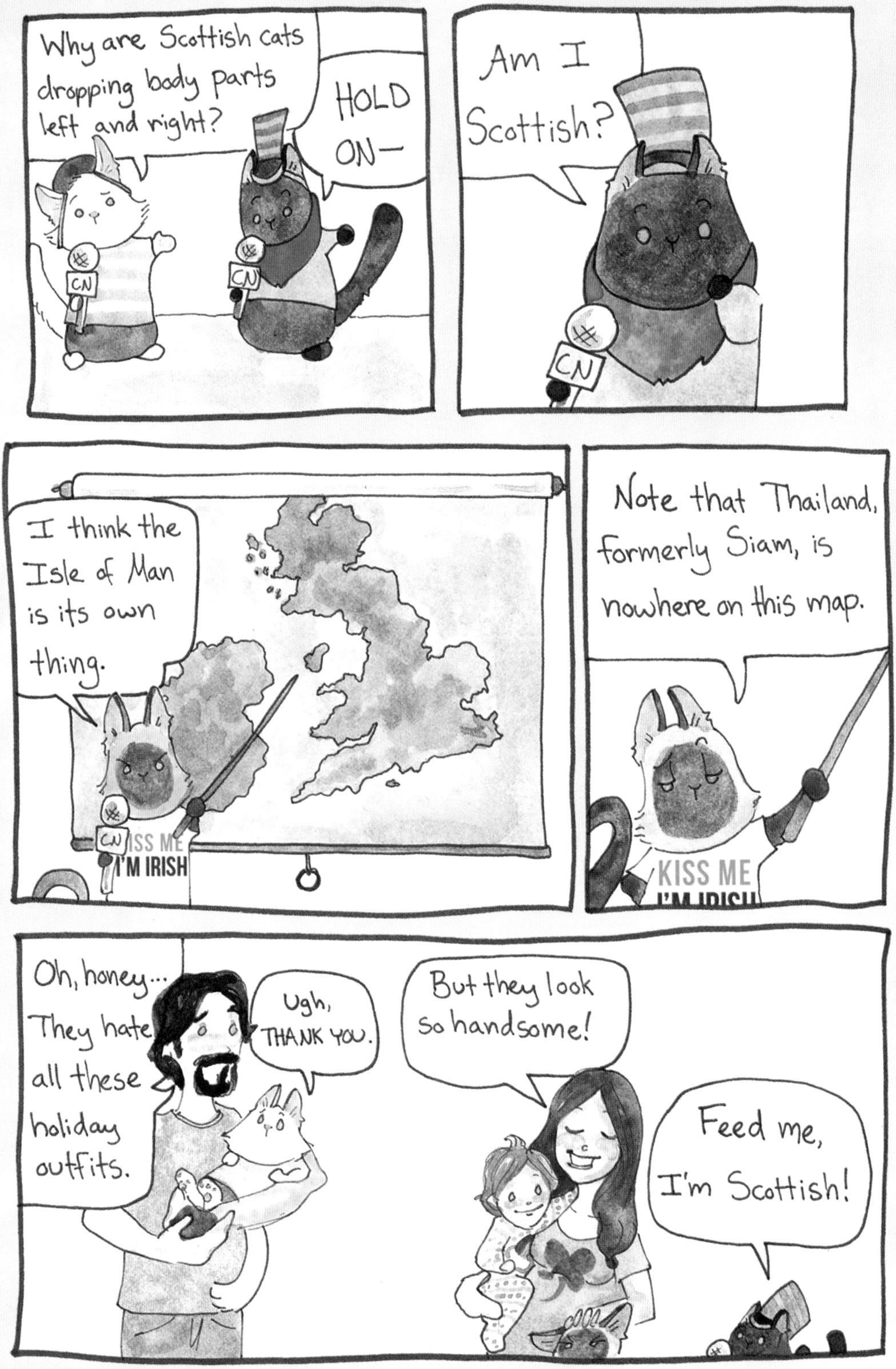
Why are Scottish cats dropping body parts left and right?
HOLD ON—
Am I Scottish?
CN
I think the Isle of Man is its own thing.
KISS ME I'M IRISH
Note that Thailand, formerly Siam, is nowhere on this map.
Oh, honey... They hate all these holiday outfits.
Ugh, THANK YOU.
But they look so handsome!
Feed me, I'm Scottish!

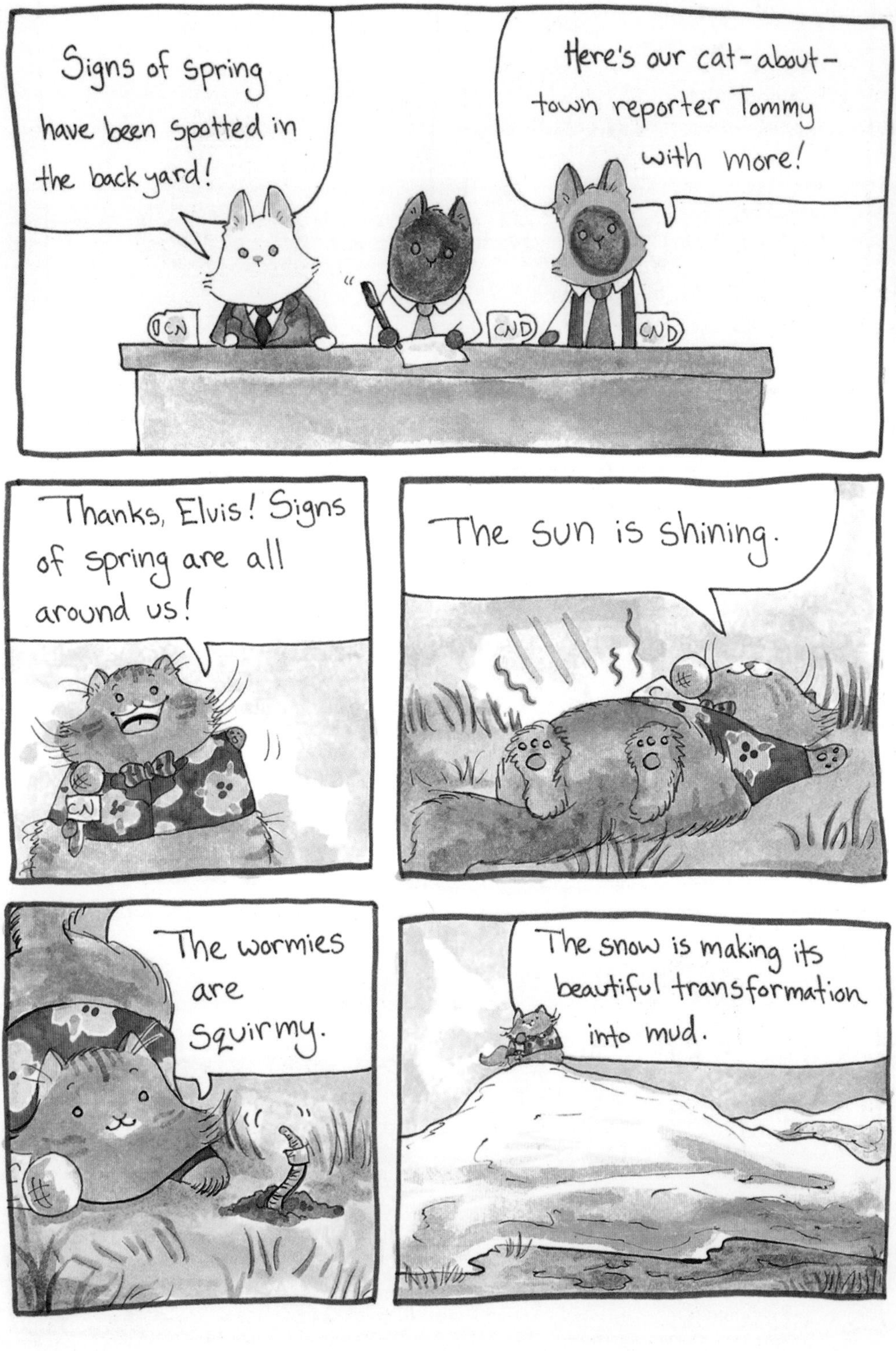
Signs of spring have been spotted in the back yard!
Here's our cat-about-town reporter Tommy with more!
CN
CND
CND
Thanks, Elvis! Signs of spring are all around us!
CN
The sun is shining.
The wormies are squirmy.
The snow is making its beautiful transformation into mud.

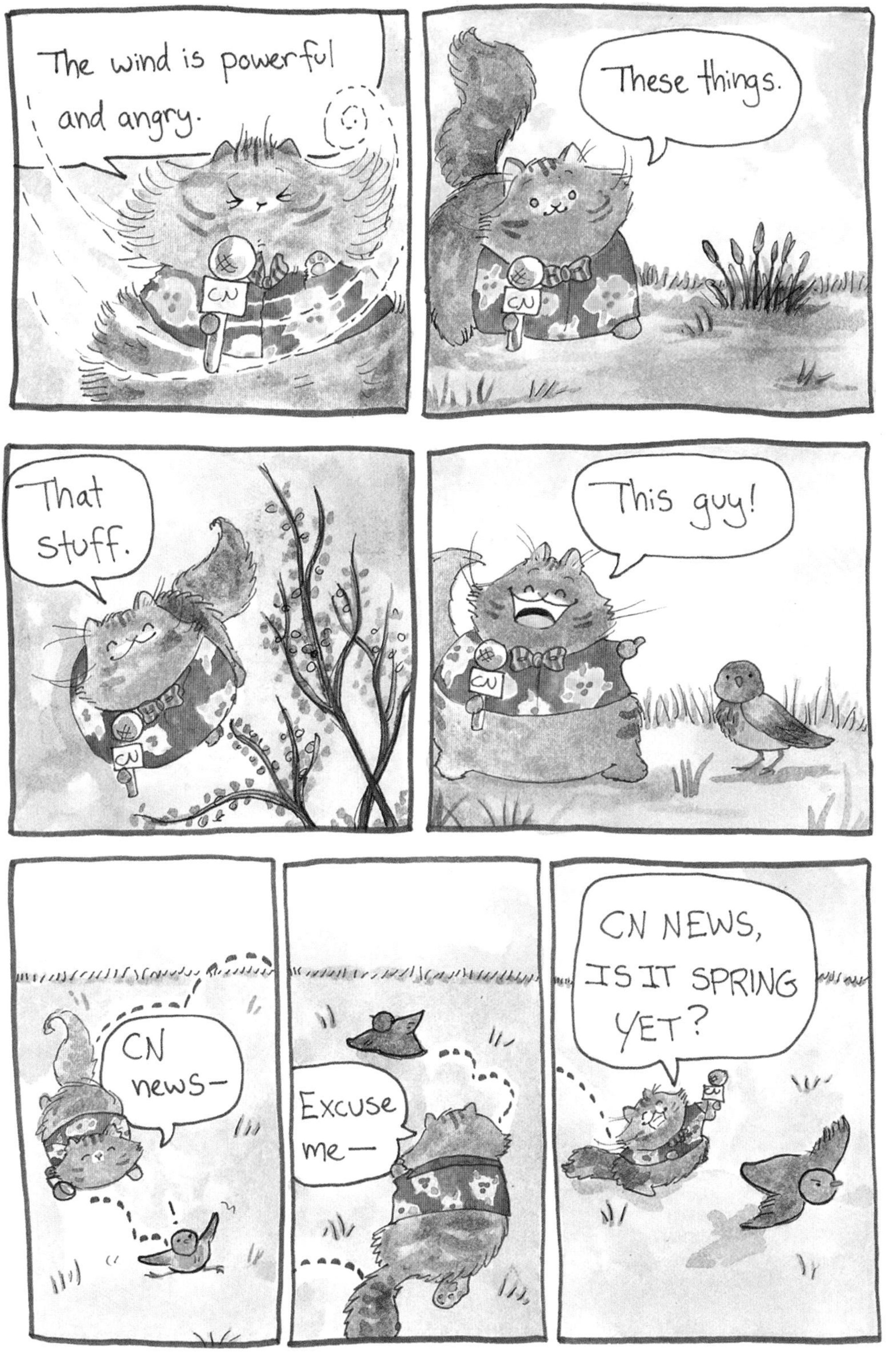
The wind is powerful and angry.
These things.
That stuff.
This guy!
CN news-
Excuse me—
CN NEWS, IS IT SPRING YET?

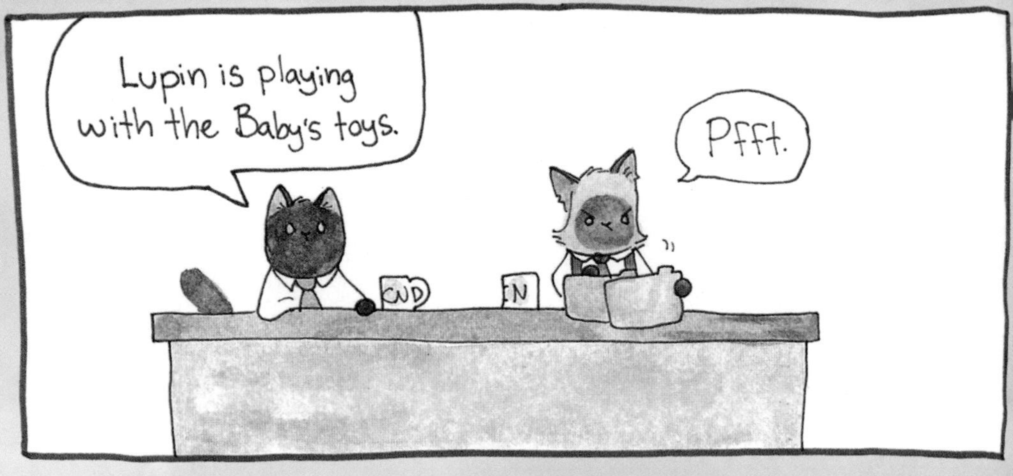
Lupin is playing with the Baby's toys.
Pfft.

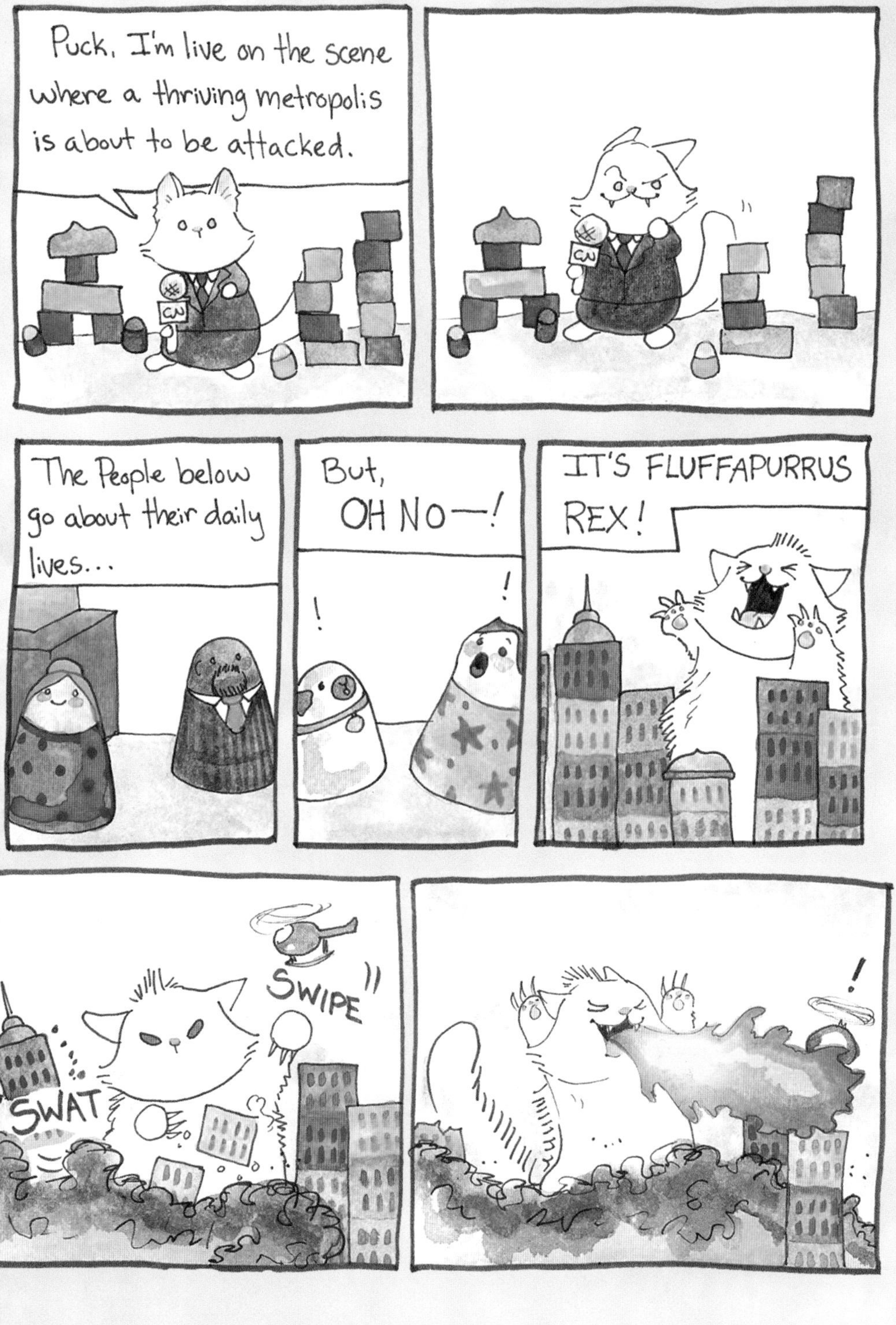
Puck, I'm live on the scene where a thriving metropolis is about to be attacked.
The People below go about their daily lives...
But, OH NO—!
!
!
IT'S FLUFFAPURRUS REX!
SWIPE
SWAT
!

TAP...
TAP...

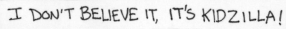

I DON'T BELIEVE IT, IT'S KIDZILLA!

KICK
KICK

OH,
STOP
IT!

FACTS

MORE FACTS

THE GOOFY STUFF LUPIN DOES ISN'T NEWS!!

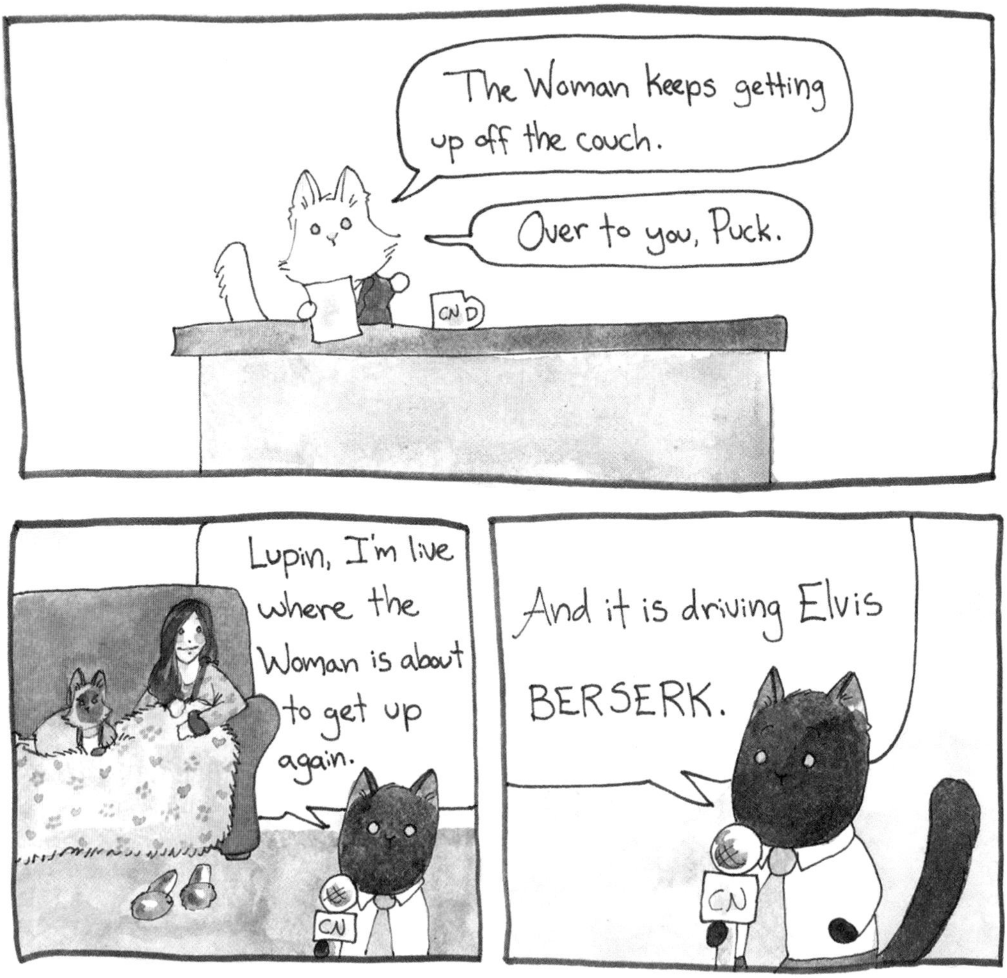
The Woman keeps getting up off the couch.
Over to you, Puck.
CN
Lupin, I'm live where the Woman is about to get up again.
CN
And it is driving Elvis BERSERK.
CN

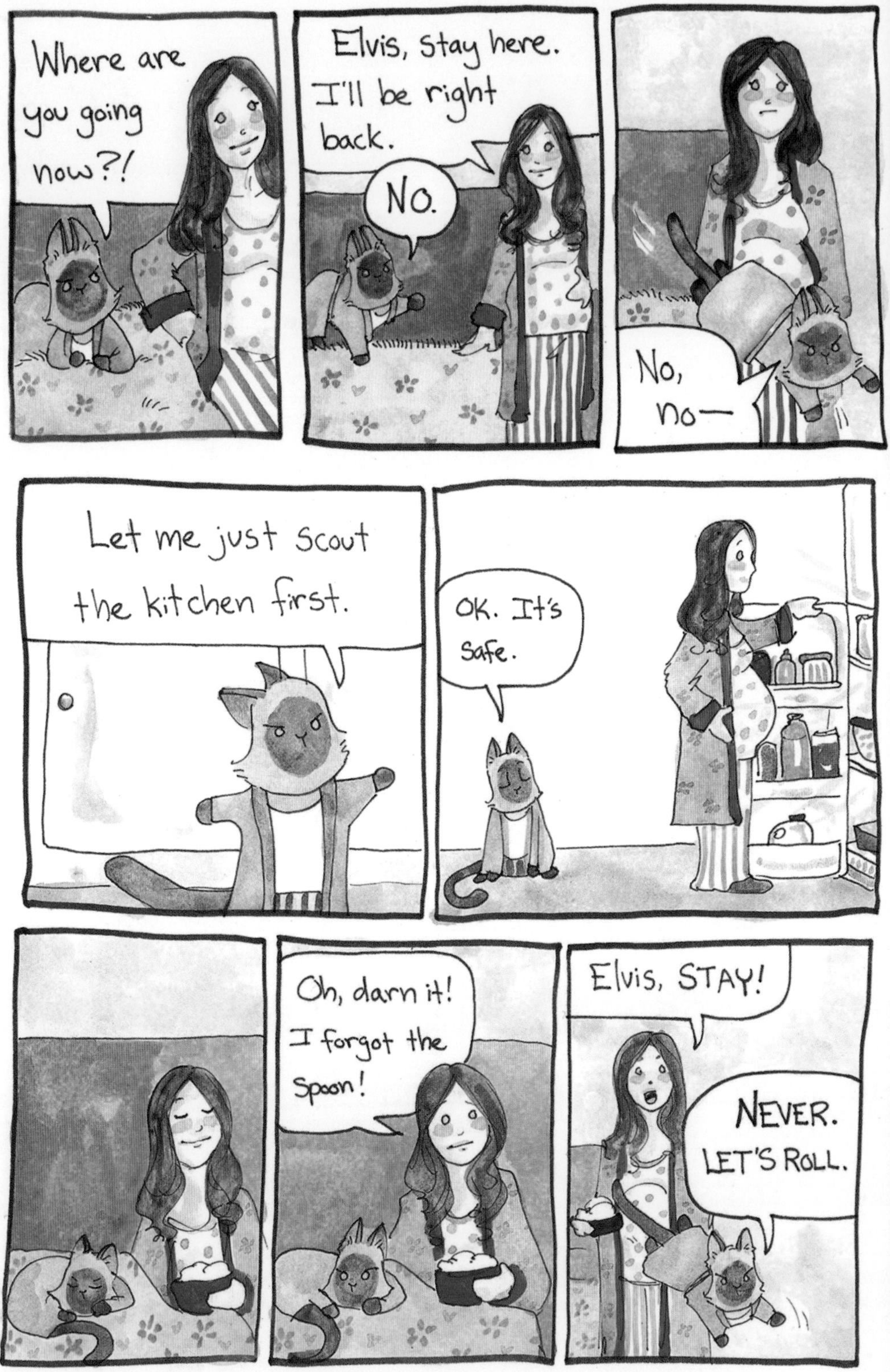
Where are you going now?!
Elvis, stay here. I'll be right back.
No.
No, no—
Let me just scout the kitchen first.
OK. It's safe.
Oh, darn it! I forgot the spoon!
Elvis, STAY!
NEVER. LET'S ROLL.

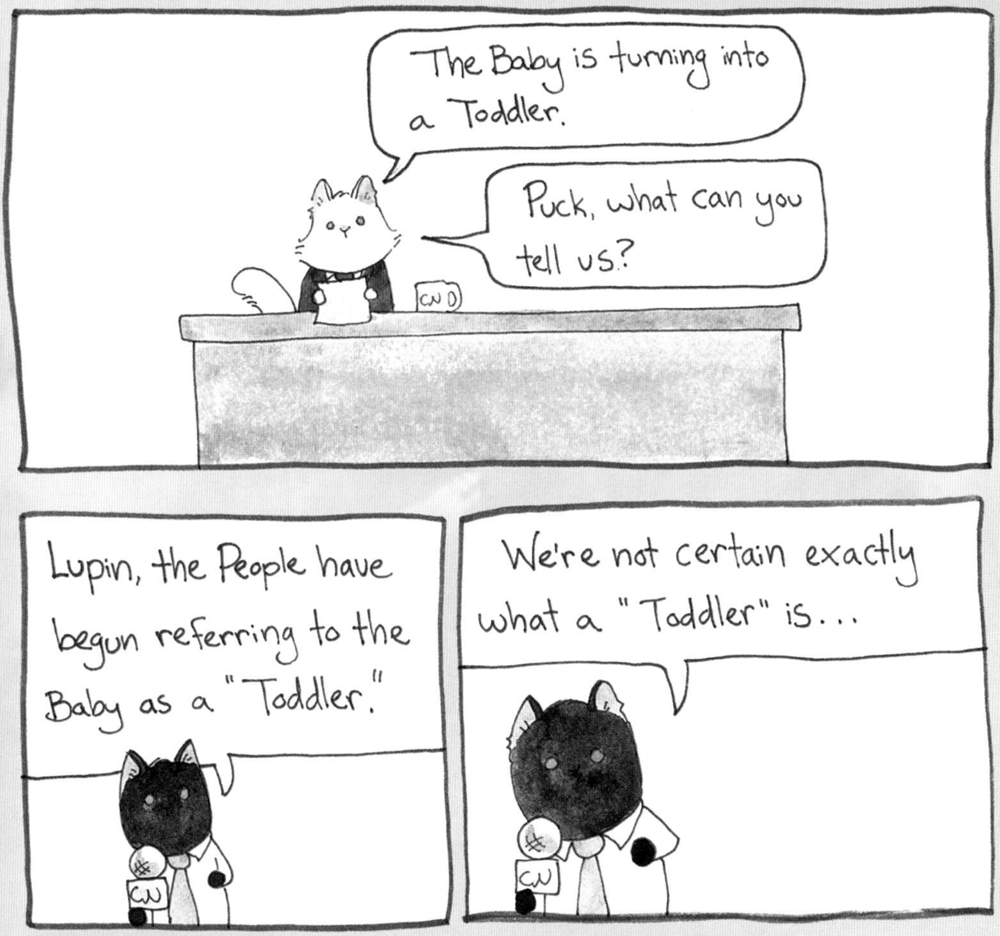
The Baby is turning into a Toddler.
Puck, what can you tell us?
Lupin, the People have begun referring to the Baby as a "Toddler."
We're not certain exactly what a "Toddler" is...

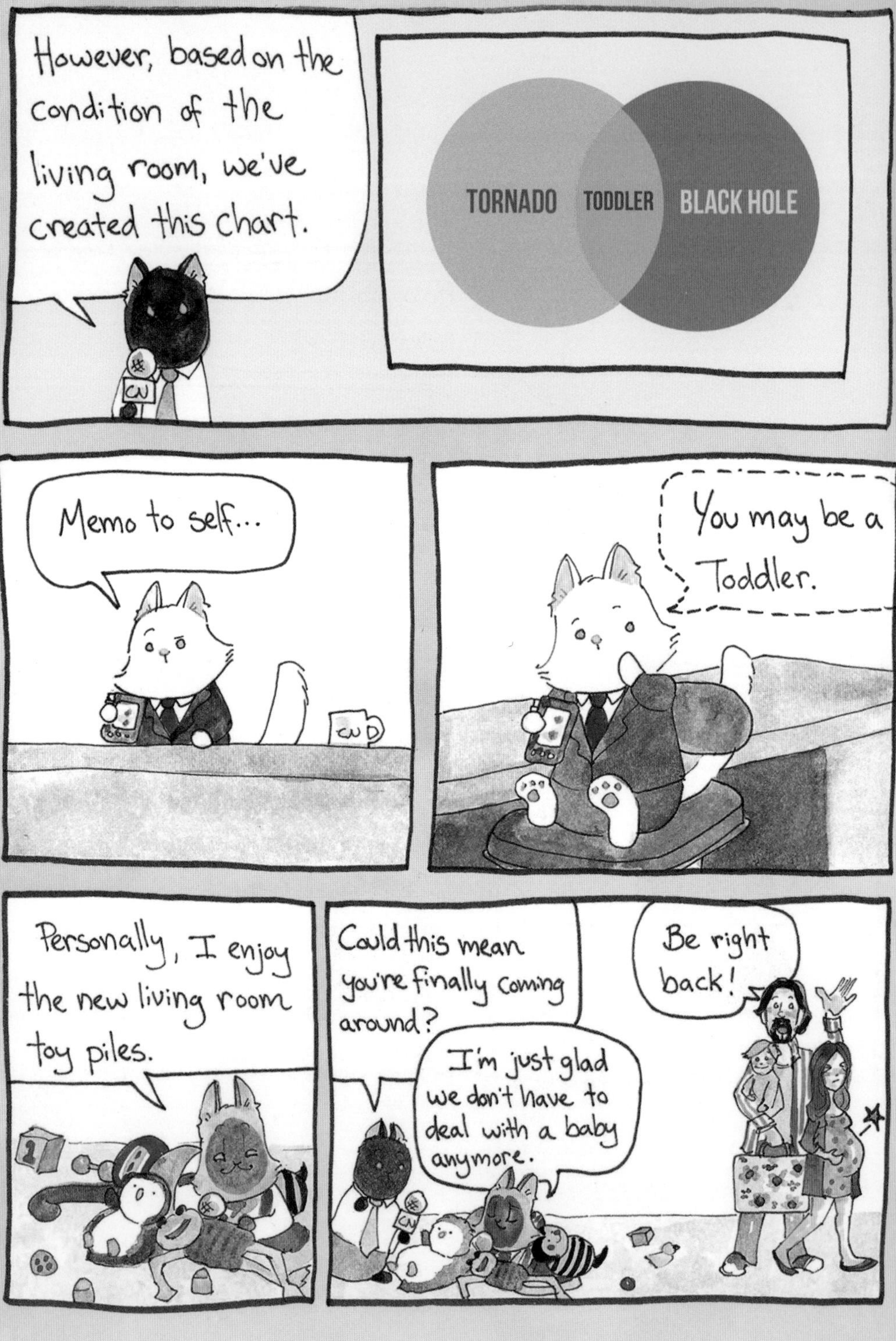
However, based on the condition of the living room, we've created this chart.
TORNADO
TODDLER
BLACK HOLE
Memo to self...
You may be a Toddler.
Personally, I enjoy the new living room toy piles.
Could this mean you're finally coming around?
I'm just glad we don't have to deal with a baby anymore.
Be right back!

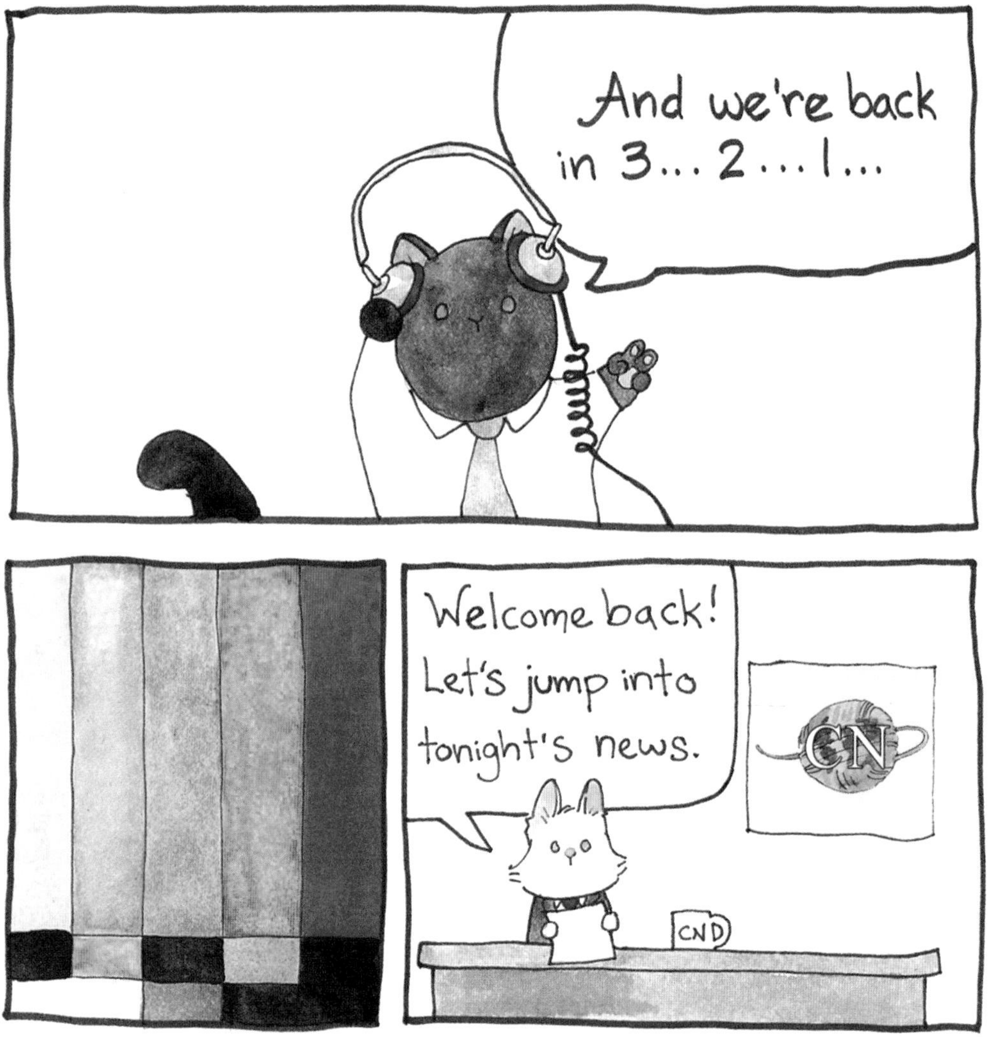
And we're back in 3... 2... 1...
Welcome back! Let's jump into tonight's news.
CN
CND

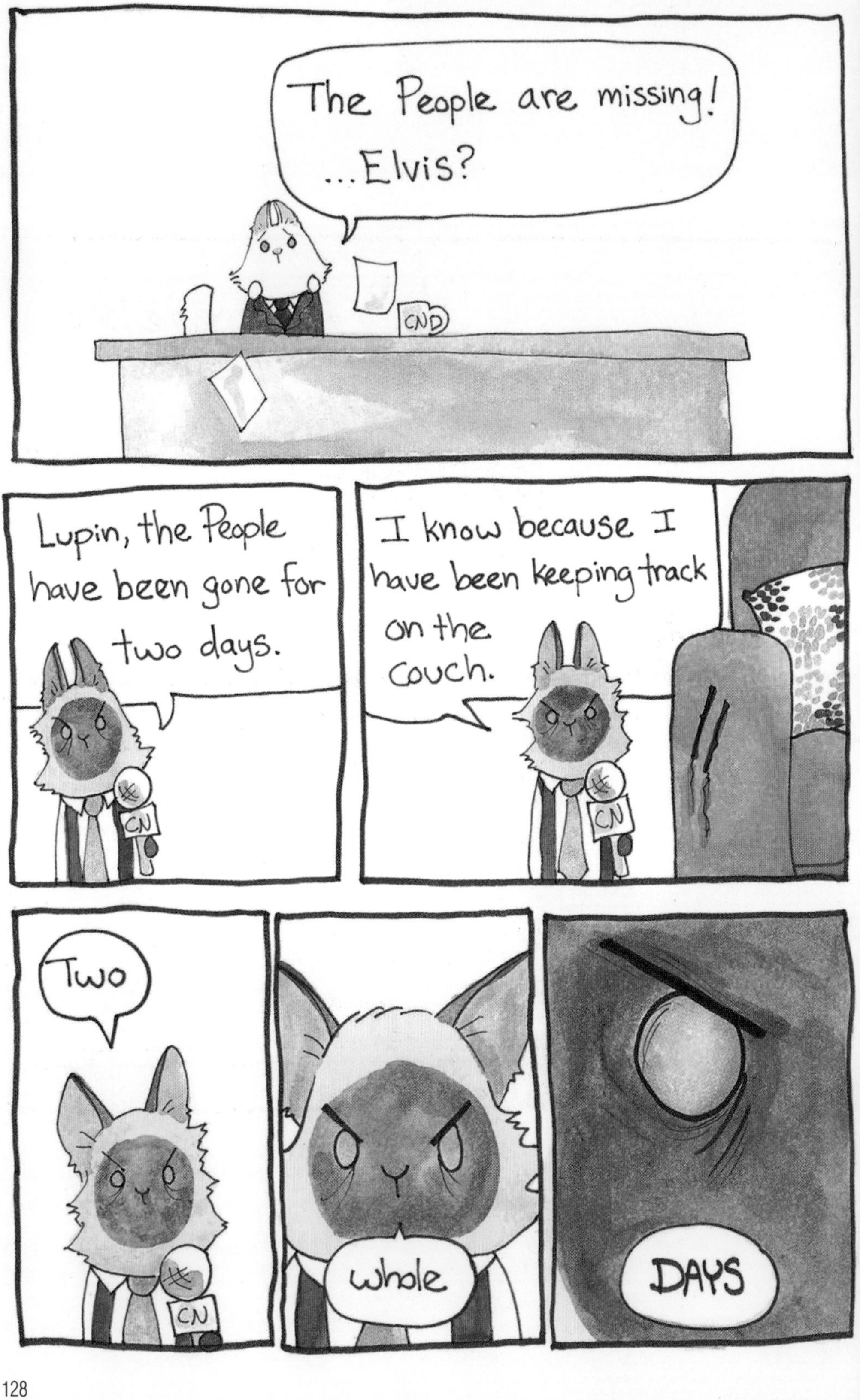
The People are missing!
...Elvis?
CND
Lupin, the People have been gone for two days.
CN
I know because I have been keeping track on the couch.
CN
Two
CN
whole
DAYS

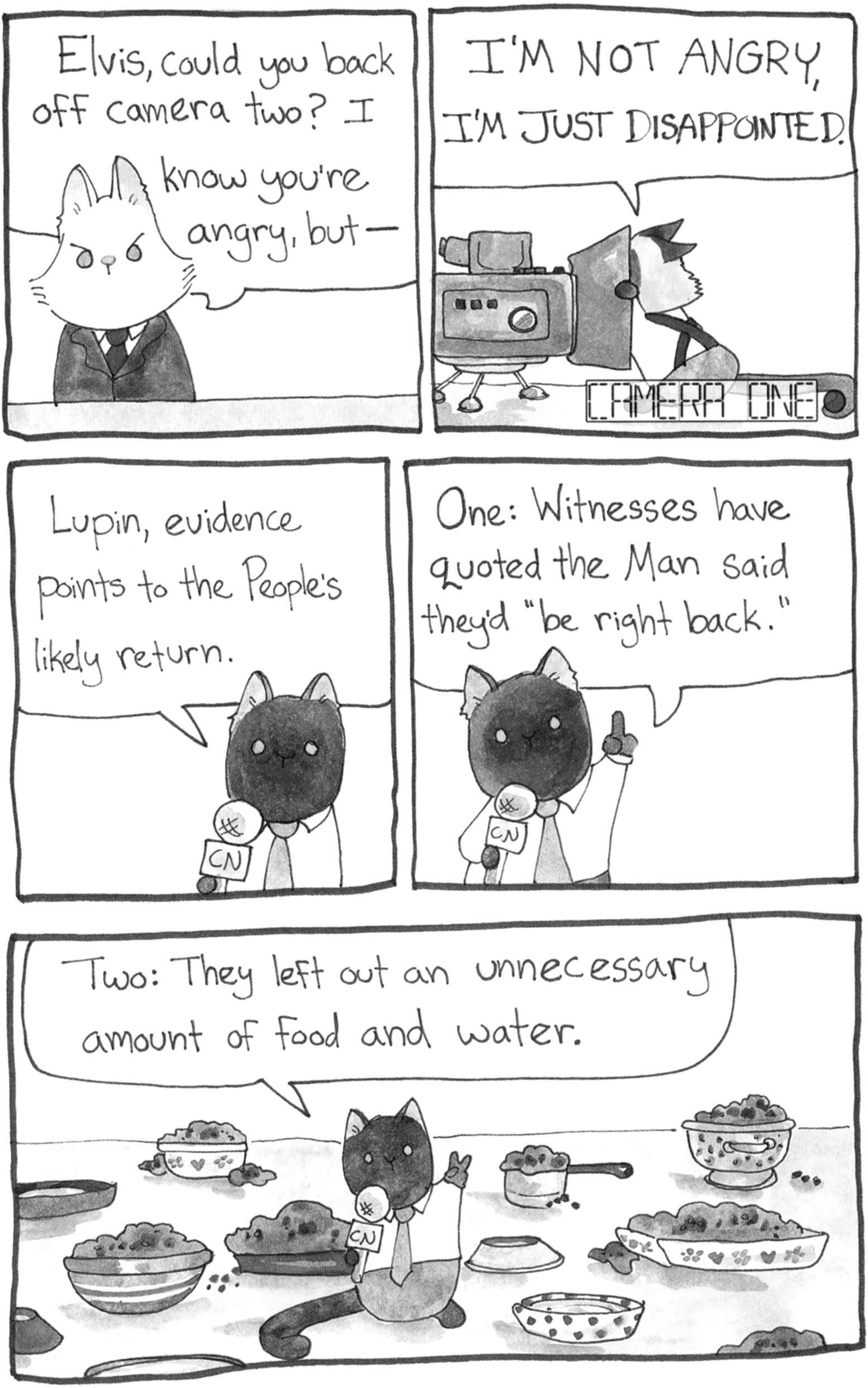
Elvis, could you back off camera two? I know you're angry, but—
I'M NOT ANGRY, I'M JUST DISAPPOINTED.
CAMERA ONE
Lupin, evidence points to the People's likely return.
One: Witnesses have quoted the Man said they'd "be right back."
CN
Two: They left out an unnecessary amount of food and water.
CN

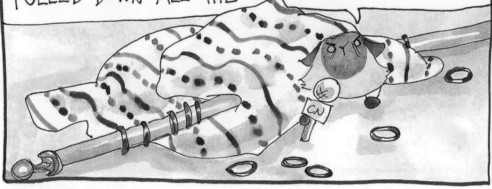

LUPIN I'M GETTING REPORTS THAT SOMEONE PULLED DOWN ALL THE CURTAINS.

Lupin, Sources indicate we have enough food for 6 weeks.

BUT THEN I ATE **ALL THE PLANTS**

For cat's Sake, will you two cool it?

Can I interest you in a colander full of kibble?

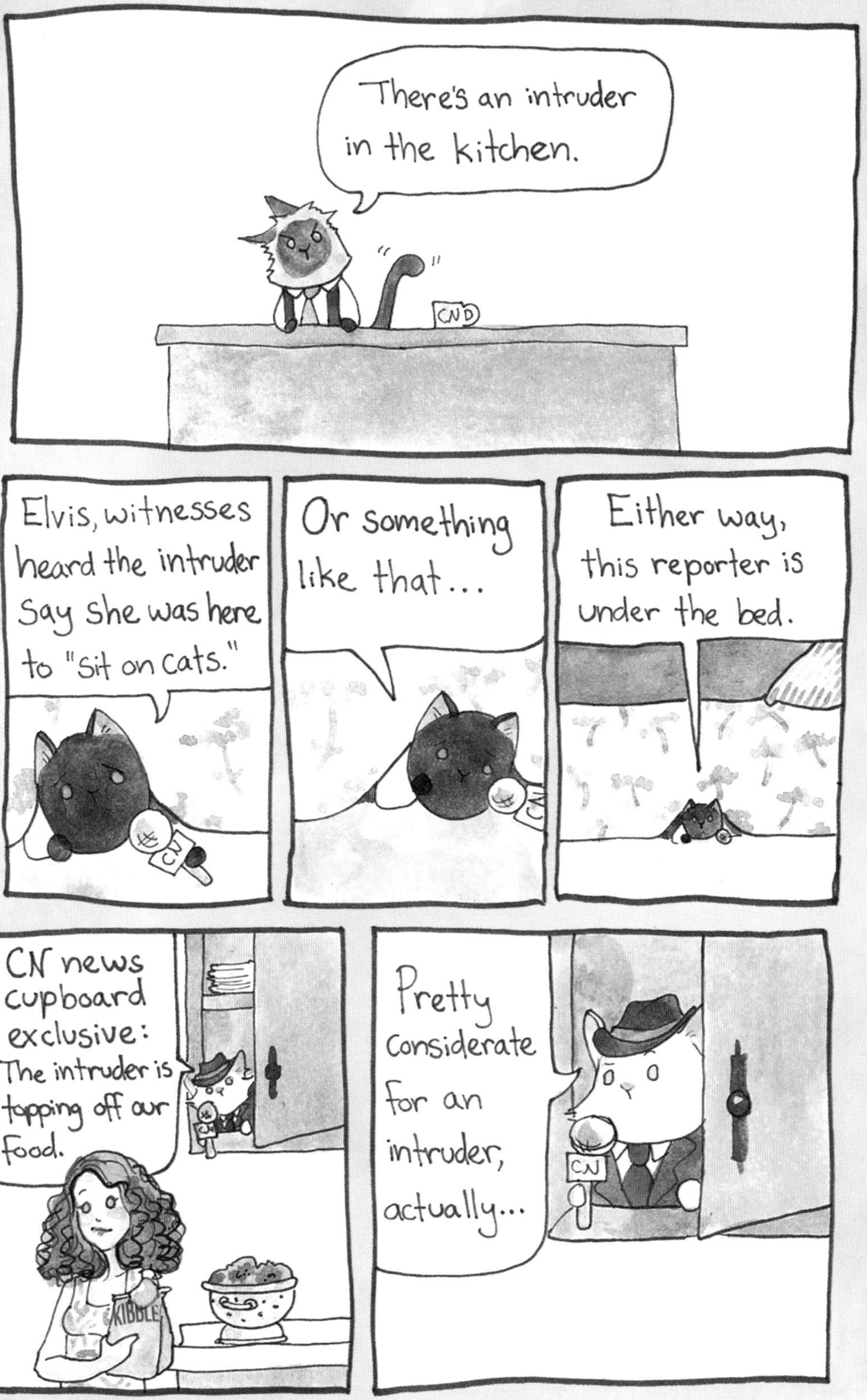
There's an intruder in the kitchen.
CND
Elvis, witnesses heard the intruder say she was here to "sit on cats."
CN
Or something like that...
Either way, this reporter is under the bed.
CN news cupboard exclusive: The intruder is topping off our food.
KIBBLE
Pretty considerate for an intruder, actually...
CN

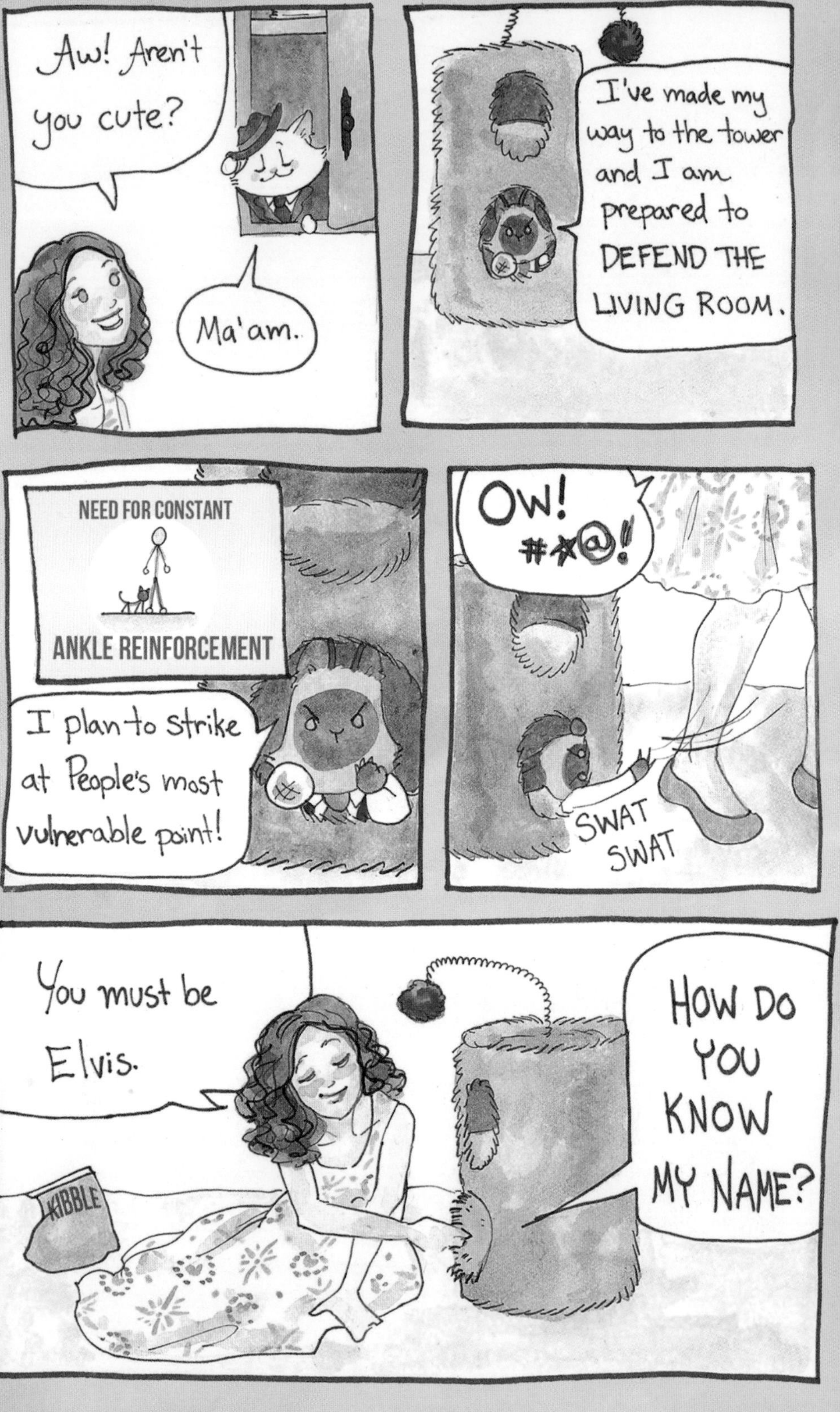
Aw! Aren't you cute?
Ma'am..
I've made my way to the tower and I am prepared to DEFEND THE LIVING ROOM.
NEED FOR CONSTANT
ANKLE REINFORCEMENT
I plan to strike at People's most vulnerable point!
OW! #*@!
SWAT SWAT
You must be Elvis.
HOW DO YOU KNOW MY NAME?
KIBBLE

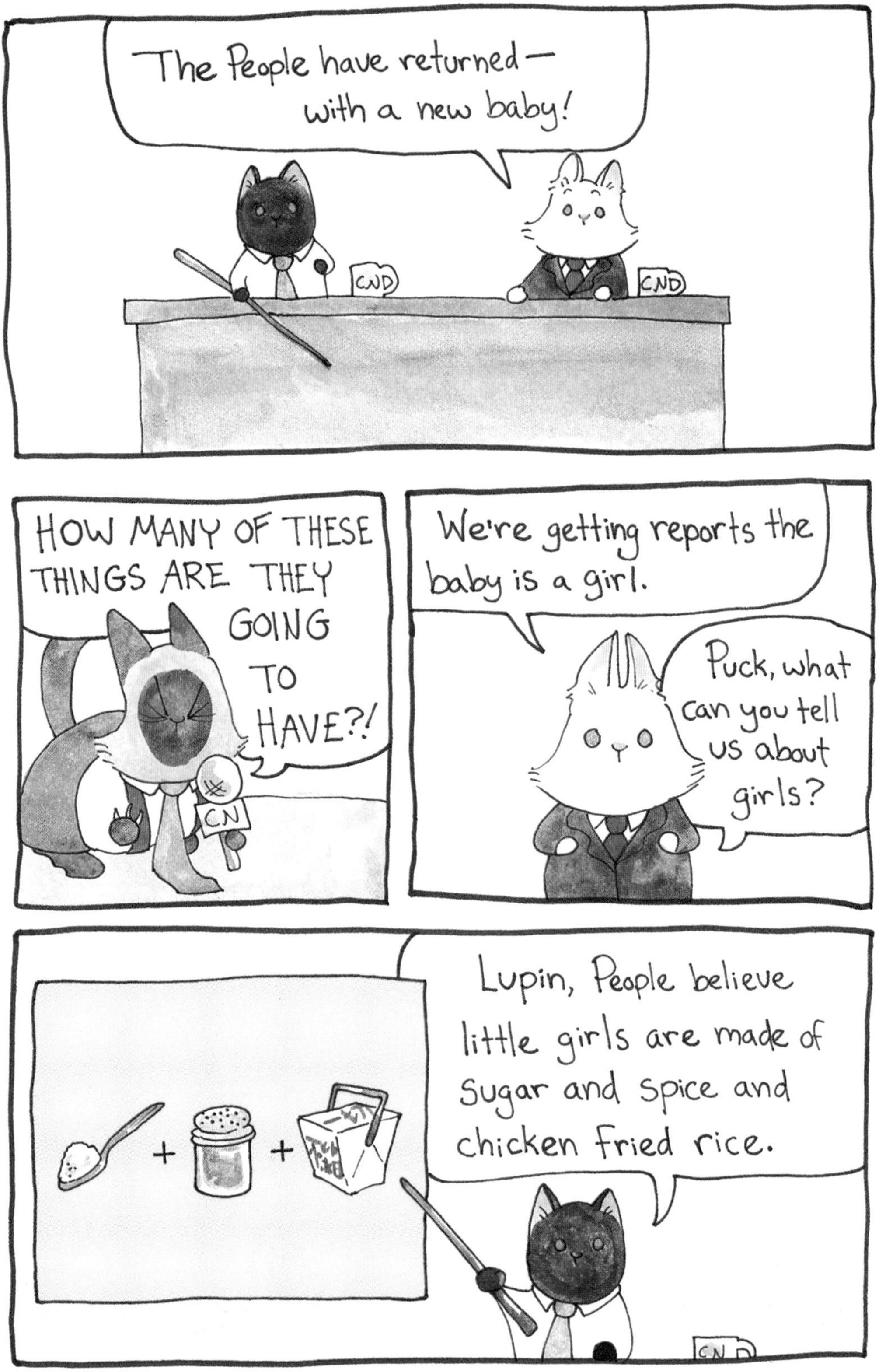
The People have returned— with a new baby!
CND
CND
HOW MANY OF THESE THINGS ARE THEY GOING TO HAVE?!
CN
We're getting reports the baby is a girl.
Puck, what can you tell us about girls?
Lupin, People believe little girls are made of sugar and spice and chicken fried rice.

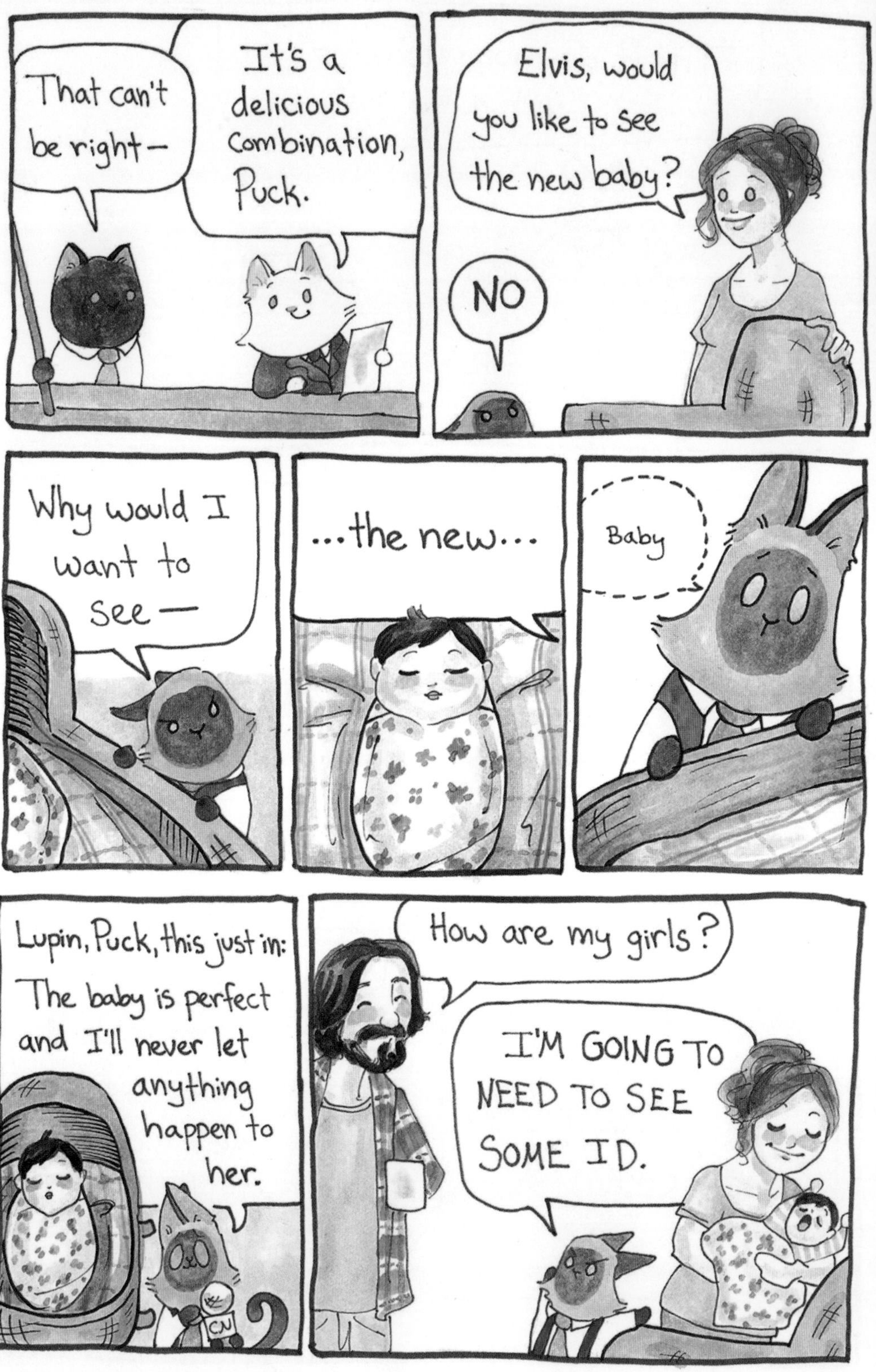
That can't be right—
It's a delicious combination, Puck.
Elvis, would you like to see the new baby?
NO
Why would I want to see—
...the new...
Baby
Lupin, Puck, this just in: The baby is perfect and I'll never let anything happen to her.
CN
How are my girls?
I'M GOING TO NEED TO SEE SOME ID.

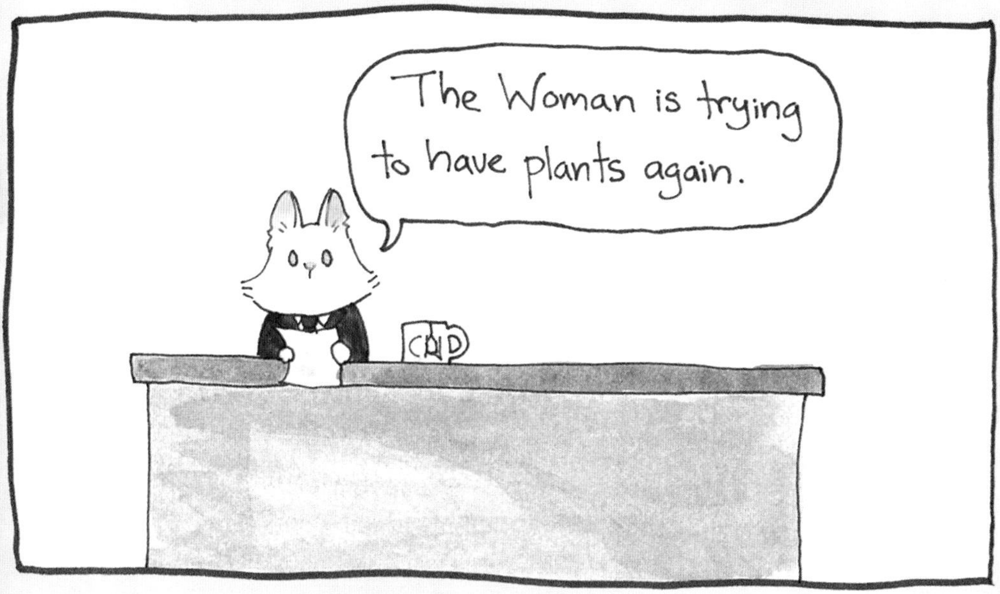
The Woman is trying to have plants again.

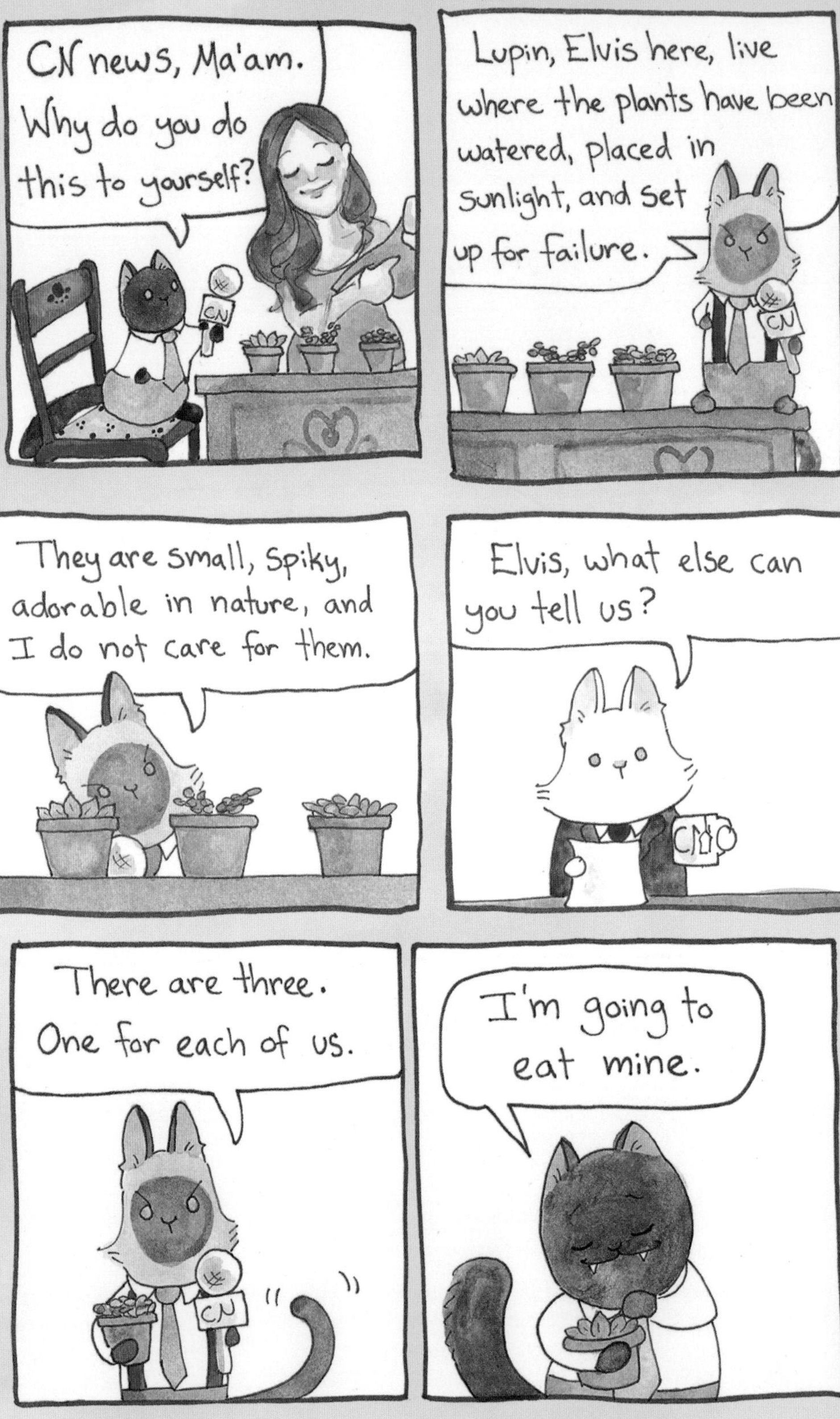
CN news, Ma'am. Why do you do this to yourself?
CN
Lupin, Elvis here, live where the plants have been watered, placed in sunlight, and set up for failure.
CN
They are small, spiky, adorable in nature, and I do not care for them.
Elvis, what else can you tell us?
There are three. One for each of us.
CN
I'm going to eat mine.

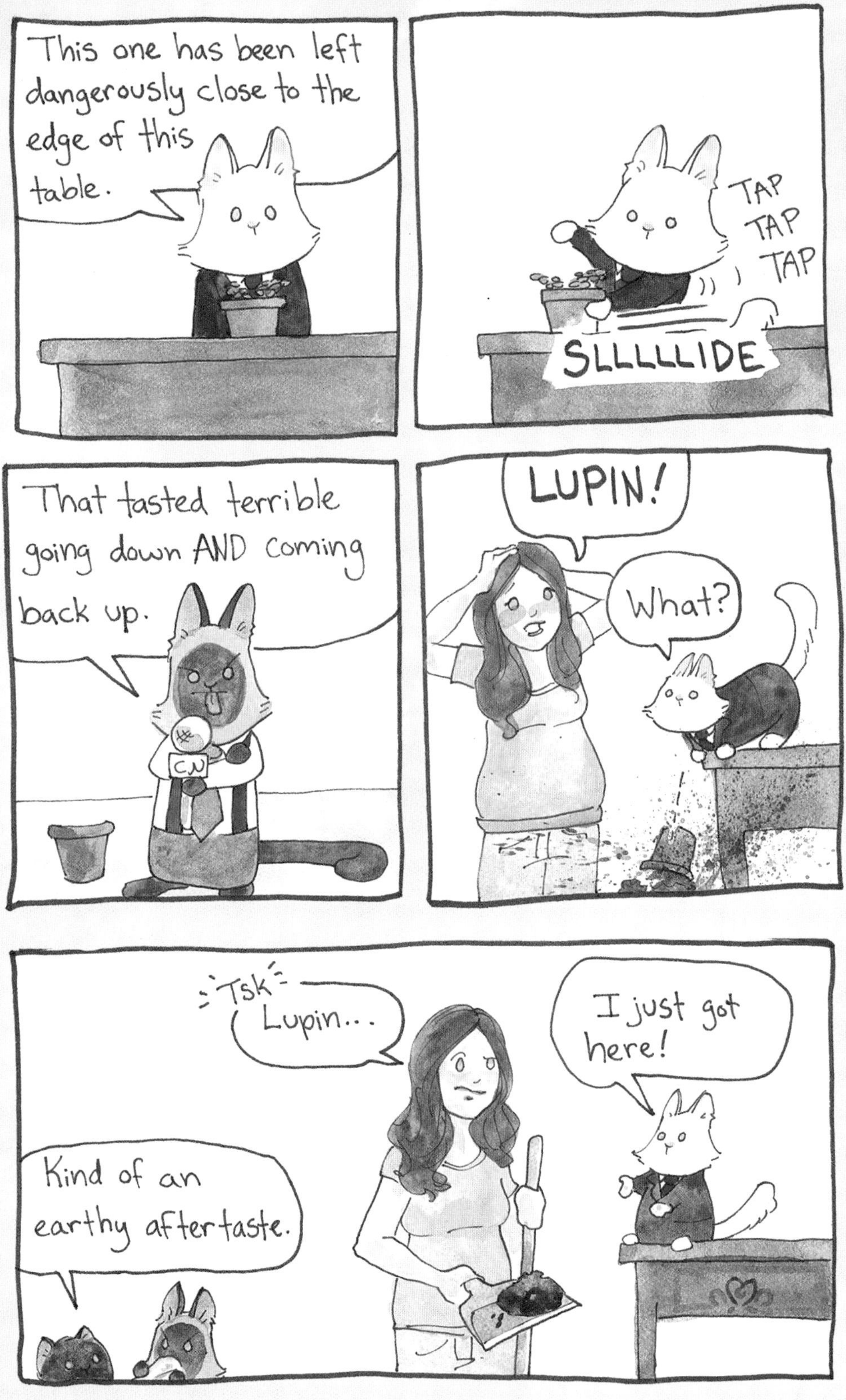
This one has been left dangerously close to the edge of this table.
TAP TAP TAP
SLLLLLIDE
That tasted terrible going down AND coming back up.
CN
LUPIN!
What?
Tsk Lupin...
I just got here!
Kind of an earthy aftertaste.

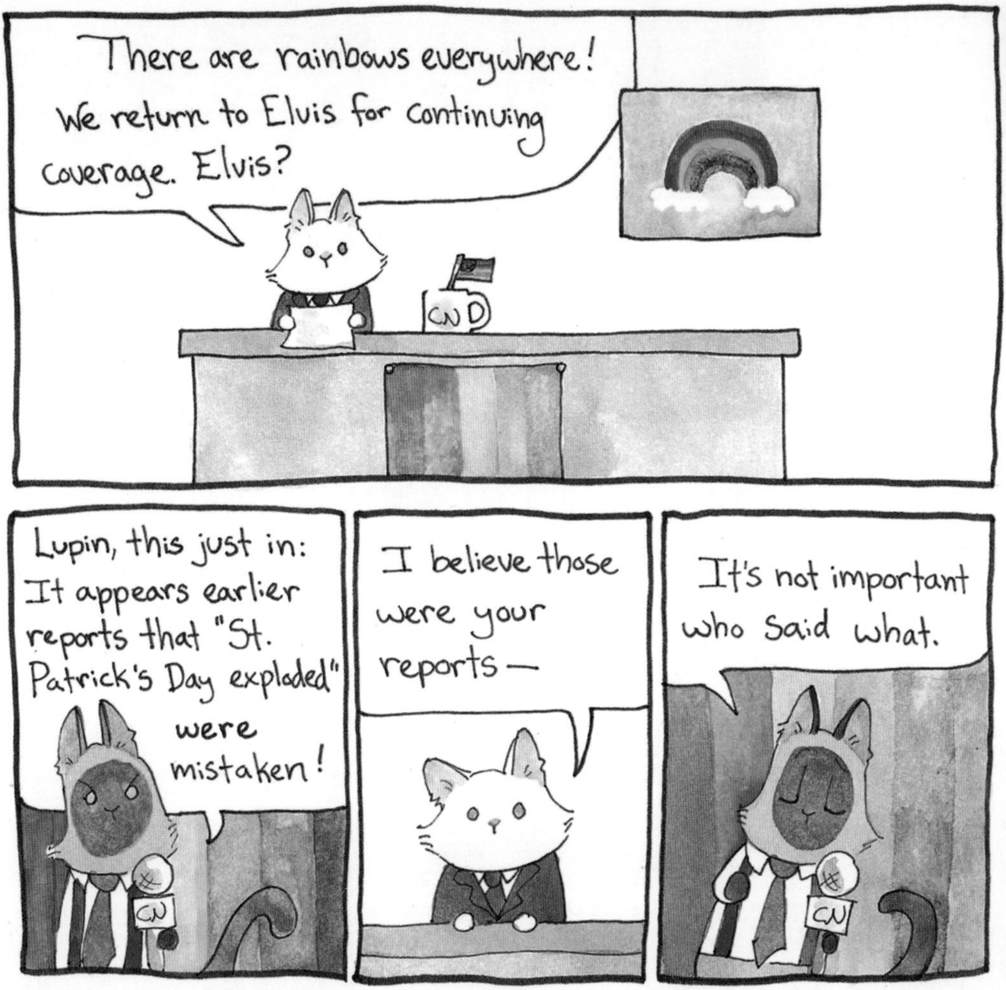
There are rainbows everywhere!
We return to Elvis for continuing coverage. Elvis?
CND
Lupin, this just in: It appears earlier reports that "St. Patrick's Day exploded" were mistaken!
CN
I believe those were your reports —
It's not important who said what.
CN

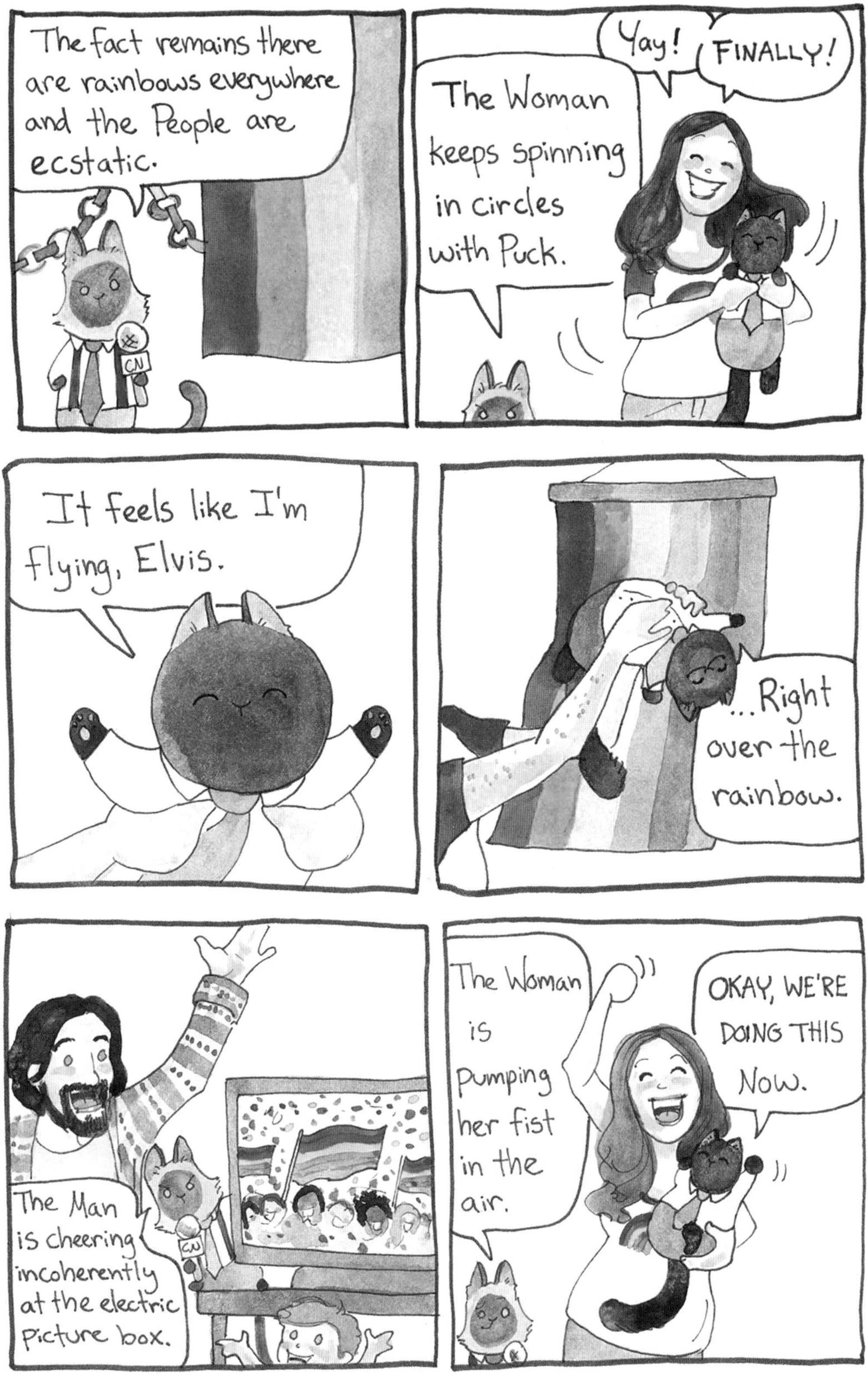
The fact remains there are rainbows everywhere and the People are ecstatic.
CN
The Woman keeps spinning in circles with Puck.
Yay!
FINALLY!
It feels like I'm flying, Elvis.
...Right over the rainbow.
The Man is cheering incoherently at the electric picture box.
CN
The Woman is pumping her fist in the air.
OKAY, WE'RE DOING THIS NOW.

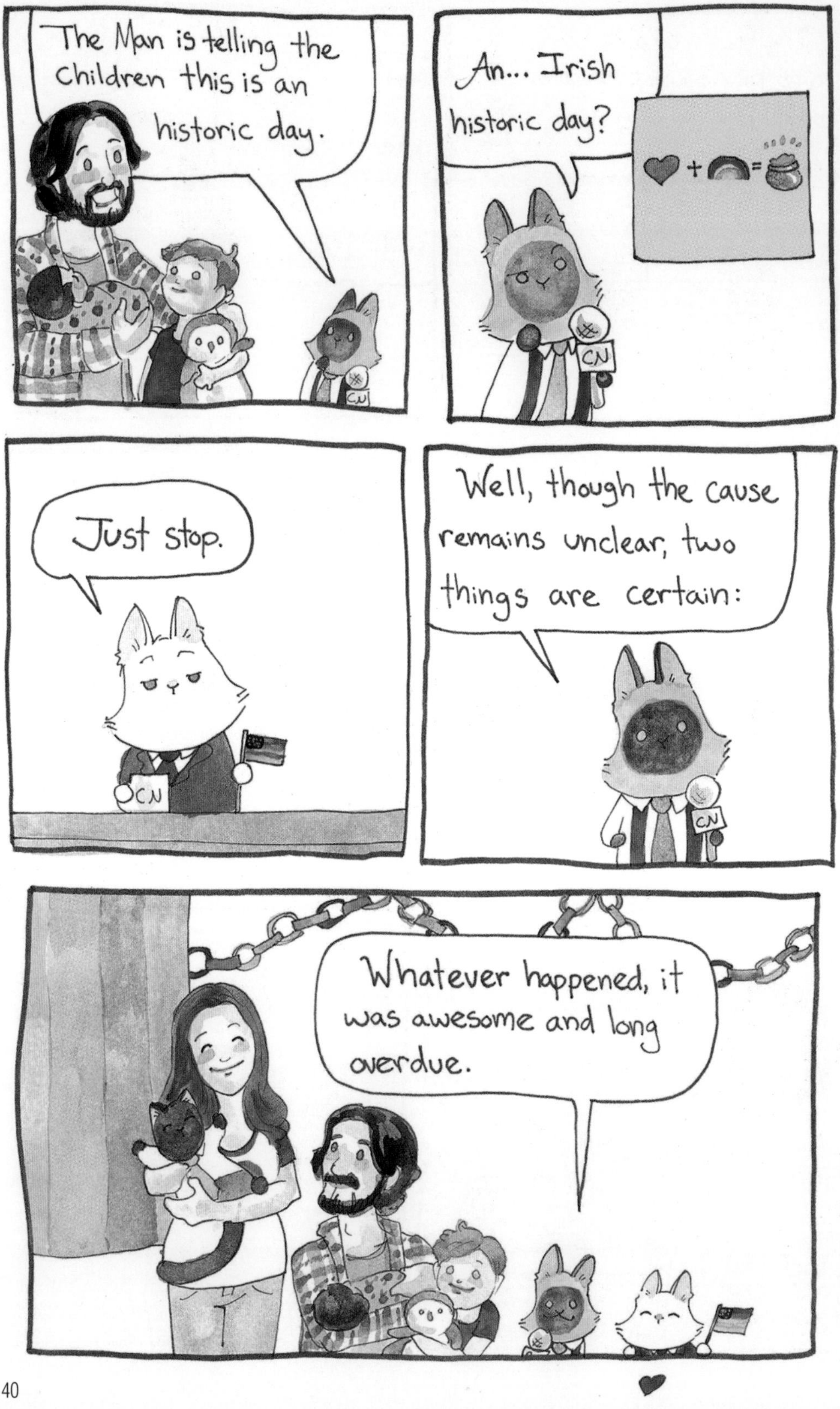
The Man is telling the children this is an historic day.
An... Irish historic day?
CN
Just stop.
CN
Well, though the cause remains unclear, two things are certain:
CN
Whatever happened, it was awesome and long overdue.

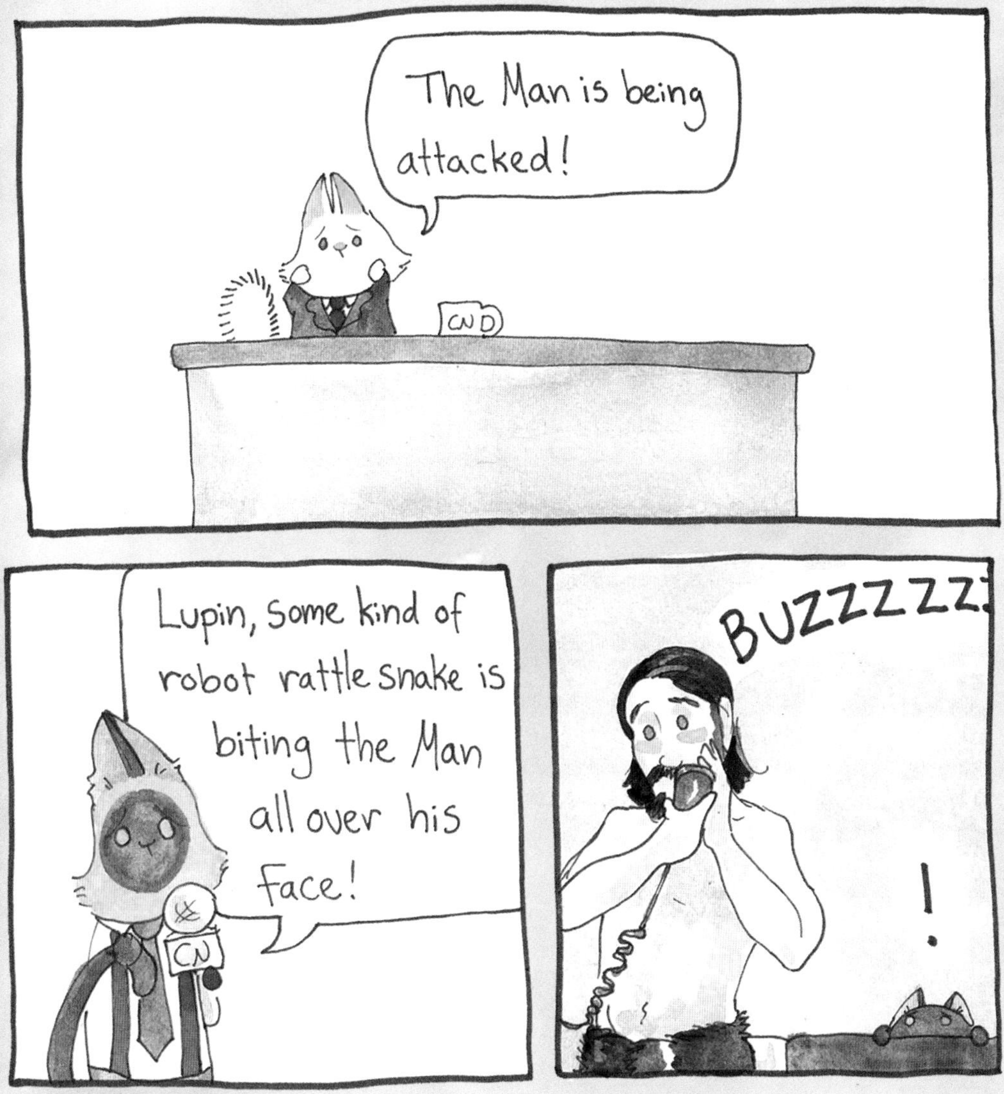
The Man is being attacked!
CND
Lupin, some kind of robot rattlesnake is biting the Man all over his face!
CN
BUZZZZZ
!

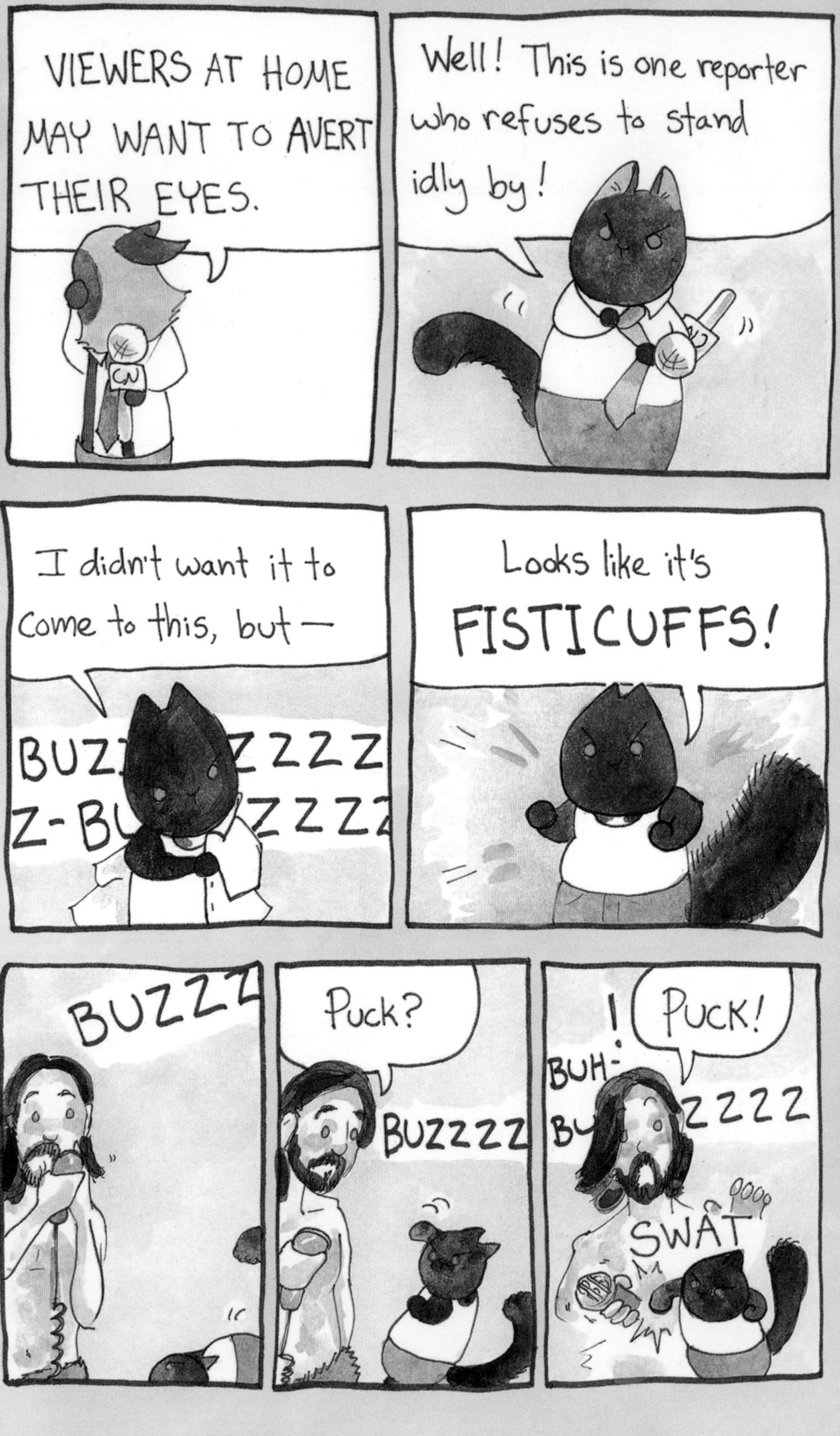
VIEWERS AT HOME MAY WANT TO AVERT THEIR EYES.
CN
Well! This is one reporter who refuses to stand idly by!
I didn't want it to come to this, but—
BUZ ZZZZ
Z-BU ZZZZ
Looks like it's FISTICUFFS!
BUZZZ
Puck?
BUZZZZ
!
PUCK!
BUH-
BU ZZZZ
SWAT

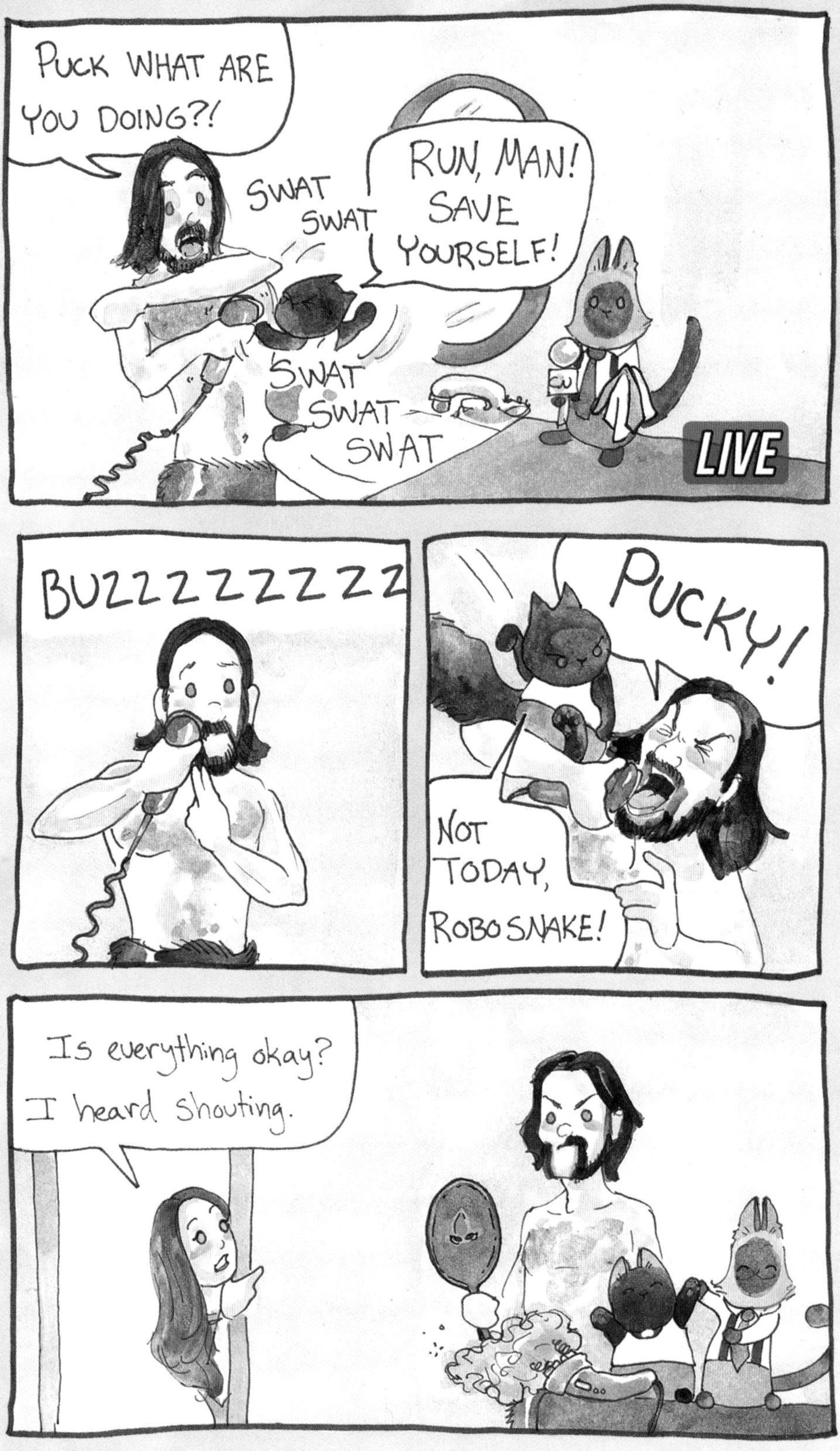
PUCK WHAT ARE YOU DOING?!
SWAT SWAT
RUN, MAN! SAVE YOURSELF!
SWAT SWAT SWAT
LIVE
BUZZZZZZZZZ
PUCKY!
NOT TODAY, ROBOSNAKE!
Is everything okay? I heard shouting.

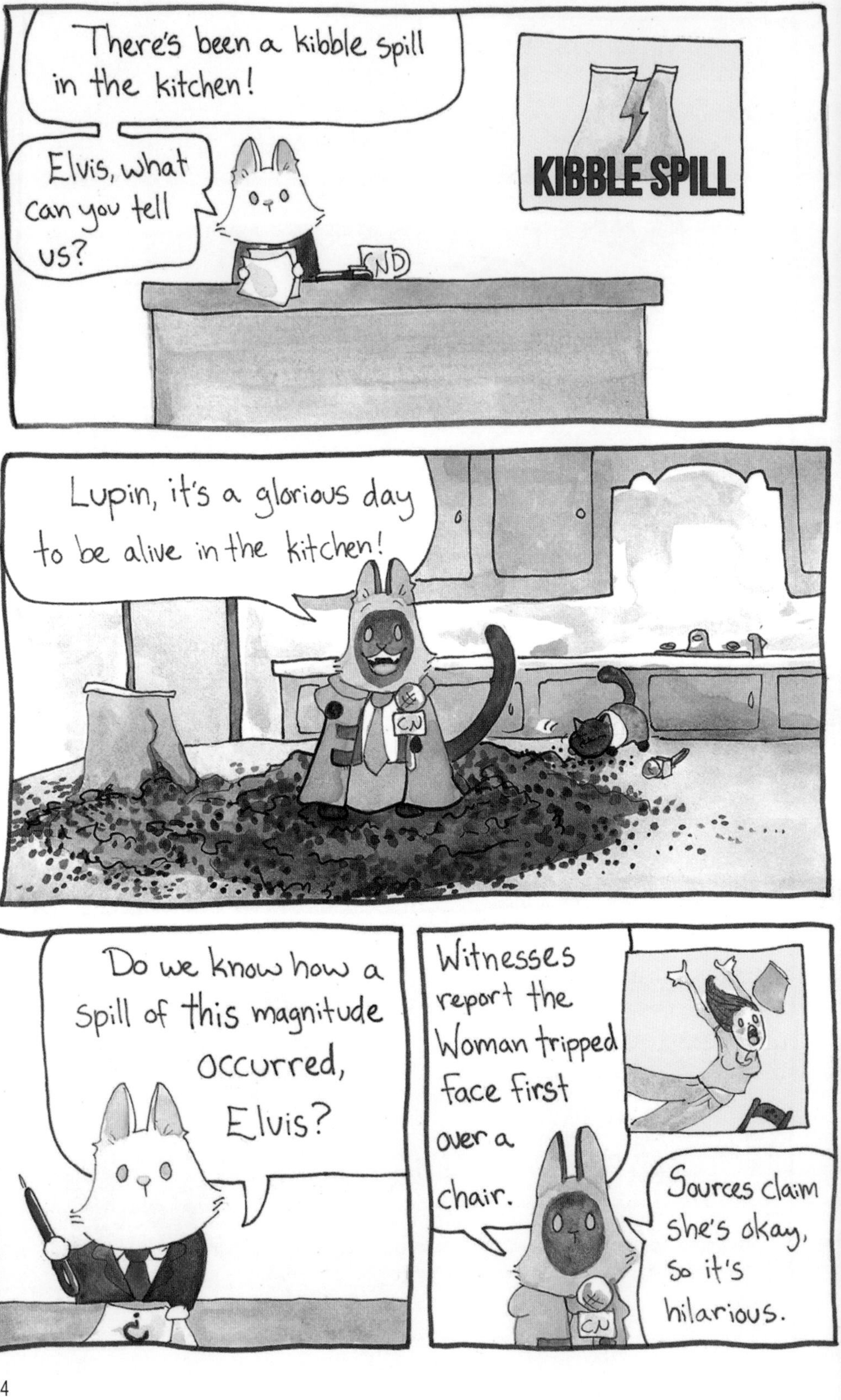
There's been a kibble spill in the kitchen!
Elvis, what can you tell us?
KIBBLE SPILL
Lupin, it's a glorious day to be alive in the kitchen!
Do we know how a spill of this magnitude occurred, Elvis?
Witnesses report the Woman tripped face first over a chair.
Sources claim she's okay, so it's hilarious.

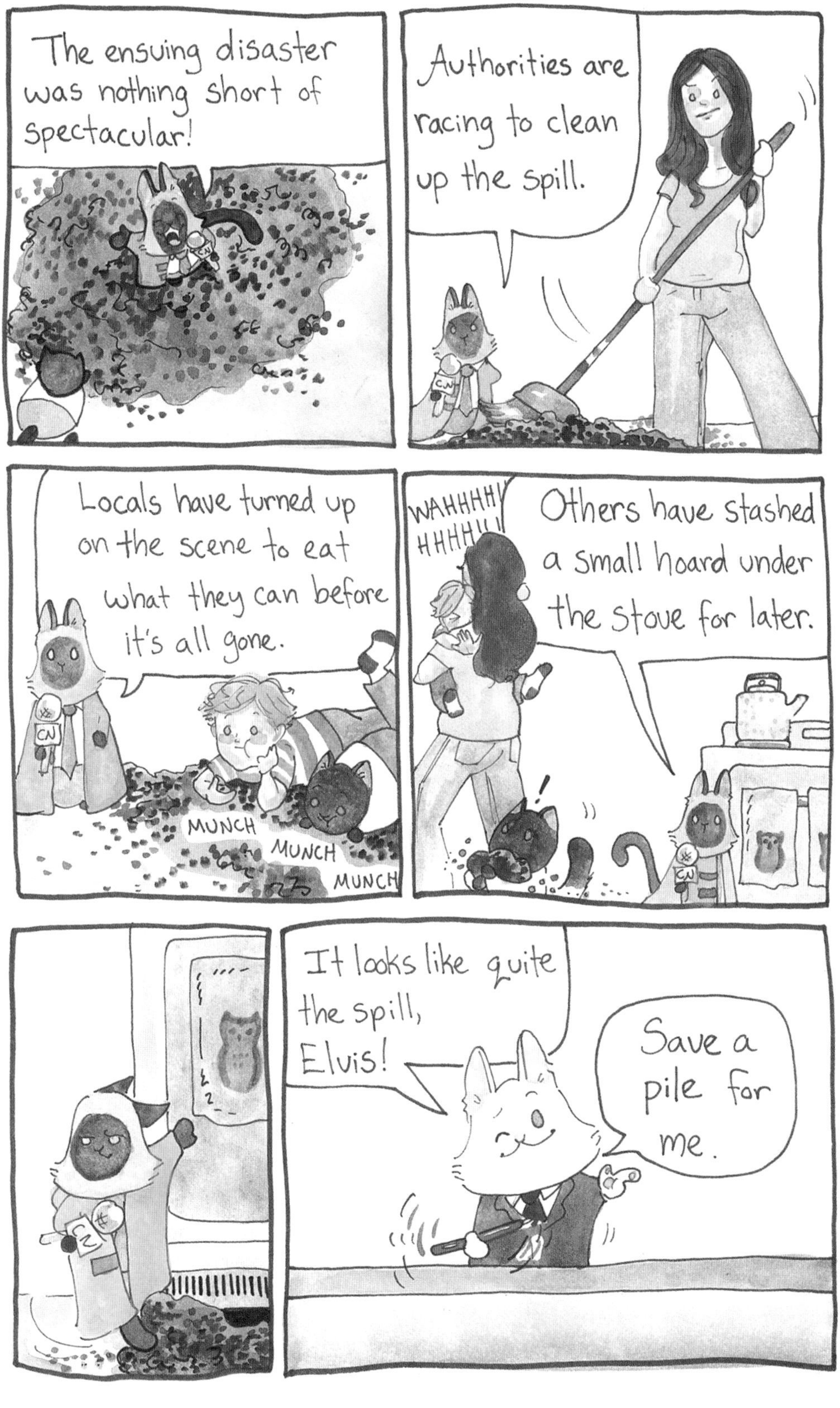
The ensuing disaster was nothing short of spectacular!
Authorities are racing to clean up the spill.
Locals have turned up on the scene to eat what they can before it's all gone.
MUNCH
MUNCH
MUNCH
WAHHHH! HHHH!!!
Others have stashed a small hoard under the stove for later.
It looks like quite the spill, Elvis!
Save a pile for me.

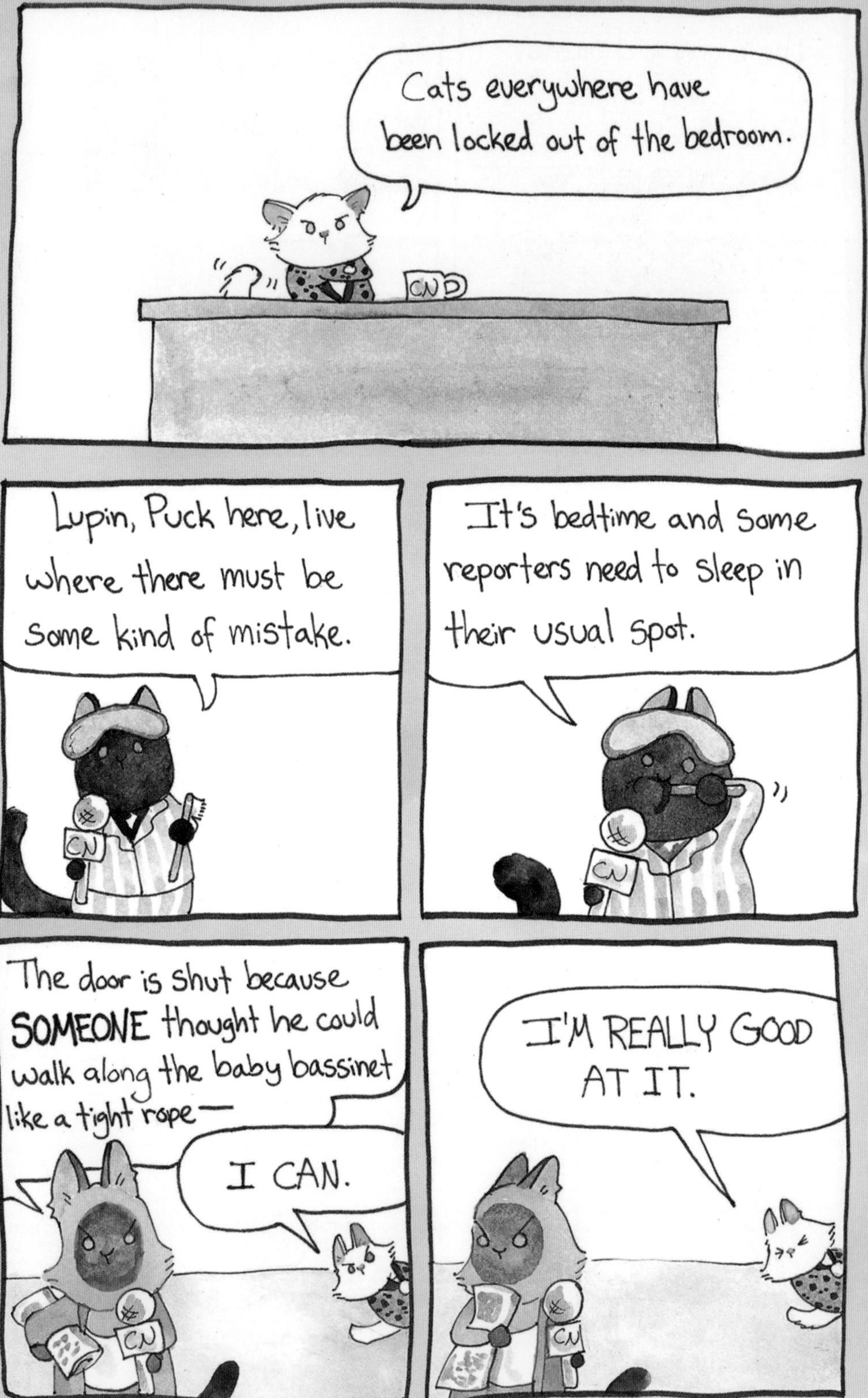
Cats everywhere have been locked out of the bedroom.
CN
Lupin, Puck here, live where there must be some kind of mistake.
CN
It's bedtime and some reporters need to sleep in their usual spot.
CN
The door is shut because SOMEONE thought he could walk along the baby bassinet like a tight rope—
I CAN.
CN
I'M REALLY GOOD AT IT.
CN

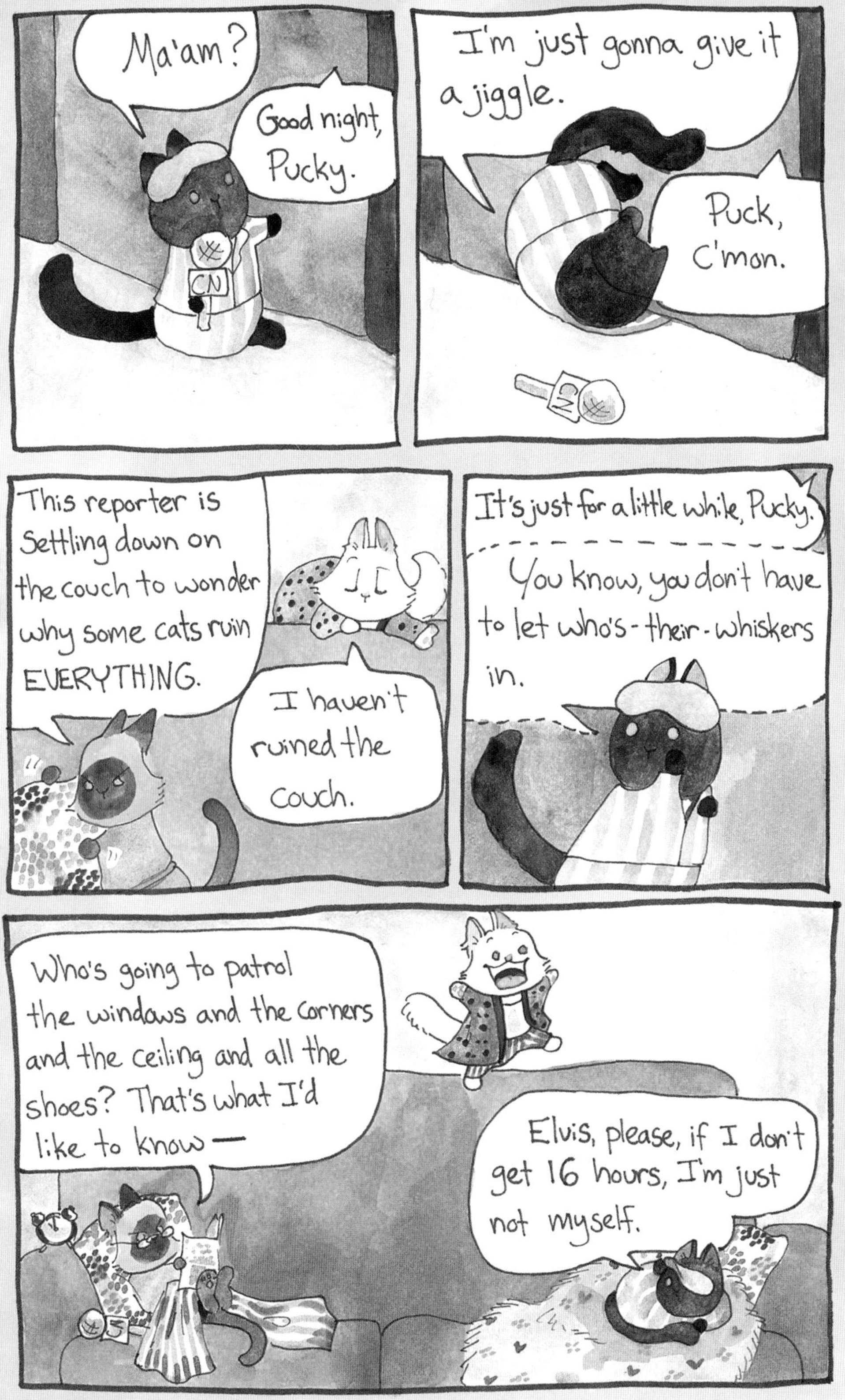
Ma'am?
Good night, Pucky.
I'm just gonna give it a jiggle.
Puck, C'mon.
CN
This reporter is Settling down on the couch to wonder why some cats ruin EVERYTHING.
I haven't ruined the couch.
It's just for a little while, Pucky.
You know, you don't have to let who's-their-whiskers in.
Who's going to patrol the windows and the corners and the ceiling and all the shoes? That's what I'd like to know—
Elvis, please, if I don't get 16 hours, I'm just not myself.

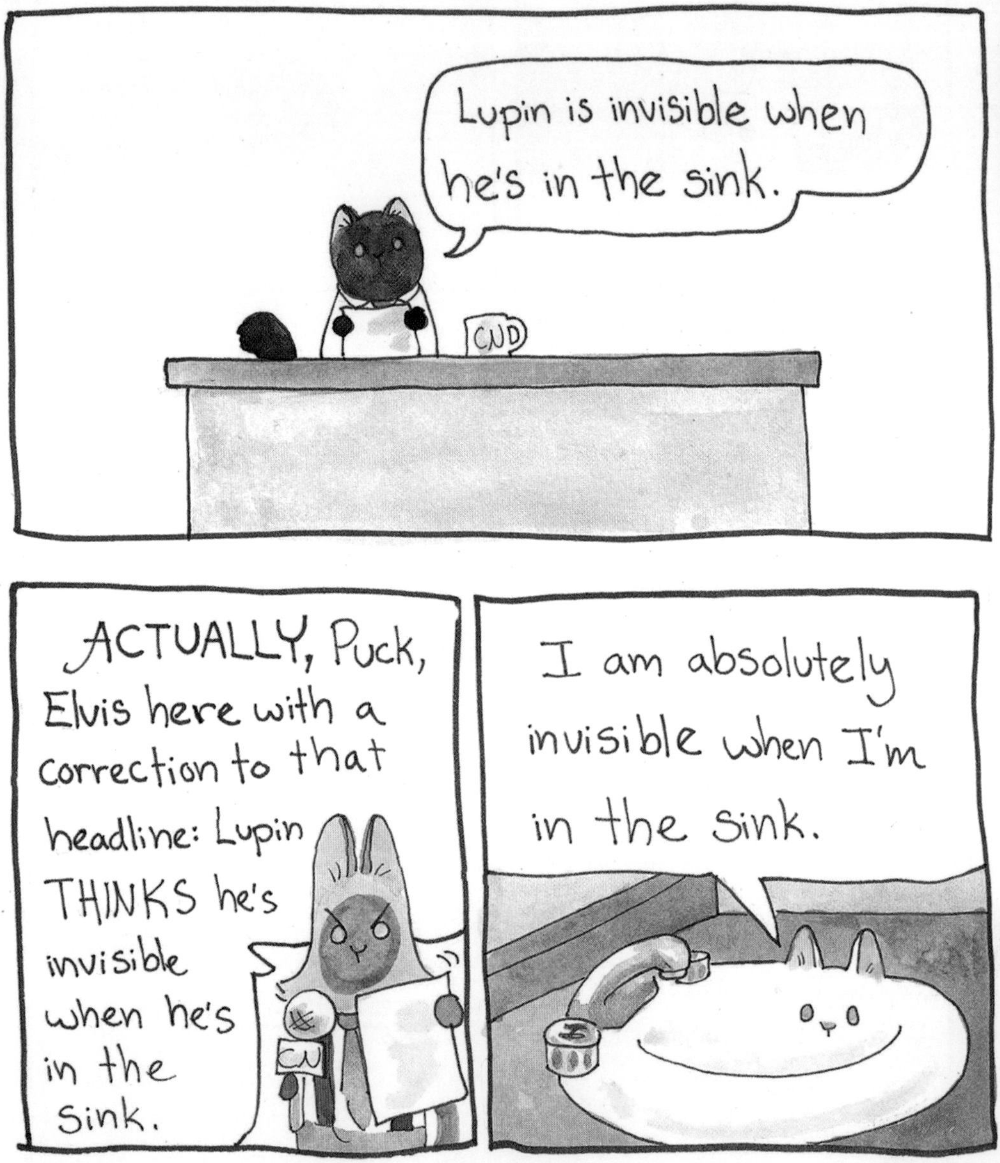
Lupin is invisible when he's in the sink.
CND
ACTUALLY, Puck, Elvis here with a correction to that headline: Lupin THINKS he's invisible when he's in the sink.
CN
I am absolutely invisible when I'm in the sink.

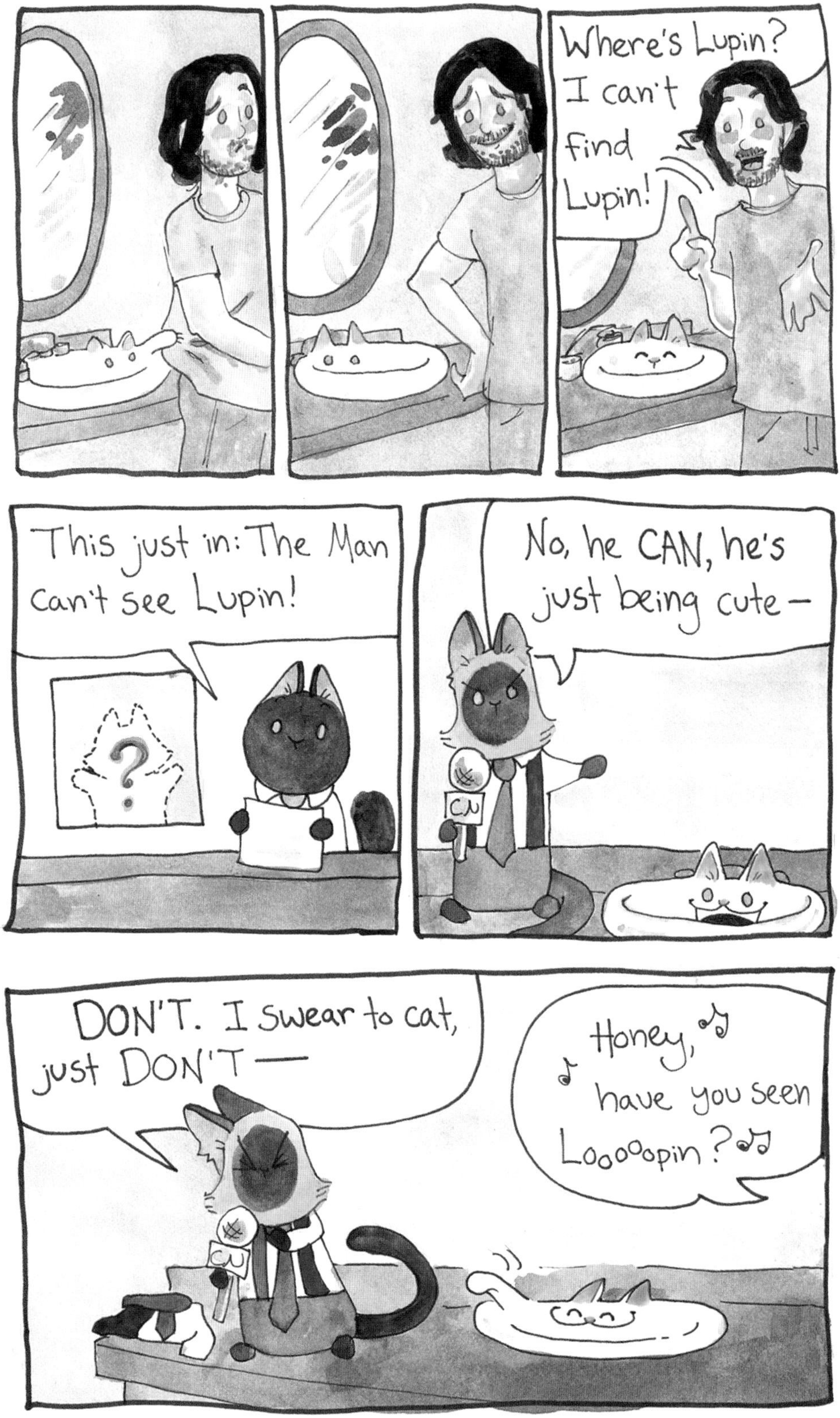
Where's Lupin? I can't find Lupin!
This just in: The Man can't see Lupin!
No, he CAN, he's just being cute —
DON'T. I swear to cat, just DON'T —
Honey, have you seen Looooopin?

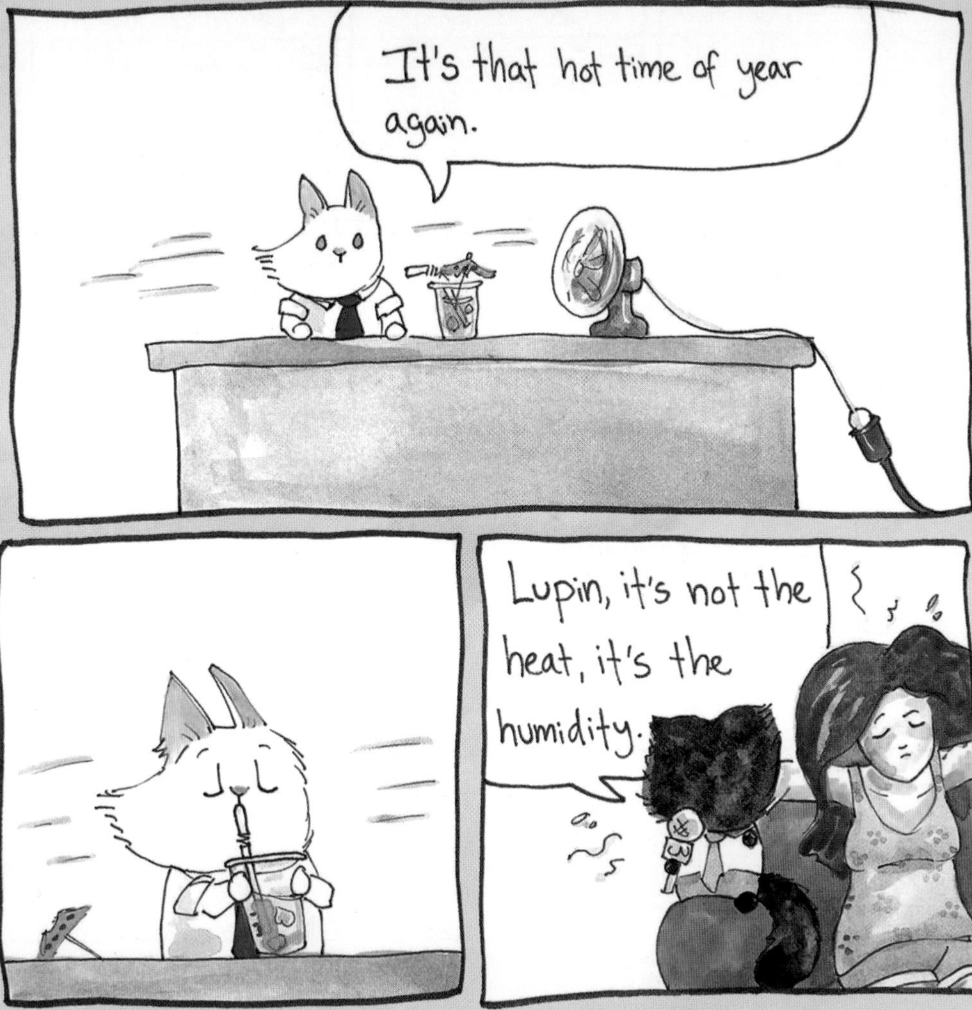
It's that hot time of year again.
Lupin, it's not the heat, it's the humidity.

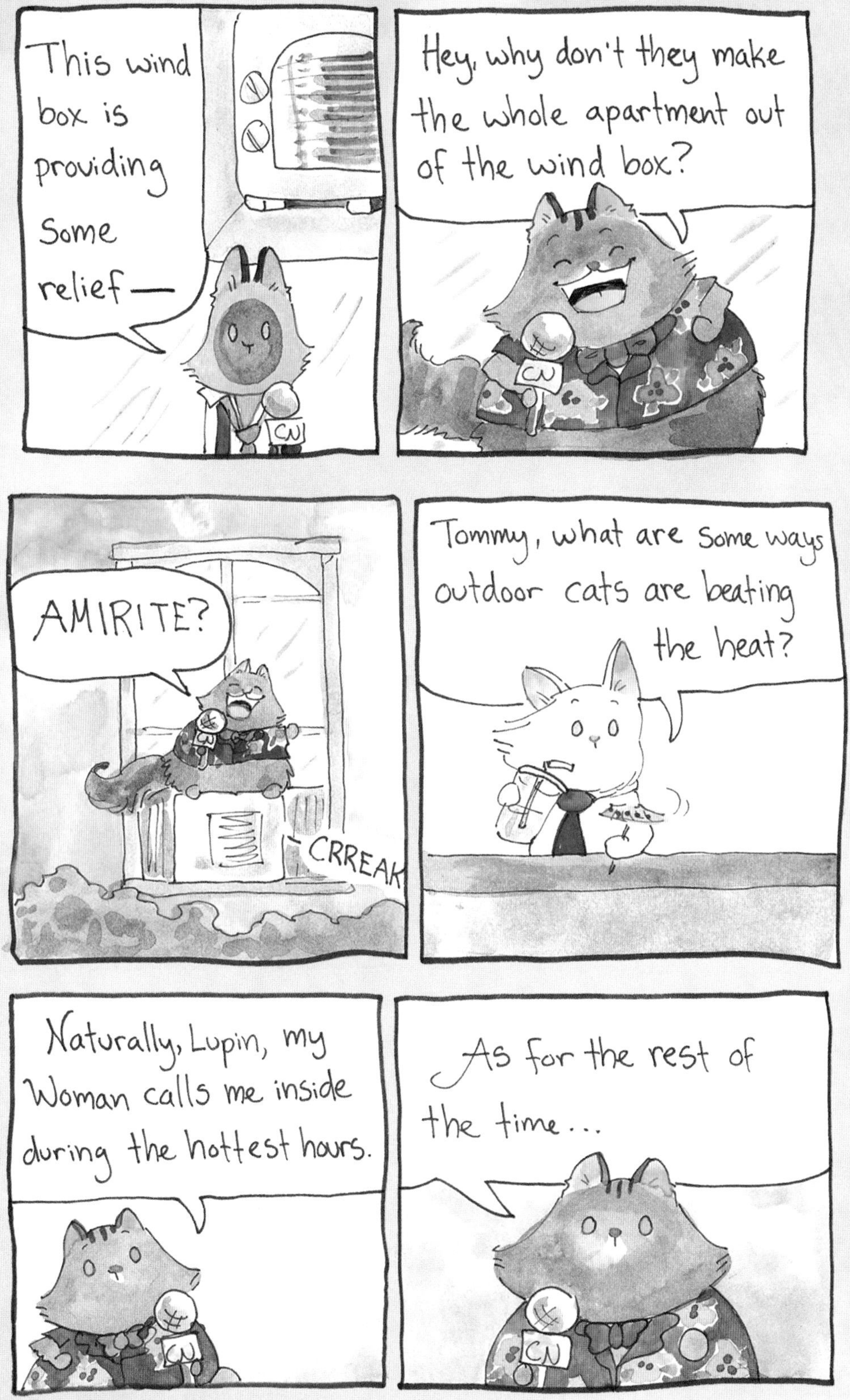
This wind box is providing some relief—
Hey, why don't they make the whole apartment out of the wind box?
CN
AMIRITE?
CRREAK
Tommy, what are some ways outdoor cats are beating the heat?
Naturally, Lupin, my Woman calls me inside during the hottest hours.
As for the rest of the time...
CN

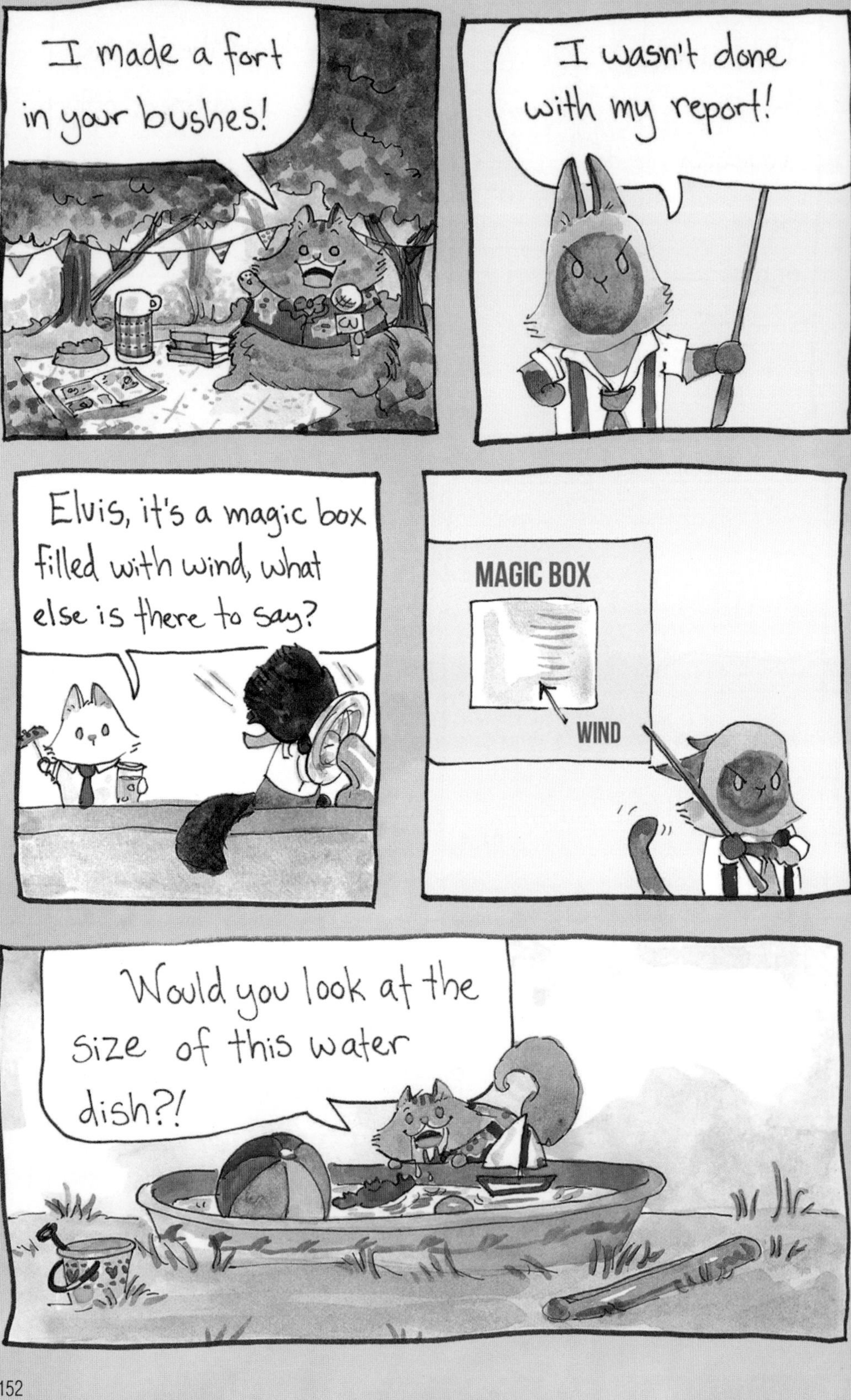
I made a fort in your bushes!
I wasn't done with my report!
Elvis, it's a magic box filled with wind, what else is there to say?
MAGIC BOX
WIND
Would you look at the size of this water dish?!

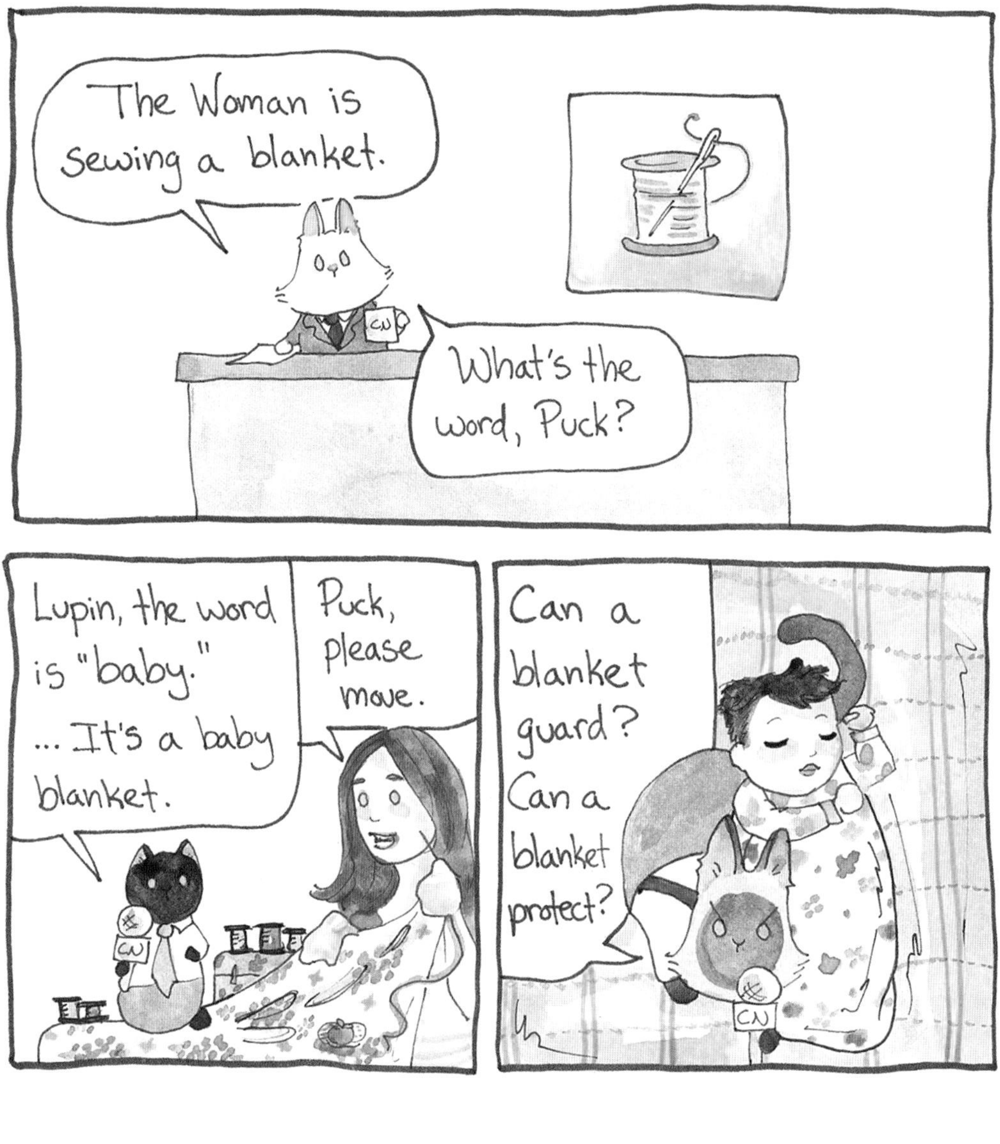
The Woman is sewing a blanket.
What's the word, Puck?
CN
Lupin, the word is "baby." ... It's a baby blanket.
Puck, please move.
CN
Can a blanket guard? Can a blanket protect?
CN

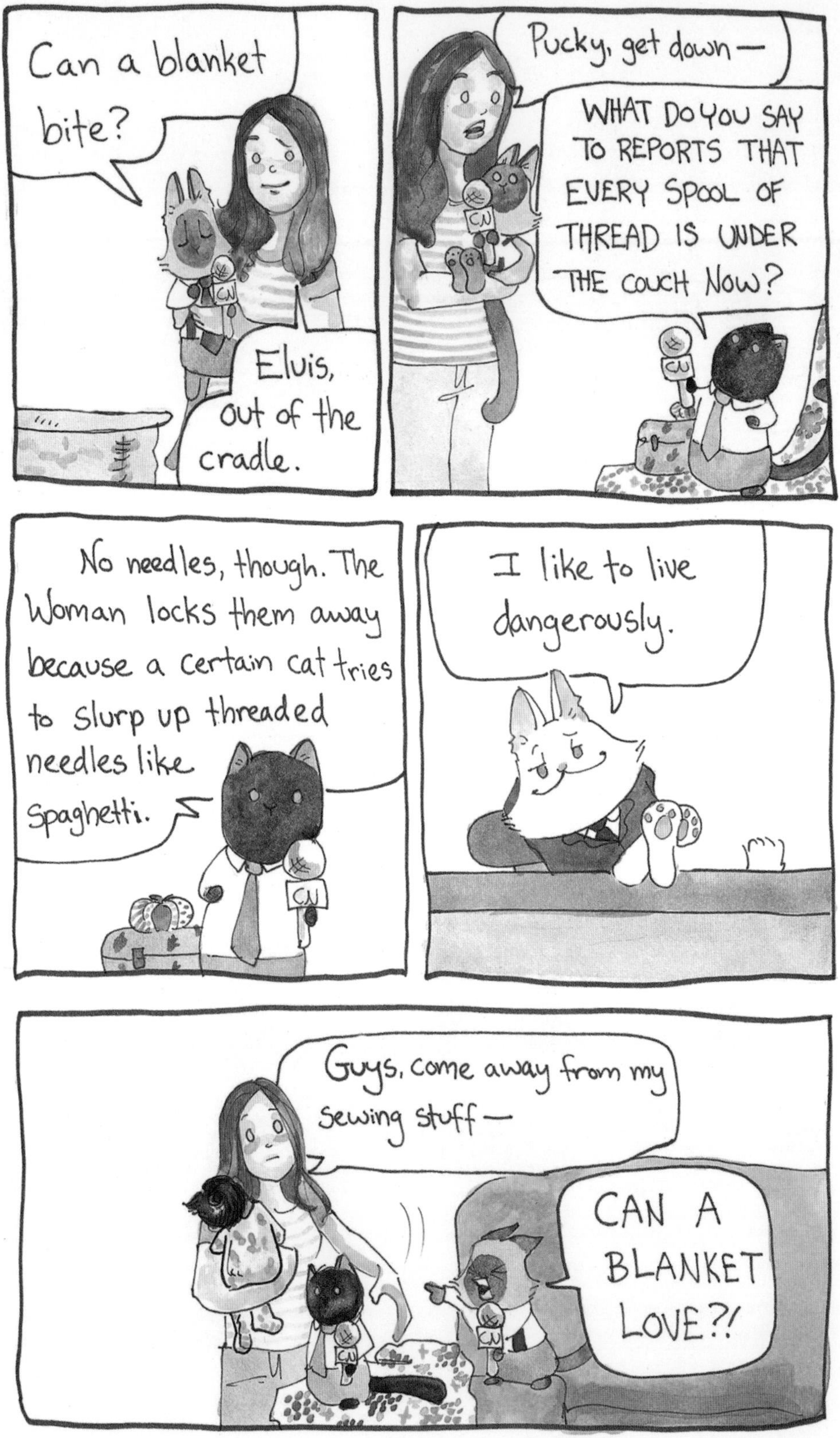
Can a blanket bite?
Elvis, out of the cradle.
Pucky, get down—
WHAT DO YOU SAY TO REPORTS THAT EVERY SPOOL OF THREAD IS UNDER THE COUCH NOW?
CN
CN
CN
No needles, though. The Woman locks them away because a certain cat tries to slurp up threaded needles like spaghetti.
CN
I like to live dangerously.
Guys, come away from my sewing stuff—
CAN A BLANKET LOVE?!
CN
CN

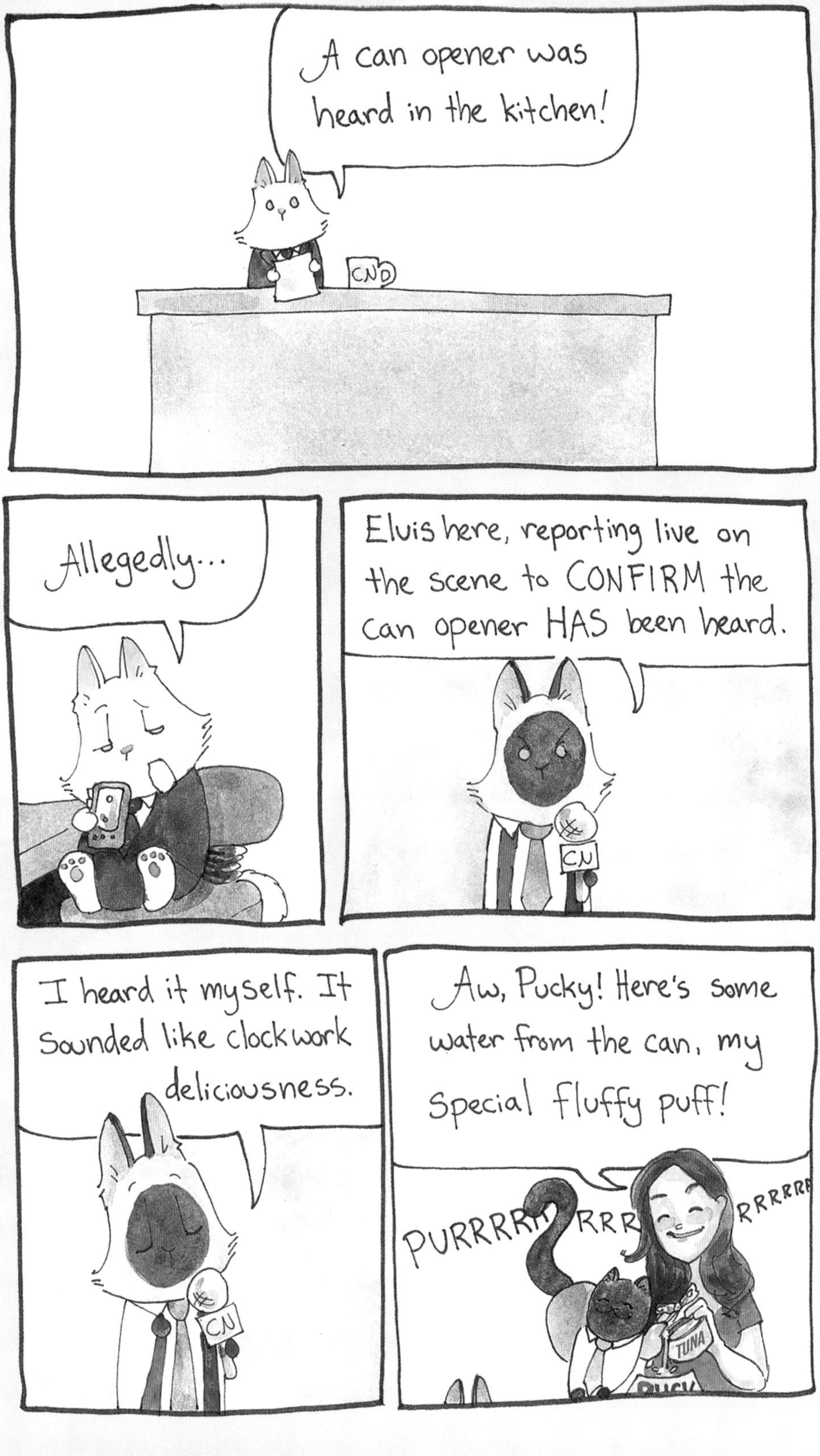
A can opener was heard in the kitchen!
CND
Allegedly...
Elvis here, reporting live on the scene to CONFIRM the can opener HAS been heard.
CN
I heard it myself. It sounded like clockwork deliciousness.
CN
Aw, Pucky! Here's some water from the can, my special fluffy puff!
PURRRRRRRRRRRRRR
TUNA

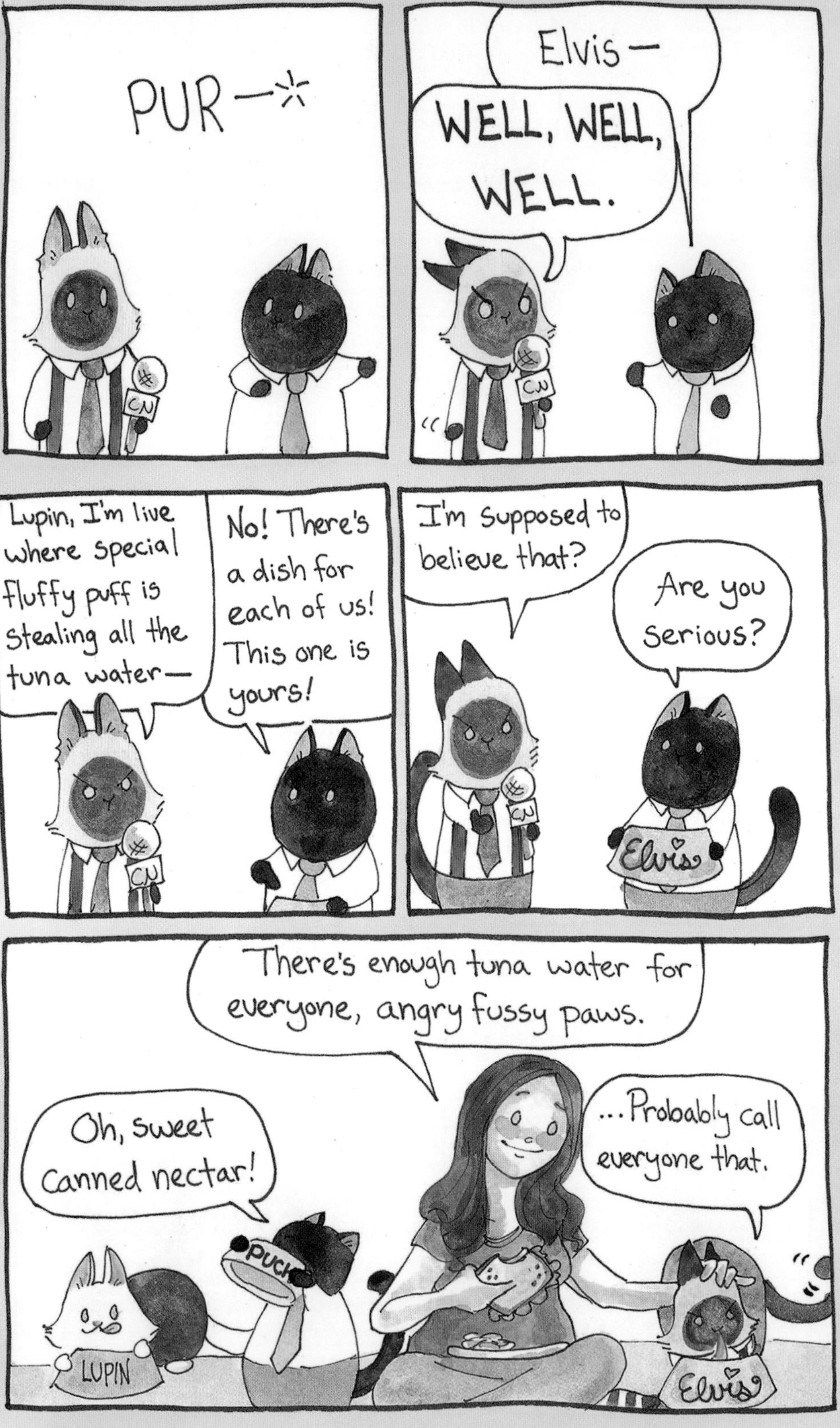
PUR—
Elvis—
WELL, WELL, WELL.
Lupin, I'm live where special fluffy puff is stealing all the tuna water—
No! There's a dish for each of us! This one is yours!
I'm supposed to believe that?
Are you serious?
Elvis
There's enough tuna water for everyone, angry fussy paws.
Oh, sweet canned nectar!
...Probably call everyone that.
LUPIN
PUCK
Elvis

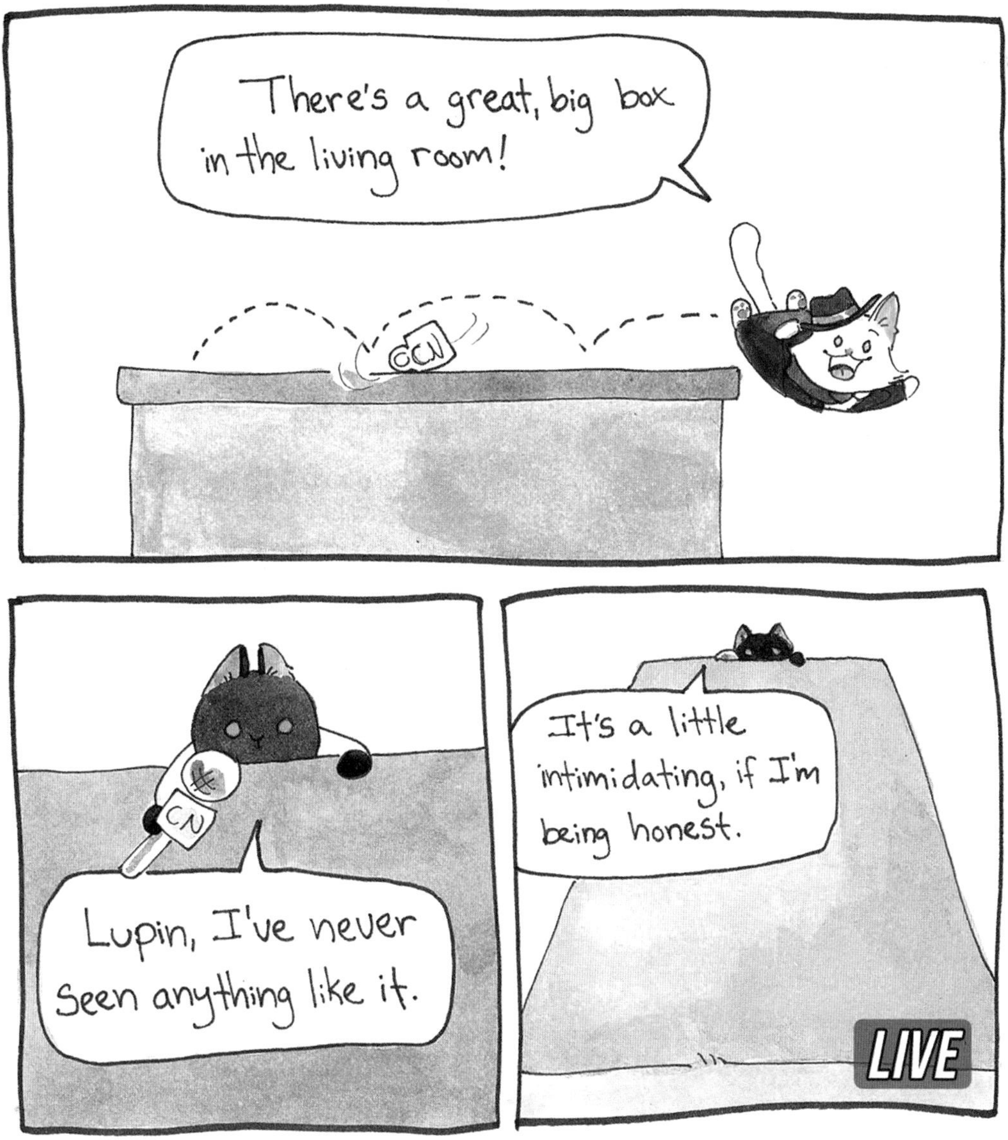
There's a great, big box in the living room!
CCN
CN
Lupin, I've never seen anything like it.
It's a little intimidating, if I'm being honest.
LIVE

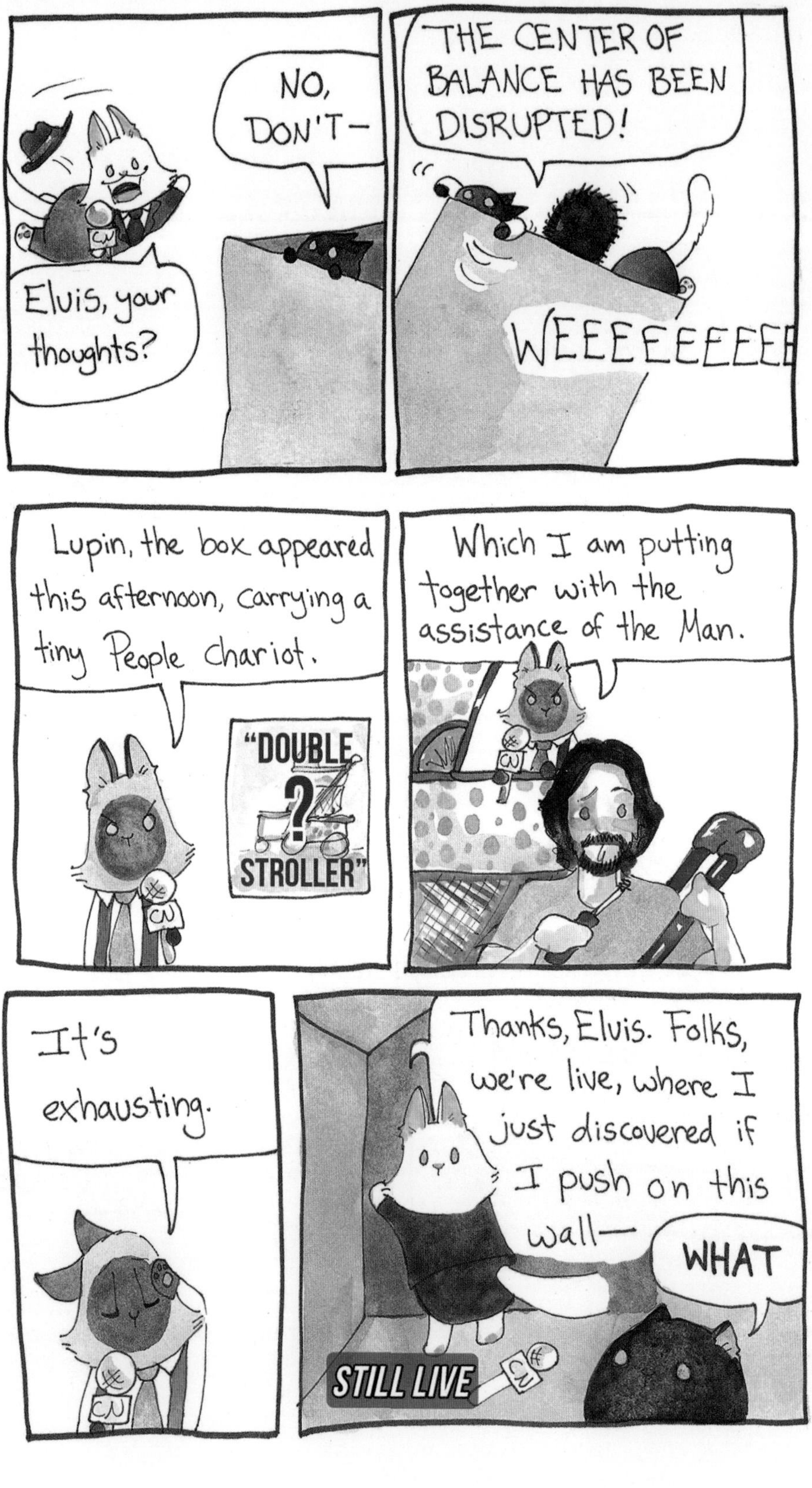
Elvis, your thoughts?
NO, DON'T–
THE CENTER OF BALANCE HAS BEEN DISRUPTED!
WEEEEEEEEE
Lupin, the box appeared this afternoon, carrying a tiny People Chariot.
"DOUBLE ? STROLLER"
Which I am putting together with the assistance of the Man.
It's exhausting.
Thanks, Elvis. Folks, we're live, where I just discovered if I push on this wall—
WHAT
STILL LIVE

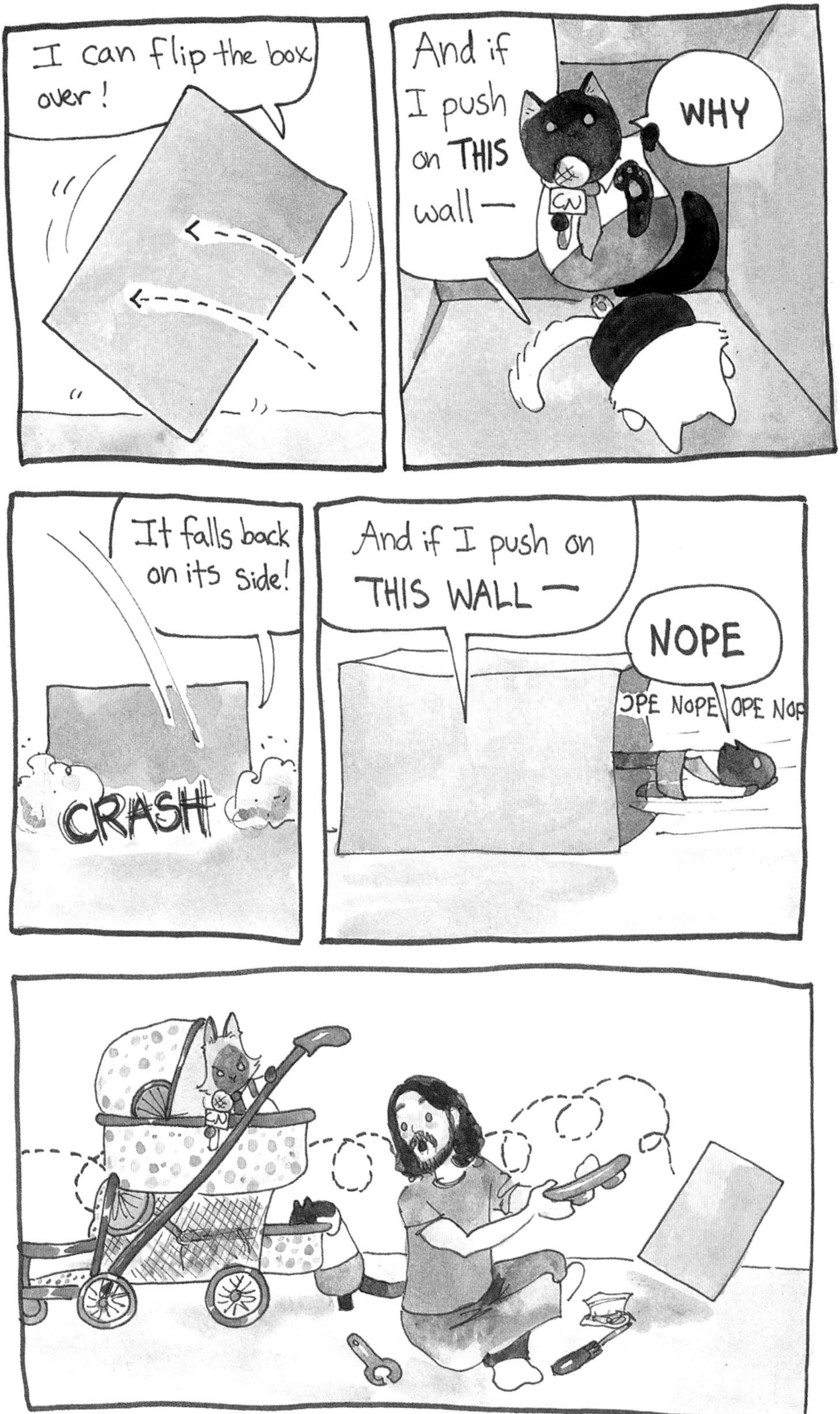
I can flip the box over!
And if I push on THIS wall—
WHY
It falls back on its side!
CRASH
And if I push on THIS WALL—
NOPE
OPE NOPE OPE NOP

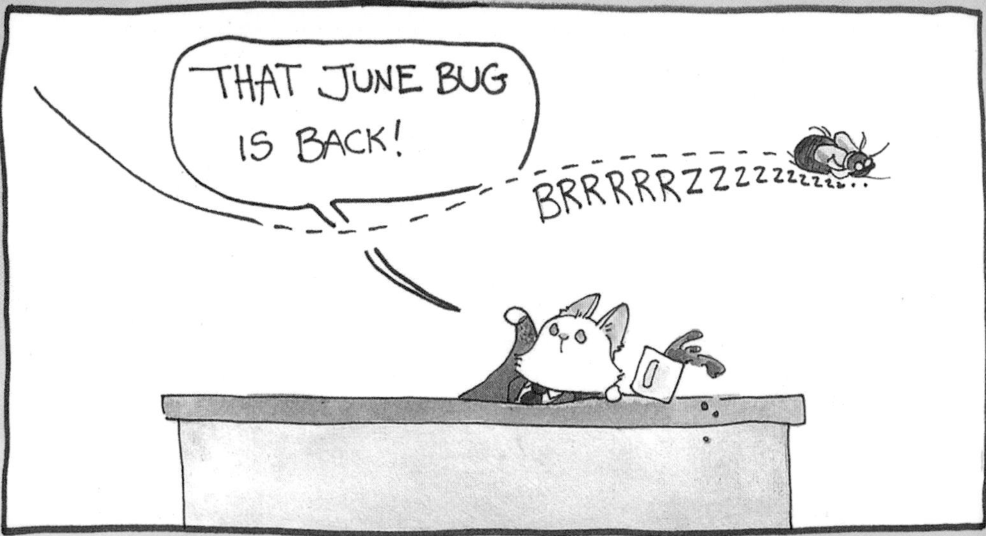
THAT JUNE BUG IS BACK!
BRRRRRZZZZzzzzzz...

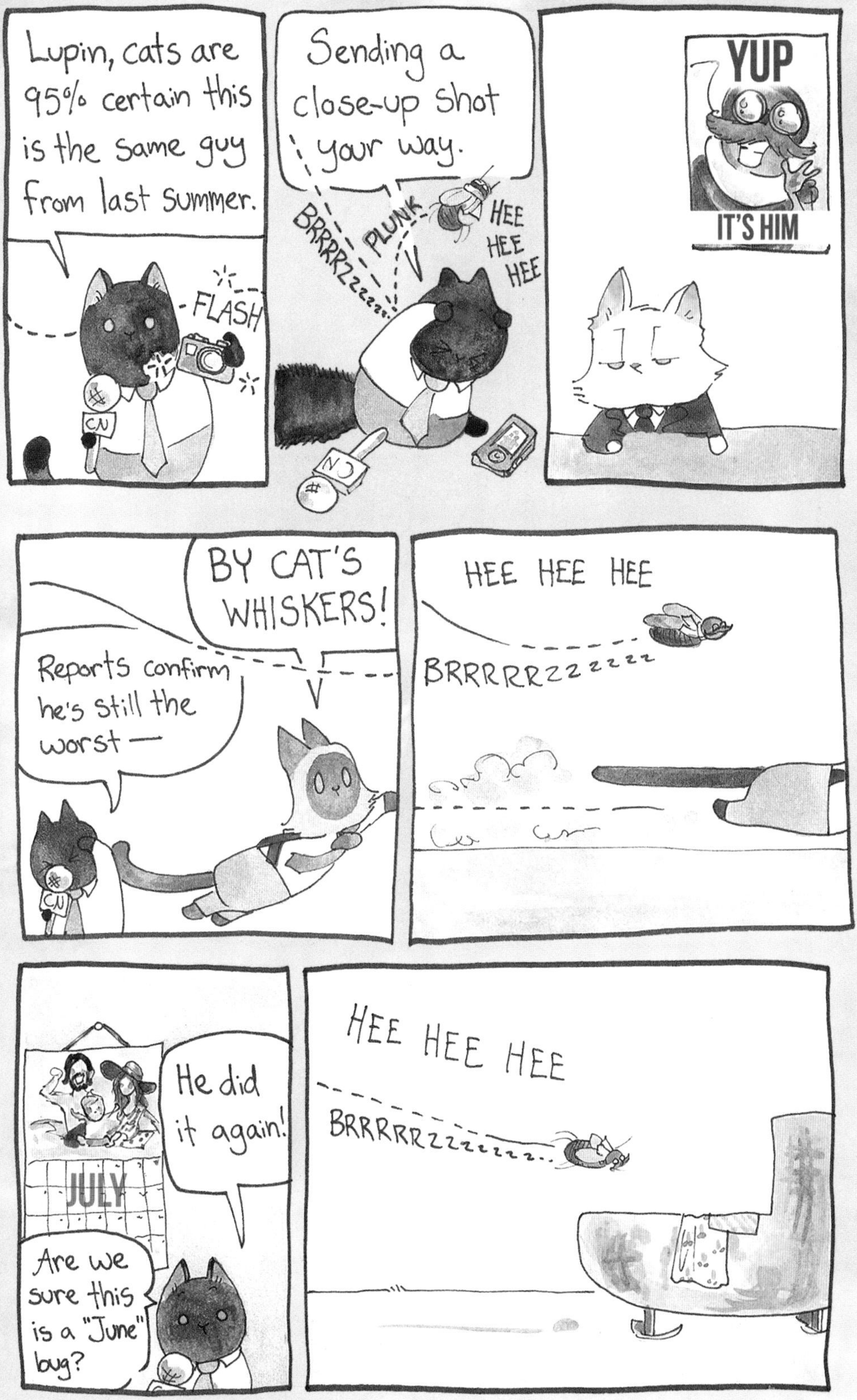
Lupin, cats are 95% certain this is the same guy from last summer.
FLASH
CN
Sending a close-up shot your way.
BRRRRZzzzzz
PLUNK
HEE HEE HEE
CN
YUP
IT'S HIM
BY CAT'S WHISKERS!
Reports confirm he's still the worst—
CN
HEE HEE HEE
BRRRRRZzzzzz
JULY
He did it again!
Are we sure this is a "June" bug?
HEE HEE HEE
BRRRRRZzzzzzz

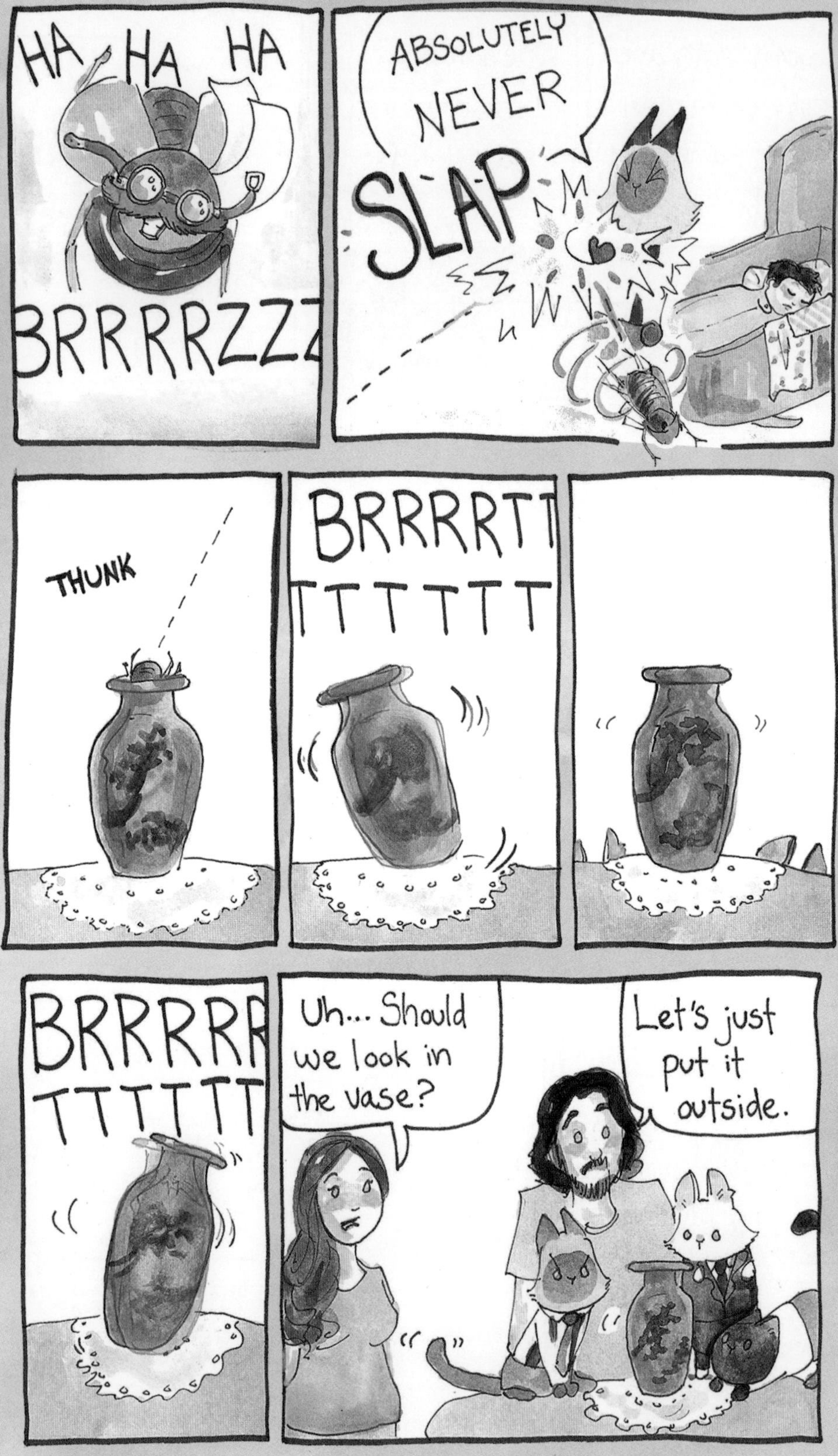
HA HA HA
BRRRRZZZ
ABSOLUTELY NEVER
SLAP
THUNK
BRRRRTT TTTTTT
BRRRRRR TTTTTT
Uh... Should we look in the vase?
Let's just put it outside.

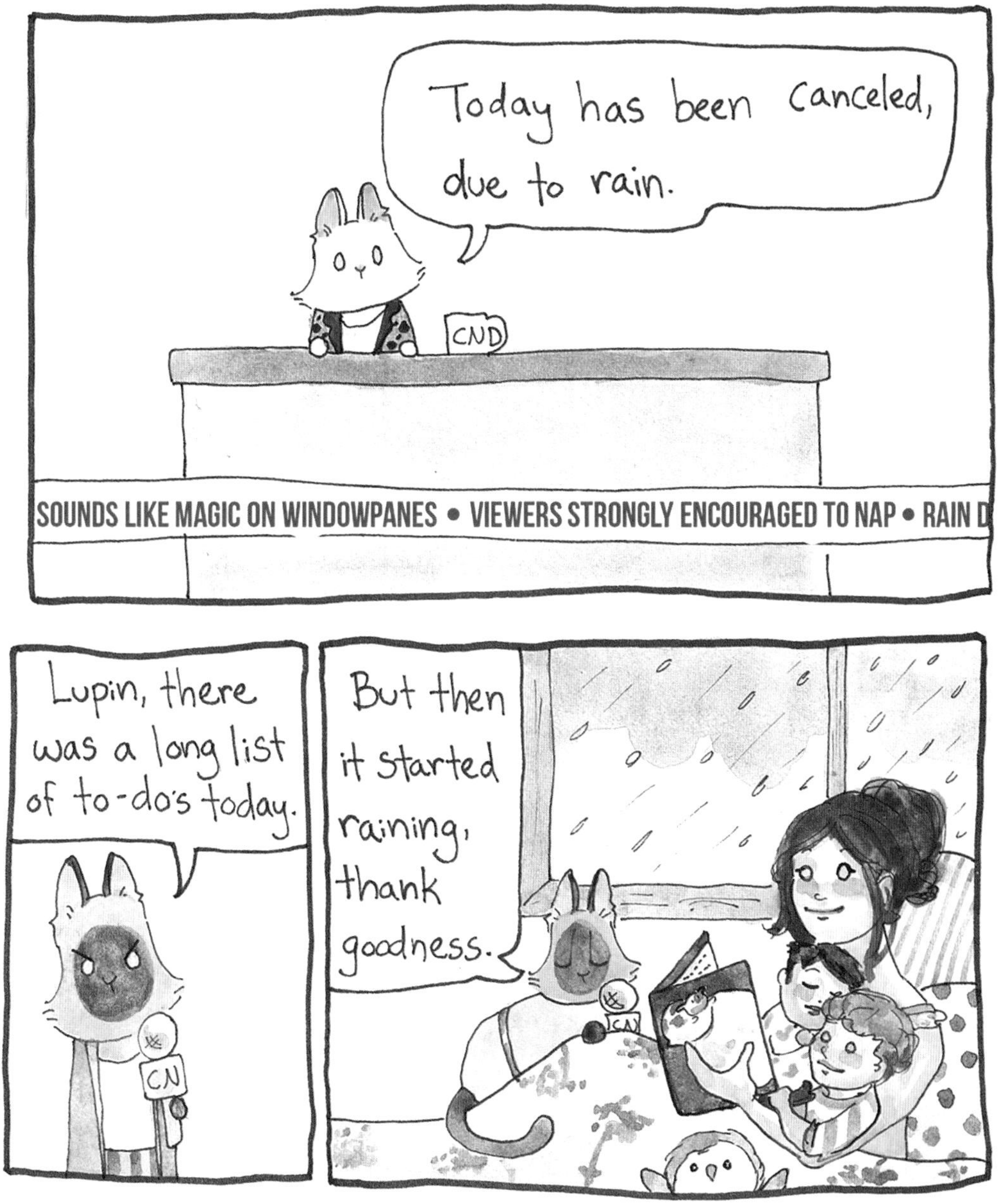
Today has been canceled, due to rain.
CND
SOUNDS LIKE MAGIC ON WINDOWPANES • VIEWERS STRONGLY ENCOURAGED TO NAP • RAIN D
Lupin, there was a long list of to-do's today.
CN
But then it started raining, thank goodness.

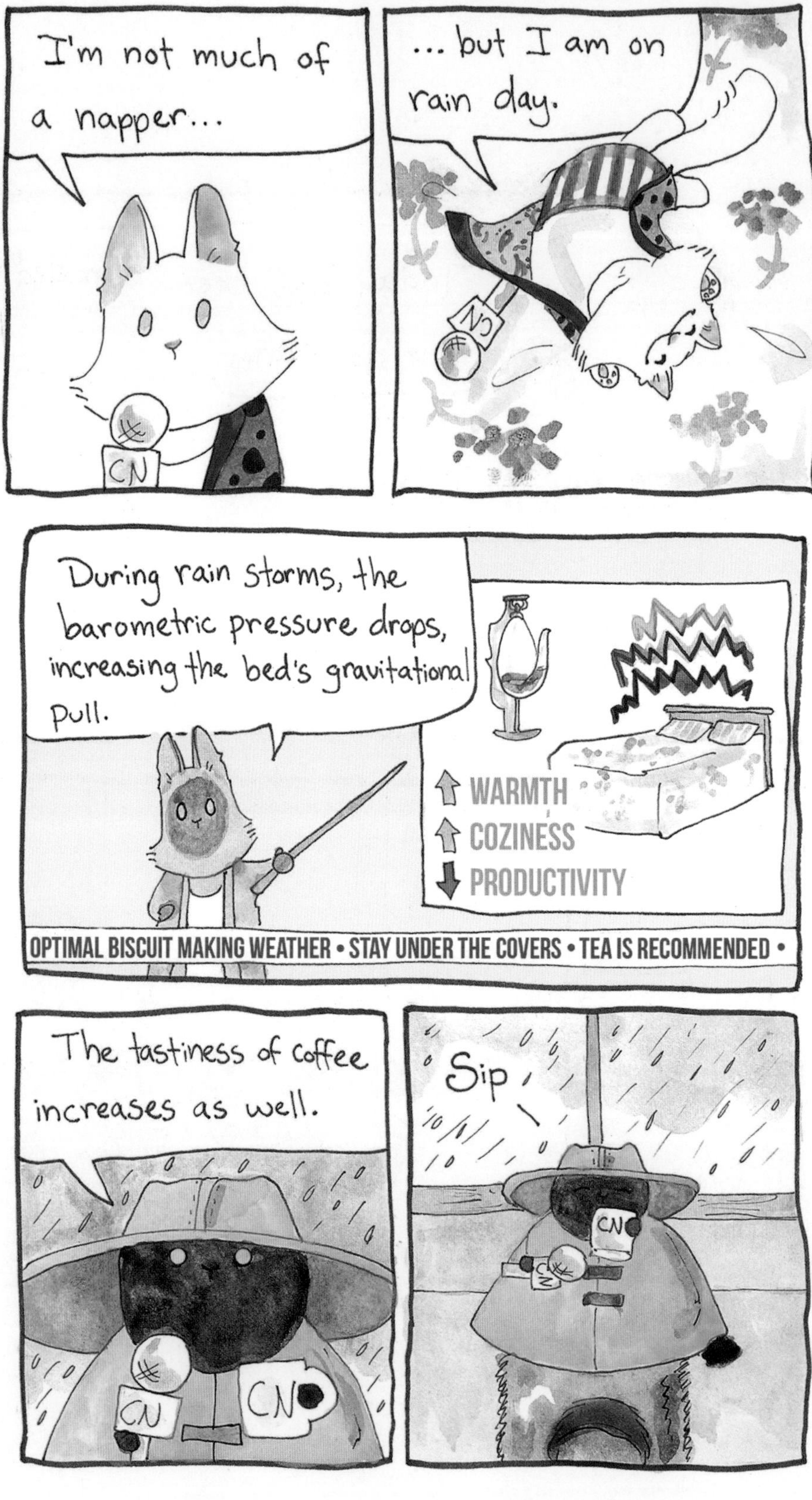

I'm not much of a napper...
... but I am on rain day.
CN
During rain storms, the barometric pressure drops, increasing the bed's gravitational pull.
WARMTH
COZINESS
PRODUCTIVITY
OPTIMAL BISCUIT MAKING WEATHER • STAY UNDER THE COVERS • TEA IS RECOMMENDED •
The tastiness of coffee increases as well.
CN
CN
Sip
CN

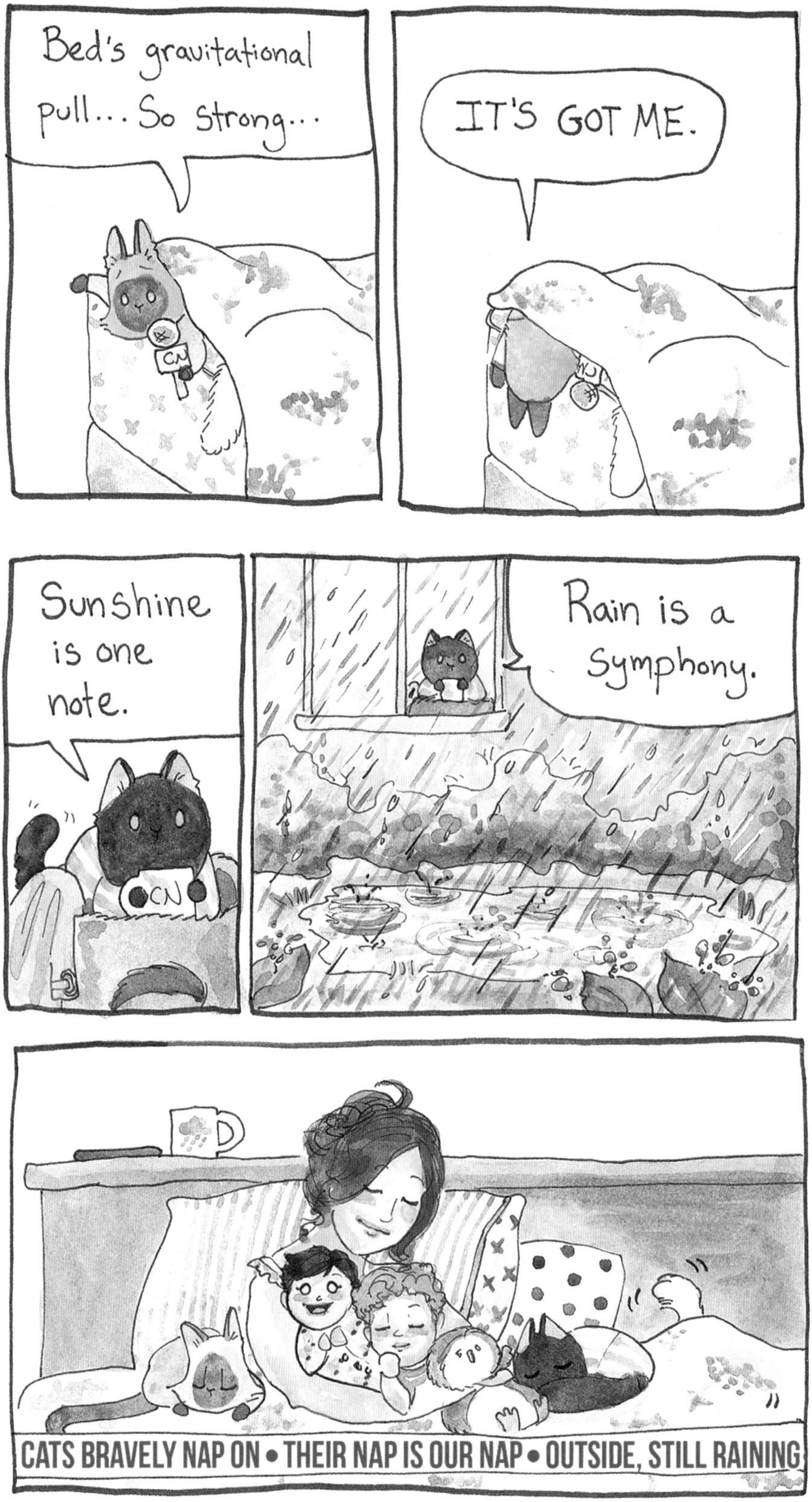
Bed's gravitational pull... So strong...
IT'S GOT ME.
CN
Sunshine is one note.
CN
Rain is a Symphony.
CATS BRAVELY NAP ON • THEIR NAP IS OUR NAP • OUTSIDE, STILL RAINING

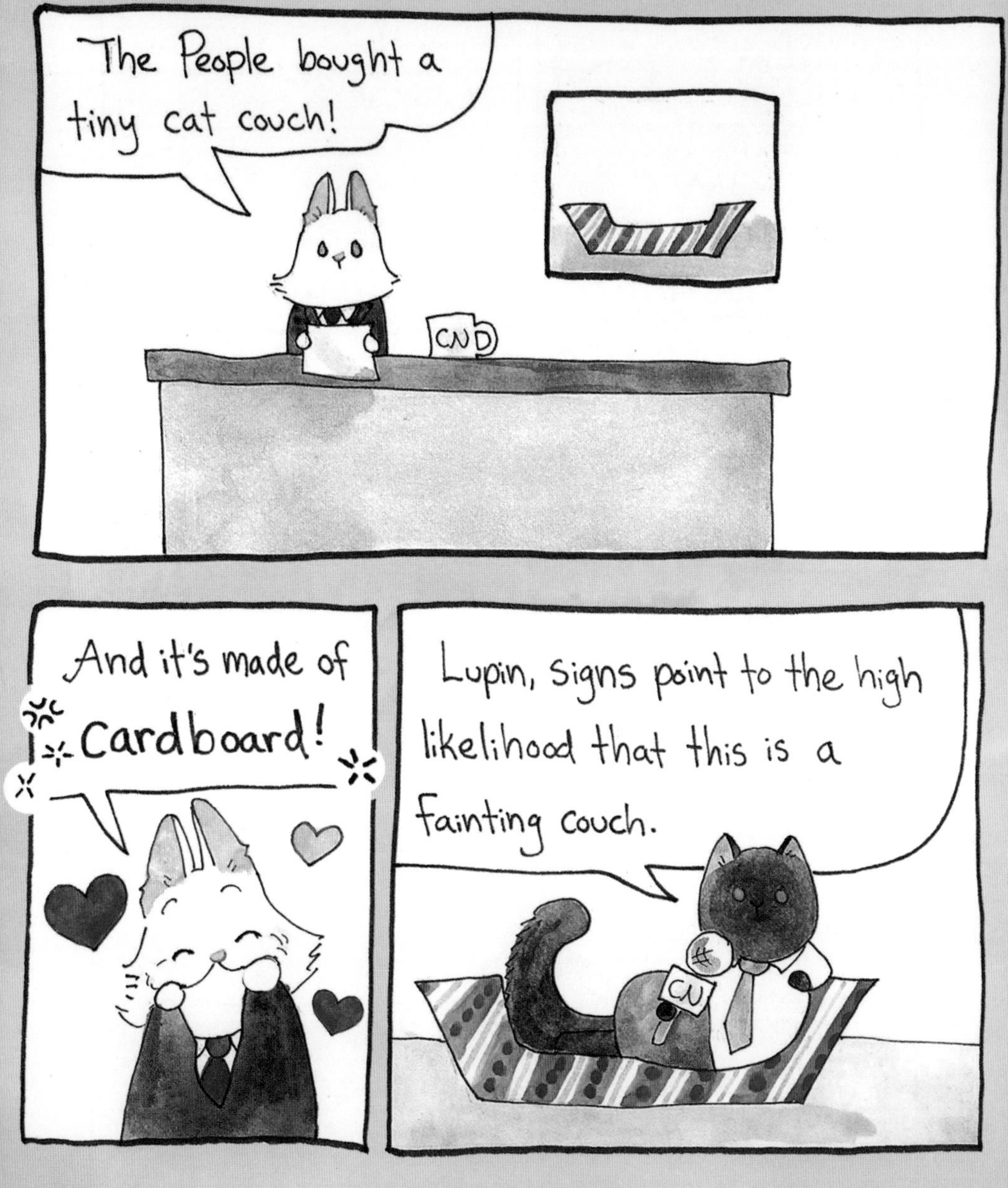
The People bought a tiny cat couch!
CND
And it's made of cardboard!
Lupin, signs point to the high likelihood that this is a fainting couch.
CN

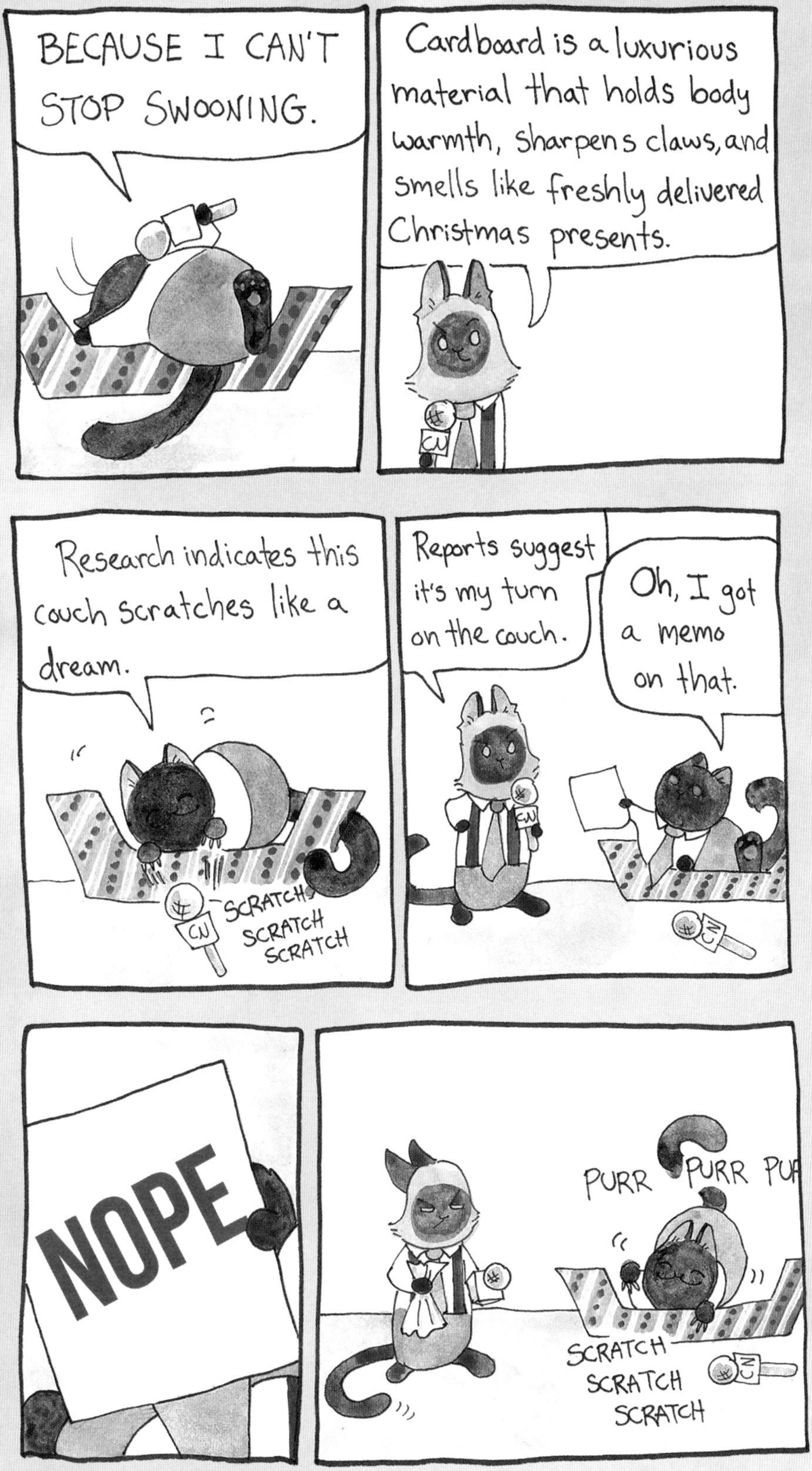

BECAUSE I CAN'T STOP SWOONING.
Cardboard is a luxurious material that holds body warmth, sharpens claws, and smells like freshly delivered Christmas presents.
CN
Research indicates this couch scratches like a dream.
SCRATCH SCRATCH SCRATCH
CN
Reports suggest it's my turn on the couch.
Oh, I got a memo on that.
CN
CN
NOPE
PURR PURR
SCRATCH SCRATCH SCRATCH

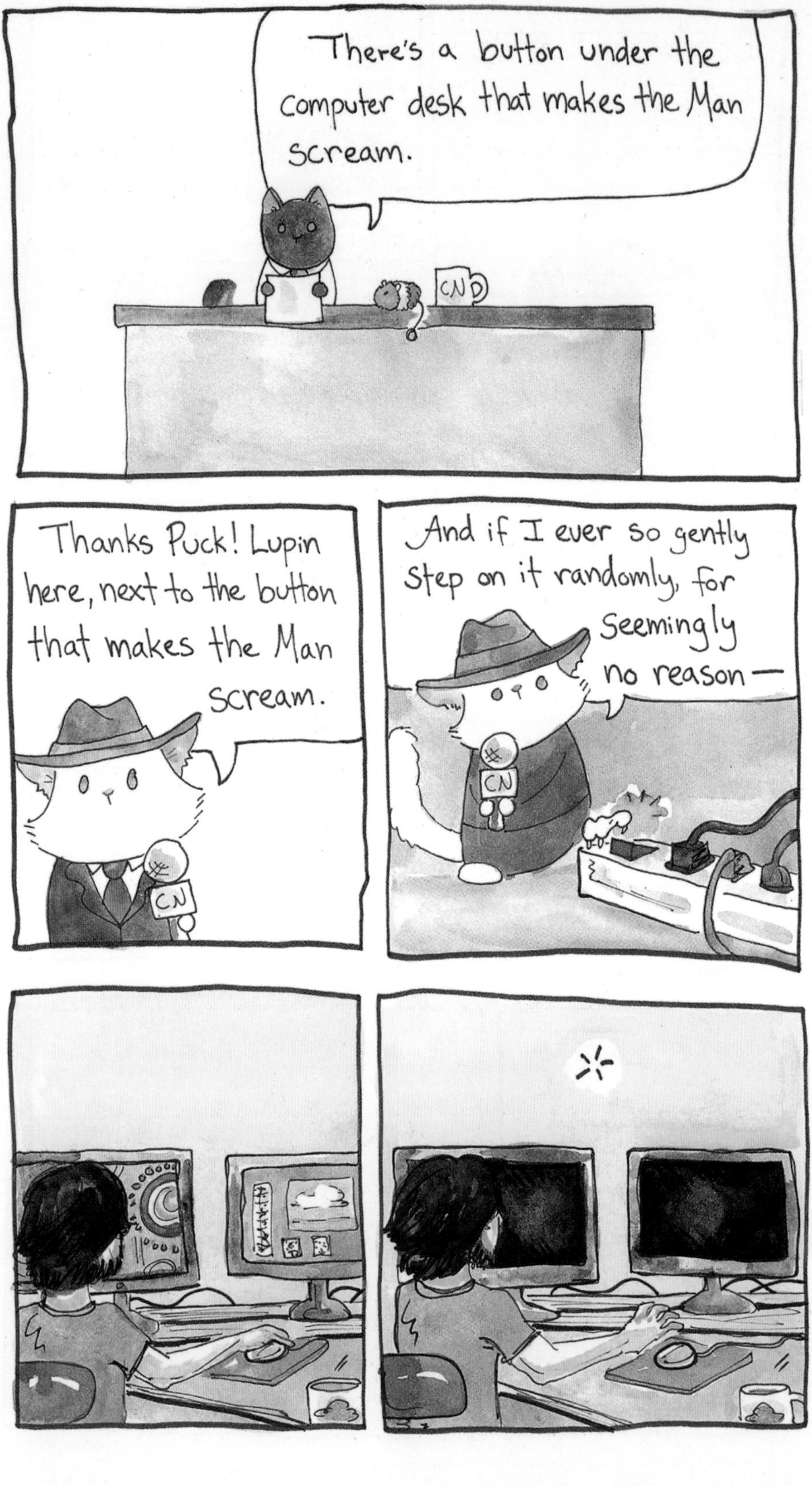
There's a button under the computer desk that makes the Man scream.
Thanks Puck! Lupin here, next to the button that makes the Man scream.
And if I ever so gently step on it randomly, for seemingly no reason—

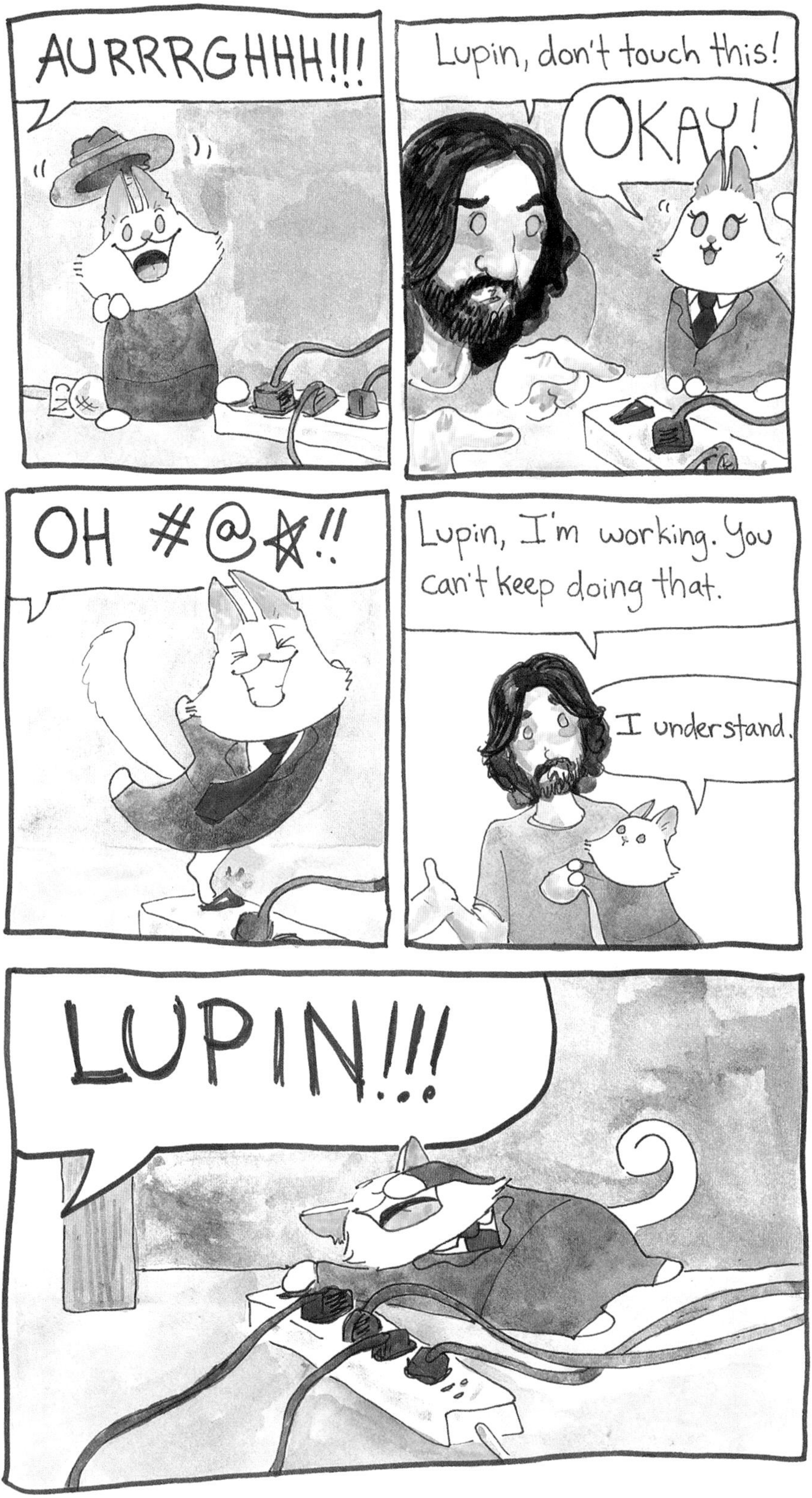
AURRRGHHH!!!
Lupin, don't touch this!
OKAY!
OH #@☆!!
Lupin, I'm working. You can't keep doing that.
I understand.
LUPIN!!!

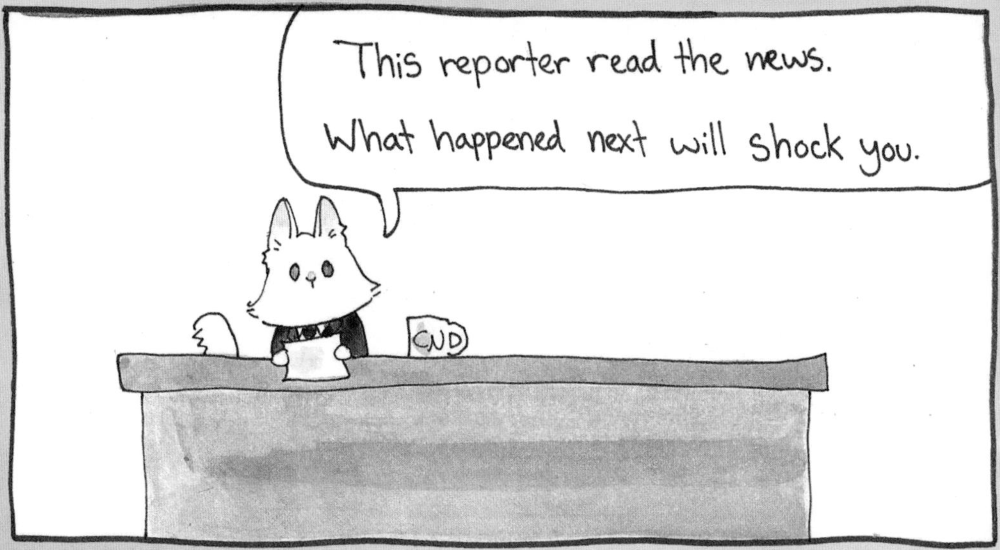
This reporter read the news.
What happened next will shock you.
CND

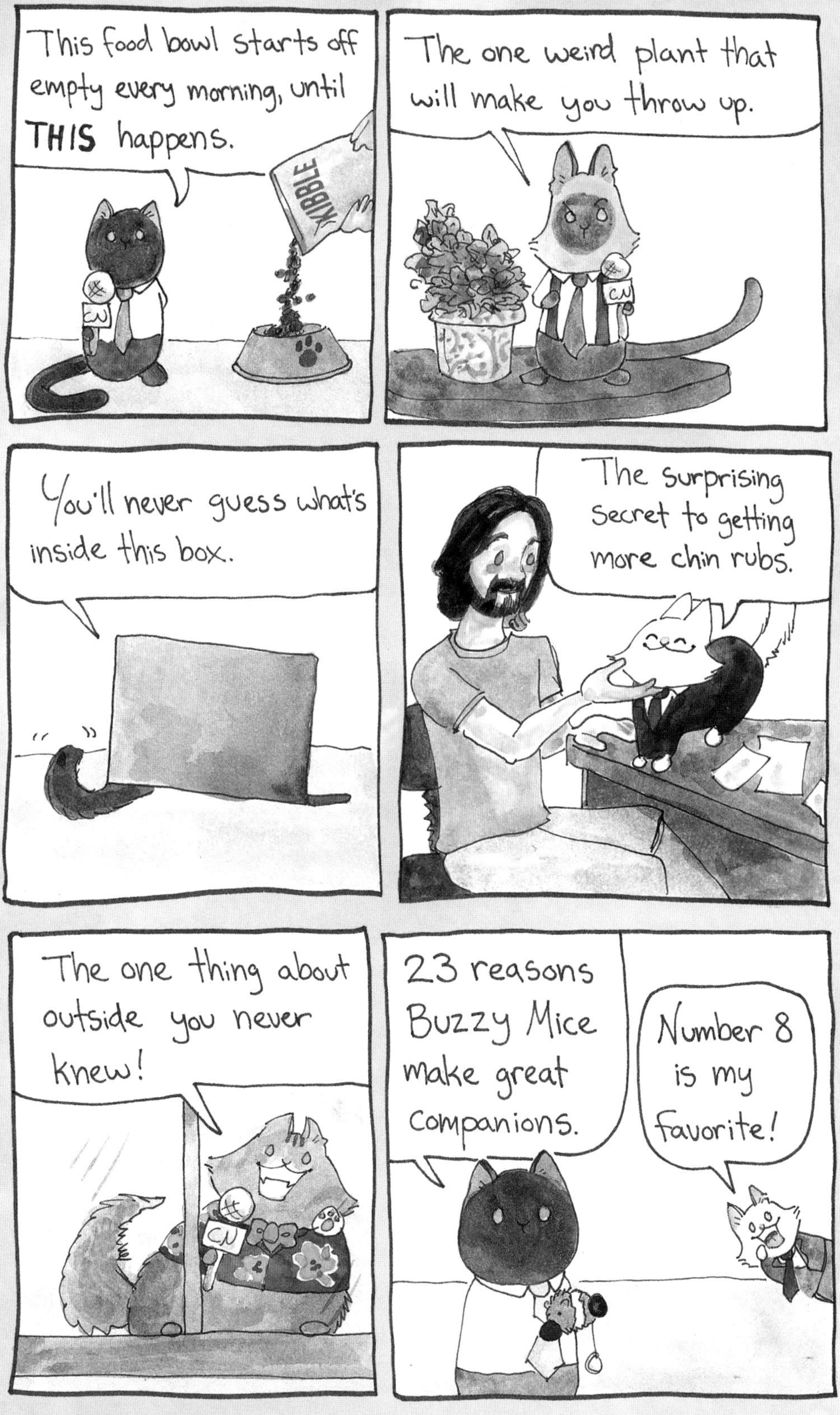
This food bowl starts off empty every morning, until THIS happens.
KIBBLE
CN
The one weird plant that will make you throw up.
CN
You'll never guess what's inside this box.
The surprising secret to getting more chin rubs.
The one thing about outside you never knew!
CN
23 reasons Buzzy Mice make great companions.
Number 8 is my favorite!

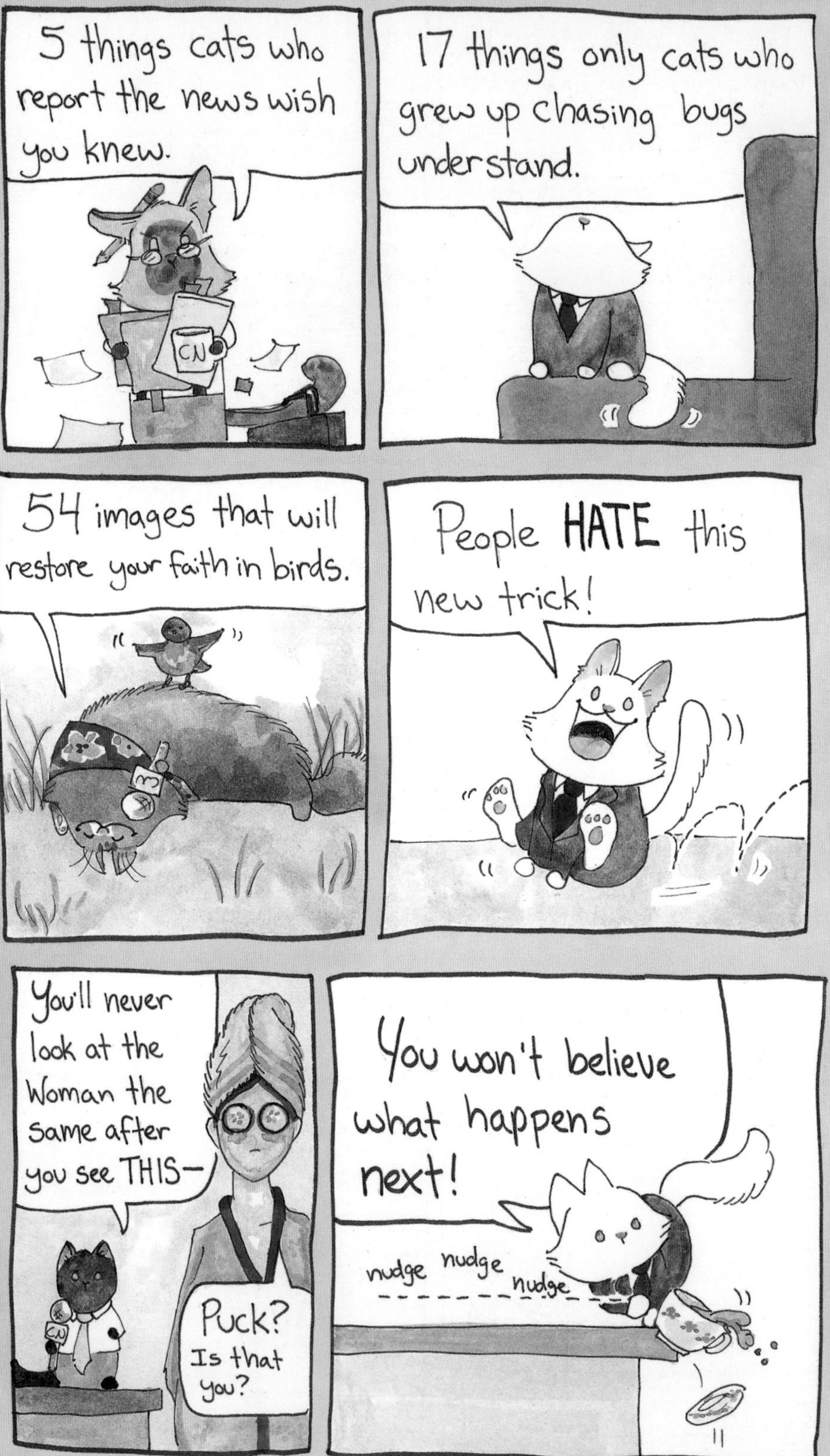
5 things cats who report the news wish you knew.
CN
17 things only cats who grew up chasing bugs understand.
54 images that will restore your faith in birds.
People HATE this new trick!
You'll never look at the Woman the same after you see THIS—
CN
Puck? Is that you?
You won't believe what happens next!
nudge nudge nudge

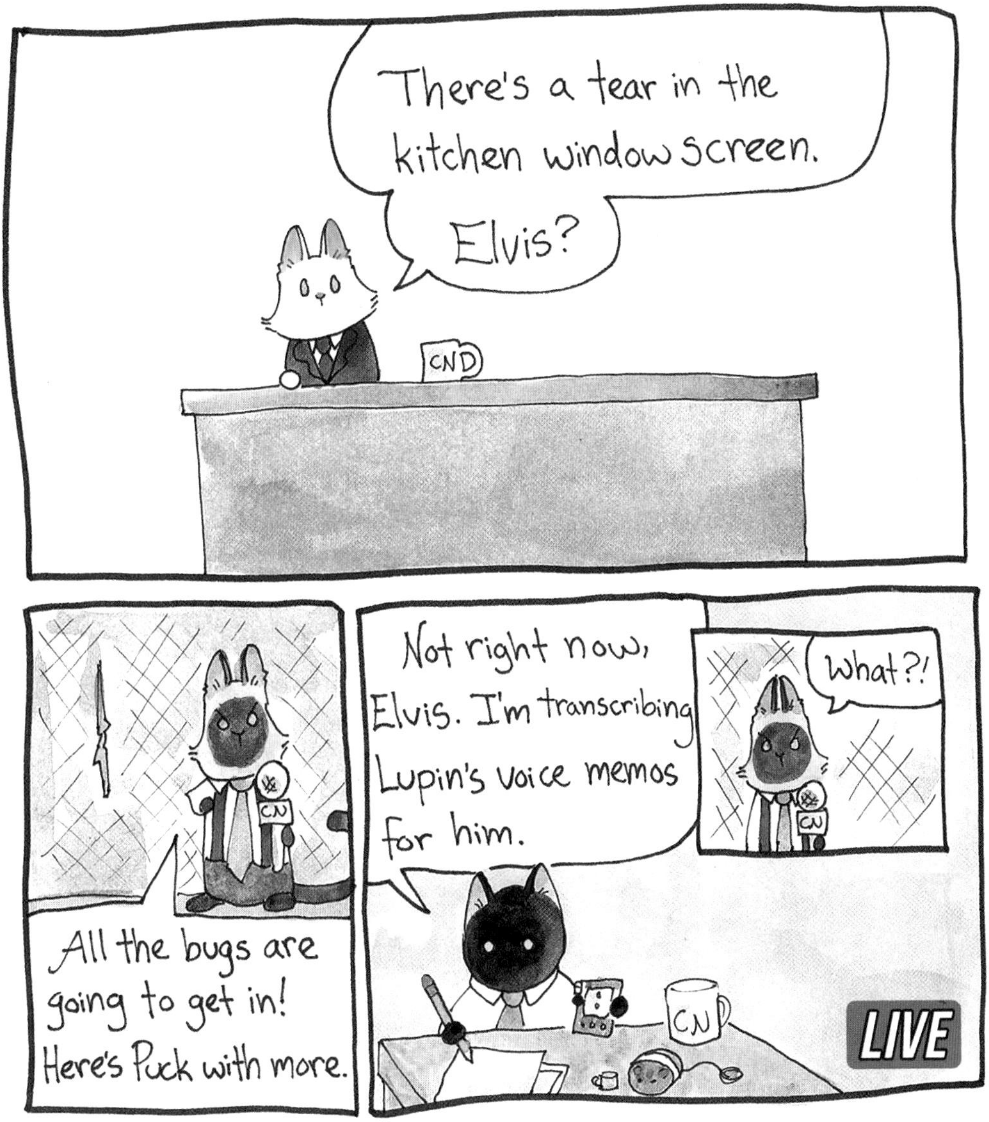
There's a tear in the kitchen window screen.
Elvis?
CND
CN
All the bugs are going to get in! Here's Puck with more.
Not right now, Elvis. I'm transcribing Lupin's voice memos for him.
What?!
CN
CN
LIVE

Lupin, why don't you just jot them down instead?

This is faster.

NO IT'S NOT, you're adding an extra step!

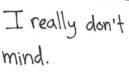

I really don't mind.

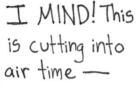

I MIND! This is cutting into air time—

Elvis, when inspiration strikes, I don't have time to look for a pen.

Just keep a legal pad and a pen nearby, that's what I do!

TALK ABOUT THE BUG

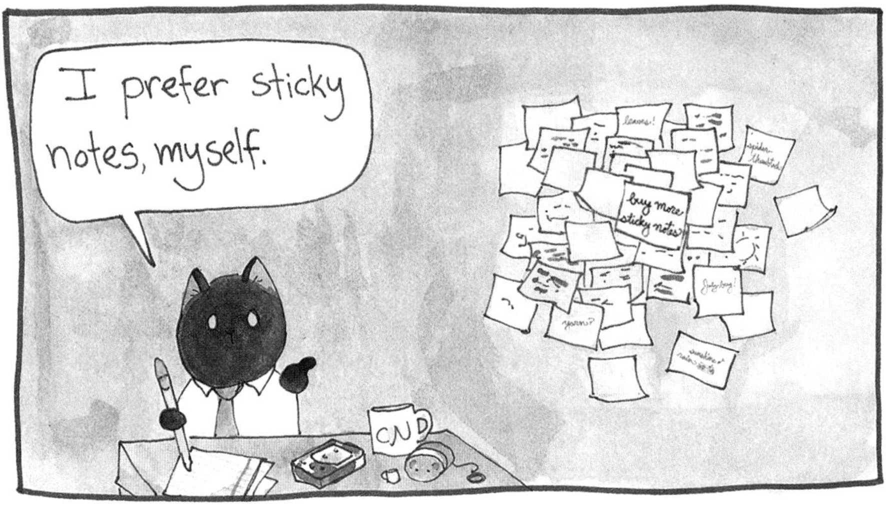
I prefer sticky notes, myself.
buy more sticky notes!

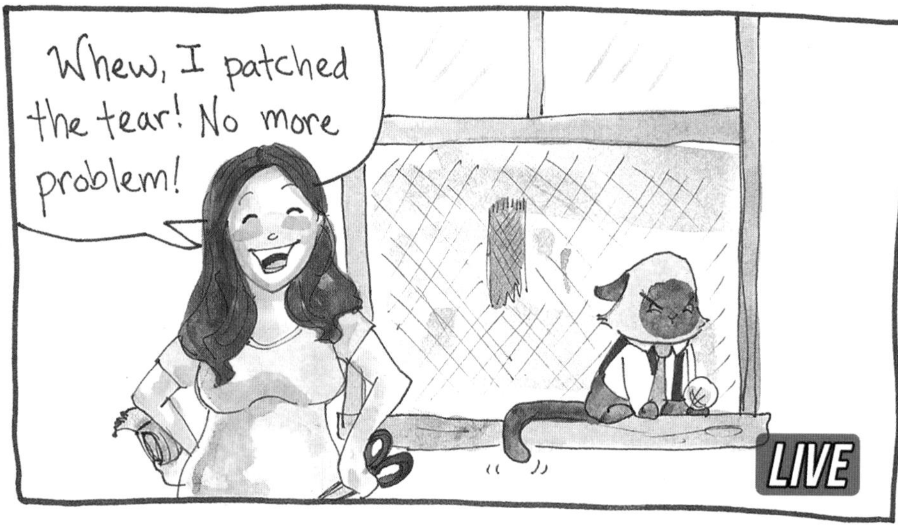
Whew, I patched the tear! No more problem!
LIVE

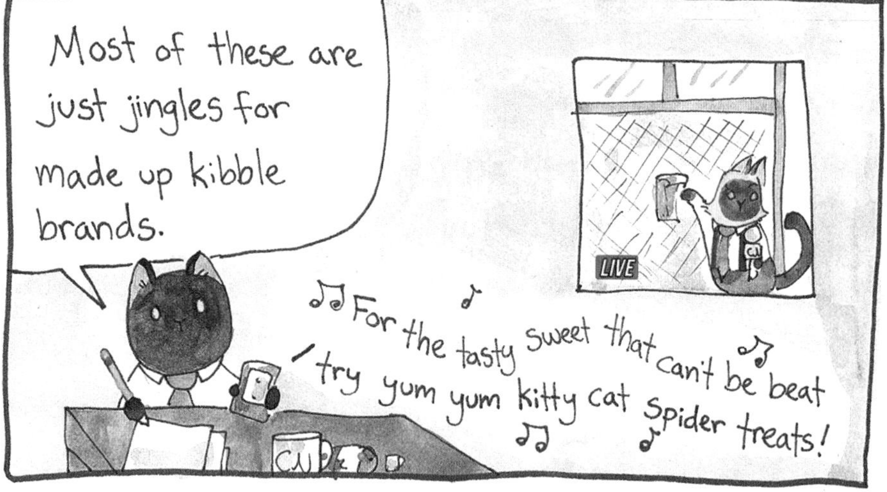
Most of these are just jingles for made up kibble brands.
LIVE
For the tasty sweet that can't be beat try yum yum kitty cat spider treats!

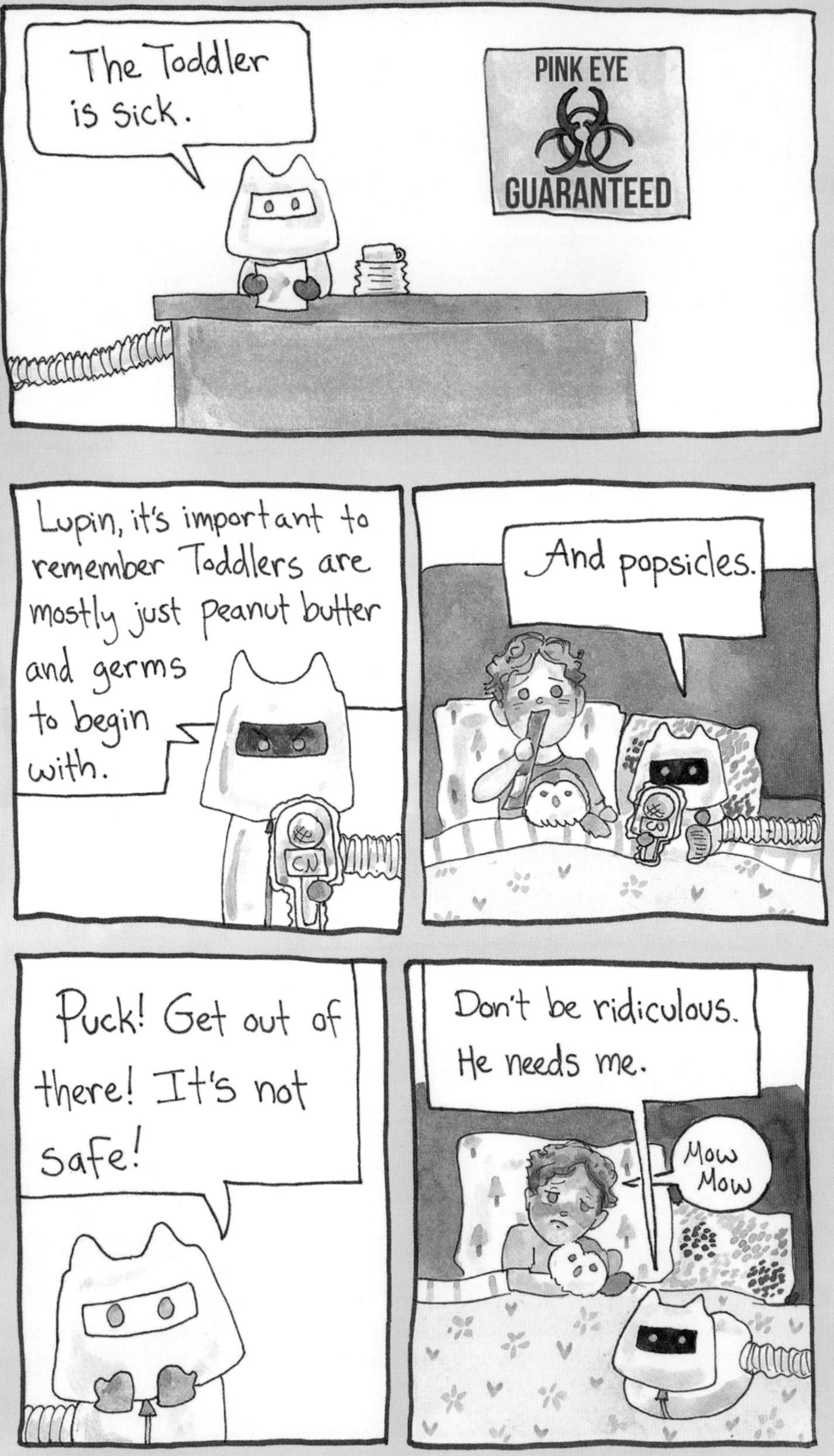

The Toddler is sick.
PINK EYE
GUARANTEED
Lupin, it's important to remember Toddlers are mostly just peanut butter and germs to begin with.
And popsicles.
Puck! Get out of there! It's not safe!
Don't be ridiculous. He needs me.
Mow Mow

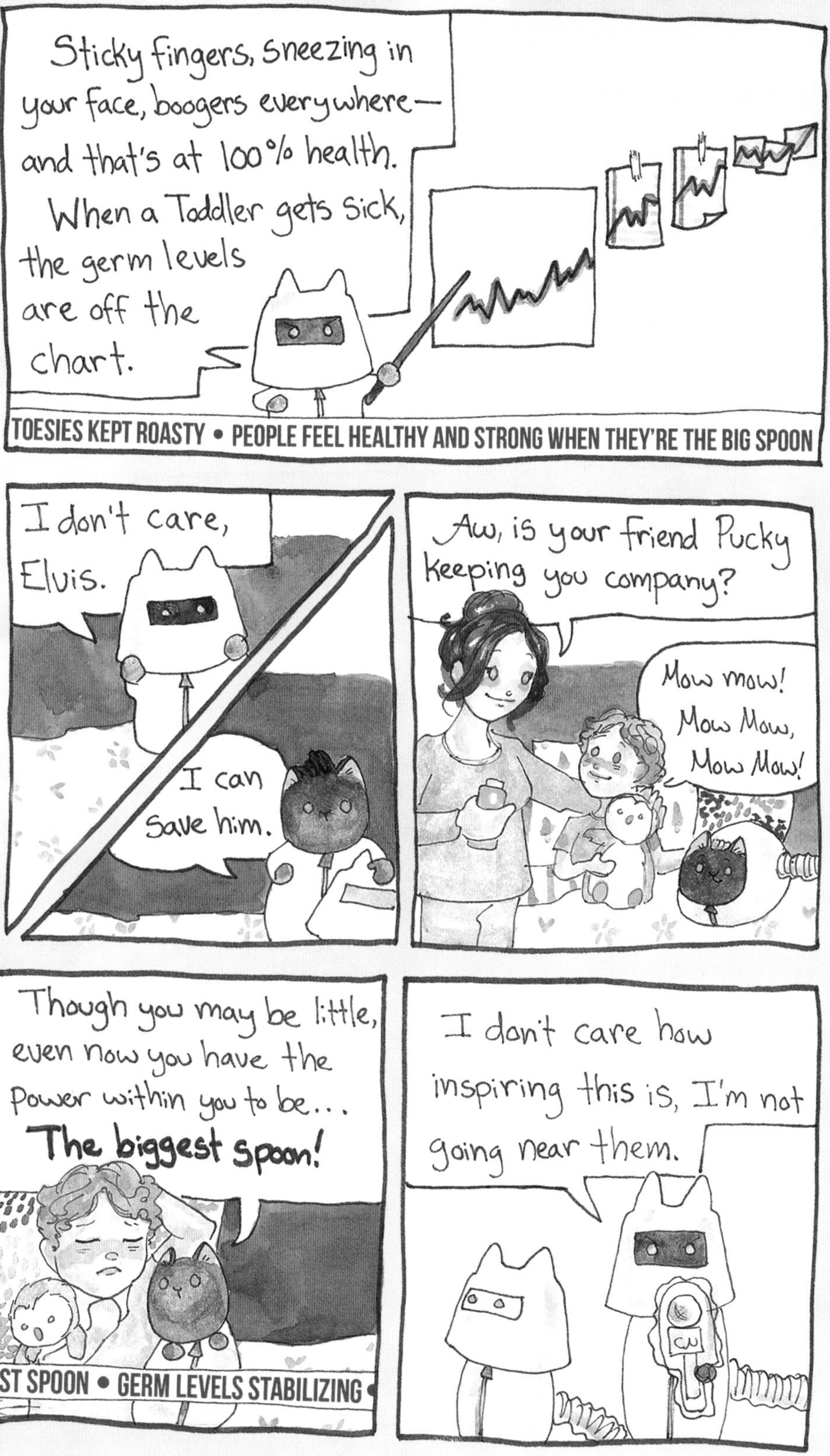

Sticky fingers, sneezing in your face, boogers everywhere—and that's at 100% health.
When a Toddler gets sick, the germ levels are off the chart.
TOESIES KEPT ROASTY • PEOPLE FEEL HEALTHY AND STRONG WHEN THEY'RE THE BIG SPOON
I don't care, Elvis.
I can save him.
Aw, is your friend Pucky keeping you company?
Mow mow! Mow Mow, Mow Mow!
Though you may be little, even now you have the power within you to be...
The biggest spoon!
EST SPOON • GERM LEVELS STABILIZING •
I don't care how inspiring this is, I'm not going near them.

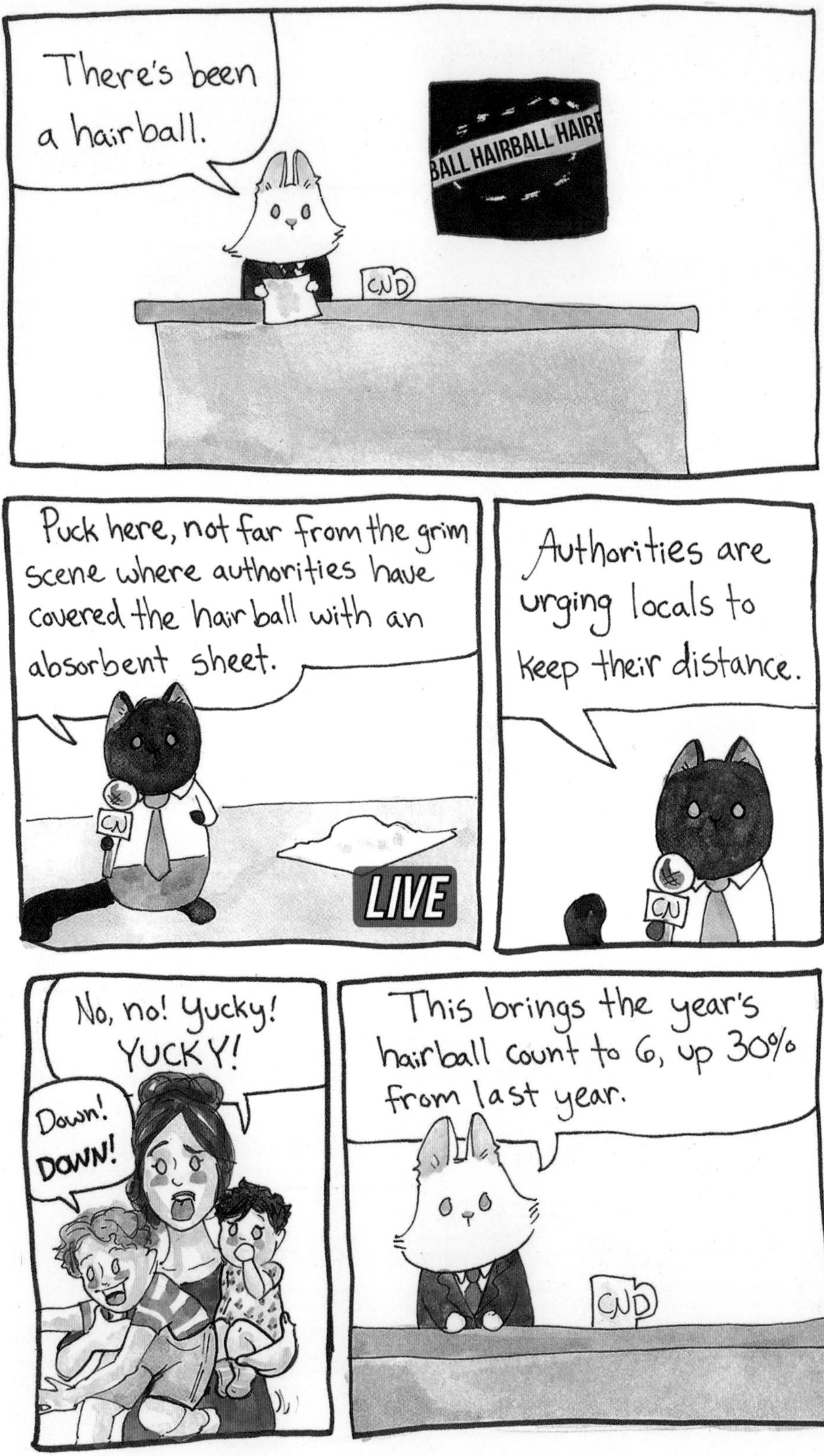
There's been a hairball.
BALL HAIRBALL HAIRB
CND
Puck here, not far from the grim scene where authorities have covered the hairball with an absorbent sheet.
CN
LIVE
Authorities are urging locals to keep their distance.
CN
No, no! Yucky! YUCKY!
Down! DOWN!
This brings the year's hairball count to 6, up 30% from last year.
CND

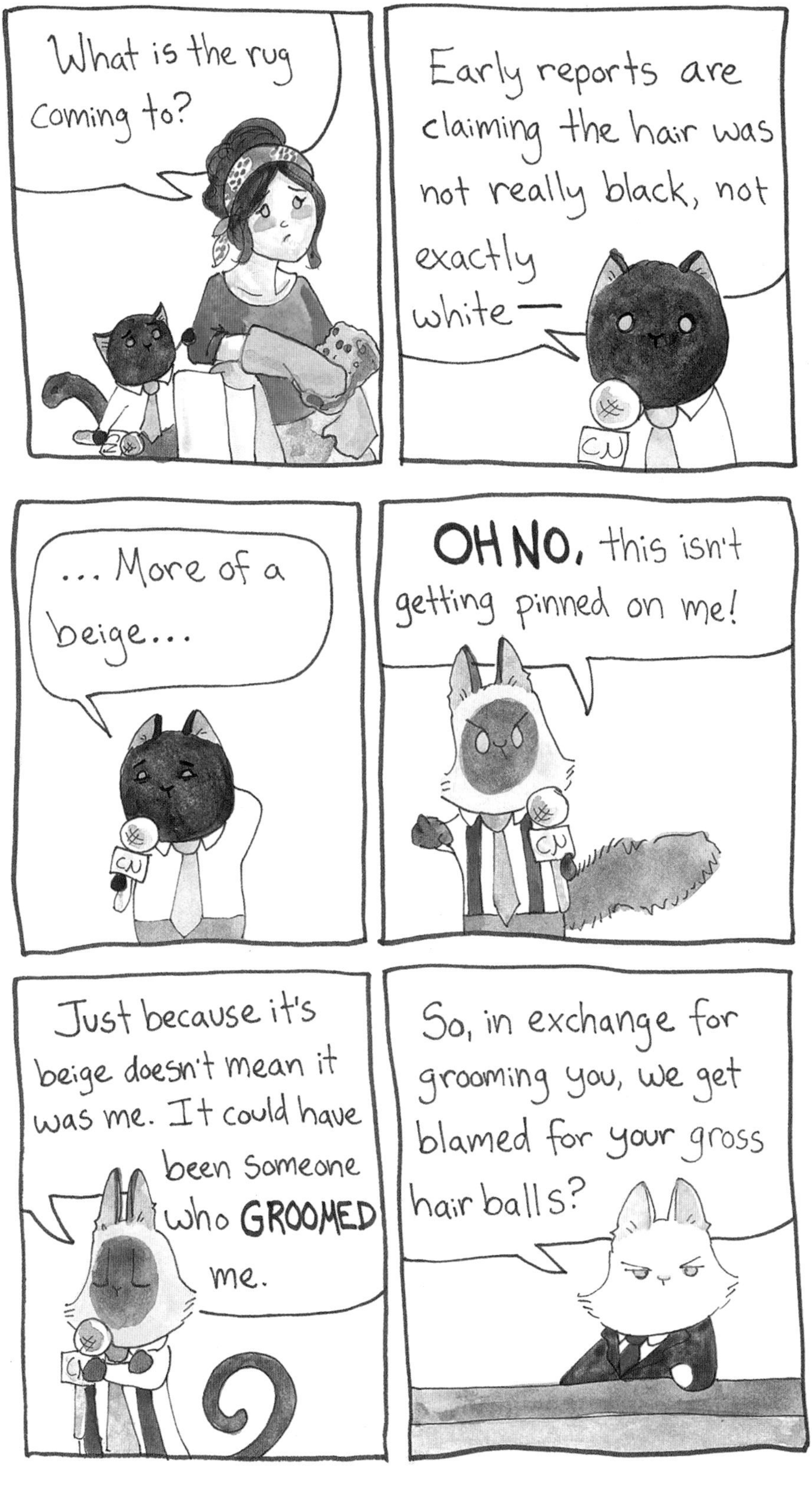
What is the rug coming to?
Early reports are claiming the hair was not really black, not exactly white—
... More of a beige...
OH NO, this isn't getting pinned on me!
Just because it's beige doesn't mean it was me. It could have been someone who GROOMED me.
So, in exchange for grooming you, we get blamed for your gross hair balls?

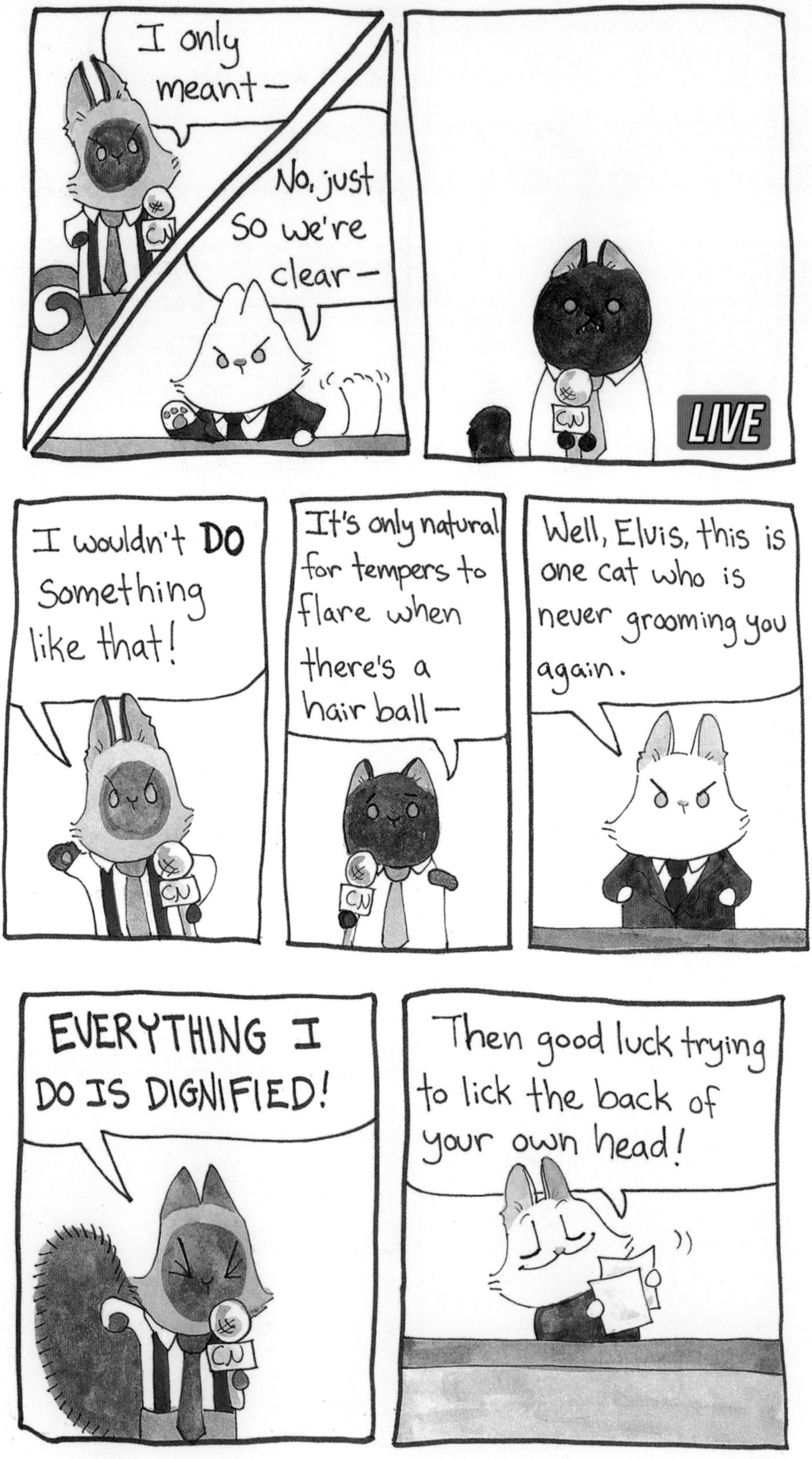
I only meant—
No, just so we're clear—
LIVE
I wouldn't DO something like that!
It's only natural for tempers to flare when there's a hair ball—
Well, Elvis, this is one cat who is never grooming you again.
EVERYTHING I DO IS DIGNIFIED!
Then good luck trying to lick the back of your own head!

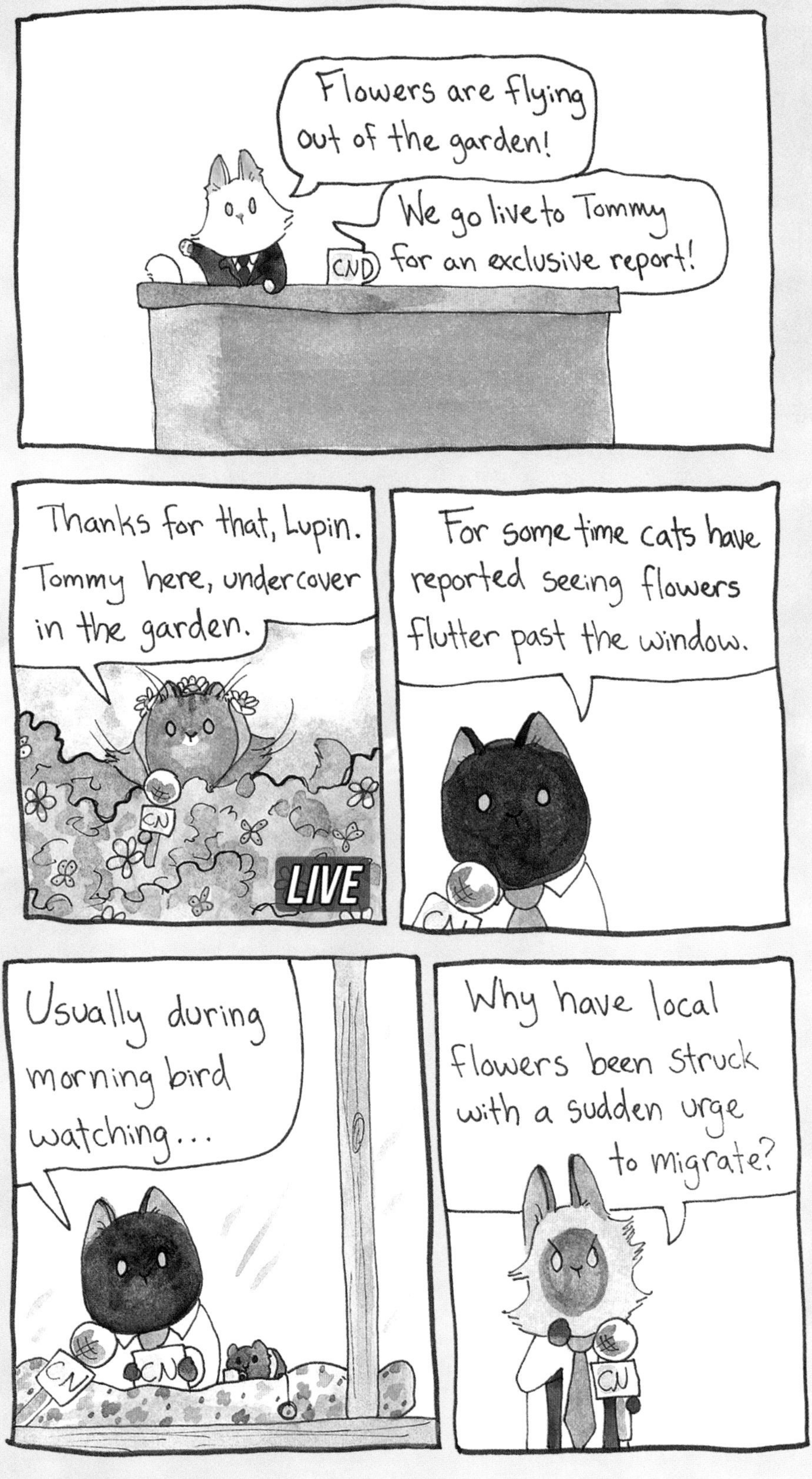
Flowers are flying out of the garden!
We go live to Tommy for an exclusive report!
CND
Thanks for that, Lupin. Tommy here, undercover in the garden.
CN
LIVE
For some time cats have reported seeing flowers flutter past the window.
Usually during morning bird watching...
CN
CN
Why have local flowers been struck with a sudden urge to migrate?
CN

Looking a little rough there, Elvis.

Can we please stick to the matter at paw?

Just sayin'.

According to reports, flowers suddenly take to the sky! One local shares their story.

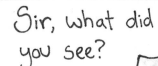

Sir, what did you see?

LIVE

!

It's happening!

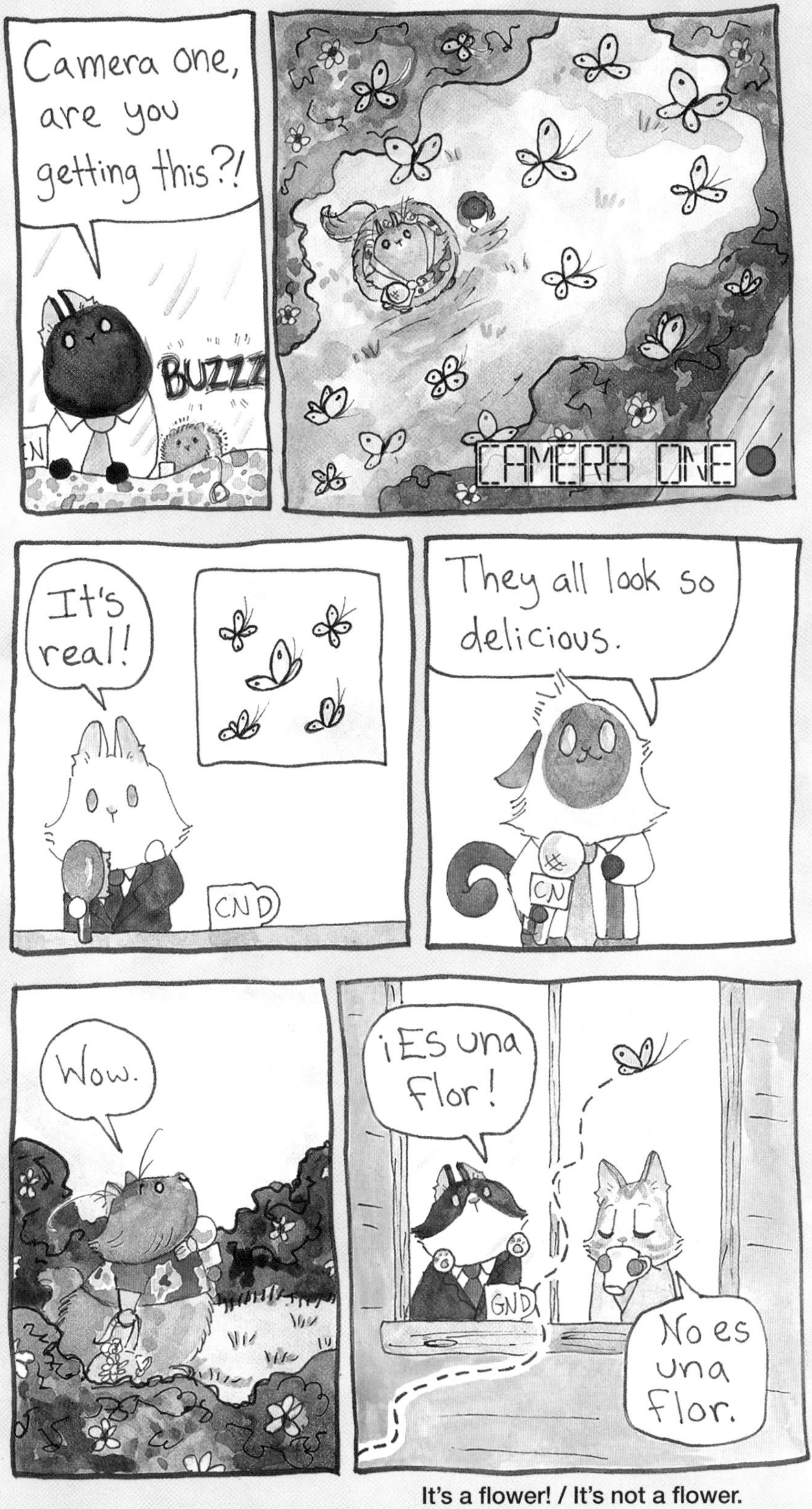
Camera one, are you getting this?!
BUZZZ
CAMERA ONE
It's real!
CND
They all look so delicious.
CN
Wow.
¡Es una flor!
GND
No es una flor.

It's a flower! / It's not a flower.

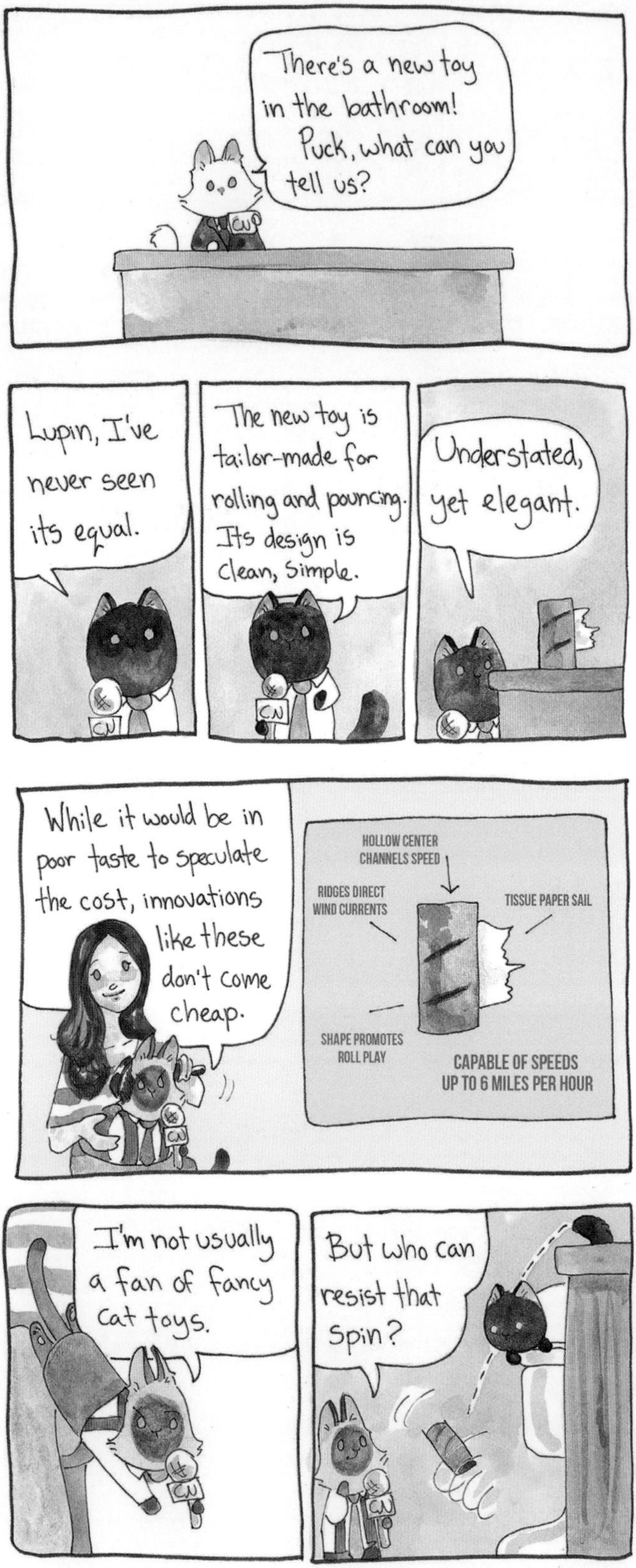
There's a new toy in the bathroom! Puck, what can you tell us?
CN
Lupin, I've never seen its equal.
CN
The new toy is tailor-made for rolling and pouncing. Its design is clean, simple.
CN
Understated, yet elegant.
While it would be in poor taste to speculate the cost, innovations like these don't come cheap.
CN
HOLLOW CENTER CHANNELS SPEED
RIDGES DIRECT WIND CURRENTS
TISSUE PAPER SAIL
SHAPE PROMOTES ROLL PLAY
CAPABLE OF SPEEDS UP TO 6 MILES PER HOUR
I'm not usually a fan of fancy cat toys.
CN
But who can resist that spin?
CN

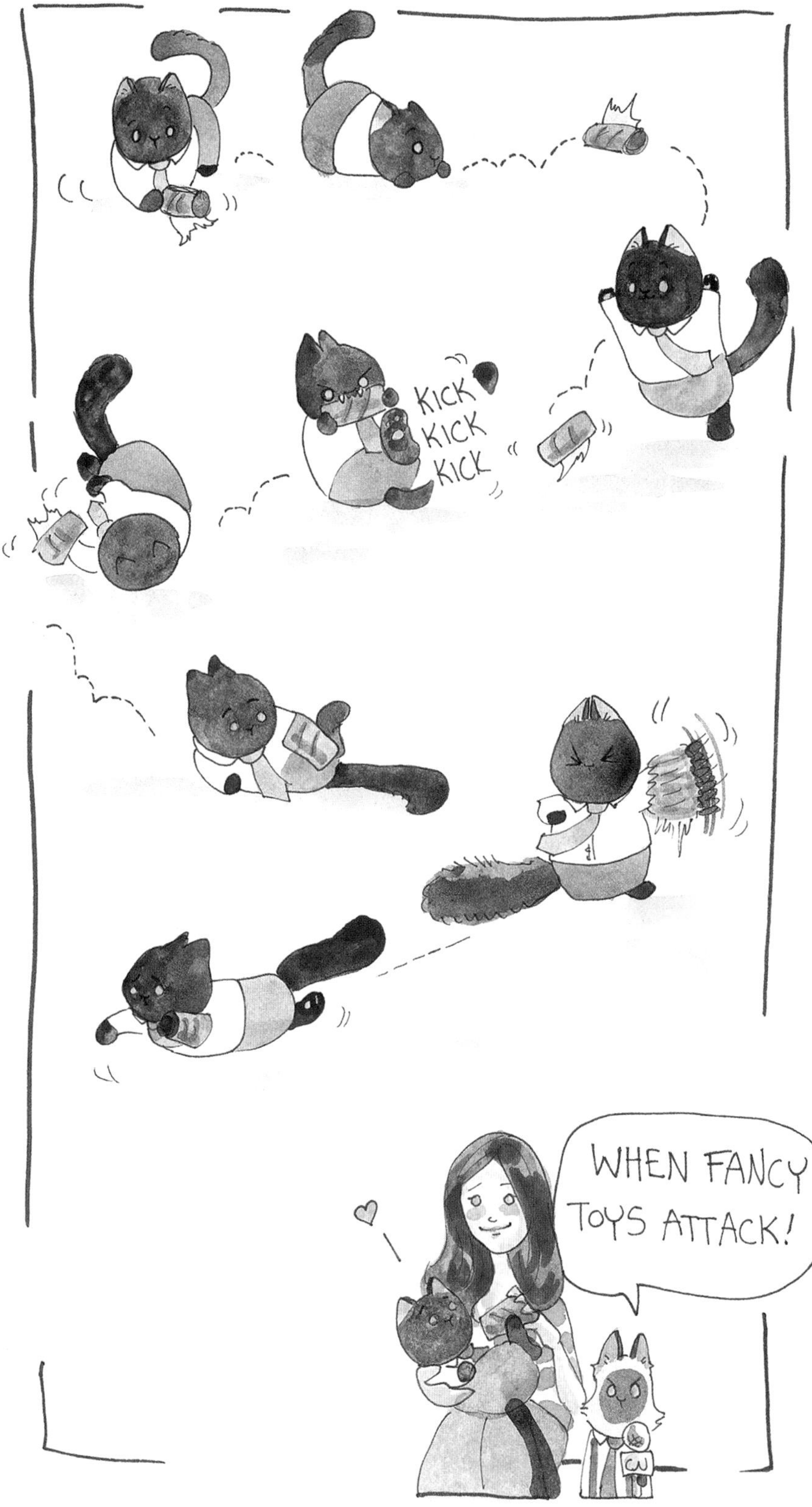
KICK
KICK
KICK
WHEN FANCY TOYS ATTACK!
CW

MORE TO EXPLORE!

Featuring cool activities and fun facts!

BREAKING CAT NEWS

MORE TO EXPLORE

Do you have your brush? Let's paint!

✦ • Georgia Dunn's
Tips to begin cartooning

1. Write, write, write! (Draw, draw, draw!)

Write stories for fun, for projects, for yourself, for your friends. Stories, poems, comics, jokes, observations, thoughts, lists, journals—everything! You have all these stories inside you, the more you tap into them, the more they will tumble out! (And the same goes for drawing!)

2. Read as many comics as you can!

Soak them up and study your favorites. Examine how the jokes and surprises are set up from panel to panel. Take in what works and question what doesn't. ("How could I make this panel funnier?")

3. Make comics! A lot of comics!

'Breaking Cat News' was probably the 40 or 50th comic I started in my life (starting when I was a kid). It was my 3rd web-comic. Make comics, share them, learn from feedback, ignore negativity, appreciate helpful advice.... And then make more comics! Nothing teaches like doing!

4. Trust in yourself, and in your stories.

You are the only person who can ever tell the stories you have inside you. There are people out there who need your stories. They will mean so much to them.

You can do this!

Georgia Dunn 2018

HOW TO DRAW THE GOOD BOYS OF BCN

Start with a pencil with a sharp point and a clean eraser. Work very lightly (I actually darkened these lines so you could see them better). Take your time and practice!

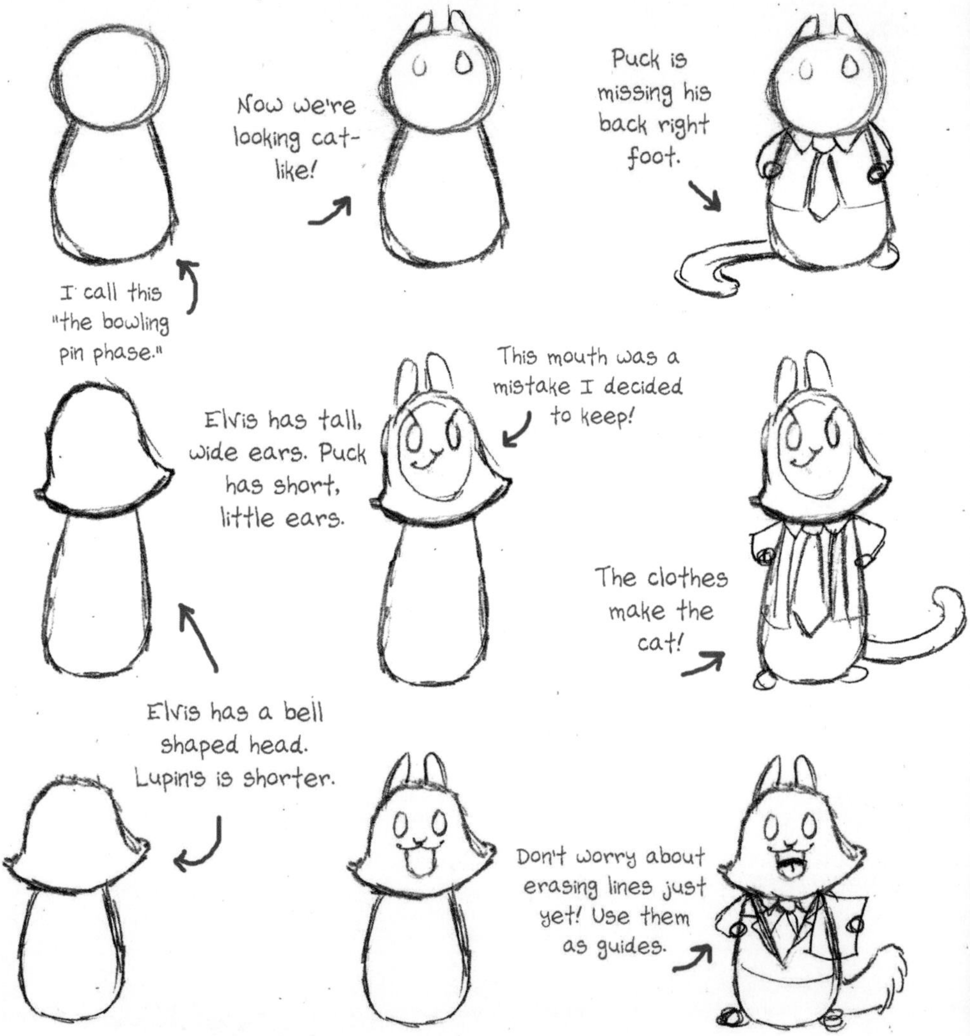

Now we're looking cat-like!
Puck is missing his back right foot.
I call this "the bowling pin phase."
Elvis has tall, wide ears. Puck has short, little ears.
This mouth was a mistake I decided to keep!
The clothes make the cat!
Elvis has a bell shaped head. Lupin's is shorter.
Don't worry about erasing lines just yet! Use them as guides.

You will make mistakes, and that's ok! Mistakes are a terrific way to learn-as-you-go. Some of the best face expressions I've drawn started off as an eyebrow or lip I got wrong and thought, "wow, Elvis looks so delighted now—"

You're ready to ink! Trace the lines you want to keep, leave the rest to erase later. If you're going to paint your drawing, be sure to use a waterproof pen or marker! You can always use colored pencils or crayons to add some color to your work, too.

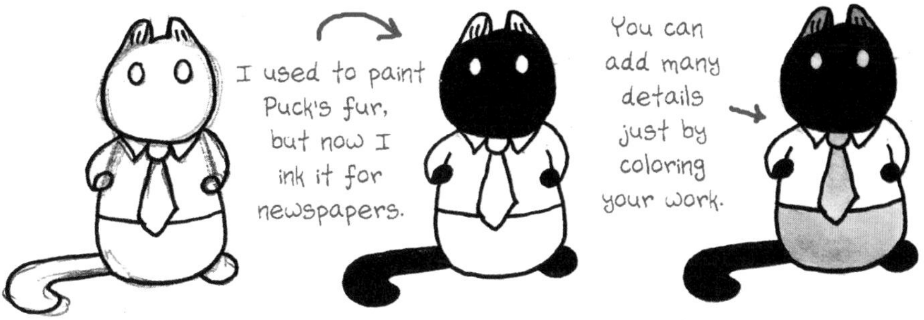

I used to paint Puck's fur, but now I ink it for newspapers.
You can add many details just by coloring your work.

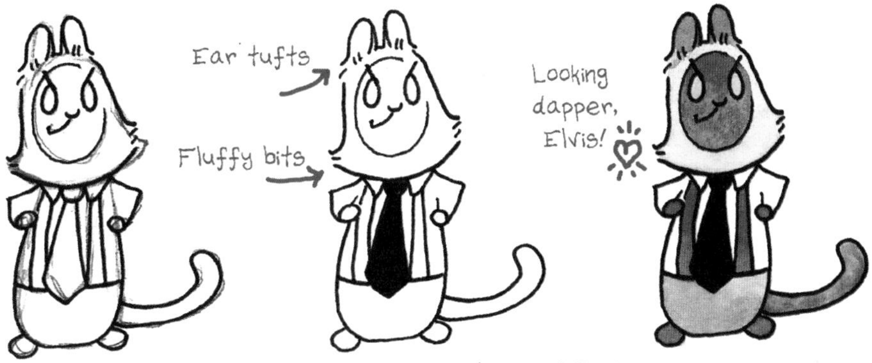

Ear tufts
Fluffy bits
Looking dapper, Elvis!

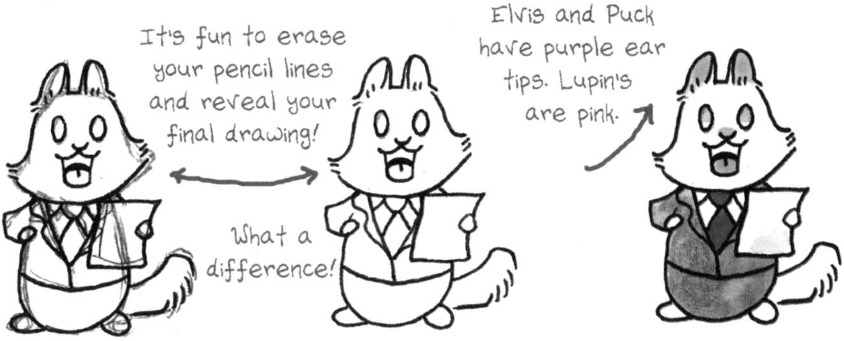

It's fun to erase your pencil lines and reveal your final drawing!
What a difference!
Elvis and Puck have purple ear tips. Lupin's are pink.

I like to add a lot of details during this stage, like Elvis's and Lupin's little "fluffy bits" on their cheeks, and the tufts of fur in their ears, too. It's fun to add fabric patterns or fur markings with paint!

DRAWING FACE EXPRESSIONS

Drawing face expressions is a lot of fun and comes with practice. Watch your most animated loved ones, and observe their features when they speak or react. Grab a mirror and make silly faces of your own!

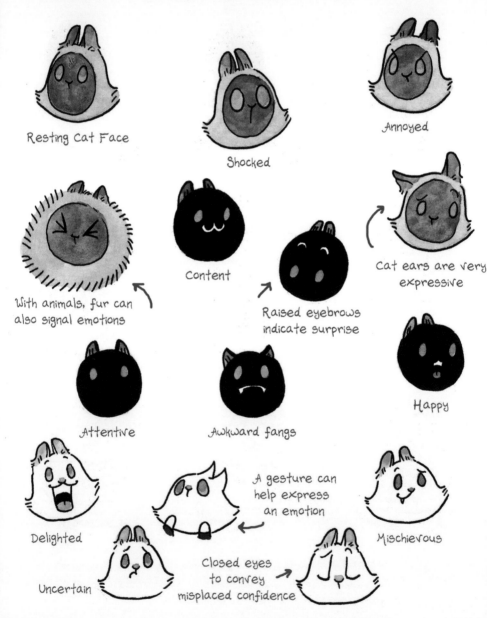

Resting Cat Face

Shocked

Annoyed

With animals, fur can also signal emotions

Content

Raised eyebrows indicate surprise

Cat ears are very expressive

Attentive

Awkward fangs

Happy

Delighted

A gesture can help express an emotion

Mischievous

Uncertain

Closed eyes to convey misplaced confidence

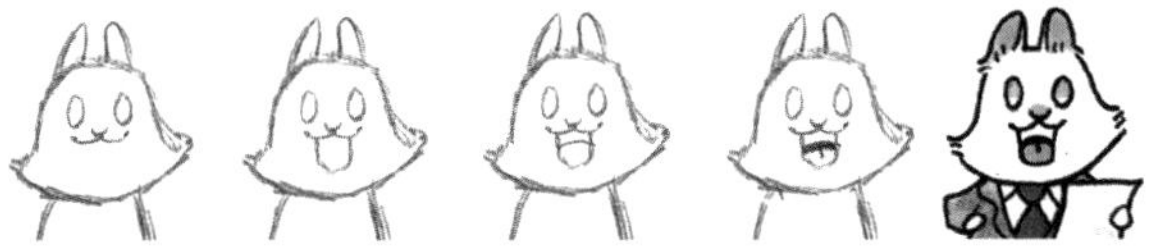

Take it one line at a time! ♡

EYES

The eyes are a window into our feelings, and eyebrows set the tone. Draw those two little dashes every way that comes to mind, and see what expressions pop out at you!

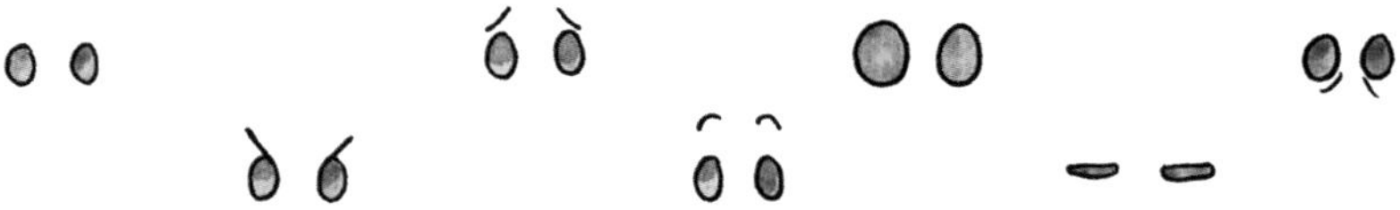

Even closed eyes are expressive. Are they happy, relaxed, purring eyes? Sleeping eyes? Frustrated and shut tight? Knowingly resting?

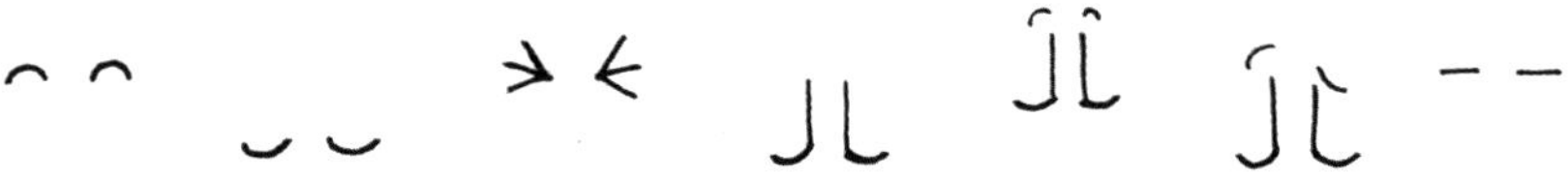

NOSE AND MOUTH

In cats, the nose and mouth work together. Think of the nose as an anchor. When it comes to mouths, every little line tells a story. Even just a short squiggle to the side can change "confused" to "perplexed."

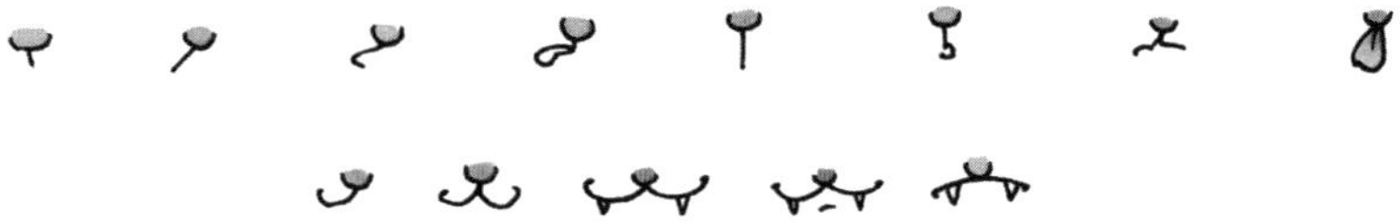

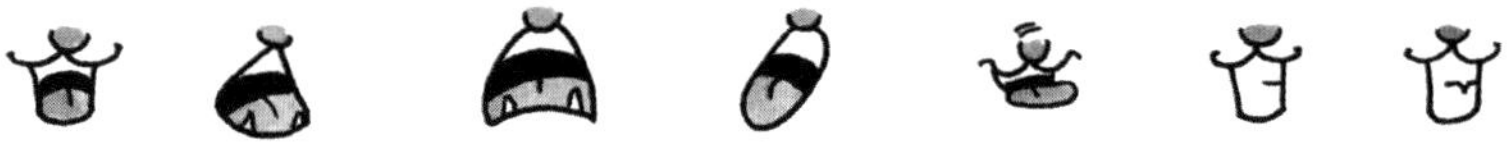

Smile Shout Gasp Yawn Snerk Proud Confident

MIX & MATCH

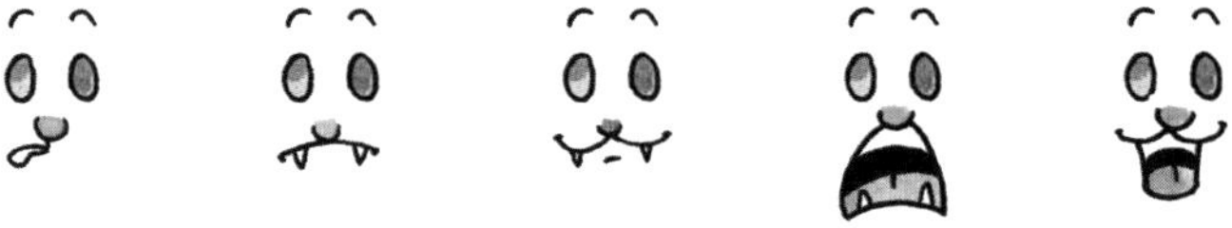

The same eyes can look very different, depending on which mouth you pair them with!

Don't worry about mistakes! Just gently erase, correct, and move on!

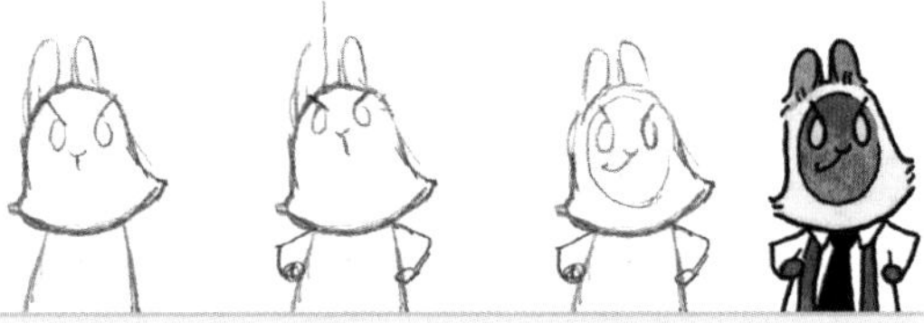

DRAWING YOUR PET AS A REPORTER

Would your pet be a hard-hitting, cynical journalist, a sensitive interviewer, a pet of adventure, or...?

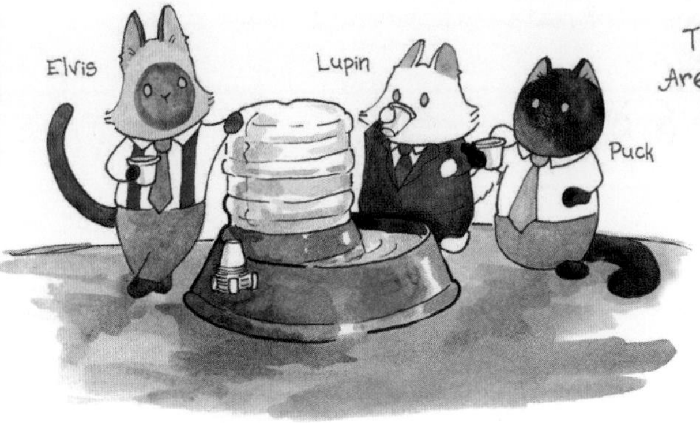

Elvis
Lupin
Puck

Take a good look at your pet. Are they tall and lean like Elvis? Short and round like Puck?

Would your pet have a big, wide smile like Tommy? Or a more serious expression, like Tabitha?

Every cat has their own unique look. Some cats are fluffy, some are sleek. Even two tabbies will have their own distinct markings, if you look closely.

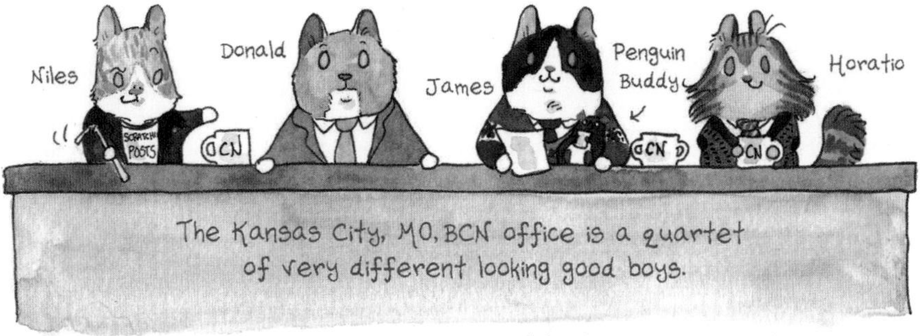

Niles
Donald
James
Penguin Buddy
Horatio
SCRATCHING POSTS
CN
The Kansas City, MO, BCN office is a quartet of very different looking good boys.

What is your pet's personality? Simple and casual? Fancy? Creative? Think about what your pet might want to wear when you pick out their clothes.

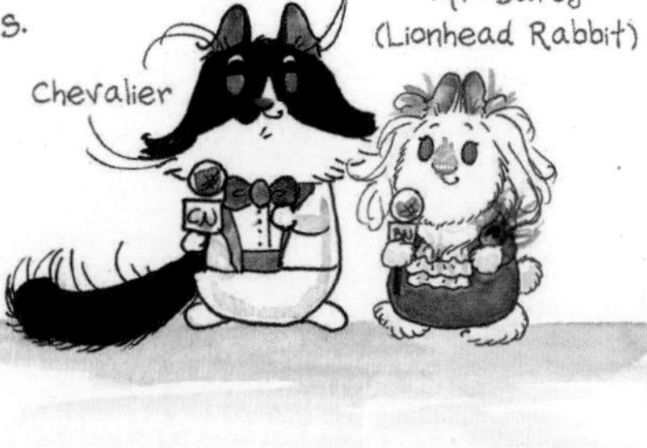

Chevalier
Mr. Darcy (Lionhead Rabbit)

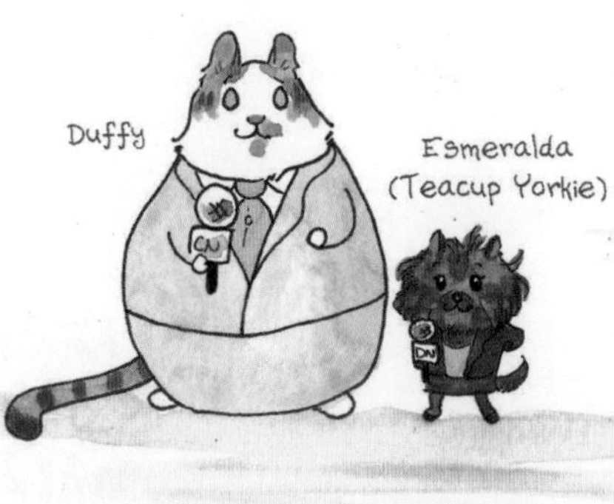

Duffy
Esmeralda (Teacup Yorkie)

Would your pet have a co-anchor?

OTHER NEWS AFFILIATES

Breaking pet news! Whatever pet you have, there's a broadcast for their stories! (And yours!)

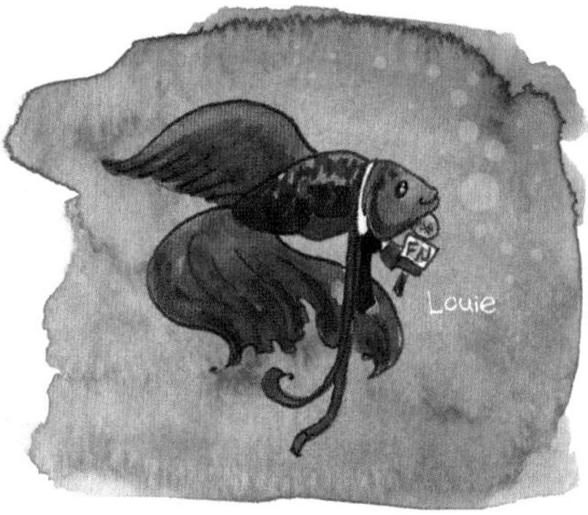
Louie

FISH NEWS

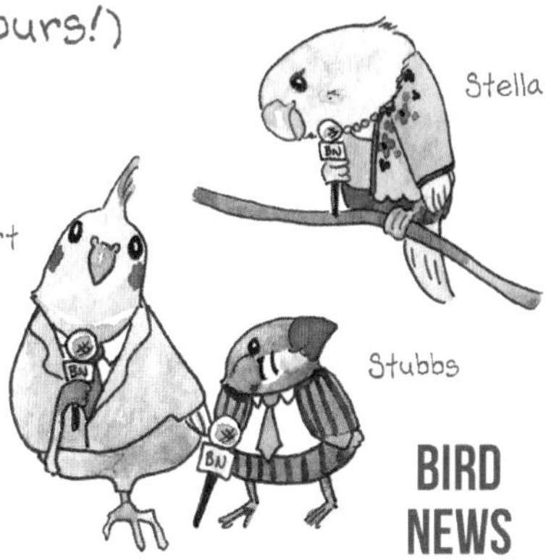
Stella
Stuart
Stubbs

BIRD NEWS

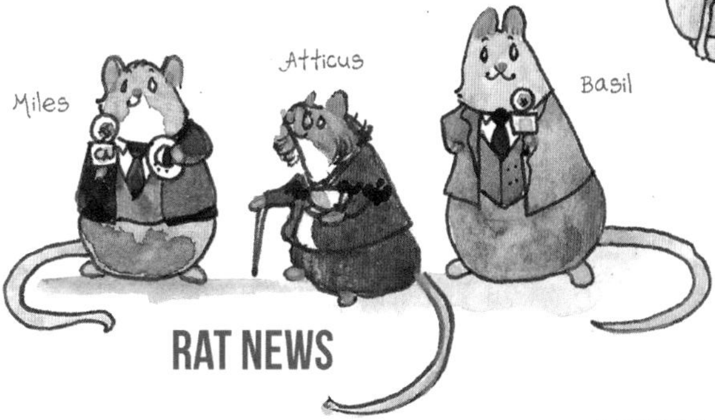
Miles
Atticus
Basil

RAT NEWS

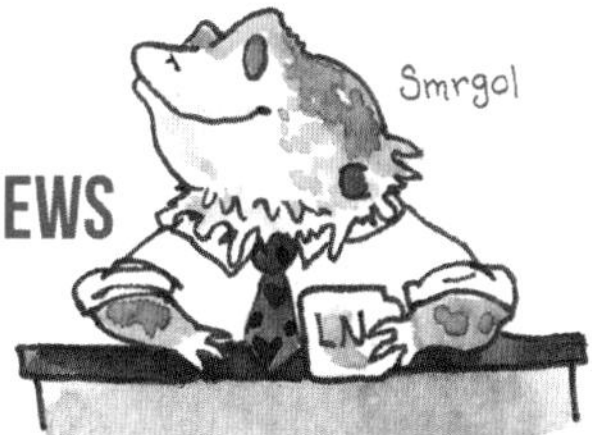
Smrgol

LIZARD NEWS

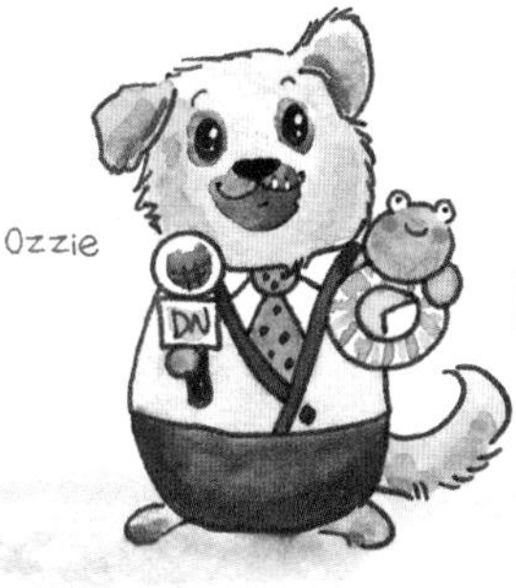
Ozzie

DOG NEWS

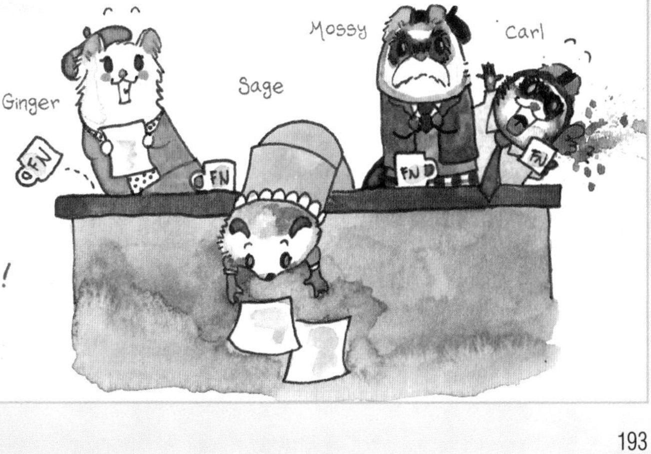
Mossy
Carl
Ginger
Sage

FERRET NEWS

And so many more! Enjoy creating your own!

TIPS FOR PAPER DOLLS

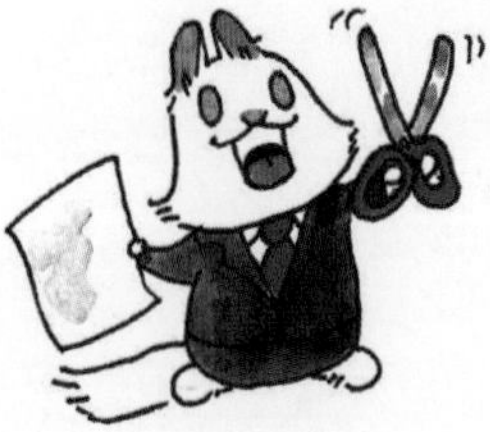

Scissors:
Safety first!
Be careful,
take your time.

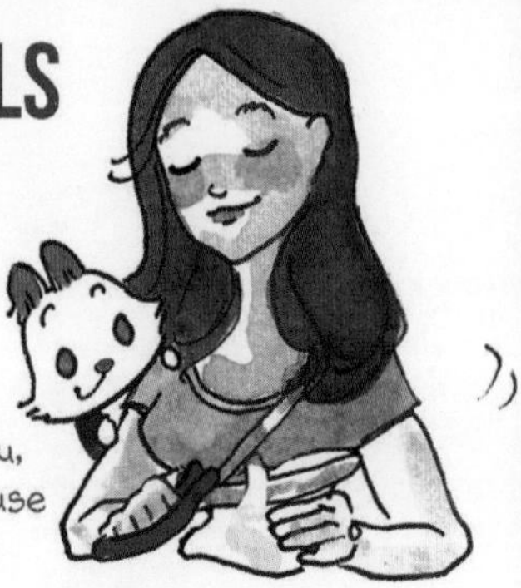

Ask someone to help you,
if you're not allowed to use
scissors. (...Like Lupin)

Make your own clothes:
Flip a patterned piece
of paper over and trace
an outfit face down. Cut it
out and you've got pajamas
or a fancy new suit! (Or
draw and color an outfit
on the tracing!)

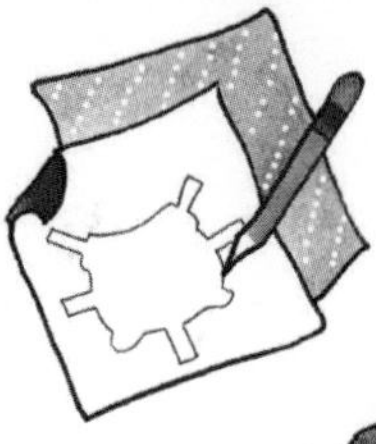

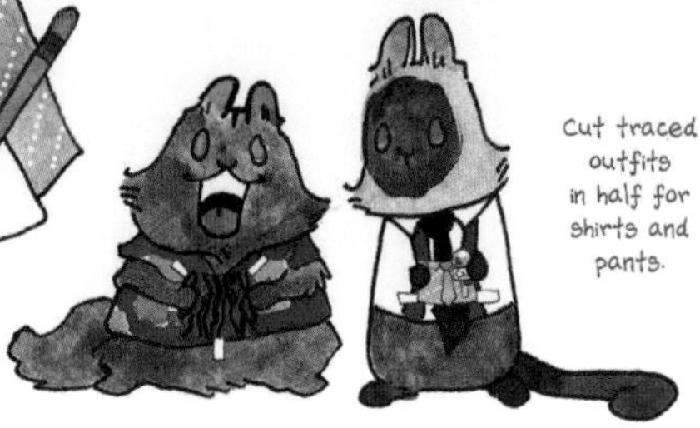

Cut traced outfits in half for shirts and pants.

Hint: Shine a flashlight behind the paper to trace exact collar lines, ties and shirt hems!

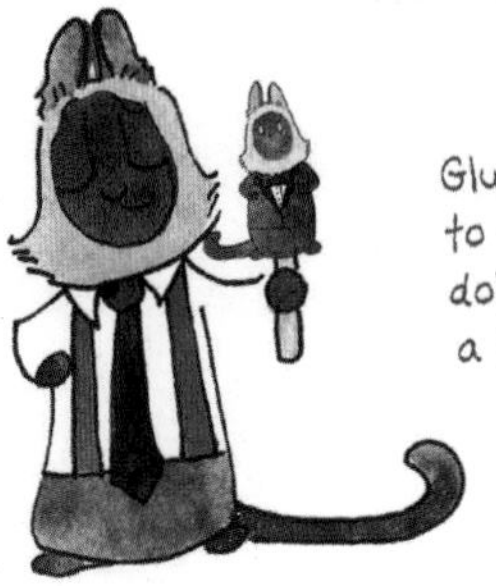

Puppets:
Glue a popsicle stick
to the back of each
doll, and you've got
a little puppet to
move around
and voice!

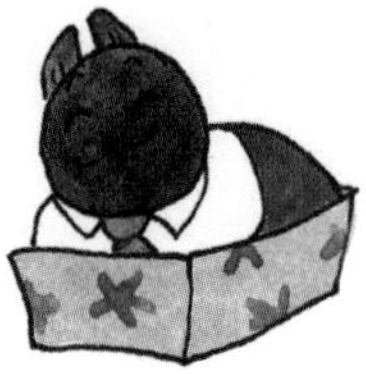

Boxes:
They're not
just for naps
anymore!
Turn any box into
a puppet theater.

Puppet Theaters: By cutting a window into a box, you can create a puppet theater! You can even make your own cardboard television and act out broadcasts inside! Delivery boxes, shoe boxes, and oatmeal containers all make great little theaters.

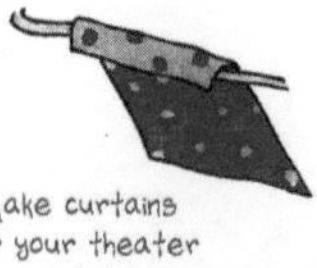

Make curtains for your theater by looping fabric over string and fastening it with glue, thread, or safety pins.

Decorate your theater with paint, crayons, craft paper, scraps of fabric, stickers—anything you have!

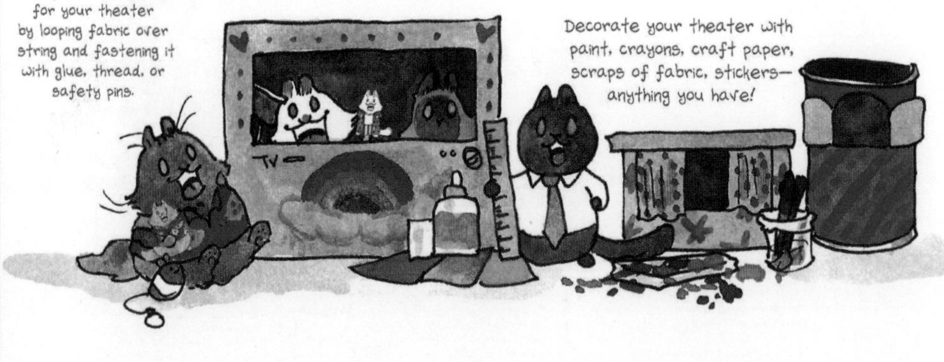
TV

BREAKING CAT NEWS PAPER DOLLS

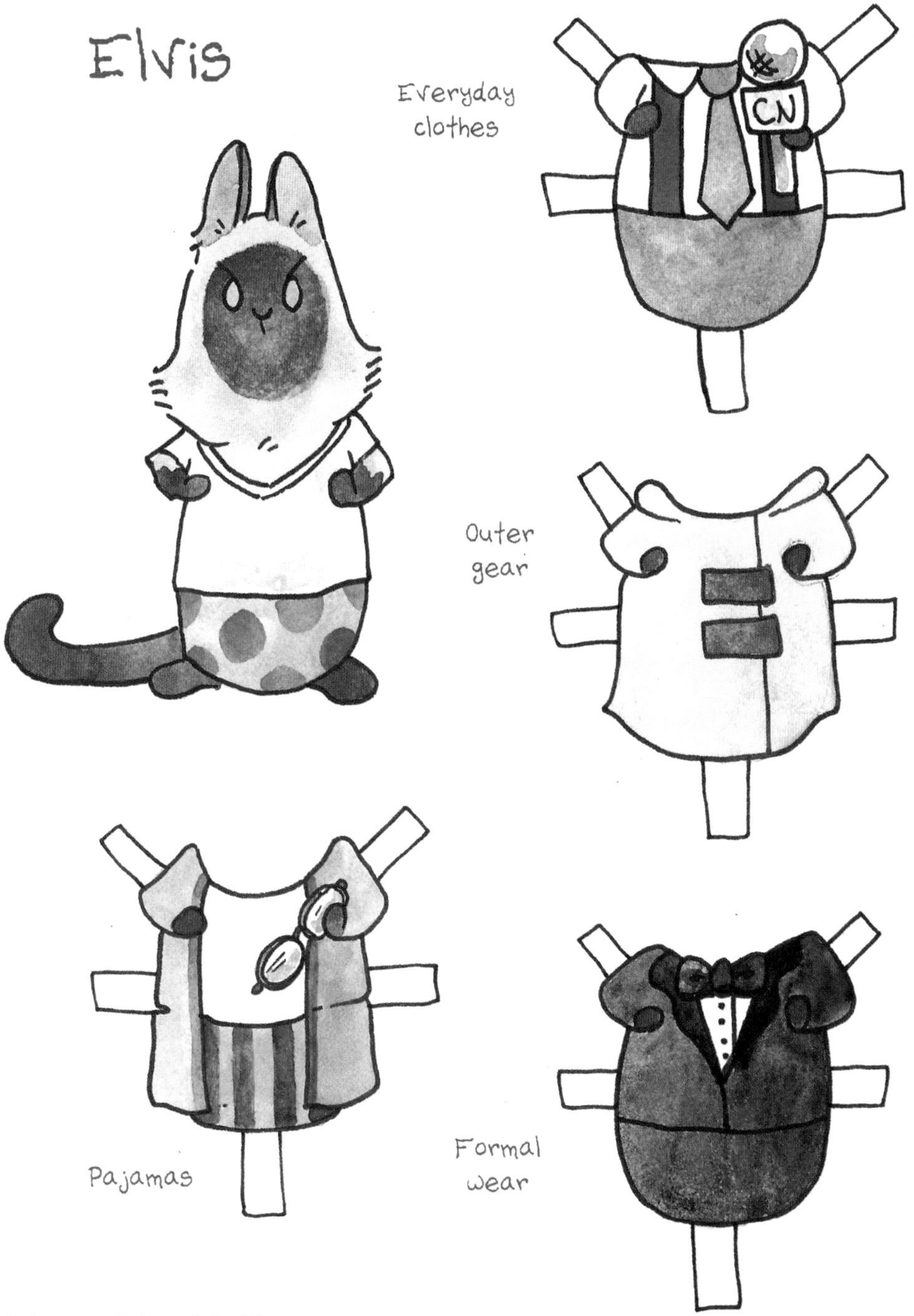
Elvis
Everyday clothes
CN
Outer gear
Pajamas
Formal wear

Cut page out along dotted line.

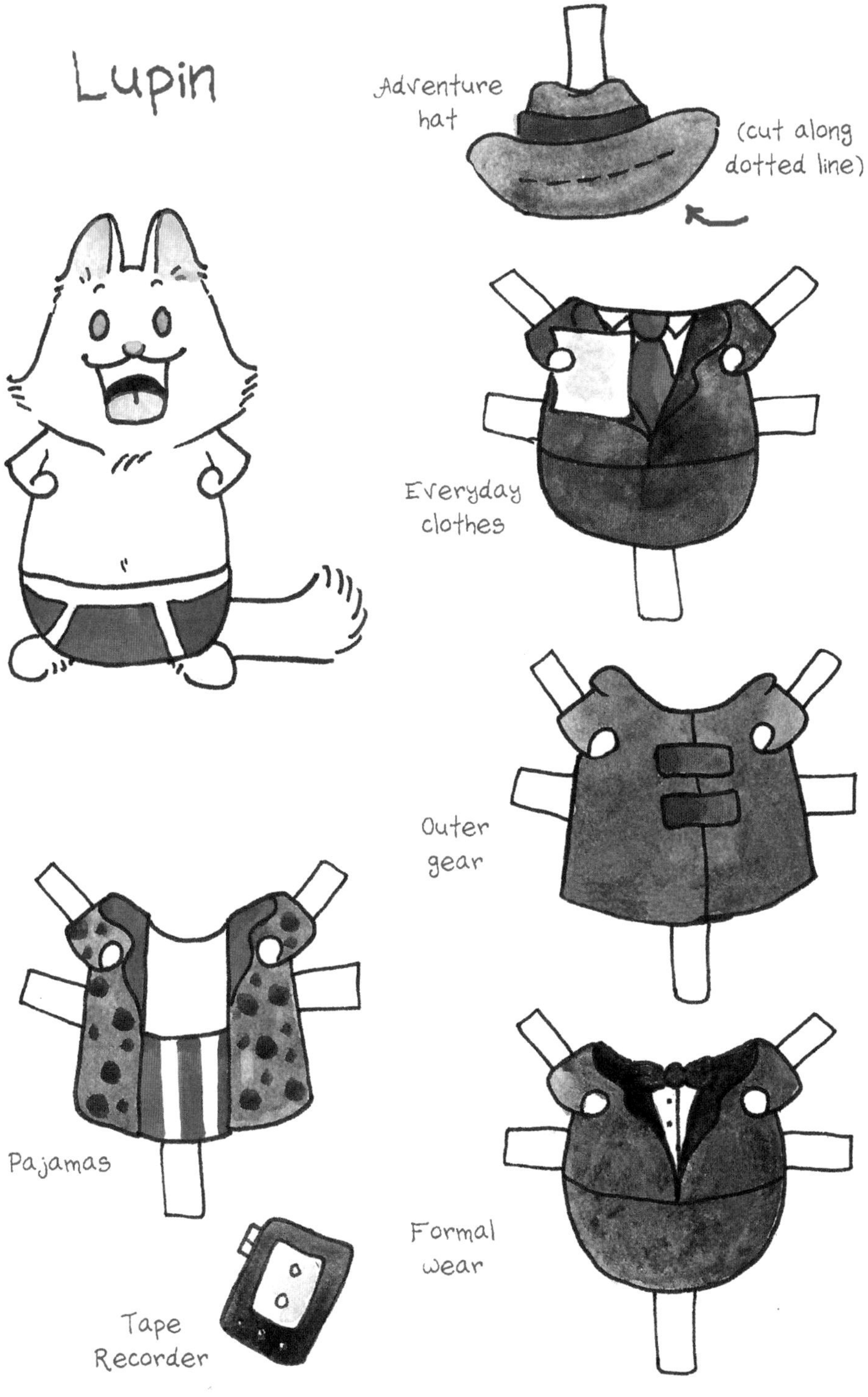
Lupin
Adventure hat
(cut along dotted line)
Everyday clothes
Outer gear
Pajamas
Formal wear
Tape Recorder

Cut page out along dotted line.

Puck

Everyday clothes

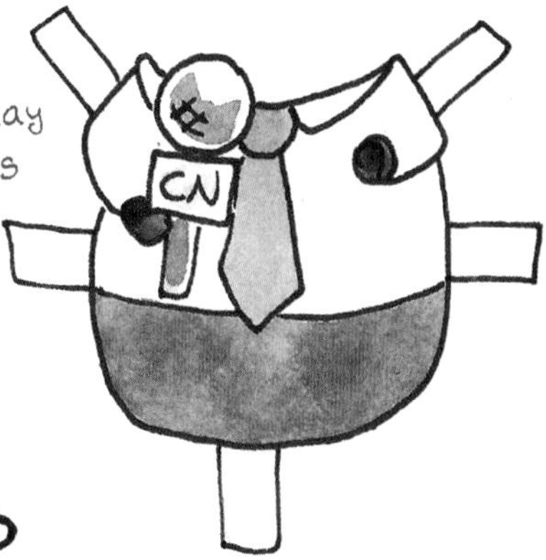
CN

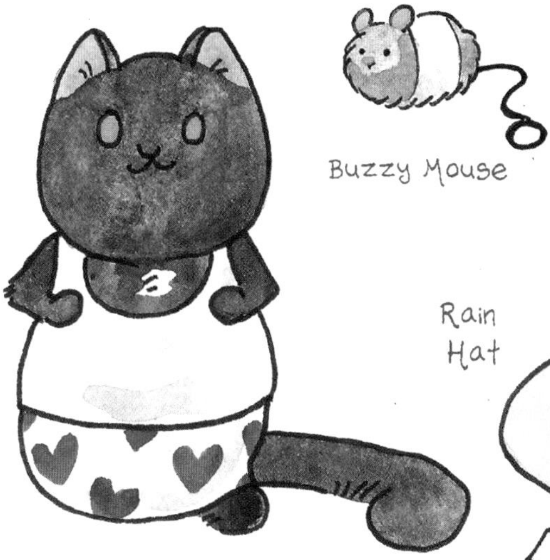

Buzzy Mouse

(cut along dotted line)

Rain Hat

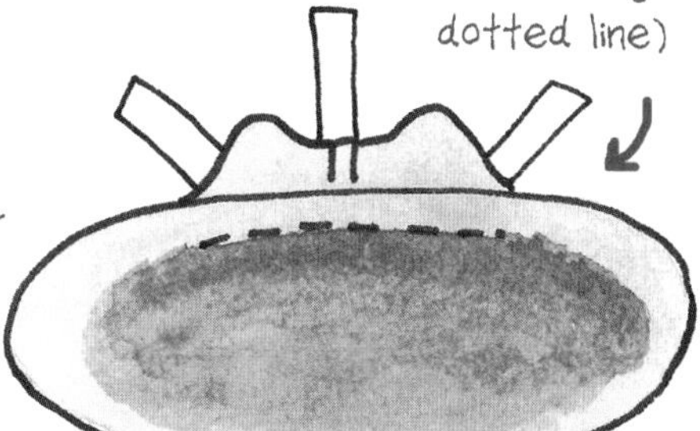

Outer gear

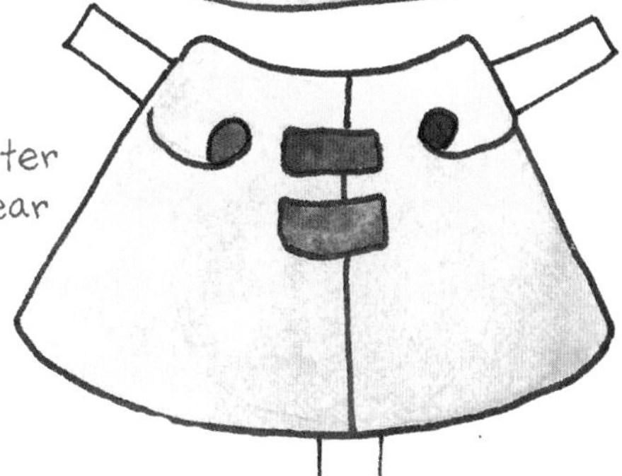

Beauty Mask

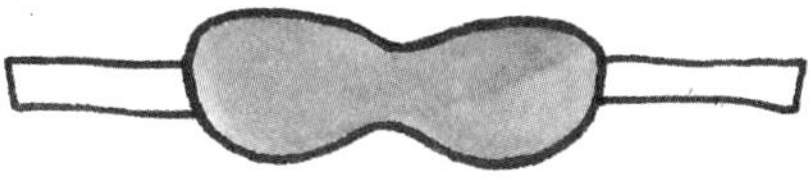

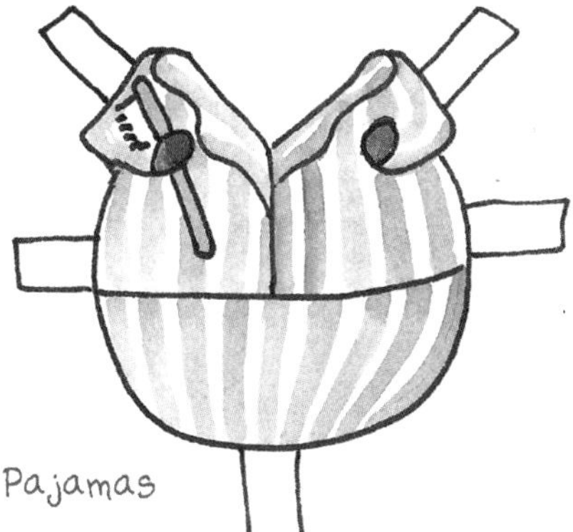

Pajamas

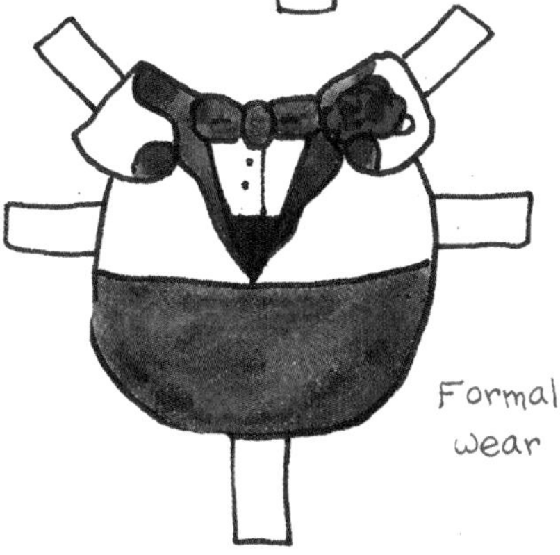

Formal wear

Cut page out along dotted line.

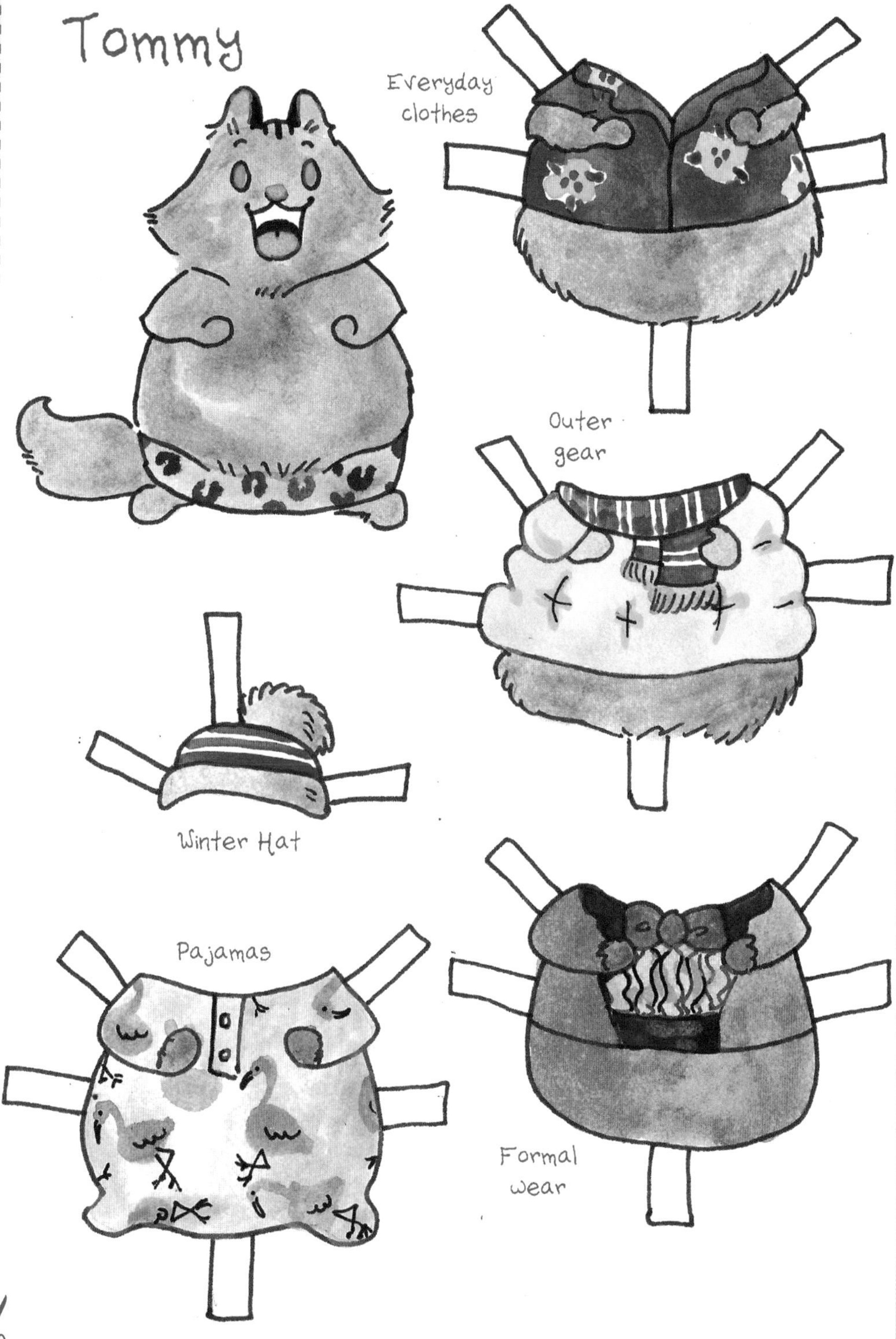
Tommy
Everyday clothes
Outer gear
Winter Hat
Pajamas
Formal wear

Cut page out along dotted line.

Props and Extras!

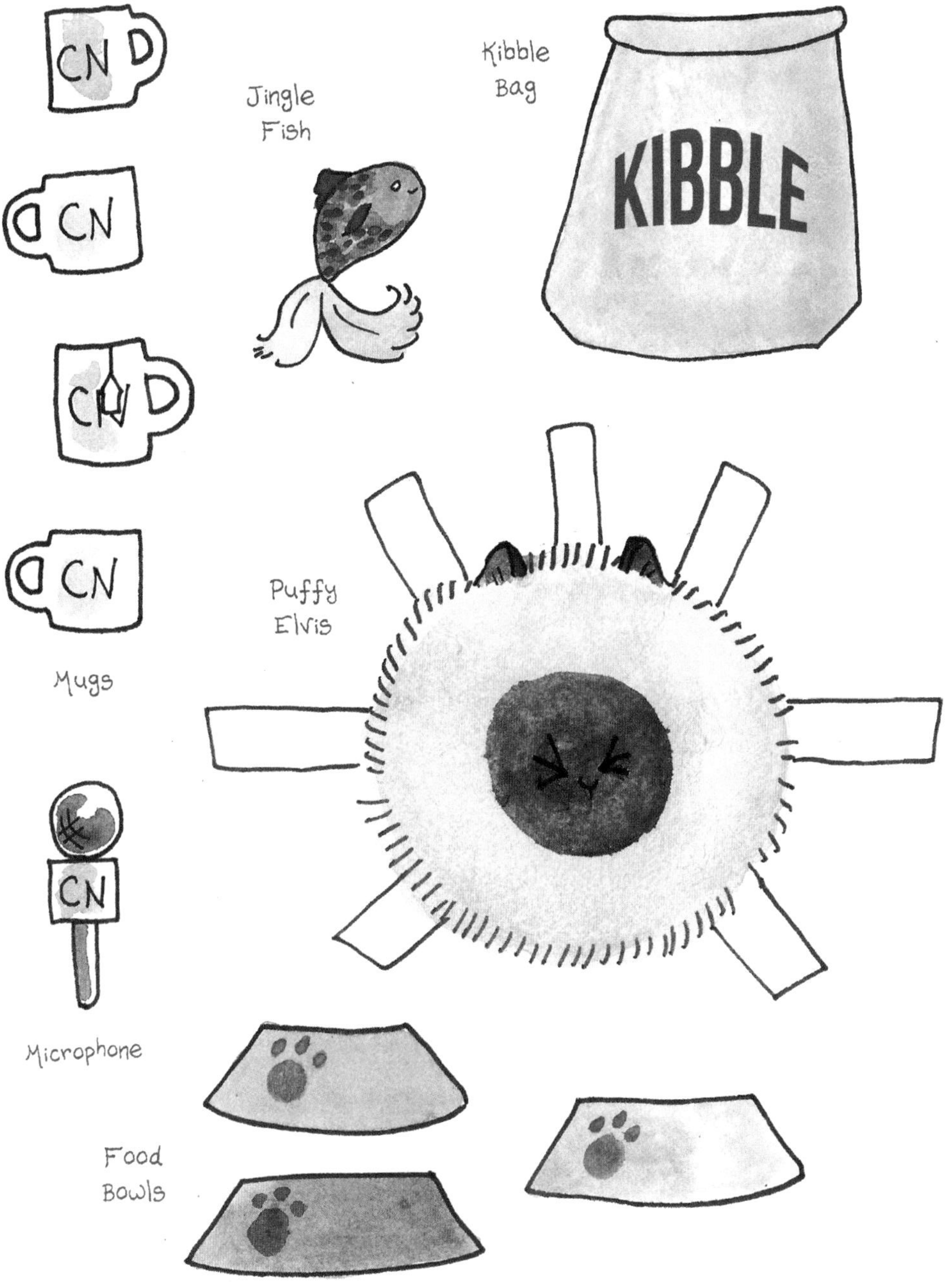
CN
CN
CN
CN
Mugs
Jingle Fish
Kibble Bag
KIBBLE
Puffy Elvis
CN
Microphone
Food Bowls

Cut page out along dotted line.

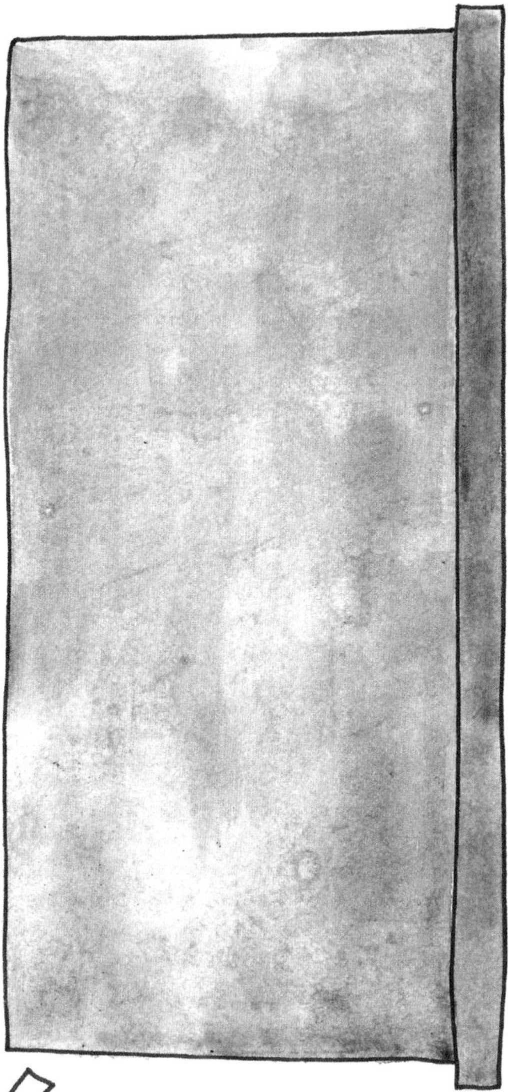

CN news
desk

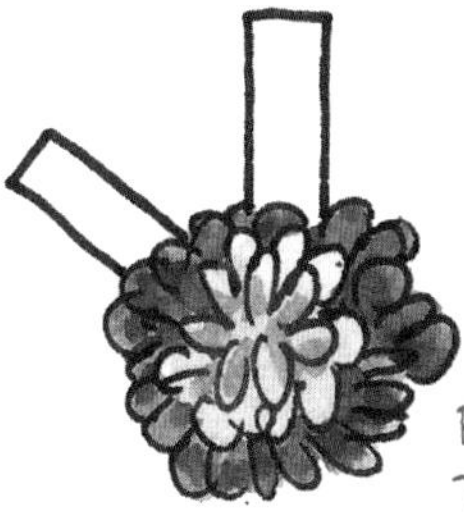

Plant of Many
Teeth's Fancy
Hat

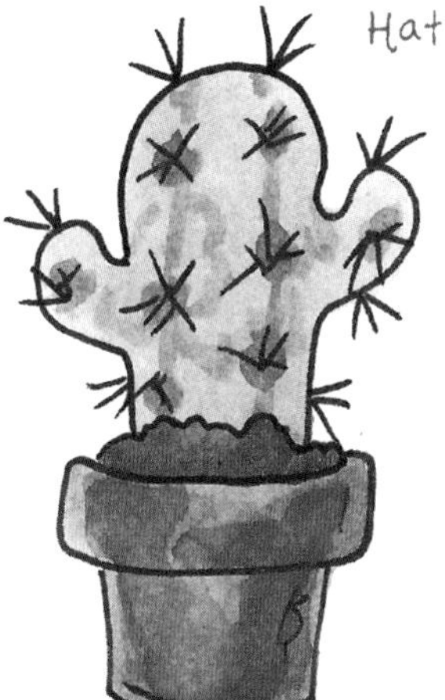

Plant of
Many Teeth

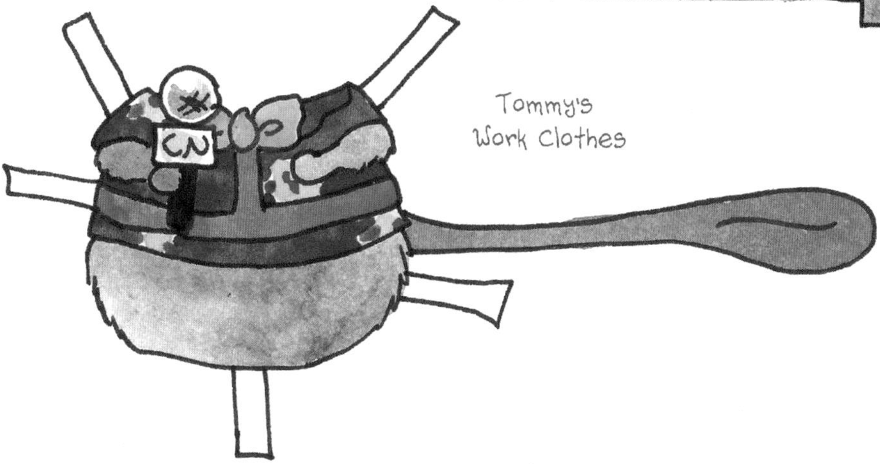
CN

Tommy's
Work Clothes

Cut page out along dotted line.